D.S. CRAIG

Reincarnated as a Familiar Volume 4

First edition

Editing by Greythorne Edits
Illustration by Yura's arts

This book was professionally typeset on Reedsy.
Find out more at reedsy.com

Contents

Acknowledgement

It's been a little over two years since I started writing Reincarnated as a Familiar. When I first started, I thought I would be lucky if even one person read the book. Now, I've written four volumes. None of this would have been possible without you, the readers. Thank you so much for giving my story a chance.

The Story Until Now

My name is Astria, and I'm an Astral Cat. I actually used to be a human, a grade school teacher, in fact. However, one day, I died in an accident and found myself surrounded by darkness. I thought that would be the end of me, but suddenly, a strange voice started talking to me.

The next thing I know, I'm in a completely different world, with magic and everything. Even more unbelievable is that I was stuck in the body of a cat! A young red-headed girl called Lesti broke the school rules and summoned me as her familiar. In fact, she almost got kicked out of school. Thankfully, it turned out that I was pretty special, and they let her stay.

It took me a while to adjust to this new world, but every day was exciting. I slowly got to know more about Lesti and my new powers. Skell, a massive black dragon that lives in the caves under the school, trained me. Lesti and I even managed to discover a new way to use magic circles to learn instruction-based magic more quickly.

But not everything went smoothly. A jealous classmate of Lesti's kidnapped me. Of course, she rescued me, but in the struggle, a malformed summoning circle was activated, and an archdemon named Thel'al showed up. We fought hard and nearly defeated him, but my power ran out at the crucial moment, and he escaped.

After that, Lesti passed her practical exam with flying colors, earning herself the second seat in her entire year. With her ranking shooting up, she moved into the first class, where she met Aurelia.

Lesti quickly became friends with the girl, and we quickly found ourselves dragged into her problems. Not only was Aurelia secretly raising an elemental hound named Fang out in the city, but she was part of a smuggling operation too. However, that wasn't her choice.

It turned out that Aurelia was actually the head of the Mori clan's daughter. She was being used as a political prisoner by Lord Dawster, who was behind the smuggling ring. Even worse, his smuggling ring had been infiltrated by Thel'al's agents.

After discovering this, we laid out a plan to crush the smuggling ring and save Aurelia, but our opponents struck before we could. A man named Ulrich brought all the gathered beasts to attack the school. He also enslaved Fang, transforming him into a massive monster.

Lesti, Aurelia, and I managed to barely rescue Fang and turn him back to normal, thanks to a little intervention from whoever had sent me to this world. However, we couldn't save the other magical beasts that had been enslaved. The headmistress was forced to put them all down to protect the school, and Ulrich got away.

It wasn't the victory we wanted, but it wasn't a complete loss either. We managed to save Fang and free Aurelia from Lord Dawster's grip. We also managed to help Fang become Aurelia's familiar.

Our challenges didn't end there, though. Just a month later, training for the Spring Tournament began. Lesti immediately challenged Alex to a sparring match and was promptly defeated. Despite all the the training we had done, the gap between them seemed to be as wide as ever.

After that, I went out to play with Fang and stumbled across a strange first-year girl named Rose, a girl who seemed to have the ability to inject magic into things. As we investigated the girl, Lesti and Aurelia quickly became good friends with her. Although, she didn't seem to like Fang or me that much.

At the same time, Lesti found out that her future husband, Augustine, would be coming to town for Elliot's birthday party. Despite the stress that information caused her, she still managed to make great progress in her research and training. Learning from the collar that had been used to transform Fang, she developed the ability to break spells down into small reusable steps.

Aurelia, on the other hand, focused on learning to channel her magical energy while I trained with Fang. The pup soon fell sick and we discovered that magical energy was building up inside him. Since he couldn't use it fast enough, the headmistress taught Aurelia how to extract it for use in her own spells.

During all of our training, we learned about Rose's secret. She had been abducted by her sponsor, Baron Arvis, years ago and her family was being held hostage. Arvis had hoped to make use of her ability to gain the power he needed to overthrow Elliot's father, Lord Gambriel. In the end, his impatience got the best of him and he turned to less than savory allies.

Chaos broke out at Elliot's birthday party. Assassin's attacked and threatened the lives of Elliot and his family. Although we had known the attack was coming, we weren't entirely prepared. The assassins drank strange potions that turned them into demons. We managed to defeat them using the abilities we had gained through our training, but there was still Baron Arvis to deal with.

Elliot led us to his father's office through a secret passage. There Baron Arvis and a group of his men had Lord Gambriel cornered. We ambushed them before they could drink the potions and were just about to capture Baron Arvis when Ulrich showed up.

He gave Arvis a special potion that transformed him into a massive demon. That demon began to rampage through the manor grounds. Lesti and I immediately went to stop it while Lord Gambriel went for reinforcements. The fight was going well until the transformed Arvis began summoning hordes of other demons.

Lesti and I were pushed to the brink, but were saved in the nick of time by Rose, who had come back to help us. Soon after, Lord Gambriel returned with reinforcements. With everyone's help we managed to survive until Lesti's most powerful spell destroyed the massive demon.

After that, Dag, who it turned out was one of Frederick's men, led us to a secret hideout. While we had been fighting Arvis, he and his men had been raiding his estates and they had managed to rescue Rose's parents. The three of them were reunited at last.

A lot has happened in the few months since I came to this world and I imagine its only going to get crazier from here. Both Lesti and I have some big challenges ahead of us. No matter what happens, though, we'll get through them together.

Prologue

Alex stood next to the riverbank near the Bestroff manor, or at least a place that looked exactly like it. The air was perfectly still around him, and the sun shone brightly overhead. No wind blew, no clouds moved across the sky, and not a single sound could be heard.

It was like the entire area was frozen in time, all except for himself and one other odd feature. Just upstream from him was a massive dam, golden liquid flowing through the partially opened gates. Cracks ran all along its surface, allowing even more water to flow forth. He grimaced as he watched the golden water pour into the river. It rushed by with incredible force, barely contained by the dirt banks.

He had seen this dream several times over the years. The first time he had seen it, he had been just seven years old. Back then, the water flowing from the dam had been a trickle, almost imperceivable. Over the years, it had slowly grown into the rushing torrent it was today.

It happened slowly at first, but recently the amount had been growing at an accelerated rate. The dream was occurring more frequently too. It had taken him some time to figure out what that dam represented, but he was sure now. After all these years, there was no way he couldn't be. It was whatever part of his soul that was responsible for holding back the flow of magic.

"You won't be able to control this much longer." From behind him, he heard a familiar voice.

Glancing over his shoulder, he saw a man who was the very definition of nobility staring at the rushing river. He was rather tall, with golden blond hair and blue eyes. His body was fit and muscular, showing that he didn't indulge in his privilege. The aura that he emitted was one of absolute authority, and yet it never felt oppressive.

The man had first appeared after his last trip back home a few months ago. He never gave a name and never answered any of Alex's questions. Instead, he just repeated the same warning each time. That never stopped him from asking, though.

"How can you be so sure? My father and my brothers have had no issue. Why should I be any different?" He waited for a moment but didn't receive an answer. "What would you have me do then?"

"The damage has progressed too far. If you keep using your magic so recklessly, there'll be no turning back." The man simply ignored him and repeated the same line as always.

Alex let out a heavy sigh and turned his gaze back to the golden water flowing from the dam. "No change, huh?"

Deep down, he knew the man was right. The torrent of water grew more quickly whenever he used his magic too much. Simple spells didn't seem to be much of an issue, but the more powerful a spell was, the more damage it appeared to cause.

Even if he knew that, he couldn't abandon his duty. He was a Bestroff, and it was his responsibility to serve the people of his territory and the alliance, even if it destroyed him. That was why he couldn't quit, even if he wanted to.

"Withdraw from the Spring Tournament."

Alex felt a chill run down his spine. The voice that was usually so calm and collected was suddenly filled with power. Turning around, he found the man glaring at him, almost as if willing him to obey.

It was the first time he had looked at Alex. Before, he had always just stared listlessly at the golden light beyond. Looking into his eyes now, Alex felt a strange sense of unease. It was almost as if he could feel an unfathomable power emanating from them.

"This is my final warning. I can do no more."

The pressure of the man's gaze locked him in place, unable to move.

Reaching out, he gently placed his hand on Alex's chest. Then, he pushed and sent him tumbling backward into the rushing river.

Just before he could be swept away by the golden rapids, Alex's eyes snapped open. Above him was the familiar ceiling of his room. For a long while, he simply laid there in silence, asking himself a single question over and over.

What in the world am I supposed to do?

Rumors

I followed Lesti through the academy as my gaze drifted across the crazy sight in front of me. All around us, the halls were filled with energy and excitement. I had never seen the academy this full, apart from right after classes. Students, faculty, and familiars alike ran about frantically, busily working on completing whatever task was at hand. The Spring Tournament was only a week away, and everyone was busy making their last-minute preparations.

"Everyone really seems amped up for the tournament, huh?" I commented as I tried my best to avoid getting stepped on in the crowded halls.

"Yeah. A lot of people consider the tournaments the real ranking system of the school," Lesti commented, her own gaze locked ahead to avoid running into anyone. "The practical exam really only tests how good you are at casting different spells. In a lot of cases, a good strategy can overcome a gap in skill."

"That makes sense, but I'm still surprised that even the lower ranking students seem into it." Looking around, I saw several faces from Lesti's old class, which were near the bottom of her year, running around excitedly. "There's no way that they'll win, right?"

"Even if they can't win, if they manage to impress a particularly powerful lord, they'll improve their own standing in life quite a bit." Lesti finally broke free from the worst of the crowd and took a deep breath before continuing. "A lot of the students here are girls or second or third sons. They won't inherit their family lands unless something happens to their elder brother. Though, in the case of girls, they'll just be married off anyway."

There was a bit of venom in her voice, which wasn't surprising given her situation. "By the way, what ended up happening with Augustine after the party? We just kind of left him outside. He didn't…"

"Don't worry. He's alive and well. Apparently, he was captured by some demons after that but managed to fight his way out." Lesti's nose scrunched up in disgust. "Everyone seems to think he's some sort of brave hero now, thanks to that."

"Wait, what about your stab wound?" I looked up at her, a bit surprised. "Wasn't the plan to get the engagement called off thanks to him attacking you?"

"It was. Unfortunately, the demon attack also blew that out of the water." Lesti slumped her shoulders, clearly disappointed. "Everyone is convinced that I got the wound fighting that massive demon that Baron Arvis turned into. Lord Gambriel said that Elliot's testimony wouldn't be enough to persuade his allies, so there was nothing he could do."

"Wait, won't he tell the council about what you said then?"

Lesti furrowed her brow. "To be honest, I'm a bit worried about that as well. Still, it seems like he's staying quiet about it for now. Lani is preparing for the worst-case scenario, so all we can do is sit back and wait."

"I see." I continued to look up at Lesti as we rounded the corner into the hall with all of the teacher's offices. She didn't seem to be stressing about the situation too much, but I was still worried about her. I wracked my brain, trying to find some words to comfort her, when I was suddenly knocked off my feet.

For a brief moment, I panicked, thinking that perhaps I was under attack. I began to channel my magical energy when suddenly I was drenched in dog drool. Tucking my ears back, I turned and hissed at my overly excited attacker, "Fang! What have I told you about surprising me like that!"

The pup didn't seem to care about my irritation and instead just did a quick play bow as his tail wagged wildly. I was still annoyed by his surprise attack, but I couldn't really stay mad at him. With everything that had been going on lately, we hadn't had much time to play. Still, I couldn't afford to indulge him right this minute.

"Alright, I get it. I can't play right now." I rubbed up against him as I passed by. "Once we're done with whatever Instructor Malkael needs, then we can play, okay?"

Fang's tail drooped slightly, but he seemed to understand. Then, from behind him, I heard Aurelia call out to us. "Instructor Malkael called for both of you as well?"

"Auri!" Lesti ran over and threw her arms around her friend before looking up at her curiously. "You're headed to Instructor Malkael's office as well?"

"Mm. He said he had something he wanted to discuss," Aurelia replied as she lazily leaned into her friend's embrace.

"I wonder if it's about the tournament?" I asked as I looked around. Even this hall, which was far less busy, was still buzzing with activity. "I guess we'll find out when we get there. Let's get going."

We walked just a little further down the hall to Malkael's office only to find the door shut. Lesti knocked on the door, and Malkael's voice called out from within, "Who is it?"

"I-It's Lesti and Aurelia. You called for us." Lesti looked over at me, a confused look on her face. It was unusual for Malkael to ask who was at his door. Normally, he would just yell at whoever knocked to come in.

A moment later, the door cracked open, and Malkael peered out. "Come on, inside. Hurry, please."

With a strange sense of urgency, he ushered us inside, barely opening the door enough for us to pass through it. The room was almost as much of a mess as the last time I had seen it, but on the far side, a small area had been cleared out near the desk. Standing nervously in the center of that space was a figure that I hadn't expected to see.

"Rose!" Lesti called out, darting across the room, nearly knocking over several piles of books in her haste. She threw her arms around the younger girl, who smiled calmly back at her. "What are you doing here? I thought you would be with your family. Did something happen?"

Lesti's expression shifted from one of pure elation to concern. Rose had only recently been reunited with her mother and father after many years. We assumed that she would be spending a lot of time with them if not heading back to the Gambriel territory with them. Thankfully, there wasn't anything to worry about.

"No, they're fine." Rose smiled softly at Lesti. "They're just busy at the moment. Lord Gambriel has made arrangements for them to set up a new shop here in the city as compensation for the damage done by Baron Arvis. He also said that he would continue my sponsorship."

Lesti's eyes lit up at her words. "So, you'll be staying here at the academy?"

"That's right. Today is actually my first day back." Rose turned her gaze to Malkael, who was straightening up some of the books that Lesti bumped into when she darted across the room. "But as soon as I arrived on campus, I was called to Instructor Malkael's office."

Malkael finished cleaning up and walked across the messy room to join us, prompting Lesti to look up at him. "So, what did you call us here for, Instructor? I'm assuming it's about the tournament."

"You would be correct, Ms. Vilia." Malkael took a seat at his desk and looked at the three of them with a serious expression. "I have a request that I'd like to make of the three of you. It's one that I'm sure won't sit well with any of you, but I'd like you to hear me out anyway. Please take a seat."

He gestured toward the bed, and the three girls sat down, each one wearing a different expression. The bright smile that Lesti had been wearing just a moment ago vanished in an instant. Meanwhile, Rose seemed nervous, her gaze flitting between Malkael and Lesti. I imagine she expected her to make a big fuss about whatever Malkael's request was. On the other hand, Aurelia absentmindedly ran her fingers through Fang's fur, her expression remaining neutral.

"As I'm sure you're well aware, word has gotten around about your battle with the demon that Baron Arvis became, as well as the assassins that attacked the manor." Malkael looked at each of the girls in turn, and they each nodded, confirming what he said. "Needless to say, it's an astounding accomplishment for a group of students to do what you three did. We here at the academy couldn't be prouder of you."

"Instructor, pardon my rudeness, but could you skip the empty platitudes and get to the point?" Lesti snapped at Malkael. I couldn't blame her either.

He was coming off as extremely condescending at the moment, and it was kind of creeping me out.

"My apologies. I simply wanted you to be aware that the following request was in no way because the academy disapproved of your activities or accomplishments." Malkael let out a heavy sigh, and an awkward grimace formed on his face. "Now then, I'll get to the point as you requested. I want you three to not use the abilities and skills you used in your battles against Arvis and his men during the Spring Tournament, or in front of the other students for that matter."

"What?!" Lesti stood up, her anger clear on her face and in her voice. "You're telling us to hold back?! After all the effort we put in? Why? What reason could you possibly have?"

"Lesti, calm down," I scolded her as gently as I could. I had never seen her this mad before, and I got the feeling that being harsh with her would just be counterproductive. "Instructor Malkael won't be able to explain things properly if you're shouting at him."

Lesti glared at Malkael for a moment longer before plopping back down on the bed and crossed her arms. Rose gently patted her on the arm, trying to ease her foul mood. Meanwhile, I turned my attention back to Malkael. While I wasn't nearly as upset as Lesti, I couldn't say that I was happy. What he was doing was as good as asking us to throw the tournament so long as Alex was participating.

Sitting up as tall as I could, I looked him straight in the eye. "Well then, go ahead, Instructor Malkael. I hope you have a good explanation prepared, though. It won't be easy to convince us to throw away all the hard work we've put in."

"Yes, I understand. Honestly, I'm not happy about this myself. But there are certain things in motion behind the scenes that I believe make this a necessary precaution to take." Malkael glanced nervously at the still angry Lesti. "You see, someone has started to spread rumors about the three of you, nasty ones at that."

"Rumors?" Aurelia tilted her head to the side as she stepped in for Lesti.

"Yes. It's utter nonsense, but the rumor goes that you've secretly been using ancient artifacts to enhance your magic. There are even accusations that the Vilia family has secretly been stockpiling artifacts against alliance law."

Malkael's statement seemed to wash away some of the anger that Lesti was feeling, and she looked at him in bewilderment now. "That makes absolutely no sense. What good would it do us to stockpile artifacts when we could sell them for money? Besides, I've never even heard of an artifact that enhances someone's magic."

"Haven't you, though?" Malkael opened a drawer on his desk and pulled out several pieces of parchment. Most contained the magic circles that had been inscribed on Fang's collar. However, one seemed to have the runes inscribed on the headmistress's staff scrawled on it. He held them out for the group to look at side by side. "Notice anything similar about these?"

Lesti stared at the parchment for a minute before her eyes grew wide. "These runes, they're the same. Why, though?"

"Well, I do have a theory on that, but I still don't have enough evidence to prove it." Malkael glanced over at me as he spoke. "It's possible that the runes used by demons and demon worshipers are the same ones that were used to create these ancient artifacts."

There was a long pause as Lesti stared at the pieces of parchment. As if unable to bear that silence, Rose hesitantly raised her hand. "Um, Instructor, if what you're saying is true, then wouldn't that mean that the ancient artifacts were created by demons?"

"No, not quite." Malkael shook his head and smiled softly at her. "There are many reasons that these runes could be the same. The ancient civilization could have stolen the technique from demons or vice versa. A third party could have developed them and passed the technique down to both. Without more study, we simply can't say for sure."

"Regardless, it's obvious from looking at this that the two things are related." Lesti finally raised her gaze to meet Malkael's. "Instructor, is this information common knowledge?"

"No, it isn't. I'm the leading expert in this field, and I haven't even reported my findings to the council yet. The only people besides me who know about it are the headmistress, Frederick, and Astria."

Lesti paused for a moment, seemingly surprised that Malkael had mentioned my name, before furrowing her brow in thought. "I see. I was thinking that whoever was spreading this rumor likely knew that I was studying the runes from the collars we had recovered from Thel'al. If they knew that they were related to ancient artifacts, then the rumors would have some merit. If the information hasn't been made public, though, then I don't think that would be the case."

As Lesti pondered who might be spreading the rumors about her, I carefully watched Malkael's reaction. He stared down at the parchment in his hands, a troubled look on his face. I could tell that he was holding something back. Most likely, he had a hunch about who the culprit might be.

"Malkael, there's one other person who might know about this, isn't there?" I probed Malkael, trying to draw the answer out of him without forcing him into saying it. He looked up at me, blinking rapidly before a pained smile spread across his face.

"Yes, you're right. There is one other person who I think might know about this." Malkael took a deep breath and steadied his gaze. "My brother, Ulrich, was researching ancient artifacts before he became a demon worshiper. He's most likely our culprit, though I don't know who he's using to spread the information."

"Ulrich, huh?" Lesti crossed her arms. "He's a rather troublesome one, creating that crazy potion that turned people into demons. I really wish we had managed to take him down before."

"Mm." Aurelia nodded in agreement, her eyes suddenly sharp and focused. It seemed like she still held a grudge against Ulrich for what he did to Fang back when we first met. "Next time, we'll get him for sure."

Malkael suddenly cleared his throat, cutting off any further discussion. "Yes, at any rate. I think you all understand the danger now. So, will you listen to my request?"

"Not a chance," Lesti replied bluntly. "I'm sure you're already aware of this, Instructor, but without the skills we've been developing, I won't be able to hold my own in the tournament against Alex."

"I understand that, but there are more important things at play here," Malkael argued back, his tone growing stern.

"Maybe from your perspective, but for me, winning the Spring Tournament will have a massive effect on my future and the future of my people. I can't afford to get scared and back down now."

The air grew tense as the two stared at each other, both refusing to back down. I was worried that it would come to this when Malkael made his request. There was no way Lesti could back down here, and Malkael was obligated to try and protect his students.

"Malkael, is hiding Lesti's abilities really the only option we have here?" It was a long shot, but I tried to move the conversation down a different path. "For example, couldn't we find the source of the rumors and discredit them, or start counter rumors of our own?"

Looking at me for a moment, Malkael let out a heavy sigh. "I suppose those are possibilities, although far more difficult. What sort of counter rumors did you have in mind?"

"Why don't we use my status as a high-level familiar to our advantage? For whatever reason, students and teachers seem to think I'm wiser than I really am. If we spread the rumor that I'm the one teaching Lesti her magic, they should believe it pretty easily, I think. We can use the same excuse for Rose and Aurelia, too, since they're both Lesti's friends."

"I see." Malkael pondered my idea for a moment. "That might work. Although, you do risk angering your fellow classmates. Many of the students from noble families have already complained about the situation regarding Ms. Vilia and Ms. Aurelia's summoning pacts."

Lesti waved her hand in the air dismissively. "If they want to be jealous and whine, then let them. People like that aren't worth our time." She quickly looked at each of the two friends sitting on either side of her. "Right, you two?"

"Mm. I was already an outsider in class anyway, so it doesn't bother me." Aurelia nodded, smiling softly back at Lesti.

Meanwhile, Rose had a slightly more conflicted expression. "I-I think I should be fine. Most of the first years just leave me alone. Wait, but what if some second or even third years come after me? What will I do then?"

I watched Rose as she began to have a miniature meltdown of her own creation. It was kind of amazing how she managed to work herself up like that over something that wasn't even likely to come to pass. Taking pity on her, I threw her a lifeline. "Don't worry, Rose. Most of the second and third-year students don't even know who you are. As long as you keep your abilities hidden until the tournament, then it shouldn't be a problem."

"Oh, right." Rose froze for a minute before blushing as she realized how much she had overreacted. Sitting up and clearing her throat, she tried her best to recover her dignity, drawing amused giggles from Lesti and Aurelia.

"So, it seems like everyone here is on board, but what do you say, Instructor?" I turned my attention back to Malkael, thinking he wouldn't have any reason to disagree with me now. However, I was quickly disappointed as he dug up some other excuse to shoot down our plan.

"Even if that's the case, how will you go about spreading this rumor of yours? You can't exactly go around spreading it yourselves, can you?"

I glared back at him, slightly annoyed. While his logic was sound, it really just felt like he was being stubborn at this point. Yet, the look in his eyes didn't seem to contain any such emotion. Instead, he looked a bit like Lesti when she was studying magic runes or coming up with a new spell. *Ah, I get it. He's enjoying this.*

For Malkael, this whole problem was like a puzzle that needed to be solved. He had offered us his own solution to it, but now he was enjoying seeing how we developed our own, even as he tried to poke holes in it. I realized as I watched him that he was the type of person who was very useful for making sure a plan was well developed. On the other hand, he would be a pain in the butt when you needed to move quickly. I wanted to just tell him we were going with our plan, but he was still Lesti and Aurelia's instructor, so I decided to play along for now.

"That's simple. We'll get Lani and Elliot to help." I made sure to meet his gaze squarely as I laid out my thoughts. "Lani has a lot of connections in the staff and faculty, so she can head the rumors off there. Most of them won't be as biased toward Lesti, so it should be fine. Elliot was hanging around us quite a bit and had that dance with Lesti, but if he frames it like he was trying to get close to her and steal her secrets, people should believe him."

Lesti looked over at me skeptically. "Lani's part, I understand, but do you really think people will believe that Elliot is some sort of backstabbing mastermind? He's far too straightforward for that sort of thing, you know."

"Yeah, I guess you're right." My gaze fell to the floor as I wracked my brain over that problem, shooting up a second later as I rebounded with another idea. "I know. We can just adjust the story to reflect his straightforward nature. Rather than tricking us, we can just have him say he came to us asking me to train him. It wouldn't even be a lie then."

"Oh, yeah. He did ask you to train him, didn't he?" Lesti slapped her fist into her palm as she remembered Elliot's request before glancing at me with narrowed eyes. "Not that you ever actually did it."

"Hey, that's not my fault!" I averted my gaze. "A lot was going on, and I'm still not sure exactly what I can teach him. I don't really know anything about combat."

"Um, is that really true?" Rose looked at the rest of us, seemingly perplexed. "I heard you say that before, but watching Astria in combat, it's hard to believe that she's never been trained."

"Yes, I've been wondering about that myself," Malkael chimed in as well. "The way you moved back when Ulrich attacked with the beasts, I wouldn't have thought that you were a complete amateur at combat."

"Well, it's not like I'm a complete amateur. It's just that when Skell taught me, he basically beat it into me. He never really taught me any techniques outside of how instruction magic and my own abilities worked." I felt a slight chill shoot down my spine as I remembered the days I spent training in the secret cave. "I don't think I could run Elliot through that kind of training either. It's not something a normal human would survive."

"Yeah, I'd rather not put him through that." Lesti shuddered next to me, a haunted look in her eyes. "I still remember some of the training that Frederick put us through as first years. I can't imagine how much worse it would be coming from a dragon."

Malkael cleared his throat, dragging our attention back to him. "While I would love to hear more about the training techniques of Frederick and his familiar, that can wait until later. Let's get back on task. For now, I think we have a fairly solid plan at this point, so I'll trust your judgment. Still, please be careful not to show too much until the tournament begins."

"We'll do our best," I replied as I jumped off the bed and started heading for the door. "I doubt it will be too difficult. We spend most of our time practicing away from the other students."

Lesti and the others stood up as well, with Rose dipping down in a quick yet graceful curtsy. It seemed she still hadn't shaken all of the habits she had picked up from being held prisoner by Baron Arvis. Lesti and Aurelia, on the other hand, simply nodded at him as they headed for the door. But just before we could head out, Malkael called out to us.

"Ms. Vilia, one last thing." We turned to find him staring at us with a rather intense look in his eyes. "Please be sure to keep your guard up in the days leading up to the tournament. If my brother is involved, then we have to assume that there is more to these rumors than simply attempting to tarnish your name, even more so if Thel'al is pulling the strings."

Lesti nodded and smiled back at him. "Thank you, Instructor, but we'll be fine. If either of them tries anything, then we'll put a stop to it."

"Mm. We won't let them have their way ever again." Aurelia calmly pumped her fist, and Fang barked in response.

Unfortunately, their bravado only seemed to cause Malkael more concern. Seeing that, I sent him my own thoughts privately. *"Don't worry, Malkael. I'll make sure they aren't reckless."*

After my reassurances, his expression seemed to soften slightly, and he nodded briefly. The group turned to head back out into the busy halls, and I followed after them. It was about lunchtime, so the girls all decided to make for the cafeteria, which meant passing through the crowded halls again.

I suddenly found myself being far tenser than before and glancing around to make sure no one was doing anything suspicious. By the time we got to the cafeteria, I felt exhausted. Realizing that I wouldn't be able to keep this up until the tournament, I started to think of other ways of keeping an eye out for bad actors. Slowly my mind began drifting off as the girls ate and chatted happily.

Old Enemies, New Spells, and Invincible Rivals

"Well, well, what do we have here?" It was about half an hour after we had arrived at the cafeteria. The girls finished eating a bit ago and were catching up with Rose when a familiar voice pulled me from my thoughts. It was a voice that I would have been okay with never hearing again, one that made my fur bristle instinctively. Turning to look at the source, I found Sebastian and a couple of other second years that I wasn't familiar with flanking him on either side.

"If it isn't the whole cheater squad together." Sebastian grinned at us with the same smug expression that he always wore whenever he picked a fight with Lesti. "What are you up to? Not using your stolen artifacts to bribe a teacher, I hope? Not even the headmistress will be able to protect you if you get caught doing something like that."

Lesti stared him down while Rose and Aurelia looked between the three of us with confused expressions. My own heart was pounding out of my chest. The image of a knife slamming into my barrier over and over flashed through my mind. In fact, it was taking everything I had to hold myself back at the moment. Just seeing Sebastian's face up close had me wanting to claw his eyes out.

Restraining myself as best as possible, I waited for Lesti to handle the situation with some cheeky comment. However, after glaring at him for a moment, her gaze grew dispassionate, and she turned away without sparing him a second glance. "Let's go, everyone. We don't need to bother with accusations from a disgrace like him."

Surprised that she had decided to ignore Sebastian, I turned and followed after Lesti in a somewhat stunned state. Looking up at her, I asked her privately, *"Are you sure it's okay to just let him go like that? He's probably one of the people helping to spread those rumors."*

"It's fine. Any rumor he's spreading won't have much credit outside whatever slimy social circle he's in. Even if his parents used their influence to keep him from getting expelled, most students know what he did. That's why he's been laying low until now." Lesti glanced back at him over her shoulder, and a slightly triumphant smile spread across her lips. *"Besides, that definitely hurt him more than fighting back would."*

I followed her gaze to see Sebastian standing there glaring at our backs, his fists clenched so hard that his knuckles turned white. For a brief moment, I felt the tension drain from my body as I realized that Lesti was right. Ignoring him and treating him as beneath her had clearly gotten under his skin. Yet, just as I started to feel better, I saw his lips mouth a wordless threat that brought me right back to my senses.

"I'll put you back in your place at the tournament."

If it were coming from anyone else, I would be willing to just dismiss something like that as an idle threat. Sebastian was different, though. He wouldn't hesitate to go to extreme lengths to get back at us. I would have to keep an eye on him during the tournament and make sure those words of his didn't come to pass.

* * *

"Wow, all of that really happened, and he wasn't expelled?" Rose stared at Lesti and me in disbelief as we finished telling her the story of what had happened with Sebastian. "Why do nobles like that exist? It's terrible."

We were sitting in a far corner of the cafeteria where our conversation wouldn't be overheard by anyone. People kept giving us strange glances, and I couldn't really blame them. We were all a bit tense after our brief run-in with Sebastian, especially after I warned Lesti about his unspoken threat. Honestly, we all looked like we were up to no good.

"Mm. They really are the worst." Aurelia nodded, her gaze stern and full of anger. I could only imagine how her people's issues with Lord Dawster had colored her perception of nobles.

"Yeah, it's a rather big problem, actually." Lesti let out a heavy sigh. "Between Sebastian, Augustine, and the Dawster family, I feel like I'm surrounded by rotten nobles. It's a wonder that the alliance can operate at all with people like this leading it."

"I would guess that having two strong enemies at your borders is preventing anything like a people's uprising from breaking out for now." I stretched out on the table as I spoke, trying my best to work the tension from my body. "Still, that will only stay true as long as the people are decently well taken care of. If some major disaster, like a famine, strikes, then it will all fall apart."

"A major disaster, huh?" Lesti's gaze grew distant, and her mouth set in a hard line as she seemed to ponder something. It was most likely the same thing that I was worried about, Thel'al. Who knew what would happen if he managed to get free of the city and started causing chaos throughout the alliance?

"At any rate, there's nothing we can do about all of that at the moment." I shook myself, trying to reset my mental state and focus back on the things we could handle, namely, Sebastian. "I think we should keep an eye on Sebastian until we can figure out what he's up to. Unless we know that, we won't be able to make any sort of preparations."

"How exactly are we supposed to do that?" Lesti looked at me skeptically. "Auri and I are both busy preparing for the tournament, and you can't do it either. You have to help Auri with her training. That just leaves Rose, and there's no way I'm letting her do this on her own. Who knows what Sebastian might do to her if he caught her?"

"While everything you said is true, I think you're forgetting someone." I looked over at Fang, whose eyes were darting about the crowd. Well, they weren't so much darting as they were following anyone who had meat on their plate. He clearly hadn't been listening to our conversation at all.

Following my gaze, everyone else's eyes landed on the carefree pup. For a minute, they all just looked at him before Lesti turned her gaze back to me, a disappointed look on her face. "Really? That's your plan? You're going to send Fang?"

"What's wrong with that, huh?!" I glared back at her defiantly as I defended my position. "He's small, people see him running around campus alone all the time, and most importantly, he can communicate with Aurelia from a distance. Sebastian probably won't suspect a thing, and even if he tries something, Fang can just call for backup."

Lesti kept her gaze locked squarely onto mine. "All of that may be true, but I think you're forgetting something rather important." She pointed at Fang, who was still completely ignoring us. "Fang has no idea how to be subtle or sneaky. I mean, just look at him. Even the other students can tell he's eyeing their food."

"That's, well…" I glanced over at Fang as I tried to come up with some counter to Lesti's argument. Unfortunately, I knew she was right. If we sent Fang as our spy, he was likely to walk right up to Sebastian and sit right next to him at the first sign of food.

"It's okay. Fang can do it." Aurelia picked up her companion, finally breaking his hyperfocus on the meat dishes passing by before she turned him to face the rest of us. "My clan trains all of our companions on stalking prey silently. I've already started working on it with him, so we can just treat it as a training exercise."

Lesti let out a slight sigh before reaching over and scratching Fang behind the ears with a small smile on her face. "Alright. I guess it's better than nothing. Think you can do that for us, Fang?"

"Rarf!" Fang's enthusiastic bark echoed through the dining hall, causing several people to turn and look at us. Yeah. Being subtle wasn't his strongest suit for sure. Still, if Aurelia said that he could do it, then I trusted her. Being his master, she knew what Fang was capable of better than any of us.

"Well, with that settled, we should get back to work. Shall we head back to the classroom?" Deciding to leave it to Fang, I dropped the subject and moved on to making sure the girls were as prepared as possible for whatever happened. However, upon hearing my suggestion, Lesti stopped me.

"Actually, Astria, there's something I wanted to test out today. Would you mind giving me a hand?"

"Well, I don't mind, but will you be alright without me for today, Aurelia?" I looked over at Aurelia, who had been busy filling Fang in on his mission.

Glancing up, she smiled softly at me. "Mm. I'll just focus on my energy manipulation for today."

"Ah, actually, I was hoping you could help me out as well, Auri." Lesti looked at her friend apologetically. "Sorry, I know you've got your own preparations to do, but you're the only person I can ask. I can't afford to show this to Elliot since I might need to use it on him at the tournament."

"Mm. No problem." Aurelia didn't hesitate for a moment and gave her a simple thumbs up.

"I-I guess I'll head back to the dorm and work on my own preparations then." Suddenly, Rose stood up and started to shuffle away, her shoulders slumped. Looking at her expression, I could tell that her mind was running wild again. Most likely, she was feeling left out because Lesti hadn't asked for her help.

"Huh, you're not coming, Rose?" Lesti looked at her friend, confused. "I was actually thinking that you could try and use this technique too if I can get it to work. After all, you managed to use Living Wall during the fight at the manor."

Rose stared back at Lesti wide-eyed. "R-Really? You think I could do it too?"

"Well, it won't be easy, but it uses the same instructions and runes that I showed you before, so it should be doable." Lesti stood up, grabbing her dirty dishes. "At any rate, showing you will be faster than talking about it. Let's get going."

As everyone gathered up their things, a thought occurred to me. *Why does Lesti need my help?* I didn't really consider myself a magic expert. She would be better off using Aurelia as a combat partner if she wanted to try her spells on someone. That only really left two reasons that she would need me. Either she wanted me to help modify another one of her spells, or she needed my ability to sense magical energy. Whichever one it was, I had the feeling that she was going to be up to something crazy again.

* * *

I watched as Aurelia dodged yet another small Aqua Sphere that had been aimed directly at her face. Yet even as she avoided that, the ground shifted slightly under her feet, throwing her balance off. Rather than letting that stop her, she used her momentum to quickly roll and spring back up to her feet before charging Lesti again. The expression on her face told me that she was deadly serious.

The usually calm and serene atmosphere that always filled the air around her was nowhere to be found, instead replaced by an intense focus and drive. I had only seen her like this once before when she had fought Alex briefly while defending Fang. The fact that she was directing that same energy at Lesti was beyond anything I had expected from this training exercise.

I guess getting hit in the face repeatedly by Aqua Spheres was enough to even get Aurelia riled up a little bit, huh?

Just as I thought that another series of Aqua Spheres cut off Aurelia's charge, forcing her to try and dodge. But there were just too many, and several of them clipped her, causing her to grimace in frustration. Meanwhile, Lesti continued the tactic she had used from the start and used the time Aurelia had wasted dodging to gain more distance from her.

"I can't believe Lesti is holding off Auri so easily." From beside me, Rose stared on in wonder as the pair continued their game of cat and mouse. "That spell really is amazing. To think that she hasn't used up all of her magical energy even after an hour with no breaks..."

I shifted my gaze over to Lesti, who was exhausted despite clearly having the upper hand. Both her and Aurelia were entirely drenched in sweat, but she was especially bad. Probably due to not being quite as physically inclined as her friend. She was panting heavily and looked like she might fall over any moment. I was used to her pushing herself, so I knew she had a little left in the tank.

As for how she had made it this far into a fight with Aurelia, that would be the effect of her new spell. Behind her, I saw the trace amounts of magical energy in the air being drawn in and forming into multiple spells at Lesti's guidance. As long as she didn't try to cast any large spells, she would never have to touch her own small magical energy reserves. That meant she could basically keep fighting as long as her body held out. Still, it was probably best to end things here before either of them got any more heated up.

"Don't you think that's about enough, you two?" I called out, putting on the best stern teacher voice that I could. "I'd say you've thoroughly tested the effectiveness of the spell at this point, wouldn't you?"

To my surprise, Aurelia was the first one to drop her guard, causing a few Aqua Spheres to hit her right in the face again. Seeing this, Lesti froze, looking at her drenched friend in horror. "Auri, I'm sorry! Are you okay?"

I was just as worried as she was, but to my surprise, Aurelia just shook her head with a smile, "Mm. The water feels nice."

Seeing her shift gears and drop out of combat mode into her usual calm self was kind of jarring. Lesti and I could only stare at her in stunned silence before Rose finally brought towels over to the two. "Good work, both of you. I'm really impressed that you both managed to keep going for so long."

"Mm. That spell really is something. I couldn't even get close to you." Auri nodded as she began to wipe the sweat off of herself.

"Yeah, I still don't think it will be enough, though." Lesti furrowed her brow for a moment before looking over at me. "How did it look anyway?"

"Ah, yeah. It seems like your theory was correct. If you stop moving, it uses all of the energy in the air around you and will stop working."

"That's what I was afraid of." Lesti's shoulders slumped a little at my assessment. "Unlike when we fought that massive demon, there just isn't enough magical energy in the air. Even if I use smaller spells, I'll use it all up faster than it can replenish."

"Still, it's not like it's a bad spell." I walked over and closed my eyes, allowing the flow of magic to take over my senses. "The magical energy in the area seems to recover pretty quickly. As long as you keep the spells small and keep moving, it will chip away at your opponents without really costing you anything."

"Mm. It's really frustrating to fight against." Aurelia backed up my sentiment, a bit of the edge returning to her expression for a brief moment as she remembered their fight. "No matter how much I dodged or defended, more and more spells just kept coming. Even if each one doesn't do much damage, it adds up over time."

Rose nodded enthusiastically next to her. "It really is impressive and doesn't seem too hard to maintain. I think even I could use it."

"Yeah, I think it will work great against foes that lack brute force, but"—Lesti paused for a long moment, closing her eyes with a frown on her face—"it's just no good. No matter how I look at it, I can't see this beating Alex or Thel'al."

Briefly, the memory of Alex's Earth Wave spell flashed through my mind. "Yeah, you're probably right."

No matter how optimistic I wanted to be, I simply couldn't deny reality. Both Alex and Thel'al had the advantage of dumping absurd amounts of magical energy into their spells. If either of them came at Lesti with everything they had, she wouldn't be able to beat them back with such weak attacks. Yet, it seemed like Lesti had forgotten something important.

"Still, I think it's part of the answer if not the whole thing." I shot her a toothy grin. "Even if you can't beat them with this alone, it buys you some room to breathe. You can use it to keep your distance and defend yourself while spending almost no energy of your own. It may even open up some chances for you to get in some counterattacks."

"I guess that's true." Lesti pumped her fist, her enthusiasm suddenly restored. "Alright, let's plan on using this in the tournament. Then, all I need to do is come up with a killer spell to strike at Alex's weak point!"

"Mm. You can do it."

"Is it really going to be that easy to come up with a spell like that, though?" Rose voiced her doubts as she stared into space, her expression thoughtful. The upbeat mood that I had been trying to build was suddenly brought crashing down around me as Lesti's shoulders slumped slightly. I shot an annoyed glare at Rose, which snapped her out of whatever train of thought she was having.

Suddenly realizing what she had done, she tried her best to recover. "I-I didn't mean it would be impossible or anything like that! It's just, does Alexander even have any weaknesses that you can aim for? All the rumors make him out to be basically perfect."

Oddly, her statement seemed to brush off whatever cloud of doubt had been hanging around Lesti. She grinned at her friend and pointed at her in a highly exaggerated fashion. "You're one hundred percent right, Rose! As far as I know, Alex doesn't have any weaknesses. He has tons of magical energy, knows how to use instruction magic, is great at hand-to-hand combat, and he's no slouch in the tactics department either. Still, we have a secret weapon we can use to find out his weakness!"

"A secret weapon?" I looked up at Lesti skeptically. "What sort of nonsense did you come up with this time? Wait, you're not thinking about trying to spy on Alex, are you?"

I prepared to cut off whatever crazy ideas Lesti had, but she stopped me with a smug grin and a wave of her finger. "Come now, Astria. I'm not that much of a fool. Besides, we don't need to spy on him. We have the perfect informant right under our noses!" Without any warning, Lesti took off running, looking back over her shoulder. "Come on! Let's get going! We don't have time to waste here."

"Wait, Lesti! Where you going?" I shouted after her, completely baffled by her sudden excited state. "You still haven't told us who this informant is!"

"You'll see when we get there! Now, come on!"

"Oh, fine! Just don't blame me when this doesn't go how you think it will!" Giving up on trying to settle her down, I took off after Lesti. Aurelia and Rose followed close behind, both seeming just as confused as me.

* * *

"Yeah, nothing like that exists."

It was about twenty minutes after Lesti mentioned her secret weapon.

She had tracked down Elliot and pulled him into an empty classroom. Apparently, her brilliant idea had been to get Elliot to tell her Alex's weakness. Unfortunately, that plan was now spectacularly backfiring in her face.

"What?! Come on, there has to be something!" Lesti glared at Elliot, her supposed secret weapon, angry that he had failed to deliver. "You're not holding out on me because you're mad that I took your number two spot, are you?"

Elliot shot her a rather angry glare in return. "As if I would do something that petty. I still owe you for helping out with the whole Baron Arvis incident after all."

"Then, why won't you tell me?" Lesti glared back at him definitely. "Did Alex swear you to secrecy or something?"

"No, it's not that. It's that I really don't know." Elliot let out a heavy sigh as he ruffled his own hair in irritation. "Look, if I knew some secret weakness of Alex's, don't you think I would have used that to beat him by now?"

"Wait, you really don't know?" Lesti's eyes widened in shock. "I just assumed you hadn't used it because of some stupid pride thing. Wanting to beat him at his best or something silly like that."

"You really know how to push your luck, you know that?" Elliot bopped Lesti on the head playfully. While Lesti rubbed the spot he had hit, he grimaced, his eyes suddenly distant. "No matter how many times I've fought Alex, I've never managed to push him anywhere near his limit. He's never struggled in any fight that I've ever seen, even against adults."

"I was afraid this would happen." I looked over at Lesti, expecting to see her looking disappointed, but instead found her brow furrowed in thought as she muttered to herself. "Lesti? Hello?"

"Never struggled." Ignoring my calls, she continued to mutter to herself for a bit longer until her eyes suddenly lit up. "That may just work!"

Suddenly turning on her heel, Lesti ran out of the room without saying another word. Completely caught off guard, I called after her as she darted out the door. "Lesti, where are you going? What about training?!"

For a moment, I thought she wasn't going to answer me, but then a second later, her head poked back around the corner. "Sorry, but I'll be doing some top-secret training for the rest of the day, so you can help Auri and Rose with their training. Oh, and thanks, Elliot. I knew you would come through in the end."

Then, with a massive grin and a quick wave, she was gone once again. Leaving the rest of us standing there stunned. Elliot turned and looked at me, the confusion written plainly on his face. "So, any idea what that was all about?"

"Not a one. It seems like she came up with some idea based on what you said." I paused, turning my gaze toward the door. "Although, I'm a bit conflicted about her keeping it a secret from me too."

"Well, I'm sure she'll tell you in due time." Rose looked down at me worriedly while trying to comfort me. "In the meantime, shall we go and do our own training?"

"Mm. Let's go. Lesti will be fine on her own." Aurelia scratched behind my ears briefly. The pleasant sensation helped to clear my head a little. They were right. Lesti would be fine. As much as I wanted to keep an eye on her, this tournament was something she would have to do on her own anyway. It wouldn't hurt to get a bit of an early start. With my feelings on the matter settled. I followed after the others as we made our way to the usual study spot.

Suspicion and Advice

Alex dodged to the side, avoiding a series of Aqua Spheres that had been fired at him. The caster rushed toward him without wasting any time, her blonde twin tails fluttering in the air behind her. Even as she closed the distance, he could tell she was forming another spell.

The girl was probably planning on releasing the spell at the same time as a physical barrage. A small smile crept over Alex's face. It was a tactic he used pretty often himself. That was also why he knew its major weakness.

Waiting until the very last moment, he lunged forward and grabbed the girl's arm. The sudden change in distance threw off the timing of her spell and gave him an opening. Spinning to the side, he kicked her feet and pulled down heavily on her arm. Her momentum sent her tumbling forward across the ground.

Yet, even as she did, she somehow managed to finish her spell. Several new spheres of water formed in the air and launched themselves at him. He was honestly rather impressed. It was hard to concentrate on a spell while taking an attack like that, especially as a first-year.

It wasn't enough to stop him, though. He started to put some extra energy into his body enhancement magic but then thought better of it. There was no reason to push things here. Instead, he just dove forward and rolled across the ground, popping to his feet as the spheres whizzed past where he had been standing.

Alex quickly formed his own water sphere and lobbed it at the girl as she rolled to her feet. Seeing the attack coming, she made to leap to the side, but he quickly cast another spell. The earth suddenly rose up and wrapped itself around the girl's ankle before hardening into solid stone.

The girl began to form another spell, probably trying to break free, but her casting speed was too slow. Unable to break the binding in time, she was splashed across the face with the Aqua Sphere he had cast, ending their sparring match. Alex quickly undid his spell, freeing the girl, and walked over to join her.

The drenched girl wrung the water out of her hair as she glared at him. "That was a cheap trick, Al."

"Using simple magic to disable your opponent isn't a cheap trick. It's efficient and could save your life on the battlefield. I know our family values raw strength, but that doesn't mean you should only use raw strength. If anything, your tactics are too straightforward, Clara."

"I don't want to hear that from the guy who won the Spring Tournament last year using only body enhancement magic." Clara puffed out her cheeks as she looked up at him. "If anything, it just feels like you're holding back when you rely on tactics like that."

Alex let out an exasperated sigh. Clara knew him far too well. As cousins, they had spent a lot of time together growing up and had often trained together. She knew that he typically wouldn't bother with little tricks and traps. It was unavoidable this time around, though.

"Stop assuming that I can just brute force everything all the time. I may have gotten away with that last year, but there are some tricky challengers that I'll have to deal with this time."

"Like Ms. Vilia, yes?" Clara's eyes lit up as she mentioned his classmate. For whatever reason, she seemed to absolutely adore Lesti, frequently going off on tangents about how great she was.

Alex decided to use that to his advantage to change the subject. "That's right. With how much she's grown over the last few months, I can't afford to not be prepared. Who knows what crazy tricks she'll throw at me?"

"I see! Of course! If anyone is going to be able to challenge you, it would be Ms. Vilia after all!" Clara looked off across the campus toward the main training grounds, her eyes full of excitement. "I wonder what kind of fantastic new spells and innovations she's preparing for the tournament. She's so innovative and brave! I can't wait."

Alex stared at his cousin in disbelief as she gushed about Lesti. He really had to wonder if they were talking about the same person. The girl that he knew, while undoubtedly brave, was also rash and just a little bit overzealous. Besides, nothing she had shown off was that innovative in his mind.

Regardless, his diversion had been successful, and Clara had utterly forgotten about his hesitancy to use more magical energy. At least, that's what he thought. Even so, she somehow managed to quickly turn the conversation back to him.

"Still, even if you have competition like her, it's weird to see you acting like this." She planted her fists on her hips and looked up at him with a concerned expression. "It just seems so out of character for you. Are you sure there's nothing else wrong?"

Alex couldn't help but smile at just how well his cousin knew him. He had even considered talking to her about his dreams. In the end, he knew it wouldn't do any good. Being from outside the main family, she didn't know about their secrets, and his dreams touched just a little too closely on those. Telling her would actually put her in danger.

So, he did the only thing he could and lied. "It's nothing. I promise. Lesti and her friends are really just that strong. They stood up against an archdemon and that massive demon at Elliot's party, after all."

"If you say so." Clara, clearly not buying it, let out a heavy sigh. It seemed like she was willing to drop the subject, at least.

Not wanting to give her an opportunity to change her mind, Alex turned and began to head toward the school building. "Come on, it's getting late. Let's head to the dining hall."

"Huh? You're going to join me?" Clara trotted to catch up with him. "Are you not eating at the manor then?"

"No. I'm staying at the dorms tonight. The head chef is busy preparing for all the tournament festivities tomorrow, so I told him not to worry about me."

"Yay!" Clara grabbed onto his arm and started pulling. "Hurry up, Al. Let's hurry up before all the good seats are gone?"

"What exactly are the good seats?" Alex couldn't help but wonder what she meant. He should have guessed the answer, though.

"The one's where I can watch Ms. Vilia, of course."

With an exasperated sigh, he allowed himself to be tugged into the dining hall by his cousin. However, Lesti was nowhere to be found.

* * *

Later that night, Alex lay on his stiff bed in the dorms, unable to sleep. It wasn't the mattress that kept him awake. He simply couldn't stop thinking about tomorrow. It was as if there was a heavy weight laid on his shoulders that he couldn't shake off.

Ever since he had that dream, he had been struggling with what to do. He had thought on it constantly but to no avail. With the first day of the tournament nearly upon him, he wasn't any closer to making a decision.

Finally giving up, he rolled out of bed and slipped out into the night. He didn't have any particular destination in mind, so he simply wandered the grounds aimlessly. However, he soon found himself instinctively heading toward the training grounds. In the end, it was always where he went when he was troubled.

To his surprise, he wasn't the only one there. As he approached, he saw a shadowy form standing in the distance. With the light from the moon being blocked by the clouds, he couldn't make out who it was. All he knew was that they seemed to be standing there simply staring at a tree, not doing anything.

For a minute, he wondered if he should disturb them, but just as he began to turn and leave, the moon peaked out from behind the clouds. The light reflected off a messy head of red hair pulled up into a sloppy ponytail.

I wonder what she would do?

As the unexpected question popped into his mind, he found himself walking toward Lesti. It wasn't until he was just a few feet away that she finally heard his footsteps. She quickly spun around, looking like a child caught stealing sweets from the kitchen.

"Lani, I can explai—Alex?! What are you doing here? How long have you been there?"

For some odd reason, her panic only seemed to worsen when she realized that it was him and not an instructor that had found her. "I just got here. Why? Am I seeing something that I'm not supposed to?"

Lesti let out a relieved sigh and plopped down on the ground. "No, it's nothing. I just wasn't expecting you to be here. What are you doing out so late?"

"Couldn't sleep. What about you?"

She looked up at him and smiled brightly, but even then, her exhaustion still showed. "Doing some last-minute training."

Looking her over once more, he noticed that she was covered in sweat. Yet, it hadn't appeared that she was doing any sort of physical training. The only other reason she would look so exhausted then was that she had exhausted nearly all of her magical energy. It was a feeling that Alex hadn't ever experienced.

If anything, it seemed excessive. The Spring Tournament was important, but it was hardly the end of the world if you lost. He simply couldn't understand why she would push herself so hard.

"Wouldn't it be better to get some rest? There's no reason to kill yourself over something like the Spring Tournament."

"Hah?" Lesti's expression shifted instantly. The bright smile she had been wearing was replaced by an angry glare. "That's rich hearing that from last year's winner. Maybe you don't understand this being the son of the most influential family in the alliance, but winning the Spring Tournament can create important opportunities for the rest of us. Especially in my case."

She quickly stood up and shoved a finger in his face. "I'm giving my all here because winning will get me one step closer to my goals."

"Goals, huh?" Thinking about it, what even were his own goals? All his family had told him his purpose was to serve and protect his people. That was the ultimate purpose of a noble, the Bestroff way.

Maybe that was good enough. It wasn't like he hated the idea. In fact, Alex was actually proud of how his family treated their noble privilege. There was just one problem. He wouldn't be able to protect anyone if he was constantly holding back.

"What would you do if there was something that was stopping you from chasing that dream, something that you weren't sure you could overcome?"

"D-Do you even realize what you're asking me?" Lesti looked at him dumbfounded for a long moment before letting out an exasperated sigh. "What's with you tonight. I feel like you're normally more perceptive than this."

"Sorry. I've got some things of my own on my mind."

"So, even the great Alexander Bestroff has things that he worries about, huh?"

She looked at him for a long moment before planting her feet with her hands on her hips. It was oddly reminiscent of how Clara had lectured him earlier. "If there's something that you don't think you can overcome, then all you can do is give it your best. Study until your brain feels like it will explode. Train until you drop. Find allies where you can. Put every ounce of your being into overcoming that obstacle."

"And if all of that isn't enough?"

A bright grin spread across her face once more. "Then, at least you won't have any regrets."

He let out an amused chuckle. The answer she had given him was just that funny. It was pure and straightforward beyond belief. Still, he didn't hate it. After all, what could anyone do outside of giving their best?

"You really are simpleminded, you know that?"

"Why are you making fun of me after I just gave you advice?!" Lesti shouted at him before pushing her way past him. "Enough. I'm going to bed. Goodnight!"

Turning around, he called out to her as she stormed off. "Hey, Lesti."

Spinning around, she glared at him angrily. "What?!"

"Thank you."

The anger faded from Lesti's face, replaced by her usual smile. "Don't go thanking me just yet. I'm going to be coming for you during the tournament."

With that, she walked off into the night, leaving him alone. The weight that he had been feeling was gone. He was still worried, but he knew what he had to do now. With a smile, he whispered a reply that only he could hear.

"I wouldn't have it any other way."

Opening Ceremony

"Come on! Move it!" I yelled back at Lesti, who was running down the street behind me.

"I'm going as fast as I can! Wouldn't it be faster if you just transformed and carried me?"

"Yeah, because transforming into a tiger and running through town wouldn't cause a panic at all."

"Ah, fine! I'll run faster, but if I lose in the preliminaries, I'm blaming you."

It was a week after our conversation with Elliot about Alex's weakness. Today was the opening ceremony and preliminary round of the Spring Tournament. Thanks to both of us sleeping in, we were running late, forcing us to make a mad dash through the crowded city streets. As for why we had slept in, it was, of course, because we had both stayed up too late making last-minute preparations for today.

Over the last week, I had only seen Lesti during meals, breaks, and the few times I had checked on her to make sure she wasn't pushing herself too hard. I still had no idea what she had been working on this entire time. She had insisted on keeping it a secret, saying that she didn't want any leaks. Whatever it was, though, she was extremely confident in it. I just hoped that it wouldn't come back to bite her.

Suddenly, a massive stone building came into view in the distance as we rounded a corner. "Is that it?"

I slowed down a little to let Lesti catch up with me. "Yeah. That's the arena. It's bigger than I thought."

The building in question wasn't really what I had been expecting. In my head, I had imagined something like a Roman coliseum. However, this building was made of pure white stone, carved with the imagery of various beasts and mages. If anything, it looked more like a theater than a place where a combat tournament would take place. I guess that was to be expected of a building in the upper merchant district, though. It perfectly fit the fancy aesthetic of the area.

The crowds only got worse, and we drew closer to the arena. Normally, access to this part of town was somewhat restricted. If you didn't look the part and didn't have a good reason for being here, the guards would turn you away at the gates. But today was an exception. Anyone from the commoner district was allowed to come and see the tournament. Thanks to that, the streets were packed to capacity.

Eventually, we came upon a massive wall of people that we couldn't find a way through. Lesti tried to call out and get people to move aside, but the crowd was so large and noisy that hardly anyone could hear her. Realizing we weren't going to make it at this rate, I transformed into my tiger form and threw her on my back. "Hold on tight!"

Almost immediately, the people standing nearby began to panic and move away from me, just like I had expected. The nearby guards, realizing something was wrong, started to move in. I definitely didn't want to get caught up trying to explain the situation to them or let the panic spread any further.

So I used Air Walk to take to the air. I didn't really have any reason to preserve my magical energy today since I wouldn't be fighting. So, I also used Speed Boost to get us to the arena as fast as possible. The guards shouted at us to stop, but I just ignored them. It wasn't like they had any way to stop us.

In a matter of seconds, we soared over the crowd, several of whom stared at us or pointed. As we drew close to the entrance, I spotted Aurelia, Rose, and Fang off to the side, away from the main entrance. They were waving at us rather frantically, so I adjusted my course to join up with them.

"Thank goodness. You made it." Rose placed a hand on her chest as she breathed a sigh of relief. "We were worried that something had happened to you."

"Sorry about that." Lesti scratched her cheek with an awkward smile. "We were both up a little too late preparing and slept in. We're here now, though, so let's get going."

"Mm. Let's hurry. The opening ceremony will be starting soon." Aurelia turned and headed toward a side entrance that appeared to be for participants.

"Even with all of those people still outside?" I asked as we followed after her.

She didn't even look back as she replied, "Mm. The seating is already full."

"Yeah. It's kind of nerve-wracking, honestly," Rose said, backing up Aurelia's assessment of the crowd. "I don't think I've ever seen so many people in my entire life."

We made our way down the hall and soon found ourselves in a small lounge. A few simple benches and basic medical equipment littered the area. Compared to the outside appearance of the arena, it was incredibly plain looking. On the far side of the room, another door led deeper inside. Next to that door, Malkael was waiting impatiently, a rather irritated expression on his face.

"There you two are." He walked across the room and gestured back the way we came. "Astria and Fang, please follow me. The rest of you head straight into the arena proper and hurry up. The ceremony is about to start."

Without even waiting for us to reply, Malkael headed back toward the exit. Rather than following, I looked back at Lesti. "Good luck in the preliminaries. Be sure you all win."

She threw me a quick thumbs-up as she took off toward the arena. "You bet. It'll be a piece of cake."

"Mm. We'll do our best." Aurelia gave Fang one quick scratch behind the ears before following after Lesti. "Be good while I'm gone, Fang."

"I'll do my best!" Rose was the last one to head out, her words seeming to be more for her own sake than anyone else's.

Once they were all gone, I glanced over at Fang, who was pouting slightly at being left behind. "Come on, cheer up. I'm sure we'll be able to watch them from the stands. In fact, we had better hurry, or we'll miss the opening ceremony."

I turned and headed after Malkael. It seemed like he had gone ahead, but I wasn't worried about getting lost. There was really only one path to get back here that I had seen. So, instead of focusing on where we were headed, I decided to ask Fang about his assignment.

"So, did Sebastian ever do anything worth mentioning over the last week?" I had been hoping to try and distract the pup who kept looking back over his shoulder after his master, but at my question, he just hung his head. Based on his reaction, I could only assume that he hadn't been able to get any good information. Rubbing up against him, I tried to cheer him up. "Don't worry about it. If you weren't able to spot what he was up to, then none of us would have been able to."

My comforting words earned me a playful lick on the face, which honestly I could have done without. Still, it seemed that Fang was in a better mood now and just in time, too. Malkael was waiting for us just up ahead by one of the few doors in the hallway. Seeing us approaching, he pulled the door open and ushered us inside.

"So, where exactly are we heading, Malkael?" I asked as I followed after him. "Are you dropping us off somewhere before you head back to the opening ceremony?"

Malkael glanced back at me. "I won't be attending the opening ceremony or taking part in the officiating for the tournament. I've been given the sole responsibility of keeping an eye on you two in order to ensure that you don't cheat."

"Cheat?! Who even suggested that we would do that?" I felt my fur bristle a little at the idea that some staff thought we might cheat. However, Malkael quickly put that idea to rest.

"It appears that whatever rumors were being spread about you and your companions weren't just being spread in the academy." Malkael wore an expression that told me he was rather annoyed at this turn of events. "Several noble houses approached the headmistress claiming they had reason to suspect foul play. She was only able to get them to back down by making some concessions."

"Well, I guess that means our plan to spread counter rumors didn't do much good then."

Like we had discussed before, we had Lani and Elliot help us combat the rumors at the school. I had seen some decent progress based on the whispers I heard when people didn't realize I was around. Unfortunately, if the rumors were spreading outside of the academy, then there wasn't much we could do, especially since we were finding out about it just now.

"Well, it's not like it was all a waste," Malkael replied as he continued to navigate the halls of the arena. "Based on the nobles who lodged their complaints, we were able to rule out quite a few factions as the source of the rumors."

"You know who it was then?" I felt a small jolt of excitement run through my body. If we could figure out who was spreading these rumors, it would make our lives a lot easier.

"Well, we still haven't been able to figure out the exact source, but it's progress," Malkael replied as he glanced back at me. "I'll fill you in on the details later. Discussing any further now would be problematic."

There was a sudden ominous tone in his voice, warning me not to press the subject any further. As we rounded the corner, I quickly came to understand why. Two guards stood at attention outside a pair of elaborately decorated doors just a short way down the hall. Based on the extra security, there had to be some important guests inside. Based on Malkael's warning, some of them were likely suspects in our investigation.

The guards eyed us carefully as we approached but seemed to recognize Malkael. We passed by them without any questions or inspections. It was far more lax than I had expected, but just as I turned to say as much to Malkael, I felt a sudden wave of magic wash over me. The sensation was so sudden and unexpected that I did a double take. However, neither of the guards had moved or cast a spell.

Malkael, noticing my confusion, glanced back at the hallway behind us. "This entire room is surrounded by a special defensive barrier that only allows those with permission from the caster to enter."

"There's a spell like that?!" I asked as I stared back at the space in awe. Closing my eyes, I could see the flow of magic, just like Malkael had said. "Wouldn't that take an insane amount of magical energy?"

"Yes. It's definitely not something that any human could cast. This is the work of an artifact that the council uses to facilitate safe meetings between lords." Malkael paused in front of the doors and looked down at me. "Now, try your best not to draw further suspicion to either you or your master."

Without waiting for my response, he pushed the door open, and we headed inside. Immediately my nose was assaulted by an array of smells, including perfumes, food, and the scent of other familiars. All around the room, various nobles mingled, accompanied by their familiars and servants.

Almost immediately, a strange tension filled the air as everyone's eyes came to fall on me. Each person's reaction to my presence seemed to vary wildly, ranging from simple curiosity to outright malice. Only one thing seemed to be constant, and that was that everyone here knew precisely who I was. Apparently, whoever had been spreading those rumors off campus had done a thorough job.

All in all, it created a rather suffocating atmosphere. It even appeared to be affecting Malkael. For a long moment, he just stood frozen in place, seeming unsure of what to do. Thankfully, one member of our party seemed to be more hungry than anything else.

Without any hesitation, Fang darted toward a servant who was carrying a tray with some sort of appetizer. Startled by his approach, the woman froze on the spot and raised the tray high over her head. I guess she had expected Fang to jump for the food, but he had been trained well, and even without his master around, he wouldn't just randomly jump on a stranger.

Instead, he came to a screeching halt at her feet, quickly plopping down into a well-rehearsed sit and turning his eyes up at the lady. It was a look that I knew all too well. Fang always looked at Lesti like that when he thought he could get attention or treats out of her. A small smile crept over the woman's face, and several of the less hostile nobles in the room giggled at the pup's antics, breaking the strange tension in the room.

The servant lady looked over at Malkael. "Would it be alright to feed him, my lord?"

Her question seemed to bring Malkael back to his senses, and he looked down at me. "You would know better than me. Would Aurelia mind?"

"I'm sure it's fine, but you have to promise not to bother the workers anymore. Okay, Fang?"

"Rarf!" Fang barked his agreement enthusiastically, his tail wagging faster than ever. Another wave of laughter passed through the room as everyone became charmed by the little pup, but there was one group that seemed to maintain their foul mood. Rather, it seemed to worsen when I had called out to Fang, and now they were glaring daggers at him.

Before I could worry too much about it, Malkael pointed over to the far side of the room. "Shall we get a good spot for the opening ceremony? It should be starting any moment now."

Without waiting for my response, Malkael headed over to a less crowded part of the room. A low wall ran across the entire far side of the room, with evenly spaced pillars supporting the ceiling above. Rows of fancy chairs had been lined up toward the center of the room, allowing the guests to sit and observe the tournament. However, the corner we were heading to didn't have any, forcing me to climb the wall to see.

As soon as I did, the crowd outside cheered loudly, startling me and causing my fur to stand on end. The room we were in was at the top level of the arena, with the stage several stories below, giving us an excellent view of the whole building. Down below, the fighting area was an ordinary raised section of stone surrounded by a dirt floor on the outside.

On the far side, a simple wooden stage had been set up. At the center of that stage was a strange magical device placed on a podium. The device was covered in runes, marking it as an artifact recovered from the lost civilization that Malkael had spoken about. Behind the device stood the headmistress, her usual stern features on full display. She waited a moment for the crowd's cheering to settle and began to speak.

"Welcome one and all to the opening ceremony of the annual Alandrian Central Magic Academy Spring Tournament!" Despite her stern expression and composed air, the crowd once again roared their approval. It was pretty apparent that the whole city was looking forward to this tournament. "Every year, we hold this tournament to give our students, the future defenders of Alandria, an opportunity to show the fruits of their studies and training. As well as to remind our foes of the might of our alliance!"

Another roar of approval shot up from the crowd at her words. It was honestly a bit surprising to me. Everything I had heard from Lesti and the others made the Alandrian Alliance seem like a rather loose group of smaller territories with no solid national identity. Yet, the crowd's reaction seemed to suggest otherwise.

"Now, without further ado, allow me to present you this year's combatants, starting with the representatives of the Bestroff territory." At her words, a neatly organized group of students walked out onto the arena floor led by none other than Alexander Bestroff. He carried a large banner with an elaborate family crest embroidered on it.

"Malkael, are all of those students hosted by the Bestroff family?" I looked over at our escort curiously as the students filtered into the arena.

"Ah, yes. Students are introduced based on the territory that they represent." Malkael gestured down at the field below. "As you can see, the Bestroff family has a large amount of influence and sends quite a few students to the academy."

"Quite a few is a bit of an understatement, don't you think?" I turned my gaze back to the field below as the Bestroff representatives came to a halt before the stage. By my account, there were around forty of them in total. It didn't sound like much, but when you considered the total number of students at the academy and the number of territories in the alliance, it was way more than I would have expected.

With Alex and the others from his area in place, the headmistress began calling the names of other territories one after the other. As I watched the various groups enter, I couldn't shake the sense of anxiety I was feeling. Officially, Lesti was the only student representing her territory. She would be out there all on her own. At that moment, I wanted nothing more than to be at her side.

I waited anxiously for some time until finally her family name was called.

"And finally, we have the representatives of the Vilia territory!"

My ears perked up as I heard the headmistress's booming voice. "Wait, did she say finally? Then that means…"

My eyes immediately darted to the entrance to the arena, where three small but familiar figures entered. In the center was Lesti, bearing her territory's crest. Her head was held high, and she was smiling brightly as if she hadn't a care in the world. Just a step behind her on either side were Aurelia and Rose.

Aurelia carried herself with her usual cool aloofness. Her steps were calm and fluid, as if the atmosphere in the arena didn't affect her at all. Rose, on the other hand, was clearly nervous. Her strides were stiff, and her gaze was locked ahead of her like some sort of robot.

Seeing the three walking together caused my chest to thrum with joy. Still, I was surprised that Aurelia and Rose had been allowed to walk with Lesti. I turned to ask Malkael what was going on, but the sound of glass shattering caught our attention before I could.

Looking to the source of the noise, I found an overweight man holding nothing but the broken stem of a wine glass. Its contents, along with the upper half, had fallen to the floor and shattered. His face was flushed red with anger, and his plump fingers were white due to how hard he gripped the broken glass. His eyes gazed down at the arena with a look of pure hatred before snapping over to me, causing a shiver to run up my spine.

The man angrily stomped over to where Malkael and I were standing, ignoring the mess he had made. "Do you care to explain what is going on here, Master Malkael?"

The man's sudden anger seemed strange to me until I heard Malkael's response. "Lord Dawster, what seems to be the problem? I'm afraid that I'm unaware of what you're referring to."

All at once, the man's anger made sense. Standing before me was Aurelia's former sponsor, Edward Dawster. His anger was the result of seeing his former bargaining chip entering the arena with Lesti under the Vilia flag. Given her people's status, her actions were as good as declaring there was a defense agreement between her people and the Vilia territory. Seeing how easily it got under his skin, I had to wonder if this had been planned from the start.

As I pondered the possibility, Lord Dawster continued his tantrum, pointing to the field below. "Don't play dumb with me! Why is one of the students that my territory is sponsoring entering the field under the flag of that backwater Vilia family?!"

"Ah, that?" Malkael's face and tone remained neutral as he replied. "I'm afraid that I know very little about the matter at hand. The headmistress bears the sole responsibility for maintaining the enrollment status of our students. If Ms. Aurelia was allowed to enter under the flag of the Vilia family, then the headmistress would had to have approved the change. I would suggest you take the matter up with her once the tournament is over."

"Why, you..." After not getting the explanation that he wanted from Malkael, Lord Dawster began to shake with rage. For a moment, I thought he was simply going to storm off in a huff, but then his eyes locked on me. "I will not wait! Once the tournament is over, the damage to my reputation will already be done. Even if you don't know anything, the Vilia girl's familiar must have been present when the decision was made!"

"Unfortunately, I was involved in no such meeting." I met Lord Dawster's gaze firmly. "Besides, even if I was, I'm under no obligation to tell you anything. I suggest you take Instructor Malkael's advice and bring your complaints up with the headmistress."

For a moment, Lord Dawster's face turned so red that he looked like a volcano that was about to explode. But just as he was about to go off, a maid stepped forward and whispered something in his ear. Immediately, the color in his face returned to normal, but the hard, angry look in his eyes remained. "Consider yourself lucky, you two. Some urgent matters have come up that need my attention. Don't think for a second this is over, though."

With that final warning, Lord Dawster turned on his heel and headed toward a door on the far side of the room. The rest of the nobles in the room gave him a wide berth as he went, clearly not wanting to be the next person to invoke his wrath. However, as soon as he had passed, several of them glared daggers at his back. He clearly had quite a few enemies even within the alliance.

"Malkael, where does that door that he is headed to lead?" I asked as soon as Lord Dawster was out of earshot.

"I believe there are some rooms and box seats set up nearby for private meetings between the lords. The tournament also acts as a summit of sorts," Malkael responded with his gaze locked on Lord Dawster's back. "Why do you ask? Hey, wait!"

Malkael finally turned his attention to me a moment too late. As soon as I had my answer, I leapt up from my perch on the low wall of the balcony out of Malkael's reach. "Sorry. I know you said to behave, but there's something I need to look into. I'll be back soon."

Without waiting for Malkael's response, I used Air Walk to head up toward the arena's roof. I knew I was going to cause him trouble by doing this, but I had good reason. Despite her best attempt at being discrete, the maid had underestimated my feline hearing. I had clearly heard her mention a specific place that I just couldn't ignore. The Forests of Dram, Aurelia's home.

Unexpected Assistance

As soon as I landed on the roof, I began to search for the box where Lord Dawster might be holding his private conference. The arena had a bowl shape, much like many modern stadiums from my world. The seats for the general public were lower and closer to the action. However, they were also exposed to the elements.

Above those were seats that appeared to be reserved for wealthy merchants. These seats sat under the noble suites and box seats on the top level, protecting them from the weather. Even so, they lacked the luxury of the suites and boxes above them, which were filled with fancy chairs, catered food, and alcohol aplenty.

I had a hunch that Lord Dawster hadn't gone very far for his meeting. He seemed like the type to make others come to him, both due to arrogance and laziness. Fortunately, it turned out that I was right, and I found him just three boxes down from the suite I had exited. It was a small box designed for two or three people. Peeking over the lip of the ceiling, I could see him conversing with another man I had never seen before. Each of them had a single servant in the room standing at attention behind them.

Unfortunately, I couldn't hear what they were saying. Straining my ears as hard as I could, I leaned over the edge of the roof, trying to get even just a little bit closer. I could just barely make out random syllables from their conversation. I was sure that if I got just a little closer, I would be able to hear them, even if it might be a bit muffled. So, I scooted just a little further over the edge, pushing my balance to its limits.

Then, just as their voices started to become clearer, I slipped and began to tumble off the roof. I immediately began to cast a spell to catch myself in a desperate attempt to avoid being spotted. However, before I could fall more than a few inches, something wrapped firmly around my belly and hoisted me back up onto the roof.

Startled, I looked back over my shoulder to find a large, dog-like creature with jet-black fur and four tails. It looked at me through its pale yellow eyes with an amused expression. One of its four tails had wrapped itself around me and prevented me from falling in a remarkable display of dexterity. While it had saved me and didn't seem aggressive, I was still leery of the creature. I was sure that I was the only one on the roof and doubted it had climbed up here normally. Yet, I hadn't sensed any magic.

As I watched the creature and tried to piece together how it had managed to get behind me without me noticing, a voice suddenly resounded in my head. "You really should be more careful, little kitty. You would have been in big trouble if I hadn't been here."

"Oh, um, thanks." I was so caught off guard by being spoken to that I randomly blurted out my thanks without thinking.

A second later, my brain caught up with my mouth, and I started kicking myself internally. This creature was clearly someone's familiar and a high-level one at that. For all I knew, he was a spy or an ally of Lord Dawster. By speaking to him, I had basically announced that I was someone's familiar.

That fact didn't seem to be lost on the creature either. His eyes widened in surprise upon hearing my voice. Yet, rather than becoming hostile or questioning, his face twisted into a smile. Or at least something as close to a smile as a dog-like creature could make. "I see. So, you're a familiar too, then. Sorry, sorry. I thought you were just a normal cat."

I was once again entirely thrown off guard by his friendly demeanor and casual tone. For some odd reason, it felt oddly nostalgic. "Oh, it's no problem. There's no way you could have known, after all. I'm Astria. It's nice to meet you."

The creature in front of me paused for a moment, his brow furrowed in thought, "Astria? I see, so you're the Astral Cat that everyone has been talking about. It's an honor to meet you. My name is Zeke."

"Zeke? That's an odd name for a familiar."

"Yes. I get that a lot. I'm originally not from this country, you see." Zeke's gaze grew distant as he turned to look down toward the crowd. "I was forcibly brought here via some sort of summoning magic. My name was given to me by someone from my homeland before that happened."

As I listened to Zeke's own story, I felt a strange sense of kinship form with him. Even if he had only been summoned from a different country and not a different world like me, we had both been ripped away from everything we had ever known. In fact, it was probably even more painful in his case since it seemed like he still had his full memories. There was a loneliness and anger in his eyes that reminded me just a tiny bit of myself.

I started to ask him about his home country, thinking that I could maybe ease his pain by hearing him out, but almost as if sensing my intentions, he cut me off. "At any rate, that's enough about me. What's a famous familiar like yourself doing playing around on the roof of the arena?"

As he talked, he walked over the edge and glanced down at the boxes below. After a moment, he turned back to me with a mischievous look on his face. "What's this? Were you trying to spy on those nobles? That's rather bold of you."

"I-I wasn't spying on anyone. I was just trying to get some exercise and slipped, is all." I tried my best to lie my way out of the situation, but even I could tell no one was going to buy that line.

Yet, Zeke's reaction surprised me. "Oh, is that right? Well then, I had better let you get back to it. It was nice to meet you, Astria."

Zeke turned and walked past me without so much as glancing down. I mentally heaved a sigh of relief and felt my body finally begin to relax. Thankfully, it seemed like he was the type of person to take things at face value. I turned and started to head in the opposite direction, thinking I had gotten away with it. However, just as I did, the familiar sensation of something wrapping around my stomach returned.

In the next moment, I experienced one of the most nauseating cases of motion sickness in my life. I was pulled what felt like no more than a foot but suddenly found myself a good ten feet away from where I had just been.

Additionally, my perspective had been entirely swapped around, changing the direction I was facing. I was now face-to-face with Zeke, who was staring at me with a deadpan look. Over his shoulder, I could see where I had just been standing.

As I tried to suppress my sudden motion sickness and piece together what just happened, Zeke began to speak. "As if I would fall for that. Do I look stupid to you?"

I tried to reply, but I was totally preoccupied with not vomiting everywhere. Noticing my predicament, Zeke set me down gently, his gaze softening. "Ah, sorry about that. I tend to forget how disorienting rift hopping is the first time."

I took a second to let the motion sickness pass before looking up at Zeke with an irritated expression. "What in the world did you do to me?! Was that some sort of teleportation magic?"

He looked down at me, the look in his eyes suddenly gaining an intensity that they had lacked before. "Teleportation? No. No. No. This is the special ability of my species. I wouldn't even classify it as magic since it doesn't seem to use magical energy. Rather, I seem to have the ability to create a rift in space-time that connects two places together."

"Oh, I see. So, you're doing something like folding space-time over on itself to connect two distant places temporarily?" Honestly, I had no idea what I was talking about. I was just repeating something I had heard at some point in my old world. I couldn't begin to explain why I felt the urge to do that instead of admitting to my ignorance on the subject, though.

Zeke, for his part, seemed somewhat surprised and was staring at me with wide eyes. But that didn't last long. A moment later, his expression shifted into an amused smile. "I'm afraid that's not quite correct. It's an excellent guess, though."

"If it was such a good guess, then why do you look like you're about to burst out laughing?" I glared at him, trying my best to seem intimidating, despite my much smaller stature. "At any rate, I don't have any more time to play around with you. I have nothing against you, but if you plan on getting in my way, then I won't hesitate to fight you."

49

"Now, now. There's no need to be so testy. I was just having some fun." Zeke flashed another amused grin in my direction. "In fact, why don't I help you out just this once. After all, familiars like us need to stick together."

I wasn't sure what he meant by that, but if he was willing to help me out, I didn't have any complaints. I wasn't sure how I was going to manage to spy on Lord Dawster otherwise. "Alright. I'll take you up on that offer, but if you try any funny business, then I'll pummel you into the ground, got it?"

"Haha. Sure." Zeke brushed off my threat as if he wasn't worried about me at all. Honestly, I was starting to feel like I was being underestimated. He quickly circled around me and laid down next to me. Then, one of his four tails snaked forward. "You just need to be able to hear them, right?"

I nodded nervously as I watched the tip of his tail floating in the air. "Yeah. That should be good enough."

"Alright, then. Here goes."

I watched as the tip of Zeke's tail traced a short line through the air, trying to see if I could notice any traces of magic in his skill. However, just like he said, his ability didn't seem to use any magical energy. The spot his tail passed through seemed to split open all on its own. It was almost as if he had cut the threads holding reality together. The tiniest sliver of a rift appeared, barely visible, even with my keen eyesight.

Then, from the other side, I heard the familiar voice of Lord Dawster. "You really are being stubborn about this, Lord Valst. The new road through the Forests of Dram will be built with or without you. I think I'm being rather generous here by offering you partial ownership of the newly claimed lands in exchange for your assistance."

"As if." Another voice that must have been Lord Valst came through the rift, dripping with contempt. "The pitiful amount of land you're offering me is hardly worth committing the atrocities you're talking about."

"Atrocities? I'm surprised that you have such a high opinion of the savages living in the forest. They've been a thorn in your side for ages, preventing you from expanding your logging operations, no?"

"That may be true, but that doesn't make it right for us to just run them out of their home. Besides, there's still the chance that they'll come back to the negotiating table." As Lord Valst replied, I could hear the strain in his voice. He clearly wanted nothing to do with his counterpart's plan, but something seemed to be holding him back from refusing outright.

"Do you really believe that?" Lord Dawster's tone suddenly shifted, carrying a bit of sympathy for his fellow lord's situation that seemed out of character for him. "Sure, things may have been going well before, but it's been two years since they suddenly cut ties with you. It's time to move on and admit that you were tricked. They never planned on allowing you to expand your logging even with restrictions. They were simply buying time to tighten their grip on the forest."

I felt my fur stand on end as I processed what was being said. Two years ago, Aurelia had run away from her home and joined with Lord Dawster to avoid her family going to war with his superior forces. Apparently, her clan had cut ties with Lord Valst shortly after that. They might have done so thinking that he had something to do with her kidnapping. However, it seemed more likely that Lord Dawster had bullied them into breaking off the negotiations. Either way, he knew exactly what had happened and was withholding that information to try and convince Lord Valst to do something horrendous.

"Perhaps that is the case, but I have the feeling there's something more to it." Lord Valst paused for a long moment. "Besides, there's also the matter of the Vilia family."

"The Vilia family?" At the mention of Lesti's family, I heard the slightest bit of doubt in Lord Dawster's voice for the first time. Most likely, he fully realized the implication of Aurelia's entrance into the arena with Lesti earlier. "What does a backwater family like that have to do with this?"

Lord Dawster's discomfort wasn't lost on Lord Valst either. I could hear the slightest bit of amusement in his voice as he replied. "Oh, you hadn't heard? I'm surprised. You're normally so well informed. Although I suppose it makes sense, you would have had to have left before me to make it in time for the tournament."

Lord Valst paused for a moment, enjoying the fact that he knew something that Lord Dawster didn't. "Just before we left, I received a letter from the

Vilia family, notifying me that they had entered a mutual defense agreement with the natives of the Forest of Dram."

For a long moment, there was nothing but silence coming from the other side of the rift. Honestly, I considered asking Zeke to open it wider just so that I could see Lord Dawster's face. But I knew it was too risky, so I pushed the desire down.

Yet, when Lord Dawster finally did reply, it wasn't anything like what I expected. "I see. Perhaps the rumors are true after all then."

"You mean about the Vilia family hoarding artifacts?" Valst replied, the skepticism thick in his voice. "I honestly can't see them doing something like that. Besides, I don't see what that has to do with what we were just talking about."

"Oh, please. Are you really that naive? The Vilia girl is clearly gathering power for something. First, it was that familiar, then the rumors about her family hoarding artifacts, and now they're suddenly making agreements with random third parties with whom they have no connections? If anything, we should be rushing to crush these allies of hers before they become a threat."

I grimaced a little at Lord Dawster's explanation. While it was true that he was withholding some information and the rumor about the artifacts was clearly false, there was some truth to his words. Lesti was working to gather power to defy the alliance, and others were starting to catch on to that fact. It was only a matter of time before it happened, but I had been hoping we would have at least one more year. Now, it was even more critical for Lesti to win this tournament.

"It's true that Lady Lesti has been making some concerning moves here lately." Valst paused, choosing his next words carefully. "Still, I'll need time to gather more information before making such a hasty decision. Going to war, even with a territory as small as Vilia, would best be avoided. We still have an archdemon on the loose after all."

"All the more reason to drive out this nuisance, so we can focus on the real problems." There was the sound of sudden movement from within the room as Lord Dawster made to leave. "I'll wait till the end of the tournament for your response and no longer. I trust you will choose wisely, Lord Valst."

A moment later, the sound of the door to the small room opening and closing rather loudly signaled the end of their conversation. Zeke's tail flicked out, and the rift he had opened was stitched closed before my eyes. Having been engrossed in listening to the two lords' conversation, I hadn't looked over at him the whole time, but now that I did, I could see a clear sense of disgust written on his face.

"Filthy nobles, always planning something." His words came out suddenly as if they were bubbling up from somewhere deep within his soul. "They think people's lives are nothing but tools to be used for their own benefit."

To my surprise, Zeke's words resonated with me more than I expected. I knew plenty of nobles who were good-natured and cared about their people. Yet, I knew just as many who were like Lord Dawster, selfish and manipulative. I had merely gotten lucky that Lesti was the one who had summoned me. If she hadn't, I might be saying the same thing he was right now.

Finding myself unable to find a response to his hate-filled words, I could only sit there as an awkward silence formed. The moment dragged on for what seemed like forever before the sound of the roaring crowd suddenly reached both of our ears. Zeke and I both snapped out of our thoughts, turning our attention to the arena below.

"Dang it. I lost track of time." Zeke was the first one to break the silence between us. "It looks like the preliminaries are about to start. Sorry, but I have to get going."

"No problem." I stood up and turned back the way I came. "I should be getting back too. Thanks for your help."

"Don't mention. It's the least I could do to help out one of my own." Zeke once again shot me an odd grin before his expression turned serious. "If you really want to repay me, then make sure you put those nobles in their place. I'll help you out in any way that I can."

I paused for a moment as I considered asking Zeke to help me out. With his power, gathering info on our foes would be much easier. Yet, I decided to hold back. I still didn't know whose familiar he was. For all I knew, he could be contracted with one of our enemies,

In the end, I decided to turn him down as gently as I could to keep my options open. "I'd rather not drag you into my problems, but I appreciate the offer."

With another flick of his tail, Zeke opened another rift and used his other tails to pull it wide enough for him to jump through. "I see. Well, if you change your mind, I'll be around the tournament, so come and find me. Later, Astria."

Then, without another word, he hopped through the rift and was gone. I stood there for a long moment, staring at the spot where he disappeared. Something told me that I would be seeing more of Zeke whether I wanted to or not.

Still, I didn't have time to worry about that. I needed to deal with Lord Dawster's plans first. My best bet was to get this information to Lani. She was more familiar with the politics of this world and would be able to come up with a plan far easier than I could. So, shaking off my worries, I turned my gaze forward and went to look for her as I said a silent apology to Malkael.

Preliminaries

L esti took a deep breath, trying to calm her pounding heart. She was standing in one of the tunnels that led into the arena with several other students and a couple of teachers. The opening ceremonies had ended a short while ago, and the order of the preliminary matches had been announced. She had hoped that she would get some time to get her nerves under control, but unfortunately, her match ended up being the first one. This would be her first time outside of practice matches fighting without Astria. That knowledge weighed heavily on her mind.

Thankfully, she wasn't entirely alone. Standing there next to her was her good friend and classmate, Aurelia. The girl, seeing Lesti glance at her, smiled gently. "I'm glad we'll be able to fight together. Let's defeat everyone, and both proceed to the main tournament."

Lesti giggled at Aurelia's uncharacteristic enthusiasm and felt her nerves relax just a tiny bit. Whether it was because Aurelia was trying to encourage her or was just nervous herself, she didn't know. Still, her friend's upbeat attitude reminded her exactly what she needed to do. Putting on a brave front, she smiled brightly back at the green-haired girl. "Yeah. Let's knock everyone else out and show them what we're made of!"

However, just as the words left her mouth, Lesti felt the icy stares of the other competitors on her back. She didn't even need to look at them to know that she had just messed up.

The preliminaries were designed to narrow the field down to sixteen contestants from each year. Eight groups of a little more than a dozen contestants would face off in a free-for-all, with the last two standing proceeding to the full tournament. The groups were drawn entirely at random, and Lesti and Aurelia had totally lucked out. Not only had they managed to get in the same match, but they had also managed to avoid some of the other strong competitors in their year, like Alex and Elliot. That meant that, unlike the other students in their block, they could fight together, giving them a considerable advantage.

Unfortunately, their exchange had clearly marked both of them as a threat to the rest of the competitors. Not only were they both near the top of their year, but they had openly proclaimed that they would be working together. The pair may as well have shouted at the others to gang up on them.

Before she could fret over their mistake, the sound of drums began to build from the direction of the arena. One of the teachers turned and addressed the group. "That's your signal. Please enter the arena and spread out as you see fit. Wait for the referee to signal the beginning of the match before you begin channeling any spells. Any questions?"

The teacher waited for a moment before leading the students to the arena. The exit wasn't far away, and soon she saw the light streaming in, causing her to wince as her eyes tried to adjust. Soon, they stepped out into the arena, and the crowd erupted in excited cheers. Their intensity surprised her, bringing back a bit of her nervousness from before. She hadn't expected them to be so riled up for a match between second-year students. Most people considered the first and second-year matches something like exhibition matches. In contrast, the third-year bouts were the main event.

As she wondered what had the crowd so worked up, the rest of the students made their way to the center of the arena. The dirt there had been raised just a few feet with magic to create the battle area. This was another special rule designed to keep the battles moving quickly. Stepping outside of this area during the match would result in immediate disqualification.

"Lesti, are you coming?" Aurelia's voice snapped her out of her shocked state, and she looked up to find the other students had already climbed onto the stage. They had spread out on either side of the arena, not leaving only two gaps, one immediately after climbing up and the other on the opposite side. Apparently, their plan was to keep her and Aurelia separated.

Seeing this, a small smile spread across her lips. Ever since she had started at the academy, others had looked down on her. For the longest time, she had felt powerless whenever it happened, but now things were different. Heading for the stage, she stared them all down with a confident grin that didn't betray the nerves she had been feeling up until now.

"Let's do this, Auri. Follow me." As she passed by Aurelia, an idea stirred in her head. If her fellow students wanted to turn this into a twelve on two, why not make it official? Marching up onto the stage, she headed straight for the center, Aurelia hot on her heels. As soon as they reached their destination, they each turned to face the students on either side of them.

The drums pounding in the background halted as the primary judge walked into the arena, an annoyed look on his face. "You two, get to your starting positions."

Rather than moving, Lesti simply pointed at each of the students lined up in front of her in turn. "We'll be starting right here. We'll take all of you on at once!"

Her declaration sent a roar of approval through the crowd, catching everyone off guard. The judge looked like he wanted to force the pair to move, but there wasn't any official rule that they had to start in a particular position. That, combined with the crowd's fervor, caused the man to shrug his shoulders. "Fine. You may all begin once I give the signal and no sooner."

Without waiting for any confirmation from the combatants, he turned and headed back off the stage. Meanwhile, one of the male students who had been staring at Lesti rather angrily finally spoke up. "You've really become full of yourself, haven't you? You really think you're so special just because you're in the first class, now? We're going to remind you just where backwater nobles like you belong."

For a moment, she could only blink at the young man. Very few students had ever openly insulted her like that, even when she was struggling at the bottom of her year. It mainly had been Sebastian and his group of lackeys. Thankfully, due to all of that group's harassment, Lesti knew exactly how to deal with stuck-up nobles like this.

"Ten seconds." She grinned at the boy confidently. "That's how long you'll all last."

"What did you just say?!!?" Just as she expected, the boy's face turned a deep shade of red as his anger overflowed. The effect wasn't limited to him either. It spread to the other students that had heard her declaration, causing their own expressions to cloud with anger.

Yet, before things could escalate further, the primary judge took the voice-enhancing magic artifact that had been used before and began to speak. "Combatants, at the ready."

She took a deep breath and closed her eyes. Behind her, she could feel Aurelia crouch into a low stance. A silent tension fell over the crowd as everyone waited for the starting signal. The moment seemed to drag on forever in her mind, even though it couldn't have lasted for more than a second.

"Begin!"

With the judge's shout, a torrent of chants was unleashed around Lesti as the other students began to cast their spells. However, the two girls in the center of the arena didn't plan on giving a single one of them time for their chants to complete. Before more than a couple of syllables had been uttered, their attack began in earnest.

Behind her, Lesti heard Aurelia utter a single word before dashing off at an insane speed. Meanwhile, she snapped the fingers on her right hand, removing the limiter she had set to prevent herself from accidentally activating her spells. In her mind, a simple magic circle lit up brightly as her magic power flowed into it.

"Explosion, repeat ten." As she uttered the words to activate her spell, the magic from the first circle flashed and connected to a second, more complicated one. It consisted of multiple smaller circles, each one used to control a different aspect of the spell.

Suddenly the air between her and the other students seemed to get sucked into several nearby points as the materials for her spells gathered. This was really just a variant of the explosive fireball spell that she had used before. But, rather than launching an explosive projectile, it created the explosion exactly where she specified.

Before her opponents could even react, the air around them was gathered into a ball of compressed gas, ignited, and quickly released. A deafening roar echoed across the arena as ten minor explosions went off right in front of the students arrayed before her. Being in the middle of their own chants and not being able to cast magic nearly as quickly, they were unable to put up even the most minor of defenses.

The blasts sent each and every one of them flying out of the combat area, shattering the magic armor spell that protected them at the same time. Not hearing the announcement that the match was over, Lesti glanced back over her shoulder, expecting that Aurelia would still be in the middle of cleaning up her foes. However, she was greeted by the sight of another six students lying on the ground outside the stage, completely stunned. Thanks to her new enhancement magic and natural agility, Aurelia had been nearly as fast as her.

Still, if that was the case, why hadn't the match been called? She looked around one more time before locking eyes with the judge. "Um, I believe the match is over, no?"

For a long moment, he simply stared at her before looking across the stage, a look of complete disbelief written on his face. Then he raised his hand and began to call the match before an angry shout from the edge of the arena interrupted him. "What are you doing?! They obviously cheated! There's no way they could have cast spells that quickly without channeling their magic before the match started."

Looking over, they found the boy Lesti had been taunting before glaring angrily at the judge while pointing accusingly at Lesti and Aurelia. "I demand that you disqualify both of them and restart the match with only the other competitors."

However, the judge ignored the boy's complaints and looked over at one of the assistant judges. A small, hawk-like familiar with piercing blue eyes sat on her shoulder. The woman looked at the familiar for a moment before shaking her head. The head judge's eyes went wide for a moment before he recovered his composure and turned to face the boy.

"We were unable to detect any use of magic in the combat area before the match started." The judge raised his hand high overhead. "Therefore, the first preliminary match is complete. Ms. Lesti Vilia and Ms. Aurelia will advance to the main tournament!"

Despite the official announcement of their victory, a strange silence fell over the arena. There were no cheers or applause, only a confused murmur. The crowd had come to see a show, and in a sense, they had, yet most of them could barely understand the astounding level of magic that they had just seen. The only ones who could were the elites sitting in their seats far above, looking down at the pair of girls with a mixture of fear and uncertainty.

Lesti stood there trying to fight the overwhelming pressure she felt coming from the crowd. Suddenly, she was acutely aware of the hundreds of eyes staring down at her, judging her. She had known that showing the full extent of her abilities during the tournament would cause some problems with her fellow nobles. But she hadn't expected the crowd to react this way. Still, she knew she couldn't falter now. She had to stay strong.

She ran over to Aurelia and hugged her tightly. "Auri! We did it! We won."

Aurelia looked down at her and smiled softly while patting her on the head, "Mm. You did great. I'm sure Astria is proud of you too. Let's head back."

Despite the strong front she was trying to put on, Aurelia had seen how much the crowd's silence weighed on her. Her kind words and gentle tone helped to ease the burden that she felt. She smiled up at her friend, her heart overflowing with appreciation.

Giving Aurelia one last squeeze filled with gratitude, she turned and headed back to the tunnel they had come in from. "Yeah. Let's go! Next up is the main tournament!"

Meeting Valst

Despite the size of the arena, I managed to find Lani rather quickly. Thankfully, she was on security detail and walking around in the open. Her bright blonde hair, combined with the distinctive academy uniform, made it easy for me to spot her even from the roof. Still, I decided to take the long route around to avoid as many eyes as I could. After all, I wasn't supposed to be wandering around on my own.

By the time I made it to her, the first match had ended, and a strange atmosphere had fallen over the crowd. Lani stood at the top of the merchant section, staring out over the crowd with a rather concerned expression. For a moment, I hesitated, wondering if I should come back later. In the end, I decided that the situation with Lord Dawster was too important.

"Lani," I called out to her while still hiding in the shadows, causing her to look around in confusion. "It's me, Astria. I'm in the shadows on your left. We need to talk."

Without missing a beat, Lani walked over and casually leaned on the pillar I was hiding in the shadow of. Then, almost as if talking to no one in particular, she started to grill me. "What in the world are you doing here? You're supposed to stay with Malkael, aren't you?"

"I know. I know." I shivered slightly from my hiding spot as I felt Lani's icy aura fall over me. "But Lord Dawster is up to something, and I figured you needed to know as soon as possible."

"Lord Dawster, huh?" As soon as I mentioned the rival lord's name, I felt Lani's anger fade slightly. "Alright, I'll hear you out. What's going on?"

I quickly ran over everything I had heard from the conversation between

Lord Dawster and Lord Valst, occasionally stopping to interject my own thoughts on the matter. "So, that's the gist of it. I was worried that this would cause some major problems for our plans, so I figured I should tell you right away."

"Well, you're not wrong." Lani furrowed her brow as she processed everything I had said. "I didn't expect that Lord Dawster would try and get Lord Valst to align with him. The two generally don't get along."

"Yeah. I got that impression. That Valst guy seemed to be really skeptical of Dawster's motives." I paused, recalling their whole conversation. "Still, I think that those rumors about the Vilia family hoarding artifacts might have done more damage than we expected. Valst seemed to be at least a little concerned about the possibility."

Lani nodded. "Well, the rise of the empire was caused by a single family hoarding artifacts and using them to invade their neighbors. It makes sense that he would be cautious. I'm sure he's also caught wind of some of the moves we've been making behind the scenes as well."

"Yeah." I paused for a moment, annoyed that even someone like Valst was close to being swayed by these stupid rumors. "Still, it didn't seem like he was fully convinced. I think there's still time to fix this if we act quickly. What do you think we should do?"

Lani paused for a moment as she considered the options. "I think our best course of action would be to approach Lord Valst directly. If we can explain the situation with Aurelia and have him meet Lesti in person, we might be able to convince him. After all, her personality speaks for itself."

"That's true." I couldn't suppress the amused chuckle that I felt as I imagined Lesti looking at the older noble with genuine confusion while he expressed his concerns. "Anyone who meets her would know that she isn't the type of person that would be interested in invading the other alliance members. Still, do you think he'd agree to meet with her, and will she even have time? She's going to be super busy with the tournament, right?"

"Well, there should be enough time between the matches that we can arrange a short meeting." Lani paused, her expression returning to the troubled look she wore when I had first arrived. "Though, I am worried about Lesti moving around with the current atmosphere."

"The current atmosphere?" I looked up at her, tilting my head in confusion. "I did notice that things were a bit quiet, but did something happen?"

Lani let out a heavy sigh. "I think the easiest way to put it is that Lesti went overboard once again."

"Oh no. She didn't kill or seriously injure someone, did she?" I grimaced as the image of a massive fireball blowing away a fellow student flashed through my mind.

"Don't worry. It's not as bad as that." Lani smiled down at me. "She held back enough to not hurt anyone, but she and Aurelia wiped out the rest of their preliminary group so fast that no one knew how to react. The crowd was really on her side before, but now that she didn't give them much of a show, I wouldn't be surprised if they turn against her."

"Oh, is that all that happened?" After hearing Lani's story, I was feeling pretty relaxed. "I wouldn't worry about that. I'm sure that by the end of the tournament, they'll all be cheering for her again."

Lani blinked a few times as she tried to maintain her composure and not look at where I was hiding. "What makes you so sure?"

"Well, it's a bit hard to explain. You'll just have to watch her and see." I glanced out toward the stage, where the sounds of the second match getting underway were starting to flow through the air. "Getting back to the problem at hand, though, how are we going to convince Lord Valst to meet with her? You think he'll listen to you?"

"Actually, it won't be me trying to convince him. It'll be you." Along with her words came just the slightest bit of Lani's chilling aura that always showed when she was angry. "I have my patrol duties, and my route doesn't take me anywhere near the noble areas. On the other hand, you should have easy access to that area of the arena."

"Wait. I get that what you're saying makes sense, but I don't really know anything about noble formalities or how to arrange a meeting between two parties. Is this really something I should be handling?"

"Don't worry. Instructor Malkael can help you with the formalities." Lani smiled gently out toward the arena, but the expression didn't extend to her eyes. The look was fairly terrifying and caused several people passing by to look at her nervously. "Just give up and consider this your punishment for wandering off when you were told to stay put."

"Okay. Okay. I get it." I decided to follow Lani's advice and give up. I knew from experience that if I didn't, I would be in for a long lecture later. "I'll figure out some way to convince Lord Valst to meet with her. Can you let Lesti know what's going on so that she's ready once he agrees?"

"Right. The headmistress mentioned that the barrier would block telepathic communication." Lani smacked her fist into her palm as though she had just remembered.

"Don't you think that's going too far? What was I going to do, give her instructions in the middle of a fight?"

"The headmistress is just trying to protect the academy and Lesti as much as possible. She didn't want to give anyone a chance to accuse you of cheating."

When she put it that way, there wasn't much I could say back. I didn't like not being able to reach Lesti, but it would probably be fine. "Well, I won't worry about it too much then. Not being able to talk to her isn't that big of a deal. There are plenty of teachers around, and Rose and Aurelia are with her too. She'll be fine."

"That's true. I guess she isn't alone." A small smile spread across Lani's lips as the words left her mouth. "Alright, leave contacting her to me. I'll figure something out. You just focus on getting that meeting arranged."

"Thanks, Lani. Leave it to me. I'll report in once everything is good to go."

Lani nodded and pushed off from the pillar she had been leaning on as she silently returned to her patrol route. At the same time, the sounds of battle erupted from the arena below, followed by the cheers of the crowd. It looked like whoever was fighting this time was giving them a much better show. Thankfully, that worked in my favor. With everyone thoroughly distracted, I began my stealthy trip to rejoin Malkael.

* * *

It took me some time to make my way back to the section for nobles where I had left Malkael and Fang. By the time I arrived, the second preliminary match was just ending. Looking through the small crowd of nobles that still remained in the main party area, I quickly found the pair right where I had left them, isolated in the corner.

Fang was still eyeing the servers hungrily as they walked by with plates of food but was holding himself back from harassing them. Meanwhile, Malkael was looking down at the proceedings below with an almost unnaturally neutral expression. Skirting the edges of the room to avoid the gazes of the other nobles, I quickly rejoined them, jumped up on the low wall at the front of the room, and looked down at the battle below.

"Welcome back." Malkael greeted me with a flat tone and surprisingly loud voice, keeping his gaze fixed on the arena below the entire time. "Were you able to find a place to use the bathroom? It took you quite some time. I was beginning to worry."

The bathroom! What in the world is he talking about?! For a brief moment, I found myself utterly flustered by Malkael's seemingly random statement. However, a moment later, I realized that he was trying to give me a proper cover story in order to avoid others being suspicious of my absence. *Still, couldn't you have come up with something less embarrassing, Malkael?*

Actually, I expected that he could have quite easily and was just using this as a chance to get back at me for running off. Either way, I decided it would be best to play along with his little game. "Yeah. I ended up having to go all the way outside in the end. I can't exactly go using a human bathroom after all."

"Yes, I suppose that's true." Malkael continued to avoid my gaze as he spoke. "Unfortunately, you missed your master's match. She put on a rather interesting performance."

"I'd expect nothing less from her," I replied as dismissively as I could to Malkael's statement. I couldn't outright say that I already knew, but I didn't want him to waste time explaining the whole situation over again.

Thankfully, he was quick on the uptake and rapidly changed the subject. "Yes. It really wasn't all that surprising for those in the know. But the second match ended up in a rather unexpected result."

I turned my attention to the arena below. The winners had just been declared and were now waving to the crowd as they headed to the exit. I immediately felt an involuntary snarl start to form as I recognized one of them. Smiling just as smugly as the first day I met him, Sebastian exited the arena without so much as a scratch on him.

It wasn't all that surprising that Sebastian won and made his way through to the main tournament. The groups for the preliminaries were random after all, and he could have gotten a lucky draw. However, he looked like he had barely broken a sweat. For the students at the top of their year, that was certainly a possible outcome. The gap between them and the bottom of their class tended to be rather large. Yet, a student like Sebastian, who was somewhere in the middle, shouldn't have boasted much of an advantage.

"What in the world happened?" I asked Malkael as my tail flicked about in irritation. "It looks like the others barely put up a fight."

"That's because they didn't. The young Master Cilias used an overwhelming show of force to overpower the other students." Malkael glanced over at me, a brief smirk appearing on his lips before he quickly returned to his neutral expression. "Although, he did have enough sense to hold back and put on a good show for the crowd at least."

I threw a dirty glare over at him. "Isn't that just because he's weaker than Lesti. If I knew Sebastian, he'd try and crush his opponents as fast as he could."

"That may be the case. It's hard to tell, though." Malkael paused and lowered his voice as he continued. "The teachers regularly discuss our students' progress, and from what I had heard about Sebastian, he didn't possess a vast store of magical energy. Yet, in this match, he was throwing powerful spells around like it was nothing. If he's been hiding things from his teachers, then it makes it hard to predict where exactly his ceiling is."

I looked down at Sebastian one last time as he exited the arena. I had been hoping to check his magical energy with my unique ability, but he was out of sight before I got the chance. I could have still tried, but it would be hard to identify him with so many people around. I decided it would be better to wait until his next match and keep an eye on him then. For the moment, I turned my attention back to the issue with Valst.

"Well, let's put that aside for now." I adjusted my position on the wall to face Malkael. "I need your help with something."

I quickly gave him the rundown of everything I had overheard, as well as what I discussed with Lani. He listened silently, his gaze fixed on the arena below. It was honestly impressive how good he was at controlling his expression. For anyone nearby, you wouldn't even be able to tell that I was talking to him.

When I finished, Malkael turned and signaled to a nearby member of the staff. When she walked over, he whispered something into her ear. She looked surprised for a moment but quickly bowed and left the room in a hurry.

"What was that about?" I asked him as he walked back over.

However, he just smiled mischievously at me. "Don't worry. You'll see soon enough."

Yet, despite his assurances, nothing happened for quite some time. We continued to watch the preliminary matches. Alex and Elliot each won their bouts easily. Meanwhile, Rose also managed to continue to the main tournament without too much difficulty as most of her opponents ignored her only to be knocked out of the ring by her surprisingly strong spells. The magic Lesti had taught her in their short time together was really paying off against her fellow first-year students.

Still, the matches I found most interesting were those of the third-year students. It was my first time seeing a mage besides Lesti or Aurelia fight with their familiar. Honestly, it was a bit disappointing. Most of the students only used their familiars like a magic battery. Out of those that didn't, a majority of them relied heavily on their familiars' special attacks and skills to try and overpower their foes. There was hardly any coordination to be seen between the many pairs fighting in the arena.

Finding the whole situation rather strange, I turned to Malkael. "Does the academy not teach students how to fight with their familiars? The difference between the third years and Aurelia and Fang is like night and day."

"The academy currently has a shortage of instructors who specialize in that type of combat." Malkael grimaced as he watched the matches below. "You may have noticed that most of the teachers at the academy don't have their own familiars. Those that do are the type of mages that tend to fight on the backline and rely on their familiars to help them sustain long-range bombardments."

My tail swished back and forth uneasily as the possible meanings of his words settled on me. Yet, before I could ask him what had happened to the familiars of those that fought up close, the female servant from before returned. Walking up behind Malkael, she held a sealed letter out in front of her. "Instructor Malkael. This is from the headmistress. She wishes for you to read it immediately."

"Thank you." Malkael quickly opened the letter and read its contents. The moment he had finished, he muttered a quick incantation causing a small candle-like flame to appear. He held the letter to the fire, watching as it slowly burned away. "Astria, we have business to attend to. Follow me."

"Hey, wait. What's going on?" I yelled, chasing after Malkael as he turned on his heel and headed out the side entrance of the room. But he simply ignored me as he quickly made his way down the hall. Fang trotted closely beside me, occasionally stopping to sniff at the doors we passed. Each one led to a small private booth like Lord Dawster and Lord Valst had used for their meeting before.

However, those rooms didn't appear to be our destination. Instead, we headed down a staircase that led to the lower level of the arena. At the bottom, we exited into a narrow but empty hallway. The entire area was well lit by magic lights and had the same clean, polished atmosphere as the booth we had come from. As we walked down the hall, I turned to Malkael. "What is this place? It seems awfully fancy for a simple hallway."

Malkael replied without looking back. "This is the direct passage to the noble area. It connects to the outside through a separate, secure entrance. The entrance we came in from earlier was specifically meant for non-noble competitors who are called upon by the lords."

"Ah, that makes sense." I thought back to the hallway we had initially used to get to the viewing area. The stonework had been much cruder, and the space had been lit by regular torches. It really was like night and day. "Still, it seems like such a waste to put all this effort into something that so few people will ever get to see."

Malkael glanced back at me, a puzzled expression on his face. "Who would care about looking at a hallway?"

"Huh? If no one cares, then why would someone put all this effort into making it look nice?" I asked as I looked back at him, equally perplexed.

A small smile crossed his face as he stopped in front of an intricately carved wooden door. "I see. I suppose that's a good point. At any rate, we'll have to leave this discussion for another time. We've arrived. This room is a special secure room for when extra privacy is needed for meetings. This door is the only access point. Lord Valst should already be waiting for you inside."

"You make it sound like you're not coming in with us." I glanced nervously up at Malkael. "Aren't you going to introduce us and make sure I don't make some stupid mistake? I already told you that I'm not familiar with noble customs."

"That shouldn't be a problem. The headmistress has arranged this meeting and taken care of the necessary formalities. Once you're on the other side of the door, the same rules we use at the academy will apply. You can speak to Lord Valst as an equal." Malkael paused and looked back down the hallway. "Besides, someone needs to stand guard and make sure that no one eavesdrops on you."

I let out a sigh of relief. Not having to worry about noble etiquette was a huge burden taken off my shoulders. "Alright. Let's do this."

As I pumped myself up, Malkael reached out and opened the door. I took one last deep breath and started to head in, trying my best to project an air of calm and confidence. Unfortunately, Fang immediately smashed any such attempts by prancing into the room happily.

His goofy stride and happy expression ultimately killed any hope in a serious or somber mood. Still, I was actually rather thankful for the pup's lack of seriousness. It helped to wash away the last of my nerves. With a slight chuckle, I stepped across the barrier, and Malkael closed the door behind me.

The inside of the room was simple but elegant. The stonework matched the polished look of the hall and noble area up above. There were no torches. Magical lights instead emitted a pale white glow across the space. In the center of the room sat two rather comfy-looking leather sofas with a table in the middle. Sitting on the couch to the left was a man who I assumed to be Lord Valst.

He was younger than I had expected, perhaps in his late thirties. His dark hair was cut short, unlike most nobles. As we walked into the room, he glanced over at us. For a moment, our eyes locked as we each tried to assess the other. As I watched him, I couldn't help but notice the heavy bags under his green eyes. He also had an exceptionally lean frame with little excess fat.

The moment felt like it might have dragged on forever. However, Fang once again came to the rescue, immediately running over to the sofa opposite Lord Valst and making himself at home. The pup's sudden reaction seemed to catch both the lord and the servant standing behind him off guard. Each of them looked at him with a confused expression that quickly turned to bemusement in the case of Lord Valst.

Seeing his expression put me at ease. If Fang being his usual self wasn't enough to set him off, then it seemed pretty unlikely that I would offend him with some minor breach of protocol. Slightly less nervous, I walked over and jumped up on the couch next to Fang.

"I have to admit. I'm rather surprised." Lord Valst leaned forward and folded his hands together as he began to speak. "When the headmistress said there was someone from the academy that she wanted me to meet, I was expecting a student."

The headmistress, huh? I glanced at the door, the other side of which Malkael stood. *Honestly, I'm not sure which one of the two is worse. I could see either one of them coming up with a plan like this.*

"I'm sorry to have deceived you, Lord Valst." I bowed my head briefly. The last thing I wanted was for Valst to think I was trying to use lies to manipulate him. "I'm sure the headmistress had her reasons for approaching the situation in this way. As for myself, I'm not familiar with noble customs, so meeting you as a member of the academy helps to put me at ease."

For a long moment, he stared at me in silence, his brow furrowed in thought. "I see. That certainly does make sense, and you seem to be sincere in your apology." Suddenly, he sat back, and the tension disappeared from his facial expression. "Very well. Let us speak frankly to each other then. I assume you have something important you wish to discuss with me?"

"Really? You're okay with this?" I asked, tilting my head to the side in confusion.

Yet, Lord Valst simply smiled back at me. "I can't say that I don't have any reservations, but Headmistress Rena has my utmost respect. If she thinks I should meet with you, then the least I can do is hear you out. Besides, I may be somewhat young for a lord, but I like to think I'm a good judge of character. I have to be in order to survive with the neighbors that I have."

"I can definitely see that being the case." I felt a fleeting spark of hope in my chest. Between Valst's current tone and his previous conversation with Lord Dawster that I had overheard, it seemed like there was a very high chance he might believe me. With that in mind, I decided to be rather blunt. "I'll be frank. Lord Dawster is lying to you about the situation regarding the Vilia territory."

Valst once again leaned forward, though this time he maintained his relaxed posture. "Oh, that's a rather bold accusation that you're making. Although, I think the same thing. Alright then, let's hear your version of the story."

Expecting a challenging round of questions to accompany my explanation, I took a deep breath before beginning. "Okay. First, the rumor about the Vilia family hoarding artifacts is completely false. It's certainly true that Lesti has jumped up in the ranks at the academy, but that's a result of her own hard work and talent."

"Hard work and talent, you say?" Valst grimaced slightly at my explanation. "You'll have to forgive me if I have a hard time believing that. While that would be a reasonable explanation under normal circumstances, the jump in your master's abilities is far too much to be explained away by pure hard work. The magic she showed during the preliminaries wasn't something that a second year at the academy should be capable of. There's something else going on, isn't there."

"Well, you aren't wrong, but I'm afraid that I can't tell you the specifics." I once again bowed my head slightly to Valst. I wanted to be as honest with him as possible, but I couldn't risk spreading the secret behind Lesti's sudden jump in power right now. She would need that advantage going forward. However, in the next moment, Lord Valst threw my plans into complete disarray.

His gaze grew stiff once more as he stared me down, the relaxed posture from before disappearing in an instant. "She's using magic circles, isn't she?"

I froze. *How does he know about that? We've only told a handful of people that we trust.* While it was true that our secret had been exposed somewhat in the fight with Baron Arvis, I didn't think that Dag or Lord Gambriel would have allowed that information to leak so quickly.

Wait, is he just testing me? No. There's no reason he would jump straight to a conclusion like that. He knows something.

My mind raced through the possibilities as the silence stretched on between us. Still, I couldn't come up with any reasonable explanation for how we had been found out. That left me with only one option. Ask menacingly.

"How do you know about that?" I sat up on the couch, narrowing my eyes as my tail began to twitch back and forth. "For your sake, I hope you have a good explanation."

"Insolent creature! You dare threaten my lord?!" Sensing my sudden hostility, the servant standing behind spoke up for the first time. She glared daggers at me, and I heard the slightest ruffling of fabric as her hands moved behind her back. It seemed like things might escalate into a fight for a moment. Thankfully, Valst defused the situation.

Casually waving his hand, he once again relaxed. "Stand down, Silvia. It's only natural that she'd be suspicious after I jumped to such an unusual conclusion."

Silvia hesitated for a moment but eventually folded her hands in front of her once more. Though she continued to stare daggers at me. I turned my attention back to Valst. Our conversation hadn't even been going on for that long, and I was already feeling exhausted. His ability to switch modes between serious and relaxed so quickly was throwing me off more than I wanted to admit.

"Allow me to explain," Valst continued. "Years ago, when I had just graduated from the academy. There was a skirmish with the nearby kingdom, and I was called up to defend the alliance. During that deployment, I met a certain commander that used magic in a very similar fashion to your master."

"That still doesn't explain why you jumped straight to magic circles," I replied as I continued to glare at Valst.

Yet, he only smiled at my impatience. "Well, that's simply what he told everyone who asked him about it. He never would tell us the specifics, though. They even dragged him in front of council once and tried to force him to talk, but he just grinned at us with that usual wicked smile of his and dared us to fight him."

"And you expect me to believe that the council just let this commander get away with it?"

"We didn't have any other choice." Valst shrugged nonchalantly and let out a heavy sigh before switching gears once more back into serious mode. "After all, it wasn't just that he was powerful. He also had a dragon on his side."

I suddenly found myself blinking rapidly as this new information sank in, and everything clicked into place. As far as I knew, there was only one man in the alliance who could claim a dragon as his ally. "It was Frederick?!"

Valst smiled at me with a knowing grin. "I see you're acquainted as I expected. Still, I'm surprised that he decided to pass on such precious knowledge to your master after defending it so zealously. He must have a lot of faith in her."

"Actually, he didn't tell us about using magic circles. That was something that we discovered on our own." I suddenly had a lot of questions. If Frederick knew about using magic circles as a shortcut for spells, why had he kept it from everyone? It would have given the alliance a massive advantage against their foes. More importantly, where in the world had he learned it?

Valst seemed to pick up on my confusion and cut my racing thoughts short. "I can't say why Commander Frederick chose to keep this information secret, but I suggest you do the same. If others find out that you've learned the same techniques as him, then both you and your master may find yourselves in serious danger. I can think of a number of lords that wouldn't hesitate to take less than noble actions to obtain power like that."

Lesti's preliminary fight flashed through my mind. If Valst had figured out our secret from that fight alone, then it was likely that others had as well. I needed to hurry up and finish things here so that I could go and warn the others. "At any rate, you can see clearly that we aren't stockpiling artifacts. If it's alright with you, I'd like to move on to the second subject that I wanted to discuss."

"Yes. That's fine." Valst paused for a moment, seeming to consider something before he started to speak once more. "Also, I'll do my best to keep your secret and dismiss any rumors that may be circulating. Frederick saw fit to defy the entire alliance to keep this info out of our hands. He's a man of integrity. If he felt so strongly, then there must be a good reason."

I nodded, feeling slightly relieved. "Thank you, Lord Valst. Now, the second thing I wish to discuss with you is Lord Dawster's activities in the forests of Dram."

"I thought that might be the case." Valst paused, seeming to consider something as he stared down at the table. "That fool wants to drag me into a genocidal purge. Honestly, I may still be forced to participate."

His sudden declaration caused me to pause. "Why's that? Now that you know the Vilia family isn't planning a war, there's no reason for you to get involved, right?"

"Oh? And just how is it that you know that?" Valst looked up from the table, a rather intense glare on his face, "I don't believe I ever mentioned my reasons for participating in Dawster's madness."

I kicked myself internally. Valst's seemingly kind nature and the constant whiplash caused by him switching between relaxed and intense had caused me to drop my guard. There was no reason that I should have asked a question like that. "Well, I guess there's no reason to hide it now. I overheard your conversation earlier today with Lord Dawster."

"Overheard? More like you were spying on us, no?"

"Well, you're not wrong. Although to be fair, I was actually only trying to spy on Lord Dawster." I bowed my head while looking up sheepishly at Valst. "You just happened to be the person he was dealing with today. I apologize for that."

Valst waved a hand dismissively. "It's no matter. I'm more concerned about how you managed to break through the security measures we had in place. The artifact that we were using should have made it so that no one outside of that room could overhear us, and I'm certain that we were alone."

My mind flashed back to my encounter with Zeke. I still didn't know who he worked for or what he had been doing on the roof. Honestly, I wanted to ask Valst if he knew anything, but I felt that telling him would cause an increase in security, which wouldn't be good for me. "I'm sorry, but that's one secret that I'll have to keep to myself."

"Very well. Let's move on then." Valst closed his eyes for a moment. It seemed like he was struggling to let the subject go, but he eventually opened his eyes and moved on. "You wanted to talk about Dawster's activity in the forests of Dram, yes?"

"Right, it's a bit of a long story, so please bear with me."

After that, I quickly filled Valst in on everything that had happened with Aurelia regarding Lord Dawster and Lesti. I left out the parts about our battles with Thel'al's minions. They didn't really seem all that important to the current situation. Once I had finished, he sat there silently, staring at the table between us for a long time.

When he finally spoke again, it was slowly and deliberately. "If what you are saying is true, then I fear that a war may be inevitable. Lord Dawster's greed seems to have gotten the better of him. He won't be stopping his subjugation of the Mori clan."

"Yeah. I kind of figured that might be the case. Based on our information, he's already invested a ton of time and effort into gaining control of the forest." I dug my claws into the sofa below me as I thought back to how he had used Aurelia as leverage against her clan.

"Yes. Plus, I'm sure he's feeling some pressure to finish things soon. The other lords in the region have been pushing back on him ever since we learned of his plans." Valst grinned at me across the table, a playful light in his eyes. "Although, now that I've heard your story, I'm guessing we have your lot to thank for that too."

I blinked at him a few times as he sharply put the pieces of the puzzle together. I wasn't entirely sure how he had managed to figure it out. Still, the fact that he managed to trace that anonymous information back to us made me grateful we hadn't made an enemy of him. Now, the only thing left to do was to try and secure Valst's help.

"Well, what if I told you there might be a way to prevent the war?" I asked as I stared straight into his eyes.

Valst looked at me quizzically before waving for me to continue. "I have to say I'm skeptical, but I'll hear you out. Go on."

"Well, the main reason that Lord Dawster is still willing to pick this fight is that he thinks he can easily defeat Vilia. But he's obviously not one hundred percent confident. Otherwise, he wouldn't be trying to recruit you to help." I felt something akin to a sadistic grin sweep across my face as my fangs bared themselves naturally. "And that's before he's even seen what Lesti and her allies can do. If she puts up a good enough show in the tournament and you ally with us, it might be enough to deter him."

"I'm sorry, but I can't agree to that plan," Valst instantly replied without even taking so much as a second to think about what I had said.

"What? Why not?!" I yelled angrily as I stood up.

His guard tensed behind him, reaching behind her skirt once more. However, he calmly raised a hand to stop her. "I mean no offense, Astria, but it doesn't matter how strong your master and her friends are. A few people don't make an army."

"You say that, but Frederick challenged the entire alliance, and they flinched. You're underestimating what we can do."

Several seconds passed as we both glared at each other. In the end, it was Valst who broke the silence, letting out a heavy sigh. "Very well. I'll give this plan of yours some consideration on two conditions."

"Master! You can't be serious!" Silvia pointed accusingly at me. "We have no reason to entertain the fantasies of a mere familiar, high-level or no."

"Silvia, I understand your concerns, and I'm not making this decision lightly." Valst's expression grew tense as he glanced back at her. "Normally, I would never consider getting involved in such a risky plan, but the alliance can hardly afford an internal war right now. Not only are the kingdom and the empire both waiting for any reason they can to invade, but we also have an archdemon hiding within our borders. We have to take some risks this time around."

Silvia fell silent and bowed her head. I was surprised to see that Valst didn't plan on rebuking her. It was clear that he valued her opinion despite her status. Still, I didn't have time to be impressed.

"You mentioned some conditions. What are they?"

Valst turned back to me and nodded. "It's rather simple. First, I'd like to meet your master. I want to judge her character for myself."

"Perfect. I wanted to ask for the same thing anyway. What's the second condition?"

"She has to beat Alexander Bestroff and win the tournament. If she's as strong as you say, it should be easy, no?"

I felt a sudden charge run through my body, and my heart began to beat faster. There it was. The goal that we had set for ourselves just shot up in importance tenfold. If Lesti didn't win, not only would she not be able to take over as lord, but her people would be forced into war. Even worse, they could potentially be subjugated by Lord Dawster. Still, despite the sudden increase in stakes, I couldn't help but smile.

"Are you kidding? That was the plan the whole time."

Quarterfinals

I left my meeting with Lord Valst tense but happy with the results. Assuming everything went well, it looked like we would be able to secure his help. All that was left for me to do was arrange for the meeting between him and Lesti. Everything else would be left up to her.

As I stepped out into the hall, a wave of annoyance washed over me as I realized that there wasn't much I could do to help her. I shook my head to try and dismiss the feeling, but it still lingered in my chest. Fang cocked his head at me before licking me right across the face. It was a little gross, but it also made me feel better. I nuzzled up against him to return the favor before a light cough reminded me that Malkael was here.

"Based on your reaction, it seems like things didn't go too terribly," he said as he glanced down at both of us.

"Yeah. I managed to secure a meeting with Lord Valst for Lesti. If that goes well and she wins the tournament, it looks like he'll be willing to help us out." I continued explaining the specific details of our agreement with Malkael. When I was done, the irritation that Fang had managed to help me brush off returned.

Malkael seemed to notice that something was wrong and looked down at me with a concerned expression. "Is there something on your mind? You don't quite seem to be your usual self."

"It's just that the entire plan seems to be in Lesti's hands this time." I stared down the hall, not looking at anything in particular. "I just wish there was some way I could help."

"I understand why you would want to help your master out, but this is an important test for her. If she really does want to become the lord of the Vilia territory, then she'll need to have both the negotiation skills and power to overcome this challenge."

I let out a heavy sigh. "I know. That still doesn't stop me from wanting to help, though."

Malkael stared at me for a moment before turning and heading back down the hall in the direction we had originally come from. "Then I suggest that we return to the viewing area. The best thing you can do for your master at this point is to keep a close eye on her potential opponents for the second day."

I trotted after him, and we quickly headed back to the viewing area. Fang, of course, ran rampant the entire time, running around and sniffing everything he could. Honestly, I was surprised by how well behaved he had been during my talks with Valst. I guess even he had enough sense to realize that he should behave himself during a meeting with a noble.

We arrived after a few minutes to a mostly empty room. After asking one of the servants, it seemed like the preliminary matches had just finished, and there was a short break before the quarterfinals. It was around lunchtime, so I assumed that most of the nobles were eating and having meetings. Looking down into the arena, it seemed like most of the crowd had gone to eat as well. Only about half of them remained in their seats.

"It looks like we have some time before the next round of matches starts," I said, turning to Malkael. "Do you think I could go visit Lesti and let her know what's going on?"

Before he could answer, Lani's voice called out from behind me. "Haven't you already caused enough trouble wandering off on your own?" I turned to find her walking toward us with an annoyed grimace on her face. It didn't reach her eyes, which had a playful light in them. "It sounds like your meeting went well. Leave contacting Lesti to me. You just sit here and behave yourself."

"I don't know what you're talking about. As her familiar, I was just following Lesti's lead." I felt my tail flick back and forth as I teased Lani back.

"P-Please don't do that. If anything, you should be the one setting her straight." Her teasing facade quickly fell apart at the slightest provocation, and her old stutter made a sudden reappearance.

"Alright. I'll try," I replied, suppressing a giggle. "Anyway, what are you doing here? Shouldn't you be out patrolling the stadium?"

"I'm on my break, so I figured I would come and see how everything was going." Lani sat down in a nearby chair and let out an exhausted sigh. "So, care to fill me in on what happened?"

"Of course." A pleased thrum reverberated through my chest. Despite how exhausted she was, Lani still used her break time to help Lesti toward her goal. It was heartwarming to see just how much she cared for her. I just hoped she didn't overdo it.

I quickly gave Lani the rundown of my conversation with Lord Valst. She sat there contemplating everything I told her with a troubled look on her face. I couldn't blame her for that. If we messed this up, we could end up dragging the entire region into a civil war. We couldn't afford to let that happen, especially with Thel'al on the loose.

Finally, Lani broke the silence. "I'm not too worried about the meeting with Lord Valst. Lesti knows how to handle herself when she puts her mind to it. Beating Alexander is another story, though."

"I get what you're saying, but nothing has really changed there." I looked back out toward the arena as my mind flashed back to the sparring match that Lesti and Alex had before the battle with Baron Arvis. Ever since then, Lesti had been working her hardest to make sure she could take him down when the time finally came. "She's going to win. She has to."

Lani stared at me with a surprised expression on her face that quickly turned into a soft smile. "Yeah. You're right. At any rate, leave contacting Lesti to me. You stay here and watch the rest of the matches. I doubt any of the others will give her much of a problem, but it's better safe than sorry."

Malkael, who had been watching us silently, spoke up for the first time in a while. "Yes. The entire plan will be ruined if she loses before even reaching the final. Instructor Lania, I suggest you get going. The preliminaries are starting soon, and you'll need to return to your patrol."

Looking around, it appeared he was right. Many of the nobles who had been away were returning, and the commoner seats below were also starting to fill. Lani stood up and nodded at Malkael. "Right. I'll be heading out then. I'll talk to you both later."

I watched Lani as she left before turning to Malkael. "So, who's the first match going to be?"

"It looks like they've just finished posting the bracket." He pointed to a large chalkboard on the far side of the arena where several brackets had been drawn.

After several months in this world, I had managed to pick up on enough of the alphabet to read simple sentences and names. "So it looks like Aurelia is up first, and she's against"—I furrowed my brow in disgust as I saw her opponent—"Sebastian, huh? I hope she beats the snot out of him."

"Actually, the first-year matches will be held before that." Malkael ignored my spiteful comment. That was probably for the best. An instructor shouldn't go around condoning violence against their students, no matter how terrible they were.

Scanning the rest of the board, I saw that Lesti's match was right after Aurelia's. If they both won then, they would end up facing off in the semifinals. The same was true for Elliot and Alex, who were on the opposite side of the bracket. Both of those were matches that I couldn't wait to see.

Everyone needed to make it through the quarterfinals first, though. I sat and watched the crowd patiently as they filtered back into the arena, and before I knew it, the time had come. The loud banging of drums echoed through the air, signaling the start of the quarterfinals.

We sat and watched the first three quarterfinal matches in silence. The first years didn't do much to rile the crowd up either. Their battles were clumsy at best. Their spells misfired when put under pressure from their opponent. One student even drained all his energy without hitting his target once.

Rose's match was the fourth and final one for the first-year students. As she entered the arena, I could see how nervous she was. Every movement she made was stiff, lacking her usual trained grace. In fact, it was so bad that she seemed to forget where she was for a moment.

"Begin!" The judge's call rang out, and her opponent began to chant as quickly as he could. Suddenly snapping back to reality, Rose looked around startled before her eyes locked onto her opponent, and her attention refocused.

She extended one hand, pointing it toward the young man on the other side of the arena. Even from up in the stands, I could feel her energy building. It appeared she wanted to end the fight in a single shot. However, her opponent had a head start and finished his spell first.

His body now enhanced via his magic, he rushed across the arena, zigzagging as he went. I was impressed. Out of all the first-year students we had seen, he was the first to change his tactics based on what his opponent did. Unfortunately for him, he had drawn a bad lot, matching up against Rose in the first round.

Even as he rushed toward her, her hand never stopped pointing toward the spot where he had initially been standing. Just as the boy reached the midway point in the arena, she unleashed her spell. "Gale!"

I felt a sudden pull as the air behind Rose rushed down and began to swirl around her. Looking at the crowd below, the effect was stronger the closer you were. She was drawing in so much air that I was thankful that the arena wasn't inside. If she had done something like this indoors, she might have caused someone to suffocate.

Once the air had finished gathering around her, it exploded outward in a cone in front of her. Bits of the arena floor were ripped up as the gale-force wind she had summoned raced across it. With the effect hitting the entire battle area, her opponent had nowhere to run. His body enhancement didn't do him any good either. He was sent flying into the opposite wall, ending the match.

It didn't seem like any of the first years would be able to put up a fight against Rose. The speed and power of her spells were just way above their level, even if the number of them she could cast was limited. Rose walked off as the surprisingly happy crowd cheered for her. It seemed like the shock from Lesti's performance earlier had worn off, and they were just enjoying the spectacle now.

Once both fighters had cleared the arena, the judges used magic to quickly patch up the damage Rose had done. As soon as they had finished, the drums began to beat once more, and Aurelia and Sebastian soon entered the arena. I glared at the back of the latter's head as he made his way to the far side. I was looking forward to Aurelia knocking him around a bit.

Sebastian came to a stop at the far side of the arena and turned to face Aurelia, a cocky grin plastered on his face. He shouted something at her, but at this distance and with the sound of the crowd, I couldn't hear him. Whatever it was, it managed to get her attention. Even though I couldn't see her face, I could tell she was now rearing to fight just from her stance. Her weight was leaned forward ever so slightly, ready to rush at Sebastian as soon as the battle began.

The judge took his position and raised his hand. A sudden silence fell over the crowd, and a strange tension filled the air. It was almost as if they could feel the anger rolling off of Aurelia down there. Just as that pressure seemed like it might become unbearable, the judge swung his hand down. "Begin!"

Aurelia exploded forward. At the same time, I felt her silently cast a spell. Magical energy flowed through her body, empowering it. The sudden increase in her abilities caused her to cross the arena in the blink of an eye. Yet Sebastian didn't seem surprised at all. He waved his hand wordlessly, and a wall of earth exploded upward, shielding him from all angles.

I stared at the wall in shock. The speed at which the spell had completed was far too fast for image-based magic. Sebastian had definitely just used instruction-based magic. Aurelia must have been caught off guard too, but she didn't hesitate. She pulled her arm back and swung. Before her fist even connected with the stone, it exploded into a million pieces as the full force of her magical energy slammed into it.

I fully expected to see Sebastian go flying from the impact, but he expected Aurelia's attack. Behind the stone wall, he had thrown up another magical barrier that deflected the stones and absorbed the remainder of the blow's energy. Even worse, he had a counterattack prepared as well. Lightning crackled off the fingertips of his outstretched hand.

"Lightning Magic?!" Malkael shouted as he lost his composure for the first time all day. "Where in the world did he learn that?"

I was just as surprised as him. Harnessing lightning like that took a lot of training and practice. One mistake and the entire thing could go wild and seriously injure the caster. However, Sebastian seemed to have complete control. I watched the magical energy flow around him, perfectly directing the lightning. I also noticed something even more terrifying.

"Watch out!" I leaned forward and shouted as loud as I could, even though I was sure Aurelia wouldn't be able to hear me. Stone walls exploded out of the ground on either side of her, creating a corridor of death. Sebastian unleashed his lightning at the exact same moment. He had cast two spells at the same time.

I stared in shock and horror as lightning arced toward Aurelia in what seemed like slow motion. The moment couldn't have lasted more than a fraction of a second, but it seemed to drag on forever. The lightning crawled through the air crackling with energy as it went. But just before it made contact with the magic protecting Aurelia, she blurred and then disappeared from my vision entirely.

The lightning flew through empty air and crashed into the barrier on the far side of the arena. Sebastian looked around frantically for his target. He found her a moment later when a shadow briefly blocked the afternoon sun. His gaze shifted up toward the source of the shadow, Aurelia, descending on him like a bird of prey.

Sebastian began to cast another spell, but he was too slow. Aurelia was on him before he could react. Her fist slammed into the magical barrier he had thrown up to protect himself. It only held for a moment before her magical energy crashed into it too. The barrier shattered instantly, and Sebastian was sent flying backward, coming to a stop just at the edge of the ring.

Aurelia didn't hesitate for a moment after knocking her opponent back. She immediately rushed toward him with a burst of speed, causing Sebastian to quickly throw up another barrier to block her attack. Aurelia smashed through it with another punch, but this time Sebastian held his ground, throwing up a stone wall behind himself to keep from being pushed out of the arena.

Aurelia pulled her arm back, aiming another punch at Sebastian's face. But before the blow could land, he threw up another barrier which was shattered immediately. The same pattern continued for several seconds, with Aurelia throwing finishing blow after finishing blow at Sebastian while he barely deflected them. It looked like she had him on the ropes.

"Something is wrong." The words slipped free from the recesses of my mind without my permission. It couldn't be helped, though. Despite the pinch Sebastian was in, he remained calm, composed, and barely seemed tired at all. Meanwhile, Aurelia was clearly growing more exhausted with each attack.

It made sense. She was basically hurling raw magical energy at her foe. It wasn't easy to optimize, and she couldn't rely on Fang for more. Still, Sebastian should have been just as worn down. Barriers used the same basic concept, and he had to be using an equal amount of energy if he was blocking her blows.

I didn't have time to think through the reason behind the difference, though. Aurelia was about to hit her limit, and she knew it. She took a giant step back and lowered her center of gravity. Magical energy surged through her body, collecting in her fist. Sebastian, seeing that a heavy blow was coming, threw up one last barrier, a look of pure concentration on his face.

Aurelia took one last deep breath and lunged forward with all the might she had. As soon as she was in range, her fist exploded forward, ready to hurl the full force of her magical energy at her foe. It raced at Sebastian's barrier with unbelievable speed. It looked like it would smash right through his defenses, but she didn't notice the trap that had been laid.

Sebastian cast another spell, one that took only a tiny bit of magical energy. A small spike of earth popped out of the ground and connected with Aurelia's fist, pushing it off course. Her attack went high and wide, just missing Sebastian and his barrier. Unable to hold back the energy she had built up any longer, Aurelia's attack erupted forward and slammed into the magical barrier protecting the crowd. It flickered and waved from the insane force of the blow, but it held.

Aurelia, exhausted of all her energy, staggered toward Sebastian as he smiled smugly at her, "I guess that's the end of tha—"

Just as Sebastian began to gloat, Aurelia took one last swing at him. There was no magic or even physical power behind the blow. It was just the defiant punch of an exhausted girl, but it landed directly on Sebastian's jaw, causing his head to snap to the side. He stood there in shock for a long moment before his face became clouded in anger.

"How dare you?!" I felt a surge of magical energy as he began to cast a powerful spell. Despite everything Aurelia had thrown at him, he still had plenty of power left. Lightning began to crackle from his fingertips, charging with more and more energy. Seeing how much he was pouring into the attack, I started to worry. If that hit Aurelia in her current state, it could seriously injure her or kill her, even with the protective spells the judges had cast.

I leaned forward, gathering my magic as I prepared to rush to her aid, only to have Malkael lay a firm hand on my back. "Don't worry, it's fine."

"That's enough." The judge calmly cast a spell as he called out to Sebastian. A magical barrier appeared over Aurelia as Sebastian loomed over her. He turned to glare at the judge but lowered his hand and canceled his spell despite his apparent misgivings.

Seeing him back down, the judge raised his hand. "The winner of the match is Sebastian Cilias!"

A loud cheer erupted from the crowd, their reaction wholly opposite of my own. My mind was racing at a million miles per hour, trying to figure out what had happened. Sebastian wasn't this strong before. There had already been a massive gap between him and Aurelia, and that was before all the training we had done. *How did he get so strong, so fast?*

As I wracked my brain trying to figure that out, an exhausted Aurelia staggered to her feet and headed for the exit. As she reached the edge of the battlefield, she came to a halt. A painful expression flashed across her face for a moment as she stared at the exit. Following her gaze, I found Lesti standing there, looking smaller and more vulnerable than I had ever seen her.

Uncertainty

Lesti couldn't believe her eyes. She had left the waiting room early so that she could be the first one to congratulate Aurelia on her victory. The sight that awaited her wasn't what she had expected, though. Rather than smiling at her cheerfully, her friend looked at her with a pained expression, her shoulders slumped with exhaustion. Even worse, Sebastian stood behind her, staring down at Lesti with a smug sense of superiority.

The moment must have only lasted for a few seconds, but it felt like forever to Lesti. She simply couldn't understand what had happened. With all of the training they had done and everything they had learned, they should both be far stronger than the majority of students. Yet Aurelia had lost to Sebastian, who was ranked in the middle of their year.

"Lesti." She started as Aurelia's voice called out from right beside her. She tore her gaze away from Sebastian's hostile stare and turned to her friend. "I'm sorry. I underestimated him and messed up the whole plan."

Aurelia's despondent words surprised Lesti. She was always so calm and confident. It wasn't like her to apologize like this. Lesti grabbed her hand and shook her head. "You didn't mess anything up. Listen to that crowd. They wouldn't be cheering that loudly if the battle was one-sided. I'm sure everyone realizes just how strong you are."

Aurelia looked at her hand for a moment before squeezing it gently. A soft smile spread across her lips. "Mm. I guess you're right. I'll leave the rest to you then. Go out there and win it all."

"Y-You know it!" Lesti tried her best to summon her usual optimism, but more than ever, the words felt hollow. It seemed like it was enough to fool Aurelia, though. She nodded and headed down the tunnel, her steps sluggish and heavy. Lesti watched her fade out of view until the sound of more footsteps nearby pulled her attention back.

She turned to find Sebastian just a few feet away. His usual air of superiority was still there, but it felt different to Lesti. Perhaps it was her imagination or her own doubts creeping to the surface, but there was an air of confidence behind that look of superiority that hadn't been there just a few months before. It sent shivers down her spine.

She expected him to taunt her, but he simply passed her by without a word. However, just as he was about to leave earshot, he called back to her, his voice dripping with sarcasm. "Good luck."

Lesti's fists clenched instinctively. She wanted to turn and shout at him that she didn't need luck, that she would put him in his place in the next round. But if Aurelia had lost so unexpectedly, then couldn't the same thing happen to her? That doubt festered in the back of her mind.

She stood there for a few minutes, waiting for her opponent to arrive and the arena to be repaired. The entire time, she could feel the crowd's eyes watching her. The memory of the strange silence that occurred after her qualifying match surfaced again.

The unease she felt from that moment, combined with the uncertainty she felt after Aurelia's loss. Doubts and fears that she thought she had long forgotten forced their way to the surface. Was her success really her own, or was it all just because of Astria? Was she really strong?

Before she knew it, it was time to begin the match. She climbed up into the arena. The announcer introduced them, and the crowd cheered, but Lesti barely heard any of it. Aurelia's pained expression, Sebastian's mocking words, and the stares of a confused crowd filled her head, pushing everything else out.

"Begin!"

The judge's shout signaling the start of the match caught Lesti off-guard. She hadn't even looked at her opponent yet. Turning her gaze to the far side of the arena, she found him reciting an incantation for a body enhancement spell. It wasn't anything special, a simple image-based spell, but the casting speed was rather good.

Lesti still had plenty of time to interrupt his casting, though. She raised a hand and pointed it at him. "Fireball!"

Her shout rang through the arena, but no ball of flame formed. Lesti stared blankly at her hand for a moment before realizing her mistake. She had forgotten to enter battle mode. Part of the danger of using keywords like "fireball" was that they would activate anytime you said them out loud. She got around this by placing a limiter on herself. Snapping the fingers on her right hand removed that limiter. If she didn't do that, then her keywords wouldn't work.

She rushed to recover, snapping her fingers to quickly enter battle mode, but the few seconds she had lost were enough for her opponent to finish his spell. He rushed across the arena, empowered by his magic, and quickly closed the gap between them. Despite the enhancement he had cast, he was nowhere near as fast as Elliot or Alex. Seeing his blow coming, Lesti stepped to the side.

A sudden burst of pain shot through her face as the blow connected, sending her staggering back. When she finally recovered her footing, she stared at her opponent, confused. Perhaps thinking that she was stunned from his punch, he rushed at her once more, pushing his advantage.

This time Lesti managed to dodge the incoming punches and kicks, but only by a hair. Her body felt heavy and sluggish as if she was moving underwater. The pounding of her heart echoed through her head as she fought off the sense of panic threatening to overwhelm her. At the same time, her mind raced to understand what was happening, parsing through all the possibilities.

Yet, no matter how hard she thought. She couldn't come up with a reason for why she was struggling so much. There were no unexpected spells in play. Her opponent wasn't using any dirty tricks. She was simply losing, unable to bring out the power that she should have.

With all the training she had done, she assumed that Alex would be her only real challenge. That was why she had trained so hard, sparring against

Elliot over and over and inventing new spells. By the time the tournament had started, she could consistently beat Elliot, whose style was a natural counter to hers. If Lesti could beat him, then she assumed she could beat anyone else.

Another blow snuck past her defenses, a solid shot to the body. She leapt back, putting some distance between her and her opponent. Thankfully, she had prepared her own magical shields over the ones cast by the judges, so she didn't take much physical damage.

That didn't stop her mind from spiraling even further into despair, though. If her opponent had been Alex, then the fight would have ended then and there. That's just how strong his body enhancement magic was. She could deal with that, though.

It was the idea that Sebastian might have defeated her just now that truly broke her heart. His face flashed through her mind even as her opponent continued to chase her around the ring. He had always been arrogant, but now he had the power to back it up.

Would she be able to beat him? Was she really as strong as she thought she was? The doubts continued to pile up in her mind as her opponent shifted gears.

Realizing that his attacks weren't doing any real damage, he started to chant spells as he fought. Lesti soon found herself being peppered with stone spears and fireballs between the punches. They were slow to activate and lacked any real power, but Lesti couldn't avoid them properly.

"Enough already! Fireball!"

Finally growing impatient, she began to throw counterattacks in an attempt to push her opponent back. A fireball flared to life between them. Due to how close they were, she had to hold back and be careful not to add too much power into the spell, or else it would blow her away too. Usually, this wouldn't have been a problem, but it slowed down her casting time in her current mental state.

This gave her opponent time to dodge, even at point-blank range. Ducking down, he slipped past the fireball and circled around to her side. The spell sailed off into the air, exploding against the magical barrier protecting the crowd. At the same time, a fist slammed into her side, sending her tumbling across the arena.

She skidded to a stop near the center. Wincing, she scrambled to her feet and froze at the sight before her. Her opponent was flying at her in a leaping strike, clearly intending to end the fight here. That's not what Lesti's gaze had locked onto, though. No, her gaze was drawn to a large, silver tiger far behind him.

The tiger, of course, was Astria. There's no way Lesti wouldn't be able to recognize her, no matter how far away she was. Time seemed to slow down as she stared into her companion's eyes. The gaze boring down on her, filled with anger, contained a clear message. "Get it together."

As she stared into those eyes, the emotions roiling around inside her came to a head and finally overflowed. All of the doubt and fear were replaced by disappointment in an instant. Astria had come to try and bail her out again.

This sort of thing always happened. In the end, she always relied on Astria to make it through. Even though Lesti had said that she would win and show how strong she was, she was making her worry again. Suddenly, her disappointment twisted and morphed into a new emotion—anger.

A massive roar echoed through the arena. It wasn't the roar of the crowd, nor was it the sound of a powerful spell. This roar came from Lesti. She screamed, venting her frustration to the world, cursing herself for being so weak. Using the anger built up inside her, she forced her body to move. Slipping under her opponent's blow, she cast a spell and swung her arm up with all her might.

Her fist slammed into his stomach, stopping him in his tracks. The punch sent him flying across the arena. He quickly leapt to his feet, her attack seemingly doing no damage. That didn't faze her, though. She had known that she wouldn't be able to defeat him with a single punch. After all, her body enhancement magic wasn't nearly as strong as Alex or Elliot's.

A strange hush fell over the arena. Lesti glared at her opponent, a fierce, determined look in her eyes. She knew he wanted to rush at her and continue his attack, but it was as if his feet were suddenly glued to the floor. He stared at her, a look of shock and fear written on his face.

On the other hand, Lesti was eager to fight. She was angry with herself—for doubting her abilities, for showing weakness to her foes, and for worrying her friends. Looking at him now, she could see just how weak the boy in front of her was. *How could I have allowed myself to be pushed into a corner by something like this?* The question echoed through her head over and over, causing her anger to flare even more.

She took a single step forward, causing him to flinch. At the same time, she began to silently form a spell, piecing the circle together from the recesses of her memory. The air in the arena grew damp as moisture gathered from the surrounding area. The temperature dropped to the point where her breath formed white clouds in the air.

Her opponent, sensing the change, attempted to charge her, but it was already too late. The moment he moved, the moisture in the air condensed rapidly, forming into a sheet of ice that covered the nearby ground, along with his legs. At first, the ice was thin. If he had reacted quickly enough, perhaps he could have broken free, but Lesti's magic worked too rapidly.

In moments, the boy's legs were covered in a sheet of ice so thick that even his magically enhanced strength wasn't enough to break it. He desperately began to try to melt the ice with fire spells, but they were image-based, and in his panic, they lacked a clear picture of his intent. The small bursts of flame didn't so much as faze the ice.

"I'm such an idiot." The words slipped from Lesti's mouth as she drew closer to her trapped opponent. The memories of her countless failed attempts to cast Ice Wall in the abandoned classroom flashed through her mind. She had practiced to the point of collapse on a nightly basis just to pull off that simple spell. Watching the ice spread over her opponent's body, it was clear that she was stronger.

That didn't mean that everyone else was going to stand still, though. Her friends, rivals, and even her enemies were going to get stronger. It was inevitable. Worrying about it was pointless. All she could do was have confidence in her own abilities and throw everything she had into overcoming the obstacles in her way.

And right now, this boy desperately trying to escape the ice was one of those obstacles. A grin crept over Lesti's face as the last of the doubts she had felt since the tournament began faded away. "You sure gave me a hard time, didn't you? Thanks for that."

Her opponent stopped trying to melt the ice and turned toward her, a confused look on his face. Lesti simply pointed a hand at him and began to form a spell. "If I had gone into my next match in this state, I would have lost for sure. If you want, I'll give you one last chance to surrender. It's the least I can do."

The boy's shocked expression shifted to one of determination. "As if I would sully the Saffos family name by surrendering. Give me your best shot."

Lesti's smile turned into a confident grin. "Alright! Don't say I didn't warn you. Let me show you what it takes to melt that ice. Fireball!" The frigid air around her suddenly grew hot as a roaring ball of flame exploded to life before her, then raced toward her opponent.

The boy began a chant of his own, but it was far too slow. Image-based magic could never keep up with the speed, precision, and power of instruction-based magic. The fireball slammed into him and exploded, sending smoke and debris flying throughout the arena.

When the dust finally settled, her opponent lay unconscious in a pool of water. Minor burns covered his body where Lesti's spell had overpowered the protective barrier that the judges had cast on him. She let out a relieved sigh. Upon seeing the explosion, she had worried that she might have overdone it and seriously injured him.

The judge walked over and took one glance down at the collapsed boy before raising his arm in the air. "The match is over. Lesti Vilia is the victor!"

A loud cheer rose up from the audience, causing Lesti to jump. After her qualifying match, the arena had been completely silent. This was her first time experiencing just how loud the cheers of hundreds could be. The sound threatened to overwhelm her, but the memory of Astria's fierce gaze flashed through her mind. She gathered herself and waved to the cheering crowd.

The moment didn't last long. The judge quickly ushered her out of the arena so they could prepare for the next match. That didn't stop Lesti from taking one last look back at a small figure on the roof. Astria still sat there looking down at her from above.

An uncontrollable grin spread across Lesti's face. This time, she had been saved by her companion, but next time she would prove that she could handle things on her own. She closed her fist tightly and extended it toward Astria before turning and heading back down the tunnel to the waiting area.

Evening Plans

I watched Lesti's figure fade into the tunnel as she left the arena. Once she was out of sight, I let out a relieved sigh. The quarterfinals had gotten pretty messy. I was worried that she would lose there for a minute, but she managed to recover. Whether or not my message got through to her was another matter, but I could worry about that later. I'd be sure to give her a good talking-to tonight before the semifinals.

Glancing over at the box seats I had escaped from, I saw Malkael glaring at me. *I guess Lesti isn't the only one who's in for a lecture. Maybe I'll take my time heading back.* I transformed back into my cat form and pretended to be observing the crowd below.

"So, that was your master, huh?" I started as a familiar voice echoed through my mind. Turning around, I found Zeke lazing around behind me. I knew for a fact he hadn't been there just a minute ago. He must have used a rift to sneak up on me. The fact that I couldn't detect when he was using that ability was rather worrying.

"Yeah. That's her." I turned around and walked away from the edge so that Malkael couldn't see me. I was already going to be in enough trouble. The last thing I needed was him grilling me about who I was talking to. At the same time, I didn't trust Zeke enough to leave my back exposed to him. *"What are you doing here?"*

"I was just watching the fights nearby and noticed your little performance, so I thought I'd come and say hi." Zeke stood, his large, canine body looming over me. Despite him being much bigger than me, I still didn't feel threatened. I

couldn't sense an ounce of ill intent coming from him. *"Do you always have to bail her out like that?"*

"Not really. It's true that she can be reckless and a bit of a handful at times, but she's surprisingly reliable." I unconsciously purred as I thought back on the trials we had been through up until now. Lesti seemed to believe that she relied on me too much, but I definitely didn't see it that way. *"We're partners, so it only makes sense that we'd help each other out."*

Zeke's eyes narrowed at my words. *"Partners? You think you're partners? I think you're misunderstanding something. As long as that pact exists between you two, you're nothing but a tool, a slave. With a few simple words, that girl can make you do anything she wants, regardless of your own will. She may not be using her authority now, but mark my words. Someday, she will."*

I froze where I stood, my eyes glued to his. On the surface, he was still calm. His voice remained steady throughout his sudden outburst, but I could see the hatred and loathing in his eyes. I didn't know where it came from but having him badmouth Lesti like that didn't sit right with me. *"Lesti isn't like that. We're companions, friends. She would never use our bond like that."*

"Are you sure?" The voice in my mind was strangely calm. Rather than anger, his tone seemed to be filled with pity. *"She's a noble. People like her are raised to manipulate, lie to, and use others. Even if she's treating you as an equal right now, there's no guarantee that it will last forever."*

"Are you trying to pick a fight with me? I already told you, Lesti isn't like that." I felt my fur begin to bristle and my tail stand on end as my anger flared. It was actually surprising to me how upset I was. If I thought about things rationally, I had only known Lesti for a few months. Besides, I had seen firsthand how cruel and manipulative the nobles in this world could be.

Yet, I trusted her completely. We had been through so much together in that short time. Even putting our lives in each other's hands multiple times. Having a complete stranger tell me that all of that was just a lie really got under my skin.

"That definitely wasn't my intention. I apologize if I made you angry." Zeke lowered his head, almost as if bowing. *"I just wanted to make sure you had considered the possibility. As someone in a similar situation to yours, I'd hate to*

see you make the same mistakes that I did."

I started to tell Zeke to mind his own business, but something about his words caught my attention. *"What do you mean, someone in a similar situation?"*

He had said something similar when I had first met him about helping out one of his own. At the time, I hadn't thought much of it. I figured he was just referring to us both being familiars. Now, I was starting to think that he might mean that I was some sort of noble hater like him.

Zeke looked down at me, seeming surprised. *"That? I was referring to how we're both humans turned familiar. Was that not obvious?"*

I blinked several times as Zeke's words hit me like a ton of bricks. My brain was simply struggling to believe what he had said. Sure, I had thought from our first meeting that there was something odd about his behavior. Still, Skell is pretty bizarre for a familiar himself. I just assumed it was a characteristic that all intelligent familiars had.

"Y-You're a former human?" Even though my mind was spinning with a million other questions, that was all I managed to squeeze out.

"That's right. One day I was just living my life, then the next thing I knew, I woke up in this body." Zeke used one of his tails to jokingly gesture toward his body. The fun mood didn't last long, though. His expression quickly grew dark with anger once more as he continued. *"Then, before I could even realize what had happened, I was bound by an absurd pact to my new 'master.'"*

"Wait, they didn't even give you a choice?! The pact is supposed to be a two-way agreement!"

"It's only two-way in the sense that it's not as effective if you don't agree to it. It can still be used to bind a familiar unwillingly, trust me."

"That's why you hate nobles so much, I take it?"

"Exactly, I'm sure you understand. Being ripped away from your old life jammed into a body like this and made to serve someone else's will. It's disgusting."

Listening to Zeke's story, everything clicked into place. I didn't know who his master had been, but they had definitely wronged him. When I thought about it, we really weren't all that different. Yet, I didn't feel the same level of resentment. Was that just because Lesti hadn't treated me like a slave or servant? It seemed like there had to be more to it than that.

I wanted to ask Zeke more about his experiences with becoming familiar, but he continued talking before I got the chance. *"That's actually why I wanted to come and see you. I'm working on a way to turn myself back into a human and escape this miserable fate. I'm making good progress too. I could always use more help, though. I wanted to see if you would like to join me."*

"I can become human again?" My heart pounded in my chest as I processed what Zeke was saying. I had always assumed that the entirety of my new life would be spent as an Astral Cat. While that had definitely caused me some pain and worries, I had mostly been able to ignore them because I had no way to do anything about it.

Now that I was presented with the possibility of becoming human again, everything I had given up on flooded me at once. Falling in love, raising a family, or even something as simple as sitting down and eating dinner like an average person would become possible for me again. I almost agreed to help Zeke on the spot.

However, something stopped me. Memories of my time with Lesti flashed through my mind, along with the promise I had made her. Would I still be able to help her if I stopped being her familiar? Remembering her struggling in her desperation as she trained on her own in that empty classroom, I couldn't imagine just abandoning her.

"I appreciate the offer, but I need some time to think about it. Did you need anything else? Besides, I need to be getting back soon."

In the end, I simply couldn't accept his offer right now. I needed time to process things, and I wanted to talk to Lesti. We had been through a lot together, and I truly considered her my partner. I couldn't simply make a decision as big as this without talking to her first.

A quick flash of annoyance flitted across Zeke's face, but he quickly dismissed it with a full-body shake. *"I see. I'm not sure what there is to think about, but very well. I'll come back another time."*

Zeke's tails flicked through the air and opened a rift behind him. Through it, I could see an alley somewhere in the city. Just before he hopped through it, he bared his fangs in what appeared to be a weird attempt at a smile.

"Actually, there is one more thing. If you're interested in learning the secret behind that boy's power, look for a tavern called The Mage's Retreat this evening. I think you'll find what you see rather interesting."

"Boy? You mean Sebastian?" I was confused by the sudden advice. Zeke had clearly been annoyed with me for not accepting his offer on this spot. It seemed strange that he would suddenly help me out like this. *"Why would you tell me that?"*

Zeke let out a heavy sigh. *"You really don't hold grudges very easily, huh? Consider it an apology for questioning your master's integrity."*

"Oh, right. I guess you did do something like that." With the sudden revelation of Zeke also being a former human, I had completely forgotten my anger at him for insulting Lesti.

He simply shook his head at me, clearly exasperated. *"At any rate, take my advice or leave it; it's up to you. I look forward to speaking to you again soon, Astria."*

Turning around, he leapt through the rift, and it closed behind him as if it had never been there at all.

I look forward to speaking to you again, huh? As his final words bounced around inside my head, I felt myself suddenly feeling nervous. I was sure Zeke would be back soon, demanding an answer. I would need to talk to Lesti sooner rather than later.

I shook myself and tried to calm down. There wasn't anything I could do about it at the moment anyway. Plus, I had other things to worry about. Lesti's meeting with Lord Valst and Sebastian's abnormal increase in power both came to mind. Shifting my focus back to those problems, I went to meet up with Malkael and Fang.

* * *

Later that evening, we found ourselves in a small, inexpensive inn near the arena. The tiny room was a simple affair with two beds and a small nightstand. It was filled with familiar faces, and magical lights floated through the air, casting shadows about the tightly packed space.

Lani stood by the door to make sure no one eavesdropped on us. Lesti, Aurelia, and Rose sat on one of the beds. Malkael, flanked by Fang and me, faced them from the other bed. Everyone had weary looks on their faces. Between the tournament, guard duty, and backroom dealings, we had all been swamped.

After meeting up with Malkael, I was lectured extensively for wandering off. Then, we stayed and watched the remaining battles for the day. Rose managed to win her match and advance to the semifinals. Alex and Elliot had done the same, both handily defeating their opponents. They would face each other in the semifinals tomorrow while Lesti would go up against Sebastian.

Which led us to why we had all gathered here. I turned to Aurelia, who was sitting between Rose and Lesti, looking dejected. "You shouldn't be too hard on yourself, Aurelia. There's no way you could have predicted that Sebastian would be that strong."

Aurelia glanced up at me and shook her head. "Mmm. If I had trained properly, I could have won."

"I'm not so sure about that." Malkael said the words that I had been holding back, causing me to throw him a nasty glare. However, he continued unperturbed. "The young Master Cilias's growth isn't natural. I suspect there was some sort of external catalyst that caused it. That's not the sort of thing a reasonable amount of training could overcome."

I continued to glare at him for being so blunt about it, but Malkael was right. Aurelia had already spent quite a bit of time training. Sure, a lot of that was spent working with Fang, but I honestly think that was best for them when you considered their future. Besides, even if she had ignored Fang and only focused on her own training, I doubt it would have changed anything.

Aurelia bit her lip, her frustration evident. Lesti glanced at her and smiled. "Look on the bright side, Auri. At least you lost to someone strong, even if it was that scumbag, Sebastian. I nearly lost to someone weaker than me because I let myself get too worked up. If Astria hadn't snapped me out of it, everything would have been ruined."

"Why do you sound so calm about the whole thing?" I turned my gaze to Lesti, narrowing my eyes at her. "Just watching you stressed me out, you know."

"I know. I'm sorry." She lowered her head, but the smile never left her face. "It's just that I think it was a good experience."

"A good experience?" Aurelia asked in a confused tone.

Lesti nodded confidently. "Yeah. It just goes to show that we can't underestimate our opponents or take anything for granted. You never know what could happen. Even if we're getting stronger, that doesn't mean that everyone else is standing still. Not to mention, you never know when we'll find ourselves in a situation where we can't use our full abilities. We need to be prepared for anything."

For a long moment, everyone stared at Lesti in silence. We were so used to her usual boastful attitude that such an insightful comment caught us completely off-guard. Malkael cleared his throat and nodded, breaking the silence. "An excellent observation, Ms. Vilia. It's true that strength alone can only take you so far when it comes to battle. Your own condition and experiences are just as much of a factor."

"Right? After today, there's no way I'm taking Sebastian lightly. I'll give it my all and get revenge for Auri!" Lesti pumped her fist into the air and smiled at Aurelia, trying her best to dispel her friend's foul mood. "I'll show them just how strong we are. When I'm done with him, there won't be a trace of that smug look of his left."

At Lesti's declaration, Rose's dainty giggle echoed through the room for a moment. Lesti leaned forward and looked past Aurelia at her. "What's so funny, Rose? I'm being serious over here, you know?"

"I'm sorry." Rose quickly suppressed her laughter and looked at the other two. "I was just thinking how silly I was being. I was so nervous today, during the tournament. The entire time I was worried that I would disappoint you both if I messed up or lost. Seeing you both now, I realize just how ridiculous I was being." She pumped her fists in front of her, showing her resolve. "I'm going to do my best tomorrow too, so make sure you cheer for me, A-Auwi!"

Lesti and Aurelia both turned to stare at Rose, whose face quickly turned a deep shade of red at her mistake. My mind raced to try and find some way to cover for her. Both Aurelia and Lesti seemed too surprised to react, and Rose's embarrassment grew worse by the second. Before I could come up with anything, though, something I never expected happened.

"Pff-hahaha!" Aurelia burst out laughing. This wasn't the reserved giggle or chuckle that I was used to seeing either. This was a full-bellied laugh that had her gasping for air after a few moments. Lesti and Rose both stared at her for a moment in shock before her laughter spread to them.

For a few minutes, our room was filled with the peaceful sounds of laughter and friendship. Honestly, I wished that moment could have lasted forever. Seeing them laughing together like that without a care in the world, all I could think was that was how things should be. Girls their age shouldn't have to worry about getting stronger, saving their families, or fighting demons. They should just live their lives to the fullest and laugh.

Unfortunately, that wasn't the reality of this world. Their laughter eventually came to an end, and it was time to get back to business. Aurelia dried her eyes and turned to Rose. "Thank you, Rose. Don't worry. I'll be cheering for both of you tomorrow, so do your best."

Looking at her eyes as she spoke, I could tell that the frustration Aurelia felt was still there. Still, there was also a steadiness that had been lacking before. It seemed like she was going to be okay. With that settled, I turned the conversation back to our main reason for gathering. "It's nice to think about tomorrow, you three, but we still have work to do tonight. Especially you, Lesti."

Lesti sat up straight and turned to face me, "I take it that means you managed to secure a meeting with Lord Valst?"

"That's correct." Malkael stepped in since he had been the one to arrange the final details. "You'll be meeting at a small tavern nearby in the commoner district. It's frequented by some of the wealthier merchants in the city and has private rooms for meetings."

"The commoner district? Not the merchant district?" Lani spoke up from her spot by the door, a concerned look on her face.

"Yes. While it would normally be more dangerous, meeting in the commoner district will decrease the chances of you being spied on. Plus, with the crowds being so large because of the tournament festivities, it'll be difficult for anyone to attack the two of you."

"The two of us?" Lesti looked back and forth between Lani and me. "Is Astria not coming with us?"

I shook my head. "I'll be looking into Sebastian's sudden increase in power. Something about it just doesn't sit right with me. The two of you will have to meet Lord Valst on your own. Besides, if I went with you, it would make it a lot harder to keep the meeting secret. The city isn't exactly overflowing with Astral Cats, after all."

"I guess that makes sense, but be careful, okay?" Lesti looked at me with a worried expression. "If Sebastian catches you, then there's no telling what he might do."

"Trust me, I know." The image of Sebastian's sadistic smile as he slammed his dagger into my barrier repeatedly flashed through my mind. That wasn't an experience that I wanted to relive anytime soon. "I'll prioritize my own safety this time around and get out of there at the first sign of trouble. At the end of the day, I'm just working off a hunch anyway."

"Good." Lesti seemed pleased with my answer, but a puzzled look flashed across her face a moment later. "Actually, how do you know where Sebastian is anyway?"

I paused for a moment, trying to think of the best way to tell them about Zeke. There was still so much about him, and I still hadn't figured out how I felt about his offer. I couldn't talk about that in front of this group. Not all of them knew that I had reincarnated. Yet, I got the feeling that keeping my conversation with him a secret would somehow come back to bite me. "Someone told me where I could find him. I think he's someone's familiar since he can speak, like me."

"A high-level familiar, then?" Malkael looked to me for confirmation as he asked. I nodded, and he scrunched his brow up in thought. "I see. There aren't many of those in the world. Even amongst the noble class, they're extremely rare. It shouldn't be too hard for us to track down this familiar's owner. Did he have any distinguishing features?"

"Yeah. He's kind of like a long-legged wolf with pale yellow eyes. What really stands out, though, is those tails of his. He has four of them, and they can open portals to other places. That ring any bells?"

"Astria, are you positive that you saw him open a portal with his tails?" Lani's voice came across as a mere whisper. I looked over at her only to find her looking at me nervously, her face slightly pale. Glancing around the room, she wasn't the only one who was suddenly tense.

Malkael's gaze was fixed on me as if he was hanging on my every word. Across the room, Lesti and the other girls were all glancing at each other with nervous expressions. The tension was so palpable that even the ordinarily happy-go-lucky Fang was pressed flat as a pancake on the bed.

"Y-Yeah. I'm sure. That power is how I managed to spy on the meeting between Lord Dawster and Lord Valst." I glanced around nervously at the others. "Is that bad or something?"

Lani nodded slowly and took a deep breath. "Right, you wouldn't know about it since it's a human legend. The creature you described is what's known as a Rift Stalker. It's been passed down in tales for ages as a creature whose presence signals coming ruin."

"I see. That explains why you're all acting so weird, at least." I looked around at the group. Judging by their expressions, most of them seemed to consider the story something like a myth or fairy tale. It made them nervous deep down, but their fear wasn't based on any sort of reality. Lani and Rose were the only ones who seemed truly troubled by my words.

Rose clung to Aurelia, shaking slightly as she did. Meanwhile, Lani clenched her fist nervously while staring at the floor. Eventually, her eyes rose to meet mine, and a simple question spilled from her lips. "The Rift Stalker, did he give you a name?"

"Yeah. He called himself Zeke."

"That confirms it then." Lani shut her eyes tightly, almost as she was trying to chase away the fragments of a bad dream. When she opened them again, her voice was slightly unsteady. "I've met the Rift Stalker you saw today once before, on the academy grounds."

Lani quickly explained how she had encountered Zeke shortly after we had met Rose and how he had been spying on her. That news seemed to disturb Rose far more than I would have expected until Lani explained that Zeke had most likely been Baron Arvis's familiar. Once I put that together, it made sense that Rose would be rattled by his appearance. She probably had nothing but terrible memories of him.

That wasn't the worst part of Lani's story, though. She explained how Zeke had managed to open a portal to the demon realm right in front of her eyes. The revelation shocked me. Having seen it in action myself, I knew that his ability was powerful, but I didn't think he'd be able to open portals to other dimensions. Did his ability not have any restrictions on it?

"Why in the world would Baron Arvis have forged a pact with such a dangerous creature?" Malkael shook his head in disbelief.

"Most likely, he thought he could control the Rift Stalker with the power of the pact," Lani replied. "When I spoke to Zeke, he didn't seem very fond of his master."

"Arvis didn't just try. He did exactly what you said. Zeke has a deep distrust of nobles because of that." I looked over at Lesti, who was busy comforting Rose. Zeke's attempts to break my trust in her bounced around inside my head. "He warned me that Lesti may one day use our pact against me."

Lesti's head snapped up, and she stared at me in shock. "I would never do anything like that! Only a monster would abuse the familiar pact to force their own will on another."

"Don't worry. I told him you weren't that type of person. Not that he believed me." I furrowed my brow in thought. "More importantly, if Baron Arvis is dead. Doesn't that mean Zeke is free now?"

"Yes. Once the master dies, the pact binding the familiar is invalidated." Lani confirmed my suspicions with a thoughtful expression on her face. "But if that's the case, then why is he hanging around the arena? Could he be looking for a new master?"

I shook my head. "I doubt it. He seems to value his freedom way too much for that. Besides, the majority of people who could form a pact with him would be nobles, and he hates them. He seems to be interested in me more than anything else. He keeps helping me out after all."

"Hmm. If the Rift Stalker has taken an interest in you, then that is rather concerning." Malkael rubbed his temples, clearly overwhelmed by everything going on. "Perhaps it would be best if you stayed with Instructor Lania and Ms. Vilia this evening after all."

"Sorry, but that isn't going to happen." I immediately rejected Malkael's proposal. We didn't have the luxury of playing things safe here. "I definitely don't trust Zeke, but he hasn't been hostile so far. Right now, Sebastian is the biggest threat to our plans. We need to figure out the trick behind his sudden increase in power and come up with countermeasures if possible."

Lani quickly rejected my proposal. "Even if you say that, I'm not exactly comfortable with you just wandering through the city on your own. If something happens, we won't be able to help you."

"I understand how you feel, but that just means I have to be careful. If it comes down to a fight, I'll just run away. Sebastian won't be willing to cause a ruckus in the middle of the city." I fixed Lani with a determined stare. I knew I was being stubborn here, but something told me that I needed to see this through.

However, that only seemed to worsen her mood. I felt a slight chill in the air as her tone turned cold. "You'll be careful? Sebastian won't want to cause a ruckus? Aren't you just making up excuses?" Lani's gaze turned into a hard piercing stare as her anger reached its peak. "The last time you tried something like this with Sebastian, you ended up getting captured, nearly killed, and an archdemon was summoned into our world. All of that happened back when Sebastian was at the bottom of his year. Do you really think things will go more smoothly now that he's stronger?"

I tried to come up with some sort of comeback, but I couldn't. Lani was right. Even if I had gotten stronger, Sebastian had too, and he was willing to use all sorts of dirty tricks to get what he wanted. All I could do was stare back at her defiantly.

The others watched our showdown in silence. Lani was pretty terrifying when she was angry, so I couldn't blame them for staying out of it. I would have to figure out some way to convince her on my own. Or at least, that's what I thought.

"I'll go with you." Aurelia broke the silence. Looking over, I found her staring at me with a determined look on her face. Lani started to reject her proposal, but she cut her off before she could. "Sebastian won't be able to defeat all three of us before help arrives."

"Assuming help comes at all. How are we supposed to know you're in danger?" Lani stubbornly held her position, but her tone softened quite a bit. I could tell she just needed one last push, and she'd be convinced. I wracked my brain trying to think of something to change her mind, but it ended up being a waste of energy.

"About that, I actually have something that might help." Lesti excitedly jumped up off the bed and ran over to her bag. After rummaging through it for a bit, she pulled out a small pendant with a leather cord and held it up. "Here we go. This should solve the communication problem."

Light reflected off the polished surface of the pendant. At first, I thought it was nothing more than a simple polished stone. However, when I looked more closely, I could see magic runes etched across the entire surface. Malkael must have noticed at the same time because his eyes went wide. "Is that an artifact? Where did you get something like that?"

Lesti puffed her chest out proudly. "We didn't get it anywhere. We made it. This is the result of all the research that I've been doing." She paused and scratched her cheek awkwardly. "Although, it's really just a proof of concept, so it doesn't do much."

"So, how does it help solve our problem?" I quickly cut in before Malkael could take us on a wild tangent. I could see his inner researcher was bubbling with curiosity. "Will it allow us to talk at a distance or something?"

Lesti just slumped her shoulders. "Are you even aware how much magical energy that would consume? All this does is glow either red or green when a keyword is spoken."

I blinked, slightly confused. "And how does that help us exactly?"

"It doesn't," she replied flatly. Then, she held up her other hand, and a second pendant fell from her grasp, dangling from her fingers. "This one will, though. It's even simpler, honestly. Catch."

She tossed the second pendant over to me. I caught it in my mouth and began trying to get the cord around my neck. Unfortunately, my lack of thumbs made that a rather difficult task. In the end, Rose took pity on me and helped me get the pendant on. She even adjusted the length, so it acted as more of a collar.

Once that was done, Lesti held the other pendant up to her mouth and whispered something. When she did, a faint green light emanated from the runes etched into the stone. Then, a second later, the runes on the pendant tied around my neck began to glow green as well.

"Astounding," Malkael whispered as he stared at the pendants in awe. I wasn't quite as impressed as he was. Coming from a world with smartphones, this seemed like the most basic form of communication available. Still, I could appreciate how big a deal this was to him. Even if it was simple, this was essentially a brand-new artifact that Lesti had created.

"So, when you speak the keyword into one, they both change colors?" I decided to confirm how these worked with Lesti despite how simple it seemed. It wouldn't do to get into trouble and not understand how it worked.

She nodded. "That's the basic idea. Essentially, a small burst of magical energy is sent to the other pendant whenever the keyword is spoken. When it receives the correct amount of energy, it changes color. You could force the color to change the same way by just providing the energy yourself, but that won't cause the signal to be sent to the other pendant, so make sure you use the keyword."

"What's the keyword?" I asked.

"To make it glow green, it's 'cat's paw.' To make it glow red, you just need to say 'demon's claw.' To turn it off, just say 'silent dog.'" As Lesti explained all the keywords, the stones turned red, and then the glow faded.

I jumped down from the bed and looked over at Lani. "I know it's dangerous, but I really have to do this, Lani. I promise that if we run into any trouble, I'll call for help."

Lani finally stepped away from the door and sighed. "Fine. You had better keep your promise, though. If I find out later that you ran into trouble and didn't call for us, you won't get off easy."

"Understood." I nodded at her and turned to Lesti. "I'm sure you'll be fine, but be careful with Lord Valst. He's smarter than he lets on, and he has a weird way of controlling the mood in the room."

"I'm sure it'll be fine. I'm more worried about you." Lesti grimaced at me before turning to Aurelia. "Make sure you keep an eye on her, Auri. Astria always tends to get herself in trouble at times like this."

"Mm. We'll make sure she stays safe. Count on us," Aurelia replied with a small fist pump, and Fang barked enthusiastically.

"Alright. Let's get going then. We don't want to be out too late." I turned and headed out of the inn with Aurelia and Fang close behind me. Despite everything I had said, I couldn't help but be nervous. The thought of what Sebastian might do if he captured me ran through my mind repeatedly as we headed into the night.

Noble Dealings

L esti stood outside the entrance of a rather large tavern in the commoner district. The building was located relatively close to the gate that led to the merchant district. Its stone surface was clean and well maintained despite being made from cheaper materials. Above the door hung a simple sign bearing the tavern's name, Cat's Cradle. The soft glow of magical light flowed out from the open windows before them.

Night had fallen across the city, but she could barely tell. Magical lights and oil lanterns lit the city streets as they overflowed with people. Music and song drifted by on the evening breeze only to be swept away by the chatter of the crowds a moment later.

Deep inside, she wanted nothing more than to explore the city and take in this unusual atmosphere. Unfortunately, that wasn't an option for her tonight. Instead, she had crept through the town dressed in commoner clothes that Malkael had prepared, the hood of her cloak pulled low over her head.

Lani stood beside her, dressed much the same, as her eyes constantly scanned the crowd for any threats. Lesti couldn't help but smile. She was more than capable of taking care of herself now, but Lani still had a tendency to treat her like a defenseless child. It was rather endearing. Although, she would still be sure to tease her about it later.

"It doesn't appear that anyone followed us." Lani's shoulders relaxed slightly as she finished scanning the crowd. "Shall we head inside?"

Lesti nodded silently in response, and they both walked through the door. Just like the exterior, the inside of this tavern was a strange mixture of the typical commoner district tavern and merchant district tavern. The materials were simple and cheap, but they were arranged and maintained so immaculately that it gave the place an entirely different feel. Between that and the difference in size, it was easy to tell that this wasn't your average establishment.

The main area they had walked into shared the same layout as most taverns in this district. It was a large open area filled with simple wooden tables and chairs. A well-stocked bar was on the far side of the room, with a doorway leading back to the kitchen. However, that was where the similarities ended.

The entire space was lit by magical lights that floated near the high ceiling. Off to either side of the room, curtains hung across doorways that presumably led to private rooms. Each door was guarded by two seasoned-looking warriors.

The servers also had a different air about them. Several women dressed in simple yet elegant blouses and skirts wandered between the tables while serving the guests. Even at a glance, Lesti could tell they were well trained. Their movements had an elegance and refinement to them that you couldn't fake. They might even be capable of serving in the manor of a lower-ranking noble.

As Lesti was taking in the strange sight, one of the waitresses spotted Lani and her and came over to greet them. Despite their somewhat questionable appearance, she didn't even bat an eye as she elegantly curtsied. "Good evening. Would you happen to have a reservation?"

"Yes. We're here to meet with Lord Stalv." Lani gave the girl the alias that Malkael had told them to use, causing both of them to grimace slightly. The name was so obviously close to Valst's actual name that it hardly served as an alias at all. It made her question just how capable this man really was. Astria had seemed to have a high opinion of him, but she wasn't used to dealing with nobles. So perhaps her assessment was a little skewed.

"I see. We've been expecting the two of you. Please follow me." The waitress smiled brightly, turned on her heel, and gestured for them to follow her. She led them through one of the curtained doorways and into a hallway lined with private rooms on each side.

Stopping in front of one such door, she rapped gently on it. "Lord Stalv, your guests have arrived."

"What are you waiting for, then? Let them in!" A loud and clearly drunk voice echoed from inside the room. The idea that she might be dealing with some belligerent drunk made her feel just the slightest bit anxious.

She frowned and glanced over at Lani, but her face was a blank slate, almost as if it was frozen stiff. It was a look that Lesti was all too familiar with. Lani was now in attendant mode. Despite how she usually acted, she was pretty good at hiding her emotions and maintaining her composure. Having served the Vilia family since her teens, Lani was exceptionally well trained. When situations like these popped up, it was as if she simply flipped a switch and changed her whole personality.

Lesti smiled at Lani's transformation and stepped into the private meeting room. The inside was decorated more lavishly than the bar area had been. Two sofas sat in the center of the space, each made of fine leather. The table was intricately carved and painted to look like the legs were some sort of living plant.

Sitting on the sofa to her left was a man taking large swigs of alcohol straight from the bottle while groping his attendant's butt. His green eyes had dark circles under them, as if he hadn't slept, and were filled with lust. However, he didn't appear to be flushed as one would expect someone heavily drinking to be. Nor could she smell the alcohol in the air.

She walked over and sat on the couch across from him, pulling her hood down to reveal her blazing red hair. When she did, Valst's facade cracked for a brief moment, and she saw the flash of fierce intelligence in his eyes. That, more than anything she had seen so far, caused a chill to race down her spine. It appeared that Astria's assessment had been on the mark after all.

Her mind began to race as she attempted to figure out the reason for Valst's little act. It didn't seem like he had anything to gain by making her question his character. More likely, this was a test of some sort. He wanted her to see through his little ruse; that much was clear. Only an utter buffoon would fall for such a simple act.

If that was the case, then was he testing her on how she would react? Lesti ran through all the possible ways she could confront his behavior in rapid succession. The majority that came to mind were those drilled into her by her tutors back in the Vilia territory. Most of them focused on trying to stay in the good graces of one's opponent by glossing over the issue or skirting around it.

For a poor backwater territory like hers, maintaining good relationships with their neighbors was essential. You never knew when you would need help from the lord of another domain due to famine, war, or natural disasters. Even though it would hurt her pride, she always had to do what was best for her people. Taking all these factors into account, she made her decision.

Looking her opponent in the eye, she smiled brightly. "Lord Valst, would you be so kind as to stop this nonsense? Such unsightly displays and petty schemes are unfitting of a Lord in the Alandrian Alliance."

She felt Lani stiffen behind her as silence fell over the room. The smile she wore didn't extend to her eyes. All that could be found there was a challenging glare, one that dared her opponent to keep pushing his luck. Valst's eyes remained locked on hers for a few seconds, silently boring into her as if searching for some crack in her armor.

She wouldn't let him find one, though. She had already failed once today. Messing up this meeting after her pitiful performance in the quarterfinals would be unacceptable.

A second later, Valst's entire persona changed. He sat up straight, placed the alcohol on the table, and waved off his maid. She moved to stand behind him without a word, her own attitude shifting on a dime as well. The pair suddenly wore sharp, focused looks on their faces. The intelligence that Lesti had only caught a glimpse of before now shone brightly in his eyes. The only things that didn't change were his clothes and the dark circles under his eyes.

"My apologies, Lady Vilia. I needed to be sure of your character before we began negotiations. When dealing with Lord Dawster, one has to have a strong enough will to hold their own, or they'll be eaten alive." An annoyed smirk flashed across Valst's face. "That's just the type of opponent we'll be dealing with this time. I hope you can forgive me."

She let out a relieved sigh. Her response seemed to have been the correct one. Despite how confident she had appeared on the surface, she didn't have much experience dealing with situations like this. Although, in the end, it wouldn't have mattered much if her answer had been wrong.

If Valst was the type of man to expect her to bow and scrape to curry his favor, then she would be better off solving the problem of Lord Dawster on her own anyway. Someone who viewed her as beneath them would never make a good ally.

"It's not a problem. I'm well aware of how the Dawster family operates. It was a constant point of stress for my parents when they were alive." Lesti smiled bitterly as the memory of her parents flitted through her mind.

"Yes. I do seem to remember the late Lord and Lady Vilia sharing their rather...frank opinions with my father during their last visit. I'm glad to see that the apple hasn't fallen far from the tree in that regard." Valst paused for a moment, seeming to consider something. "In fact, if you don't mind, I'd like to suggest we drop the formalities so that we can proceed apace."

"That works for me. I can't stand having to mince words and act all proper. It's such a waste of time." Lesti shook her head, an exasperated expression on her face. "Honestly, if there's one thing that I'm dreading the most once I take over the lordship from my uncle, it's that."

Behind her, she felt Lani twitch. She probably wanted to lay into her for revealing such a vital part of their plans so casually, but she held herself back. As an attendant, she had no right to speak here if her lord didn't permit it first. Lesti glanced back at her, an amused smirk on her face. "Well, you heard him. If we're going to drop the formalities, then you can speak freely as well, Lani."

"Have you never heard of keeping your cards close to the chest? Even if Lord Valst seems trustworthy, you could show just a tiny bit of caution, you know." Having her restriction lifted, Lani didn't hesitate to tell her exactly what she was thinking.

"Hahaha. You and that familiar of yours really are a pair, you know that?" Before she could even explain her reasoning to Lani, Valst burst out laughing.

"First, she threatens me because I know the secret behind your magic. Then you just come out and tell me you're going to defy the council and become lord of the Vilia territory?! Could you two make up your minds?!"

"Astria threatened you?" Lesti spun back around to stare at the cackling lord in disbelief. Astria had conveniently left that part of the story out. Still, Lesti was sure she had her reasons for what she did. "I'm sure she was doing what she thought was best for me at that time, so I hope you won't hold it against her."

"Ah, not at all. Although, Silvia here might be a little slower to forgive her."

Lesti smiled as she glanced up at the maid behind Valst. She was wearing an irritated scowl on her face as she stared down at her lord. All of the seriousness from before seemed to have dissipated. The room suddenly felt much brighter and more cheerful. This must have been what Astria was talking about when she said Lord Valst had a weird way of manipulating the mood in the room.

"At any rate, we should get down to business. I'm sure you have a lot of preparations you need to take care of for tomorrow." Just as quickly as before, Valst switched gears again. "I believe we can skip right past that nonsense about your family hoarding artifacts. It wasn't something your parents would have done, and you clearly aren't that sort of person either."

"Right. So, the question then is how do we deal with Lord Dawster." Lesti leaned forward, doing her best to keep pace with Valst. "Now that we have a mutual defense agreement with the Mori clan, he can't make any moves on his own. I'd say our best course of action would be to publicly denounce his claims that my family is looking to rebel."

"Yes. That certainly does seem like the best course of action." Valst seemed to agree with her proposal, but Lesti noticed a hesitation in his voice. Something was bothering him.

She tried to think about how Dawster might be able to counter their rebuttal, but the only way she could think of was through sheer numbers. While the family was powerful and influential, they weren't well-liked. She didn't believe they would be able to get a large number of territories to back their claims in such a short time.

"Is there something about my proposal that you don't like?" Lesti decided the best course of action was to simply ask Valst for his thoughts. Based on his reaction, there was likely something she was missing. She couldn't afford to make a mistake because she was worried about looking dumb. Her people's lives were on the line.

"It's about the rumors that gave rise to all of this, about your family hoarding artifacts." Valst paused for a moment collecting his thoughts, his brow furrowed as he stared at the empty table in front of them. When he finally looked up at Lesti again, he posed a question to her. "Dawster may be using those to his advantage, but he isn't the one who's spreading them. Do you have any other enemies that we should be wary of?"

"Ah. I see." Lesti's eyes lit up with realization. "If whoever was spreading those rumors has enough influence and backs Dawster's claims, we might be in trouble." She thought back to her recent interactions with other nobles. Only two stood out in her mind. "The only people that I've made enemies of would be Augustine and Sebastian. If I had to venture a guess, I would say the Cilias family is the more likely candidate of those two. Augustine already had a bad reputation, so his claims wouldn't hold much weight."

"The Cilias family, huh? That could certainly present a problem. They're close to the border with the Kingdom and wield enough influence to gather others to their cause quickly."

Lesti looked back over her shoulder at Lani. "Do you think that Lord Gambriel would be willing to execute our plan early if it came down to it?"

Lani nodded, her expression unchanging. "Based on my latest information, Lord Gambriel has already made arrangements to enact our plan at any given point. The Cilias family and their allies won't be able to move against us so easily."

"Well, as you heard, it seems the Cilias family won't be able to interfere, even if they want to. The only threats that we'll need to worry about are those north of this city." Lesti turned back to Valst with a mischievous grin on her face. He stared at her in silence for a long moment before an amused smile of his own emerged.

"I don't know what you've got up your sleeve, but if Lord Gambriel is involved, then it must be big. I really do pity that uncle of yours. You must be running him ragged with these schemes."

She puffed out her chest proudly. "No need to worry about that. My uncle is an extremely competent man. If it wasn't for his age, he would probably have been made lord instead of marrying me off to Augustine."

Valst chuckled, a sudden weariness appearing in his eyes. "Yes. He certainly is a capable man. Our trade negotiations last summer showed me that much." The fatigue in his eyes faded, and a sudden pressure crashed down on Lesti as he looked at her. "Make sure you learn as much as you can from him. His experience and perspective will be invaluable if you truly wish to take over the lordship."

Lesti sat up straight and nodded. The sudden change in Valst's attitude completely caught her off-guard. It was so different from what Astria mentioned and what she had seen that she hadn't expected it at all. She was very glad that this man was going to be her ally and not an enemy.

Seeing that his point had gotten across, Valst relaxed and leaned back in his seat. "Good. Then, let's get back to the matter at hand. I think we should have a contingency plan in case we're wrong about who is spreading the rumors. What do you think of expanding your mutual defense agreement with the Mori clan?"

"Expanding it? What do you mean?" She cocked her head to the side.

"I'm saying that we should also get other territories to sign mutual defense agreements with the Mori clan. Right now, Dawster is using the mutual defense agreement you have with them as proof of your ambitions for rebellion. But if you were to broker defense deals with other territories in the region, then…"

"He wouldn't be able to cast suspicion on us anymore!" Her excitement got the better of her as she followed along with Valst's suggestion, and she ended up shouting unintentionally. She blushed briefly while Valst stared at her with an amused smirk. Clearing her throat to wipe away her embarrassment, she continued, "I certainly don't object to that plan, but I don't speak for the Mori clan. I can arrange a meeting with their chief's daughter, but the rest will be up to you."

"That's a start. We should move quickly, though. The more time we take, the higher the chance of Lord Dawster coming up with some counter plan becomes."

"I agree. If it works for you, I can arrange for her to meet you tomorrow during the first semifinals match."

"That would be perfect. We can use the same meeting room where I met your familiar today. Malkael will be able to show her the way." Lesti breathed a sigh of relief at Valst's words. The final arrangement now in place, she prepared to excuse herself. As she did, Valst leaned forward, a sharp look in his eyes. "Now, with the main topic out of the way, I'd like to discuss our trade agreements as well as a few other topics."

She paused, a sense of dread welling up from deep within her. Almost reflexively, she tried to divert the discussion. "Um, if you wish to discuss such matters, then you'll need to talk to my uncle. He's currently in charge of all the major decisions for the Vilia territory."

A pleasant, friendly smile that didn't extend to his eyes flashed across Valst's face. "That won't be necessary. After all, I'm speaking to the future lord of the Vilia territory, am I not? It might take a while for our agreements to come into effect, but I think you'll find that I'm a very patient man. Now, shall we begin by discussing the exchange of agricultural goods?"

Lesti looked up at Lani, her eyes begging for some escape from the current situation. All she found there was a cold look that said, *"This is what you get for opening your mouth without thinking about the consequences."* Heaving a heavy sigh, she turned back to Valst, put on her best poker face, and began what was sure to be a long night of negotiations.

Sebastian's Secret

"Looks like this is the place." Aurelia and I stood in the streets of the merchant district, staring up at a sign with the words "The Mage's Retreat" written in fancy script. The roads were still packed with people despite the late hour, and a festival-like atmosphere filled the air.

Fang wasn't with us at the moment. We wanted someone to keep an eye on our surroundings. Given his dark fur colors, it was easier for him to stay concealed, so we had given him the job. He was currently keeping an eye on things from a nearby rooftop.

"Mm. How do we get inside, though?" Aurelia asked.

I followed her gaze to find two well-armed guards standing on either side of the door. It seemed like an unusual amount of security for a tavern, even during an event like this. Although, when I considered that a noble family might be staying here, it made more sense. We could probably assume that there was even more security inside.

I glanced over the building, looking for a way in. Even though I had called it a tavern, that was really only the first floor. The entire building was three floors, with the second and third floors serving as an inn. Most likely, it was frequented by wealthy merchants and poorer nobles who couldn't afford their own manor here in the city.

Still, that made me wonder what Sebastian's family was doing here. They might not be the most powerful family in the alliance. Still, from my understanding, they weren't low-ranking like Lesti's family. Now wasn't the time to be worrying about that, though. I shifted my focus back to observing the building.

All of the windows appeared to be plain with only shutters and no glass, so we might be able to sneak in through one of those, but I wasn't sure how we would hide once we were inside. As I pondered the problem, one of the guards spotted Aurelia and me standing in the crowd and started watching us. Apparently, we had been loitering for too long. Before I could say anything, Aurelia turned on her heel and walked away.

After we were some distance down the street, we ducked into an alley. Aurelia looked down at me with a complicated expression. "Sorry. I think you're going to have to sneak in alone."

"Yeah. I was thinking the same thing. I think that's the only way that we get past the security and don't get caught." I gazed back in the direction of The Mage's Retreat. "I just wish I knew the layout better. Even if I get inside, I don't know where to find Sebastian."

Aurelia just tilted her head at me. "Couldn't you just use your magic sight to figure out where he is?"

I shook my head. "It might work, but I'm not sure if I can identify Sebastian anymore. He's so much stronger now that I doubt his magical energy looks the same as it did before."

"Mmm. He should be pretty easy to find," Aurelia replied with a bitter look on her face. "There aren't that many mages with the magical energy to fight like he did."

"I guess that's true." I took a deep breath and paused for a moment, trying to think of other options. When nothing came to mind, I nodded and turned my gaze up to meet Aurelia's eyes. "Alright, I'm going in. Stay nearby, and I'll call for you if anything happens."

"Mm. Be careful, Instructor." Without waiting for my response, Aurelia turned and pulled her hood low over her head before blending into the main street crowds. Seeing her disappear like that took me back to when we first met. I didn't have time to reminisce, though. Using Air Walk, I leapt up onto the rooftops and headed back to the inn Sebastian was supposed to be staying in.

We hadn't gone very far, so I was there in under a minute. The building I was standing on was only two stories, so I had an unobstructed view of the third floor directly across from me. Toward the front of the building, a single window stood open. Inside, the warm glow of candlelight illuminated a portly man sitting at the small desk, filling out some sort of journal or ledger. The door behind him was shut tight, but that wouldn't be a problem for me.

I began to construct a simple wind spell in my mind using the techniques Lesti had taught me. I added runes to gather the air nearby and direct it, careful to restrict the power way down. I felt my magic go to work, pulling in the air from nearby and condensing it.

A moment later, I fired the small blast of condensed air into the man's window, blowing out the candle. Using Speed Boost, I accelerated myself to move as fast as possible without damaging the buildings and leapt into the window. Once inside, I rushed across the room and used Air Rake to open the door and slip out. As soon as I had cleared the doorway, I jumped up into the rafters above.

All of this happened in a single moment, so the portly man barely had any time to react. From inside the room, I heard his terrified voice. "What in the world?! Who's there?!"

Then, a few seconds later, his eyes must have adjusted to the dark, and I heard him get up and creep slowly toward the door. The hallway was dimly lit by lanterns, so I ducked further into the shadows to make sure he wouldn't see me. Peeking out of his room, he looked around hesitantly, scratching his head in confusion when he didn't find anything. A moment later, he closed his door again, leaving me alone.

As soon as I was sure that no one else was coming, I hopped down from the rafters and made my way toward the stairs. I didn't run into anyone else until I was almost to the first floor. Based on the loud chatter and laughter I could hear coming from below, it seemed like nearly everyone was still enjoying the festivities that came along with the tournament.

Creeping down the stairs, I came to a landing where they reversed direction before finally arriving on the first floor. Even better, it was located at the back of the building near the dead center of the main tavern area. It was the perfect spot to scope out the place before continuing my search. I crouched low in the shadows and peered out over the room.

The main area was rather expansive, with a surprisingly high ceiling supported by thick, wooden beams. Down below, a series of tables were spread throughout the room in the same open style you might expect to find in any ordinary tavern. However, each table had a surprising amount of space between it and the others. Clearly, this place wasn't worried about packing in tons of guests.

Unlike the hallways above, this area was brightly lit and even sported some magical lights floating low over the customers' heads. The entire place had a very bright, clean atmosphere that lacked the usual roughness you would expect from such an establishment. If I had to describe it, I would say it was classy without feeling stuck up.

Directly across from me was the entrance leading to where Aurelia and I had been standing before. On the wall to my right sat the bar and the door to the kitchen behind it. The wall behind the landing I was on had a couple of doors as well, but they didn't seem to be getting much traffic, so I wasn't sure where they went. To my left, though, I noticed a series of what appeared to be private booths.

The construction was a bit odd, to say the least. Rather than an entire wall, the area was blocked off by a three-quarters one, and a simple curtain covered the doorway leading back there. It was as if the place had been built to be one massive open space, and then they had later gotten the idea to create private rooms.

As I scanned over the main area, I didn't see Sebastian or anyone that looked like they might be related to him. That meant they either had to be in the private dining rooms or upstairs in their bedrooms. Considering how lively it was downstairs, the former seemed more likely.

Looking around to ensure no one was watching, I leapt up into the large wooden rafters above. Once I was sure that I was firmly out of sight, I closed my eyes and began scanning the area with my magic sight. Despite restricting my range to help, my vision was assaulted by an excessive amount of golden energy as the staff, guards, and guests moved about the building.

Thankfully, Aurelia had been right. The majority of the people in the building didn't have much magical energy. Most of them were even weaker than Lesti, allowing me to distinguish between everyone despite the large number of bodies. As I checked the private rooms, I found a group of ten or so people near the back with more magical energy than most.

Within that group, one person, in particular, stood out. They weren't entirely on the same level as Alex, but a large amount of magical energy flowed out from their soul at a steady rate. That wasn't the only reason that they stood out, though. There was something off about their magical energy, something alarming.

I honestly hoped that it wasn't Sebastian, but the evidence was all to the contrary. Based on the spells he had used during his match with Aurelia, it couldn't be anyone else. There was no one else in the area with enough magical energy.

As I scanned the area and tried to figure out the best way to get closer, I suddenly felt a chill run down my spine. Wrenching my eyes open, I spun around on the spot, but there was nothing there. The feeling had only lasted for a second. Yet, I was sure at that moment that someone or something incredibly dangerous had been watching me. Almost immediately, my mind jumped to Zeke and his ability to open portals. I had never felt such a strong aura off of him, though.

Taking a deep breath, I forced myself to relax. Whatever it was I had felt, it was gone. There was nothing I could do about it now except to be on my guard. Turning back around, I jumped across the rafters and headed to the back of the private area. After a few seconds, I came to a stop on one of the large rafters above a small party of well-dressed nobles. Sitting in the middle of that group was none other than Sebastian himself.

Even though he had won his way through to the semifinals today, his expression wasn't one of joy or even his usual smug self-importance. He stared at the food in front of him with a stiff grimace and ate in silence. In fact, the entire room seemed to be filled with odd tension.

Even the waitress seemed to be walking on pins and needles as she dropped off another round of drinks. She had barely set the mugs in front of her guests before she fled the room as quickly as possible, leaving the group to continue their awkward silence. Then, almost as if he couldn't stand it anymore, the young man sitting next to Sebastian grabbed his mug and raised it high over his head.

"H-How about a toast? To Sebastian making it to the semifinals!"

Yet, no one at the table reached for their mugs. Some of them even visibly winced at his suggestion. At the end of the table, an older man with hawk-like features similar to Sebastian's glared at him angrily. "There will be no toast. After the shame he brought upon our house, this is the least that I expect of Sebastian."

"But Father, it's the semifinals of the Spring Tournament." The young man spoke up once more, his gaze pleadingly shifting between Sebastian and the older man, whom I presumed to be Lord Cilias. "Even I wasn't able to get that far in my time at the academy. It truly is a great accomplishment. His opponent today was no slouch either. I'm not even sure I could have beaten her. Surely, his performance today warrants some celebration?"

"Celebration?" Lord Cilias scoffed at his older son. "What about this situation warrants celebration? The fact that we're stuck staying in this miserable inn meant for merchants or low-ranking nobles? Or perhaps you're referring to how even our closest allies hardly want anything to do with us now? All the power and influence we've built up over generations has been put at risk by the actions of a foolish, self-centered child. Yet, you want me to celebrate because he managed to beat some girl from a primitive forest tribe?"

"Father, I know Sebastian made a mistake, but..." Sebastian's older brother continued to plead with their father, an almost desperate look on his face.

"Claudius, it's fine." It was Sebastian that cut his brother off, never looking up from his plate as he did. "Father is right. My actions have done severe damage to the reputation of the Cilias family. That damage has delayed and even ruined some of Father's plans. Simply making it to the semifinals isn't enough to undo all of that."

"Then what are you supposed to do?!" Claudius was clearly upset, his voice cracking as it rose to a near shout. His gaze whipped from Sebastian back to Lord Cilias. "Shouldn't you at least give him some path to redemption,

Father? Or do you plan on having him spend the rest of his life with this shadow hanging over his head?"

Lord Cilias paused for a moment, his stern gaze locked on Sebastian. "Destroy the archdemon that you released upon our world. That's the only way to restore your name. If you can manage that, then most will be willing to overlook your transgressions. Some may even hail you as a hero."

"You can't be serious," Claudius replied in a hushed tone. "There's no way Sebastian can do that. He'll be killed for sure."

"That would be sufficient as well. If he died fighting the archdemon, then his sins would die with him." Lord Cilias stared at his sons with a blank expression. His tone was flat, making it hard to tell what he was really thinking. I'm sure he had his own reasons for saying the things he did, but his words caused my fur to bristle with anger.

I was no fan of Sebastian. After what he did to me, I thought that he deserved whatever was coming his way. But this man was supposed to be his father. What sort of father could sit there and tell his own son to go fight a battle where he was sure to die with a blank expression like that? If anything, I was starting to see why Sebastian had turned out like he did.

Claudius stared at his father, his shock written clearly on his face. An oppressive silence had fallen over the room at Lord Cilias's words. Whether it was because they were like me and found his words too cruel or thought that what he was saying was true, no one could say anything back to him.

Several agonizing seconds stretched on for what felt like forever until Sebastian himself finally broke the silence. "Father is right, Claudius. The only way to restore my own name is to clean up my own mess and slay the archdemon myself. If I can't even do that, then I'm a failure as a noble. Father would be better off to disown me."

"Sebastian…" Claudius stared at his younger brother, his expression filled with a mixture of complex emotions. I couldn't blame him there. What Sebastian was saying made sense, but that didn't make it any more possible. Lesti and I might have managed to survive our first encounter with Thel'al, but I wasn't foolish enough to think we could beat him as we were now if he went all out. Lord Cilias had basically given his own son a death sentence.

"Everything will be fine, Brother. First, I'll beat Alexander Bestroff and win the tournament to prove my strength. If I can beat a monster like that, then I can surely do something about the archdemon." Sebastian smiled at his brother reassuringly before standing up. It was an expression that I wasn't used to seeing on him, considering that all he did was gloat and taunt his peers at the academy.

Lord Cilias nodded as he eyed the pair with a sharp glare. "Don't get too far ahead of yourself, Sebastian. You have to face the Vilia girl tomorrow. She already stood against the archdemon once and survived. Taking her lightly will be your downfall."

Sebastian scoffed. "That girl is nothing without her familiar. I'll beat her into the ground tomorrow and remind her what her place is."

Ah, there's the Sebastian that I know, right on cue. I was just starting to get over my anger a little too.

"Now, if you'll all excuse me. Tomorrow is going to be a long day, and I need to prepare." Sebastian quickly bowed and excused himself. Leaving the room, he walked out into the main tavern area and to the staircase, an attendant hot on his heels. However, just as he reached the bottom of the stairs, he paused for a moment, then sent the attendant back to the party.

It seemed odd, but perhaps there was something that he didn't want them to see. As the idea crossed my mind, my heart began to beat just a tiny bit faster. I waited for Sebastian to disappear up the stairs before I followed him. Unsurprisingly, he went directly past the second floor and up to the much nicer third floor usually reserved for low-level nobles.

I followed him up the stairs and peeked around the corner. Sebastian walked to the far end, where the hallway ended in a T. Rather than turning left or right, he opened the door directly in front of him and slipped in. I waited for a moment to make sure the coast was clear and then followed after him.

Coming to a stop before the door, I began to look for a way in but quickly noticed that it wasn't even completely shut. It was cracked just enough for a small animal like myself to squeeze through. A pale steady light shone within the room; it was as if I was being invited in. No, I most certainly was, but how did Sebastian know that I was here?

I hesitated for a moment as I considered retreating, but there was no way I could do that. I still hadn't learned anything about Sebastian's newfound strength. I couldn't go back without any new information. Bracing myself for a possible trap, I pushed through the cracked door into the dimly lit room beyond.

The inside was rather large for an inn in the city. While the construction was simple, the decorations and furnishings were clearly a cut above. The bed sat off to the right with a mirror, dresser, and space to change. On the left, a desk and chair sat against the wall. Flowers and art decorated the walls, clashing with the simple construction.

In the center of the room was a small sitting area with a couch and two chairs surrounding a small table. The sofa faced the door, and sitting there, staring at me, was Sebastian. He was still wearing his academy uniform and wore a calm expression. Just like I thought, he had known I was here. The only question was how.

As I pondered that, I heard the door close behind me. Before I could even spin around, I felt a hand close around my throat. I reflexively leapt away, my fur standing on end, and turned to face my attacker. Standing right where I had been a moment ago was a creature that was both familiar and unknown to me all at once.

What was before me was most certainly a demon. The signature ash-grey skin and void-black eyes were enough to tell me that, but there was something strange about this one's body. All along the creature's left side, metal plates were fused with its skin. The metal itself was unfamiliar and had a strange sheen to it that gave it a murky appearance.

What appeared to be a crown or headdress of some sort was fused into the demon's skull as well. Both the crown and the other plates had an insane amount of text inscribed into them in small letters. No, they weren't letters. They were magical runes. Half of this demon's body was covered in runes.

As I took in the demon's appearance and prepared myself for a fight, Sebastian let out a heavy sigh. "Rha'kul, I thought I told you to stay hidden. Look, you've put our guest on guard."

"Ah. How rude of me." The demon named Rha'kul turned to face me and bow. "I didn't mean to startle you, but I simply couldn't ignore this lovely little trinket you were carrying."

Rha'kul held his hand up. From his fingertips dangled the stone Lesti had given me to contact her in case of emergency. It wasn't the stolen artifact that my eyes locked onto, though. Instead, I found my gaze fixed on the demon's right eye, which had come into view when he had turned to face me. If you could even call it an eye, that is.

Sitting in his right eye socket was an orb made of the same strange metal as the plates fused into the rest of his body. An incredibly dense series of magical circles were inscribed into the metal with a single rune at the center of them all. The orb wriggled around erratically in his skull, almost as if it had a mind of its own.

The eye locked onto the small, polished stone as it dangled from the leather cord. "Such a simple little magic device. Truly the work of a beginner. There aren't even any runes here to prevent erosion or breakage. Which means this has to be new. Did your master make this?"

"That's none of your business. More importantly, what in the world is a demon like you doing here?" I glared at Rha'kul, my body still primed for a fight. I had already let him sneak up on me once. I couldn't afford to let my guard down again.

Rha'kul's magical eye swirled around in its socket for a moment before fixing on me. Then almost as if it was the most obvious thing in the world, he replied, "I was summoned, of course. How else would a fallen being such as myself be allowed to walk this world once again?"

"Summoned?" I turned to stare at Sebastian in astonishment. "What in the world are you thinking?! You summoned another demon?!"

Sebastian simply grimaced, his gaze slowly drifting over to the demon. "Rha'kul, what in the world are you going and spilling all of my secrets for? And you." Sebastian turned to glare at me. "Where do you get off lecturing me while you sneak around and spy on me?"

"You expected me to see what is perhaps one of the first magical devices made in thousands of years and ignore it?!" Rha'kul looked at Sebastian in mock astonishment. "That's simply impossible, Master. I have no choice but to investigate something like that!"

"Master?!" I glared at Sebastian even harder than before. "Are you serious?! You went and summoned a familiar. After everything that happened, you were stupid enough to try that again?!"

"I was foolish to rely on a commoner last time." He looked at me smugly. "I should have taken matters into my own hands in the first place. Everything went much more smoothly once I did."

"Smoothly?!" I turned to look back at Rha'kul. While it did seem like he was playing along for now. There was no way a creature with magical artifacts fused into his body was going to be controlled so easily. I needed to make Sebastian understand that. "Do you really think that summoning another dangerous demon can be considered things going smoothly? Even if the binding is working correctly, that doesn't mean that you can control him. The moment you drop your guard, he'll be free to wreak havoc."

"Wreak havoc? That won't happen." Sebastian arched an eyebrow at me. I started to protest, but he held up a hand to cut me off. "I'm under no illusions that I can control Rha'kul. As you can see, he disobeys my orders with rampant disregard for my authority. Still, his objectives aren't the same as Thel'al. In fact, they line up rather nicely with my own."

I glanced over at Rha'kul, who was nodding enthusiastically along with Sebastian's words. Them being on the same page didn't give me any peace of mind, though. After all, I didn't trust Sebastian in the least. Their objectives lining up just worried me more, if anything.

Still, something did seem a bit odd. All of the demons that I had met up until now had a strange, almost inhuman cruelty about them. I didn't sense any of that from Rha'kul. His speech alone was far calmer than that of his kin. He also didn't seem to share in their trademark high-pitched laugh that always grated on my ears.

Despite all of that, I couldn't just let a demon go wandering free. I fixed my gaze on Sebastian. "I'll have to tell the headmistress about this, you know? Don't be surprised if you get disqualified from the tournament."

"Now, that would be a problem," Rha'kul's voice whispered into my ear as his hands once again wrapped around my throat.

My blood ran cold, and my mind froze. I hadn't even seen him move. How had he gotten behind me so quickly? Not even Thel'al had been this fast. Even if he had been holding back and toying with us in that first fight, this was on a completely different level.

As my panicked mind scrambled to find some escape from the situation, I began to call out to Aurelia, only to stop myself at the last second. There was nothing she could do here. She wouldn't be a match for any opponent that could get behind me like this.

Rha'kul didn't move an inch, continuing in a low, even tone that sent chills down my spine. "I'm not much of a fighter myself, but I do happen to have a few tricks up my sleeve. I'd rather not have to use them on your master and her companions, but I can't have you interfering with our plans. Not until we manage to gain the power that we need to kill those monsters. So, I'll have to ask you to hold your tongue. Understand?"

His words struck me as odd. He claimed to be not much of a fighter, but he managed to move so fast that I couldn't even see him. If he wasn't lying, then perhaps that was one of the tricks he was talking about. Either way, as I was now, there was nothing I could do against him. Swallowing my pride, I forced myself to slowly nod.

As soon as I did, I felt the pressure fade from around my neck, replaced by a slight weight that had been missing since I entered the room. I looked down to find the signal stone Lesti had given me hanging there once more.

But there was something different about it now. For a second, I stared at the stone, confused before I finally realized what it was. I carefully glanced back at Rha'kul, who was still standing behind me. "There are more runes on this than before, aren't there? What did you do to it?"

A sharp-toothed grin spread across his face. It was similar to his demon brethren in its creepiness and somehow lacking the malice they usually had. "I simply added some extra features. After all, I need to make sure I can keep an eye on you and make sure you don't break your promise. Don't think about removing it either. If you do, then I'll have to assume that you're trying to hide something from me."

When in the world did he get time to make modifications to this thing?! I continued to eye Rha'kul cautiously as I thought back over our conversation. I hadn't noticed any strange movements, nor had I seen him using any magic. Then again, it had been the same when he had suddenly appeared behind me, so there was a good chance that he was somehow blocking my normal abilities.

As I pondered all of this, Sebastian finally spoke up again, his voice dripping with a smug sense of superiority. "Now that that's settled, would you mind leaving? I need to rest before my match tomorrow. Not that I expect it to be any sort of challenge. Without you covering for her, Lesti is basically useless."

I instinctively bared my fangs at Sebastian and hissed. "I don't think you have any room to mock her when you had to summon your own familiar just to stand a chance against her."

"I could beat that little wretch even if I hadn't summoned Rha'kul," Sebastian scoffed. "Just look at her performance earlier today. It was absolutely pathetic. Someone at the top of our year nearly losing to a no-name student like that is unthinkable. Now, if you have nothing else to say to me, get lost."

"Actually, there is one more thing." I forced my body to relax and looked Sebastian directly in the eyes. I needed to make sure he understood what exactly he was dealing with here. If he didn't, then I would have to find some way to deal with Rha'kul, even if it meant calling in Frederick.

"Well, what is it?" Sebastian squirmed uncomfortably under my firm gaze, seemingly disturbed by my sudden shift in attitude.

"I'm sure Rha'kul is the one responsible for the sudden growth in your magical energy but has he told you what it's doing to you?"

Sebastian stared at me for a moment, a look of surprise on his face. However, he quickly recovered his composure and dropped his usual smug attitude. For once, he responded to me earnestly. "He did. We've taken precautions to make sure that the corruption doesn't spread as well."

Reaching up, he quickly pulled aside his shirt, revealing a magic circle tattooed onto his chest. The magic runes glowed with a faint light. I nodded, satisfied with his answer. From what I had seen, he wasn't unaware of the risks of what he was doing, and it didn't seem like Rha'kul was deceiving him. At least, not in any obvious way.

"Fine. I'll leave it at that for today, then." I turned and walked across the room, glad to be putting some distance between myself and Rha'kul finally. Using Wind Rake, I pried the window open before turning back to the pair. "That being said if I ever think that you've gone too far. I won't hesitate to put you down."

Sebastian didn't turn to face me, so I turned and leapt out of the window into the dark alley below. As I did, I heard Sebastian's voice one last time. "I'll leave it to you if it comes to that."

Doubts and Overcoming

"It truly was a wonderful battle. It was so noble of you to give your opponent a chance to show their abilities like that. I'm sure you could have crushed them in an instant if you wished to."

Alex smiled politely at the young noble lady who was happily chatting him up. The evening celebrations were well underway in the Bestroff manor. The hall was brightly lit with magical lights that flitted about the room. Numerous delicious dishes were spread along neatly prepared tables.

Everyone was wearing their best evening wear. Even Alex and Clara had been forced to change despite having competed earlier in the day. Socializing was an essential part of the Spring Tournament festivities for the noble class. Various nobles looking to earn his favor had been heaping praise upon him for hours now. It was honestly rather annoying.

"Of course. An opponent like that would never present any real challenge for our Al."

He glanced over at Clara, who puffed out her chest with pride. He wished she would stop encouraging these people. While it was true that he had easily won his quarterfinals match, he felt this sort of talk was rude to his opponent. Besides, other matters complicated his feelings as well.

Controlling his magic was turning out to be more complicated than he expected. The preliminaries had gone mostly to plan. His opponents had tried to gang up on him, but their attacks were uncoordinated, and he was able to easily pick them off one by one.

The quarterfinals had been a different story, though. While his opponent hadn't been particularly strong, he certainly hadn't been a pushover either.

Typically, he would have simply used his magical energy capacity to overwhelm such an opponent. With his condition, that was too risky.

Instead, he had planned to slowly wear them down with weaker spells. However, even when casting these spells, he had found it hard to control the amount of energy he used. It was as though his magic had a mind of its own and wanted to be used. Suppressing it had taken quite a bit of concentration. He wasn't sure he would be able to do it against a stronger opponent.

The young woman, egged on by Clara, continued to heap praise on him. "Yes. I'm sure that he'll defeat the Gambriel boy just as easily."

"I wouldn't be so sure. Elliot may have lost his rank as second in our class, but he's still a force to be reckoned with." He furrowed his brow as he tried to figure out how he would combat his long-time friend without overusing his magic. "Dealing with him is going to be quite the problem."

"Oh, not only strong but modest too?" The young lady fanned her face. "A man after my own heart."

"Arrogance has led to the ruin of many good men. I simply wish to avoid the same trap." He smiled stiffly at the woman, wanting nothing more than to get away from her advances, but it would be rude for him to simply dismiss her. He needed some excuse to leave.

Thankfully, Clara seemed to pick up on his distress. "Al. Isn't it about time for us to retire? We have to be at the arena rather early tomorrow, you know."

The young woman looked at him pleadingly. "So soon? Can't you stay just a little longer?"

He almost felt bad. In any other circumstances, he might have stayed and chatted with her for a while longer. Tonight, he simply wasn't in the mood for such things.

"I'm sorry, but Clara is right. We must retire soon. It wouldn't do for a representative of the Bestroff family to be late after all."

The woman politely curtsied. "I suppose that is true. Then, I wish you the best of luck in the tournament tomorrow, Alexander. I'll be cheering for you from the stands."

"Thank you. I'll do my best to live up to your expectations." He bowed quickly and then made his exit along with Clara.

As soon as they left the party, a pair of servants fell in step behind them. To his surprise, Clara waved them off. Apparently, she wanted to talk about something.

For a long while, they walked the halls of the manor in silence. It wasn't until the sounds of the party had faded entirely that she broke the silence. "Is everything alright, Al? You've been acting strange all evening."

Glancing over, he could see her looking up at him with concern. "Strange? What do you mean?"

"You're normally better at deflecting the conversation and getting away from annoying nobles and ladies like that. I had to step in several times tonight to bail you out."

"Is that all? You worry too much. I'm just a bit tired, is all." He shrugged, trying his best to dismiss her concerns.

Clara wasn't having any of it, though. She stepped in front of him and came to a halt, glaring up at him. "No! That's not all! The way you were fighting today was weird too! I understand needing to use some tactics against stronger foes, but why did you hold back like that in the preliminaries and quarterfinals? I won my matches faster than you."

Silence filled the hall for a long while as he tried to come up with some excuse for his performance today. In the end, he knew there was no point. Clara simply knew him and what he was capable of too well. She wouldn't believe any lies that he told her.

With a heavy sigh, he decided to just tell her the truth. He grabbed her by the wrist and pulled her into a nearby room, closing the door behind them. No one could overhear what they were about to discuss. It could cause a huge ruckus if it got out.

Once they were both inside the room, he turned and fixed Clara with a harsh glare. "This conversation has to stay between just the two of us. Do you understand?"

She simply nodded, her expression full of concern. "If you say so, Al."

"Alright. I'm holding back because I'm afraid something terrible is going to happen if I use my magic like normal. I'm trying to avoid using too much magical energy."

"Something terrible?" Clara tilted her head to the side, clearly confused by his statement. "Like what?"

He shook his head. "I don't know. All I know is that it won't be good."

"Al, you're not making any sense. Why would using your magic be dangerous? You've been doing it for years."

Alex paused for a moment, trying to think of the best way to explain it. In the end, he decided to use the same analogy from his dreams. "Imagine your magical energy as a massive lake, being held back by a dam. If that dam opened too wide, what would happen?"

Clara scrunched her brow up in thought and looked down at the ground. "The river would overflow, right? What exactly does that mean, though?" Her gaze shot up to meet his, suddenly panicked. "Would it destroy your body?!"

He blinked in surprise. He hadn't expected her to take him this seriously. Yet, here she was, trying her best to understand his concerns despite how crazy they sounded. "W-Well, I'm not sure. I've never felt any sort of pain or anything like that, so I don't think it will damage my body. If anything, it just feels like I might lose control."

She placed a hand on her chest and let out a relieved sigh. "Thank goodness. Still, that's not something you should take lightly. Have you talked to your father about this? I'm sure he would understand if you said you wanted to withdraw from the tournament."

To his own surprise, Alex didn't hesitate the slightest in his response. "No. I can't do that."

Clara stared at him for a moment, dumbfounded. "Why not? You're not doing this because of some stupid honor thing, are you? You'll bring more shame to the Bestroff name by losing control than you will by withdrawing, you know."

"I just feel like I have to overcome this."

Clara glared at him angrily. He couldn't blame her for that. Her suggestion was the most reasonable course of action, but Alex simply couldn't bring himself to do it. Of course, there was the pressure he felt to live up to the expectations that had been placed on him, but what was driving him was something far simpler.

He didn't want to lose. Over the last few months, he had watched how frighteningly fast Lesti had grown as a mage. She had battled an archdemon and then rocketed up from the bottom of their year to take the second position.

At first, he had thought it was a fluke, but she didn't stop there. When he had tried to cut down the transformed Fang, she had saved him and then created a spell to bind him as Aurelia's familiar. Then, she had fought that massive demon that Baron Arvis had transformed into. It was just one incredible feat after the other with her.

Others put all of the success on Astria, but he knew better than that. Even if her familiar had taught her the spells, she was still the one who had to memorize and cast them. Besides, from what Elliot had told him, she constantly studied and trained like mad. In the end, her successes were the results of her own efforts.

What sort of obstacles had she overcome to get to where she was now? How many more would she have to overcome going forward? He couldn't even begin to imagine. Still, he knew one thing for sure. If she could overcome the obstacles in her path, then so could he.

"Ever since we were kids, I've never struggled with anything, you know," he continued, trying his best to explain his feelings to Clara as she continued to glare at him. "No matter what problem came along, I was always able to break through with brute force."

"Of course, I don't see the problem. Those with power are obligated to use it in service to their people. That's the Bestroff way."

"Exactly." He turned and walked over to a nearby window, looking at his own reflection in the glass. "Yet, look at me now. My own power has become my downfall because I can't control it. I'm obligated to use my power for the greater good, but I won't be able to do that in my current state."

Turning back to face Clara, he clenched his fists tightly. "That's why I can't withdraw. I have to overcome this obstacle. I have to learn to fight while controlling my power. Otherwise, I won't be able to move forward."

She let out a heavy sigh. "I'm not going to be able to talk you out of this, am I?"

"I'm sorry, but no."

"Fine, but we need to tell your father about this. That way, if something goes wrong, he'll at least be prepared."

She turned to leave the room, but he grabbed her by the wrist. "No. I'll talk to him myself. Listen, Clara. You can't tell anyone what we talked about tonight, understand?"

"What? Why?" Clara looked at him, completely confused by his sudden stern warning. That wasn't all that strange. Nothing they had talked about seemed like a huge secret. It was closely related to family secrets, though. He worried that if his father found out how much she knew, then he might decide she was a risk.

He gripped her wrist just a little bit harder, willing her to understand. "Promise me that you won't tell anyone what we talked about tonight."

She paused for a moment, looking him up and down like he was mad. Then, her gaze sharpened as she came to some decision. "Alright. I promise I won't tell anyone, but if I find out you didn't talk to your father, then I'll come and drag you out of the arena myself. Got it?"

He nodded and smiled at her, releasing her wrist at the same time. "That's fine with me."

"Good. Then, get going." Clara opened the door to the room they had ducked into and stepped out into the hall before looking back at him worriedly. "Be careful tomorrow, okay? There's no shame in retreating if it means you live to fight another day."

"I know." Alex smiled at his childhood friend. "I'll be careful. I promise."

With that, Clara turned and left, leaving Alex alone with his thoughts. He stood there for a long moment, simply trying to suppress the anxiety he was feeling. The decision he was making was most definitely the wrong one, but he couldn't forget the words Lesti had said the other night.

Tomorrow, he would put every ounce of his being into overcoming this obstacle. Even if he failed, he wouldn't have any regrets. At least, that was what he hoped.

Interlude: Escape

Frederick's footsteps echoed through the endlessly branching tunnels of the cave system around him as he hurried forward. Several magical lights swarmed around him, lighting the dark path ahead. Unlike the other areas of the cave system, this particular section was dry, and the walls were smooth, almost as if the tunnels had been carved.

A moment later, the path opened up into a large cavern with several smooth tunnels branching off of it. Unlike the tunnel he had just been in, though, Frederick wasn't alone here. A fierce grin spread across his lips as he glared at the small group of demons that were standing guard. *"Skell, I've found them."*

"Kyiiii!"

No sooner had he called his partner than one of the demons let out a fierce shriek and charged him. It moved faster than any average person, the corrupted magic flowing through its body enhancing all of its physical capabilities. Frederick was used to far faster opponents, though. Before the creature could move more than a few steps, he snapped his fingers. A fireball materialized out of thin air and slammed into it with an explosive force, reducing it to a smoldering heap.

Unfortunately, the combination of the creature's shriek and the explosion warned the rest of the fiends of his presence. High-pitched shrieking began to echo from each of the tunnels before him, growing louder and louder with each passing second. The remaining demons in the room eyed him wearily, clearly trying to buy their time until reinforcements arrived.

Frederick didn't have time for that, though. He quickly scanned the tunnels in front of him, watching the guards' reactions as he did. As his eyes passed over one particular tunnel, they tensed. That was his target. Without a single word, he rushed toward it. The demons stepped forward in a desperate attempt to cut him off, but he never gave them a chance.

"Water Blade. Repeat four."

Frederick took advantage of his environment when choosing his spell. Despite how dry the area was, the air in the caverns was still filled with plenty of moisture. Gathering that together, he pressurized it into a thin blade with his magic before launching it at his opponents at high speed.

The blades passed through them as if they weren't there at all, cleaving them in two. They continued on, cutting deep into the walls behind them before finally stopping. His path clear, Frederick pushed forward without a moment's hesitation. The shrieking sounds were getting louder.

As he rushed ahead, the noise became unbearably loud until a wave of demons exploded from the darkness. The creatures threw themselves at Frederick desperately. Strangely, though, none of them attempted to use magic against him. That made his task all too easy.

"Chain Lightning."

Frederick pointed a single finger towards the waves of foes before him and called the name of his spell. A brilliant flash of light exploded forth from his fingertip. In an instant, the lightning he had called forth passed through the creatures before him, reducing them to charred husks.

Stepping over the remains, he continued to push forward as fast as he could. Wave after wave of demons spilled forth from the darkness ahead of him. He mercilessly cut them down, flinging spell after spell at them. Something about their mindless brute force attacks seemed odd, but there wasn't time to stop and think about it. He could hear even more enemies coming from behind. Even Frederick would struggle to make progress if he allowed himself to get pincered in a small tunnel like this.

After felling dozens and dozens of demons, Frederick finally broke out of the tunnel and into a large cave. Hearing the hordes of enemies closing in behind him, he quickly used magic to seal the entrance and carve a small air vent. Once Frederick was sure he wouldn't get ambushed from behind, he turned and examined the space around him. As expected, this cavern wasn't natural.

The stone was excessively smooth, the floor was flat, and the ceiling above formed a perfect dome. The entire cavern was so large that Frederick's lights barely covered a portion of the space. Summoning more, he sent them to the far corners of the area.

To his surprise, the cave around him was mostly empty. Based on the reactions of the demons guarding the entrance, he had expected to find Thel'al here. Clicking his tongue in agitation, he muttered under his breath, "Did I pick the wrong tunnel?"

However, just as he started to consider turning around, something on the far side of the cavern caught his eye. A glint of light, reflecting off of something metallic deeper within. Keeping his guard up, Frederick moved across the cavern. As he drew closer, the object in question came into view.

"What is this?" Muttering under his breath, he furrowed his brow. Standing in the deepest part of the cavern was a strange, tube-like object, about eight feet tall, with thick metal rings at the top and bottom. Those rings were connected by several sturdy metal pillars. Both the rings and the pillars had a strange sheen to them and were covered in an incredibly dense number of magical runes.

Frederick circled the device, carefully studying the runes and trying to determine their purpose. However, many runes were used in ways he hadn't seen before. There were even more that were unrecognizable. As he rounded to the back, he found that the runes were incomplete. Apparently, this was a work in progress.

Frederick stepped forward to examine the runes in more detail when an unfamiliar voice suddenly rang through his head. *"Ah, well, this is certainly a problem. I was supposed to get this place cleaned out before you arrived."*

He immediately tensed, preparing to cast a spell as he scanned the area, searching for the source of the voice. As his eyes scanned the room, he found that the entrance he had sealed before was still blocked off. The room itself seemed to be empty as well.

A strange unease welled up within Frederick. With his years of experience in combat, he knew that this was a dangerous situation. There were just too many unknowns here. Continuing to assess his surroundings, he calmly called out to Skell. *"Looks like I've got some company here. Hurry up. Make your own path if you have to."*

"I'm on my way." Skell's response was short but filled with a blood lust that made Frederick's heart pound. His partner had been growing more and more unstable as they had searched the caves. Being isolated in this dark, dingy place for so long wasn't good for a dragon, and Skell's own feelings toward Thel'al didn't help matters either.

Before Frederick could contemplate his friend's situation further, he finally spotted the likely source of the voice. A tiny, almost invisible shimmer floated in the middle of the room. If he hadn't been looking for something, he never would have noticed it. He thought about launching a preemptive attack but decided that it was better to try and buy time for Skell to arrive.

Looking straight at the shimmer, he called out confidently, "How long do you intend to stay hidden? You're the one who called out to me, aren't you?"

For a brief moment, there was silence as he continued to stare at the spot he expected his opponent to emerge from. Then, the silence was finally broken by an amused voice in his head. "Wow. You actually managed to find me. I can see why Thel'al is so scared of you."

In front of his eyes, the shimmer suddenly became a tear in the fabric of reality. Barbed hooks slid through the rip and pulled it wide enough that a man could step through it. From the other side, a tall, wolf-like creature with long legs and four tails stepped through.

"So, it's the Rift Stalker that Lania reported, huh? Zeke, was it?" Frederick eyed his opponent up carefully as he recalled the information he had received from the headmistress.

Zeke's yellow eyes stared right back at him, a strange, human-like grin spread across his wolf-like features. "Oh. So you've heard of me? I'm honored. To think the one person that Thel'al fears would know about little old me."

"It's my job to eliminate threats like you after all." Frederick glanced at the tails flitting through the air energetically behind Zeke. Those were the biggest threat. According to Lania's report, Zeke would use them to redirect your own spells back at you from strange angles. A clever trick and a difficult one to get around.

He didn't think it was impossible, though. As far as he could tell, Zeke appeared to use his tails to open rifts, and while they were quick, they could only open so many so quickly. If you could attack rapidly enough and from enough directions at once, the creature wouldn't be able to open enough rifts to counter everything.

As Frederick thought all of this through, the grin on Zeke's face turned from a humorous one to a vicious snarl. "You? Eliminate me? I hope you aren't underestimating me like that other woman did. The brute force tactics you're all used to using here won't work on me."

The sudden change in Zeke's attitude surprised Frederick. Lania's report had mentioned it as well, but the Rift Stalker really did appear to hate being looked down upon. "Ah, that reminds me. She also mentioned that you used counter magic. Still, I think your confidence is unfounded if that's the only trick you have up your sleeve. Counter magic is certainly rare, but it's not like I've never faced it before."

Zeke tilted his head to the side, looking confused for a moment. A second later, a flash of realization crossed his face. "Ah, I do remember that teacher lady mentioning something like that. I still have no idea what she was talking about, though."

"I see. So, it's not counter magic, then. Well, it doesn't matter anyway. Your time is up." A fierce grin spread across Frederick's face as the cave around them began to rumble. "Let's see how that confidence of yours holds up against this. Fireball, repeat one hundred!"

Frederick launched his attack. A series of fireballs began to flash into life all around the cave, preparing to pummel Zeke from every direction. At the same time, the rumbling reached its climax when the wall to Zeke's left exploded as Skell blasted his way through and lunged at the Rift Stalker, jaws spread wide.

Frederick expected Zeke to panic or even to try and run away, but he simply glanced sideways at Skell as if he were unimpressed. A moment later,

Skell and all of the debris created when he burst through the wall slammed into the ground, pinned there by some invisible force. At the same time, the fireballs that Frederick had prepared suddenly fizzled, causing the cavern to grow dim once more.

"What?!" Frederick stared at Zeke in shock as he realized that he really had underestimated the Rift Stalker. Counter magic was one thing, but countering so many fireballs instantly was absurd. And pinning a full-grown dragon down at the same time? It was unbelievable.

Frederick didn't have time to sit around and be impressed, though. With Skell pinned down, he was on his own against an extremely dangerous opponent. Another spell quickly formed in his mind, Lightning Bolt. At the same time, he prepared to cast a barrier in case the spell was redirected at him. Everything was ready in an instant. All he had to do was say the keyword.

At that exact moment, there was a sudden change in the air around him as it shifted subtly. He opened his mouth, but all that came out was a strained gasp. He couldn't breathe. Zeke's eyes moved from Skell to him, a bored look on his face. "I warned you that you couldn't beat me, didn't I? Yet, you still tried to pick a fight with me."

The Rift Stalker finally moved for the first time since he had entered the room, slowly moving toward Frederick. Skell strained and struggled against the invisible force holding him down, but no matter how hard he tried, he couldn't move. Frederick quickly snapped his fingers in a desperate attempt to keep Zeke at bay, but the fireball that appeared fizzled in an instant.

He considered trying to run, but there was nowhere to go. He had sealed the only entrance himself, and the breach in the wall Skell had created was blocked by his massive body. His mind racing, Frederick stood there gasping for air as Zeke approached him, his tails flicking through the air menacingly.

Frederick took a fighting stance. He was a mage, but he had been trained in hand-to-hand combat in the military. Even if his magic was taken away from him, he could still put up a fight.

Zeke, seeing this, rolled his eyes. "Would you give it up already? I already told you that I'm not here for you, didn't I?"

With an annoyed look, the Rift Stalker's tail flicked through the air, and he pulled open another rift, stepping through it in an instant. "I'll be taking this with me now if you don't mind."

Frederick whirled around to find Zeke standing next to the strange artifact he had been studying when the Rift Stalker had arrived. He pulled open another rift. On the other side, Frederick could see a dark room filled with worn, moss-covered stones. Thick roots broke through the walls in some places. Zeke used his tails to lift the artifact and slide it through the rift into the room beyond.

"Mission accomplished." Zeke turned and started to head through the rift after the device but paused and turned to face Frederick at the last second. "Ah, right. I would suggest that you don't try and follow me or anything like that. I'm being somewhat lenient here since I didn't have orders to kill you. If you get in the way of my plans, though, I won't hesitate to put both of you down for good."

Frederick, unable to speak, simply glared back at him. Zeke sighed and headed through the rift. "Well, have it your way, but don't say I didn't warn you. Until we meet again."

As soon as the rift closed, Frederick felt the air around him return to normal. He was still left gasping and trying to catch his breath for several seconds, but he could breathe once again. At the same time, Skell wearily pulled himself to his feet. Through ragged breaths, Frederick checked on his partner. "Are you alright?"

Skell glared angrily at the spot where Zeke had disappeared. "I'm not injured. Whatever strange spell that little whelp used, it only acted to hold me in place. It was as if there was a massive weight placed upon my back."

"I see. That's good." He could still sense the underlying rage that had been building up inside Skell, but Zeke's strange magic had apparently been enough to snap the dragon out of the worst of it. "Then, do you think you could take care of the remaining demons in the entrance tunnel? I need a moment to catch my breath. Once you're done, we'll head back to the surface."

Skell nodded before turning away with an angry snort. "Leave it to me."

As the dragon shuffled off to his next task, Frederick began to try and put his thoughts together. First, it was clear that Thel'al and Zeke were working together. Taking that into account, it was safe to assume that the archdemon was no longer in the city. But it didn't appear that the Rift Stalker was entirely under his control. There's no way Thel'al would have allowed the two of them to live when they were so clearly beaten.

Frederick shivered slightly as he reached up and touched his throat. "It might be better if we can get him on our side."

The thought slipped unconsciously from his lips. Defeating Thel'al was already a tall order, but if they had to try and fight Zeke with his strange magic, they wouldn't stand a chance. They needed to find some way to either create a rift between the two so they could fight them separately or even get Zeke on their side.

However, no matter how hard Frederick thought about it, he couldn't figure out what Zeke's motivation for working with Thel'al would be in the first place. He was already powerful and could use his rifts to go anywhere he wanted. "What does he get out of this relationship?"

As the sounds of screaming demons rose in the background, he carefully recalled how Zeke had reacted to everything that had happened. The familiar face of a certain Astral Cat flashed through his mind. There was something oddly similar about the two, despite their completely different personalities. Perhaps it was time they paid Astria a visit again.

That would have to wait, though. First, he would need to report what had happened to the council. Not only was Thel'al loose, he now had the means to appear anywhere he pleased. Security around the arena would need to be tightened. The various territories would need to be notified as well. There wasn't a second to lose.

Preparations

"So, he's summoned a familiar after all." Malkael let out a heavy sigh as I finished up my report. Aurelia and I had returned to the inn as fast as we could. However, only Malkael and Rose were here when we arrived, the latter of which was already passed out soundly on one of the beds. It was already rather late, so I decided to go ahead and fill Malkael in on what I had found, leaving out any information about Rha'kul.

"I thought that might be the case, and I'm sure the headmistress had her suspicions as well." Malkael continued as he rubbed his chin in thought.

I was surprised that he thought the headmistress already knew what was going on. "If she knew he had summoned a familiar, why hasn't she said anything?"

"She can't," Malkael replied bluntly. "After she allowed both Ms. Vilia and Ms. Aurelia to keep their familiars and not receive any real punishment. There's no way she could punish Sebastian. Basically, anyone could summon a familiar at this point, and there's nothing she could do about it."

I tucked my ears and lowered my head a bit. "I guess we've caused her quite a few problems, huh?'

"You could say that again." Malkael nodded. "It's been nothing but problem after problem since you showed up. Although, I suppose that's not your fault, or even Ms. Vilia's for that matter."

As I thought back to everything that had happened since I had been pulled into this world by Lesti, I realized we might actually be more to blame than Malkael gave us credit for. While we hadn't directly summoned Thel'al, we certainly had played a part. Plus, we had constantly been sticking our noses into problems related to the archdemon ever since then. Although, sometimes that wasn't on purpose.

Still, if I had to do it all over again. I don't know that I would have been able to make any different choices. If we hadn't done what we had, both Aurelia and Rose might not be around, not to mention Fang. Most likely, we would continue to cause a lot of problems for the headmistress and keep getting ourselves into even greater dangers.

The memory of Rha'kul's fingers wrapped around my throat flashed through my mind sending a shiver down my spine. I needed to come up with some way to counter him. But there was only one way I could think of to do that, and I was still hesitant to go that far.

Before I could pursue the thought further, the door to the room was pushed open, and an exhausted-looking Lesti stumbled inside. "We're finally back!"

Before I could even say anything, she stumbled over and collapsed face-first onto the bed next to me. I pawed at her playfully. "Looks like Valst really put you through the wringer, huh?"

"He certainly did. I think it was a good learning experience for her." Lani walked through the doorway, a wry smile on her face. "Lord Valst is certainly very thorough in his negotiations."

"It was hell," Lesti muttered, never looking up from the mattress she had her face buried in. "Every time I thought we were done, he would bring up some other topic and nitpick every minor detail of the deal. I thought I was going to be there all night."

"I can definitely see that. At any rate, don't go passing out just yet. I still need to tell you what I learned about Sebastian." I leaned down and nuzzled against Lesti.

"Alright, alright. I'm up! Let's hurry up and get this over with. Lani, could you close the door, please?" Lesti sat up and stretched, her exhaustion showing.

Lani moved to shut the door, but Malkael held up a hand to stop her. "Instructor Lania and I actually need to report to the headmistress. A messenger arrived where you were all away. We'll be heading straight to the academy now that you're back." Malkael stood up and headed to the door. "I've already heard the details on Sebastian's situation from Astria, so I can fill you in on the way."

Lani's expression turned concerned, but she only nodded. "Alright. Let's go then. Astria, I leave Lesti to you."

"Don't worry. I'll make sure she's prepared for tomorrow." I watched as the pair headed out the door, closing it behind them. Once they were gone, I turned to Lesti. "I wonder what's going on that they'd need to report to the headmistress this late?"

Lesti simply shrugged. "No idea. It might have something to do with the tournament or with the search for Thel'al. There's nothing we can do either way. So, what did you learn about Sebastian's new power?"

"First, I need you to understand that what I'm about to tell you is top secret. That goes for you too, Aurelia. If what I'm about to tell you gets out, then there's a very good chance that we'll all end up dead." I glanced between the two girls, keeping my gaze as stern as possible.

Both Lesti and Aurelia seemed to understand just how serious I was. They both sat straight up and stared at me with tense expressions. Once I was sure that they both understood, I started my story, leaving absolutely no details out. I even told them how Rha'kul had modified the artifact Lesti had given me and was probably spying on us right now.

Once I had finished, Lesti scrunched up her face with an annoyed look. "After all of the grief he gave me for summoning a familiar, he just goes and does the same thing. What a jerk." Lesti let out a heavy sigh before turning to me, her expression thoughtful. "Still, none of that explains how Sebastian suddenly got so much stronger. I can understand having more spells at his disposal, but what about his increase in magical energy?"

"About that. Do you remember those assassins who turned into demons at Elliot's birthday party? Well, I think that Rha'kul did something similar to Sebastian. His magic is partially tainted, like a demon's."

"Are you serious?!" Lesti shot up out of her seat, a determined look on her face. "We have to stop him then, before he ends up transforming like them!"

153

Aurelia silently stood up from her spot on the other bed and nodded. I felt a sense of pride well up inside me at their reactions. In her last match, Aurelia had just been beaten down by Sebastian, and Lesti had been tormented by him in her old class. Yet, here they both were trying to go to his aid as if none of that had ever happened.

A small thrumming echoed through my chest as I shook my head. "That won't be necessary. Rha'kul already inscribed a magic circle on him that seems to be holding back the worst of the corruption. There's no guarantee that it's totally safe, but Sebastian shouldn't be in any immediate danger."

"I see." Lesti slowly sunk back into her seat, still seeming troubled. "I guess there's not much we could do anyway based on what you said. This Rha'kul character sounds like more than we can handle at the moment."

"Yeah." I shook myself in an attempt to keep from remembering the encounter again. "I think you're better off focusing on beating Sebastian. Rha'kul seems to have some sort of grudge against Thel'al. Until he's taken care of, I think we can get by just keeping a close eye on Rha'kul's actions."

"I guess you're right. So, based on what you've told me, Sebastian's increase in strength comes from two things." Lesti held up two fingers and pulled the first one down. "First, he's got a new array of powerful spells that Rha'kul has taught him. Based off how easily he got behind you, we'll have to assume Sebastian might have some spells we've never even heard of at his disposal."

"Mm. Not only that but he's also got enough magical energy to use those spells at will," Aurelia chimed in with her own experience from her match with Sebastian.

Lesti nodded as she pulled down her second finger. "Right. I doubt he has as much energy as Alex, but we should assume that he has more energy than most of the students at the school. So, how do we go about beating him, then?"

I dipped my head in thought for a moment before looking back up at Lesti. "What about the strategy we came up with for beating Alex? It should be just as effective against Sebastian, right?"

She shook her head. "It would work, but then I wouldn't be able to use it against Alex. He's too skilled for me to be able to pull that off if he knows it's coming."

"I guess that's true." I flicked my tail in frustration. There were several ways that I could imagine Lesti gaining an edge in the Sebastian fight, but I didn't think I had time to teach any of them to her. Plus, they all involved using knowledge from my old world, which I was still hesitant to teach her about.

The little bit that I had taught her to help make her fireball spell more efficient had been so effective, it was a bit scary. Simply helping her properly fuel the flames had resulted in a massive increase in power. At the same time, the magical energy required to use the spell had plummeted. If I taught her about more physics and chemical reactions, what would she be able to do, and how would those revelations affect this world?

As I struggled with my own thoughts, Lesti glanced down at me and flashed me a bright smile. "I guess I'll just have to beat him the old-fashioned way. If I stick to my most efficient spells, I should be able to keep up with him in terms of magical energy. It's not like he's as crazy overpowered as Alex, right?"

I closed my eyes, recalling the magical energy that I saw flowing through Sebastian. "That's true. If anything, his magical energy generation should only be slightly stronger than Aurelia's. I think the main reason that she lost was she burned through her own magical energy much faster than him."

"Mm. I was careless," Aurelia replied, pursing her lips in frustration. "His barriers broke easily enough, but they never seemed to end."

"Yeah. Now that you mention it, Sebastian was able to throw up barriers repeatedly without getting tired." I thought back to Aurelia's match with him. "How was he able to do that anyway? I've used barriers quite a bit, and they use quite a bit of magical energy if you use them to take blows head-on like that."

Lesti crossed her arms over her chest and tilted her head to the side. "Maybe Rha'kul taught him some trick to make them use less magical energy?"

"Mm. That's probably the case," Aurelia chimed in as a sleepy Fang crawled into her lap and yawned. "Based on what Instructor said, I think he probably

155

has tricks like that for all of his spells."

"So, I should assume that his magical energy usage will be at least as efficient as mine, if not better. This is going to be tough if that's the case. That's one of my main advantages after all." Lesti flopped back down on the bed. "Any time I try to hit him with a spell, he'll just throw up a barrier. If his magical energy usage is as efficient as we think, I won't be able to turn it into a contest of stamina either."

I was out of ideas. There just wasn't enough time to prepare something. Frustrated, I scratched at my neck, where the cord was rubbing against my skin. As I felt the stone hanging from my neck shift around, I looked down at it. The polished surface was covered in such a dense number of magical runes now that it was almost scary. I wanted to figure out some way to turn this thing off, but even Lesti couldn't figure out how it worked. There was even the possibility that it had some sort of trap built into it that would cause it to explode or something if we tried to deactivate it.

"That's it!" I jumped up on the spot, causing both Lesti and Aurelia to start.

"What happened? Did you figure something out?" Lesti asked with a skeptical look on her face.

"Yeah, I did." I felt my tail begin to flick through the air behind me as the plan fully formed in my mind. Hopping off the bed, I headed for the door. "Come on. Let's head outside. I'll explain once I get there."

"Wait, Astria. What about Rha'kul? Isn't he spying on us right now? Won't the plan get leaked?" Lesti hopped up off the bed despite her protest and started following me. She must have thought that I already had some solution to the problem.

Fortunately, I didn't need one. "I don't think he'll leak our plan to Sebastian. Their end goal is to defeat Thel'al, and if they can't even beat us in a fair and square fight, then they won't stand a chance against him. Besides, I think he enjoys causing trouble for Sebastian. He is a demon, after all."

Lesti smiled mischievously as she followed me out the door. "Well, then I guess we'll just have to help him out with that."

I wasn't sure if she had picked up on my plan or if I would have to explain everything from scratch. Either way, it was still going to be hard to pull off. This wasn't the sort of thing you usually practiced at the academy. I braced myself for a long night as we headed out into the already dark city.

* * *

"I-I did it." Lesti gasped out the words as she lay on her back, staring up at the night sky above. We were back on the academy training grounds. At first, we had considered finding some dark alley or something to practice in but had changed our minds. After all, this was really the only place in the city where you could do this type of training without disturbing anyone.

Lesti had just finished perfecting the technique that I had come up with to counter Sebastian. Honestly, I was impressed that she had managed to pull it off. Admittedly, it was right up her alley, but it was still last minute. It just went to show how strong she was.

I walked over to join her, rolling onto my back to stare up at the stars with her. With a playful smile, she reached over and used a finger to tickle my exposed belly. I had the strange urge to bite at her hand, but I managed to suppress it somehow.

Honestly, I should be rushing her back to bed. It was already extremely late, and there were only two matches before hers tomorrow. There was something that I needed to talk to her about, though. I wasn't sure I would get another chance before we headed to the arena with everything going on.

For a long moment, I just laid there next to her, trying to find a way to broach the subject. In the end, I decided the direct approach was the best. "Hey, Lesti. What would you do if I found a way to become human again?"

Lesti glanced over at me before turning her gaze back to the night sky. "Is something like that even possible?"

"Zeke seems to think it is. The truth is that he's a former human like me. Apparently, he's working on a way to turn himself back into a human."

Lesti propped herself up on her arm and turned to look at me, a concerned look on her face. "Shouldn't you have told Malkael or Lani about that? What if he has advanced knowledge like you do?"

"I probably should have, but I didn't get the chance." In truth, I shared her concern concerning Zeke's knowledge. "I'll try and talk to them about it tomorrow. For now, let's stay on topic. What would you do?"

"What would I do, huh?" She laid back again, spreading her arms wide on the grassy field. "More importantly, what do you want to do?"

"Me?"

"Yes, you." Pulling me into the crook of her arm, she began to absentmindedly scratch behind my ear. "You may be my familiar, but before that, you're my friend and partner, and I want you to be happy. Rather than worrying about me, you should be thinking about yourself at times like this."

"I see." For a long moment, I stared up at the stars, trying to collect my thoughts. Everything was happening so quickly that I wasn't sure how I felt. There were a few things that I did know, though, so I tried giving voice to those.

"If I'm being honest, there are some things that scare me about being a familiar. Will I ever be able to fall in love or have a family? If I did have kids, would they be like me, or would they just be ordinary Astral Cats? At the same time, I don't want to abandon you."

Lesti's hand stopped, and she sat up again, scooping me up in her arms as she did. Looking up at her face, I could see a strange, conflicted look on her face. It only lasted for a moment, though. A second later, she was grinning just like she always did. "I guess that just means that I need to win the tournament tomorrow and prove to you that I can take care of myself. Then, you can go back to being human."

"Why do you make it sound so simple!" I kicked myself free of Lesti's arms and leapt to the ground. "Didn't you just say that we're friends, partners even?! If I go back to being human, I might not be able to use magic. I could be as weak as a commoner, you know!"

"That's fine. Even if you're weak, we can still be friends, and I'll always consider you my partner." The grin from before was gone, replaced by an awkward smile.

"I guess that's true." Even if I did end up becoming just a normal human being, it didn't mean I had to stop helping Lesti. It just meant that I wouldn't be able to fight with her anymore. Yet, there was still something about that that left me unsettled.

Lesti, noticing that I still wasn't convinced, picked me up again and looked me in the eyes. "I can't say that I understand how you feel, so I won't pretend to. Just promise me that you won't hold back for my sake if this is really what you want. I don't think I could deal with that happening again."

I felt a twinge of guilt in my chest as I recalled how Lesti felt after her parents had died and Lani had turned down the teaching position at the academy to watch over her. It was really unfair bringing that up. I slapped at her halfheartedly with my paws before finally giving in. After all, what else could I do after she said that to me?

"Alright, I promise."

Setting me down, she turned and headed toward the entrance of the academy. "Good. Let's head back then."

I followed after her silently, an uneasy feeling in my chest.

* * *

"Doesn't this feel familiar?" Lesti shouted from my back as we raced through the city.

I glanced back at her, slightly irritated. Although, it was primarily due to the lack of sleep. We had stayed out until early in the morning, practicing so that Lesti could execute the plan during the match today. Thanks to that, we had once again slept in and were running dangerously late. If it hadn't been for Rose waking us up, we might have slept through the whole thing.

So, I again found myself racing across the rooftops over the early morning crowds heading to the arena in my tiger form. I was going a bit slower due to having Rose on my back as well. Just like yesterday, I was drawing a lot of attention. Only this time, people seemed to recognize us. Quite a few people were pointing excitedly, and a few even cheered as we passed.

Thankfully, the inn we had stayed at the evening before wasn't very far from the arena, and we arrived with a bit of time to spare. Still, as I leapt down by the participants' entrance, I was met with the stern glare of Malkael.

"Are you trying to be late at this point, or is there some sort of curse that you have that I should know about?" Spinning on his heel even as he lectured us, he headed into the arena. "Let's get going. Rose's first match is starting soon."

We followed Malkael down the tunnel toward the waiting room. Quickly coming across the door leading to the suite we used yesterday, He and I parted ways with the girls there. "Good luck, you two. I'll be rooting for you from upstairs, so make sure you win."

"I-I'll do my best." Rose tried to sound confident, but it was obvious she was extremely nervous.

Lesti smiled at her friend's awkwardness and threw her arm over her shoulder with a grin. "Come on, Rose. You have to be more confident than that. We're definitely gonna win!"

She then threw her other hand up into the air with a shout. Rose blinked at her a few times before smiling and throwing her own hand in the air. "Y-Yeah. We'll definitely win. Just you watch."

Lesti and I could only snicker at how she still managed to stutter. Still, there was a firm resolve in her eyes now. She was definitely ready. Now I only had to worry about Lesti. She was acting confident, but our plan had been thrown together at the last minute, and we had barely mastered everything necessary in time.

Not to mention the fact that she was going into this match sleep-deprived. Even as she worked on pumping up Rose, she was also leaning on her. Depending on how long the bouts before hers took, she would have some time to rest, but it likely wouldn't be long enough.

"Get going, you two. Otherwise, you'll be late." Malkael finally urged them to move on and directed me through the door on the side. They turned and headed down the tunnel without looking back, chatting happily as they went. I watched them nervously for a moment before turning and following Malkael down the hall.

We didn't get very far before he dropped a bombshell on me. "We need to talk. There's been a change in the situation with Thel'al. He's escaped."

"Escaped?! What does that mean?" I stopped walking and looked up at

Malkael, a nervous chill running down my spine. "I thought Frederick was tracking him down in the caverns? Where could he escape to that Skell couldn't hunt him down?"

Malkael held up a hand to stop my barrage of questions. "We received a report from Frederick late last night. Thel'al used the power of the Rift Stalker to relocate himself and the main bulk of his followers. We haven't been able to figure out where he fled to yet. Although, we expect it's somewhere up north based on what Frederick saw through the rift."

"So, Zeke is working with Thel'al after all. I guess our plan won't work then." I shook myself, trying to escape the feeling of the room pressing in around me. The news that Thel'al was on the run and Zeke was working with him had really rattled me. It also made me really question the offer he had made me before.

"Actually, there may be some hope there after all. Although, it comes with some bad news as well. Frederick and Skell encountered the Rift Stalker down in the caves." Malkael paused and took a deep breath, a very stiff expression on his face. "They were both soundly defeated."

I stared at Malkael with a blank expression. My mind understood the words he had just said, but for some odd reason, I just couldn't process their meaning. Frederick and Skell had been defeated by Zeke?

"Are they okay?!" I practically shouted at him as I finally overcame my shock.

"Yes. They are both quite well, if in a foul mood." A wry smile formed on Malkael's face. "In fact, they were so energetic that they were sent on a tour of the alliance. After all, someone had to warn the territories of the potential danger while their lords are absent."

"That's good to hear." I let out a sigh of relief. If they were healthy enough to travel around, they probably didn't need me worrying about them. "So, what's the good news then?"

"The good news is that the Rift Stalker didn't finish them off. Based on that, we can assume that he isn't directly under Thel'al's control. The archdemon would never have let them get away. He considers them far too dangerous."

161

"I suppose that makes sense. Zeke did seem to value his freedom quite a bit as well." I pondered Zeke's motivations for a little while, but I kept getting hung up on the fact that he had managed to beat those two. No matter how hard I tried, I simply couldn't imagine Skell and Frederick ever losing.

No. That wasn't true. There was one way that I could see them losing, but it also scared me even more than the thought of facing Thel'al. Taking a deep breath, I closed my eyes and asked a very important question. "How exactly did they lose?"

Malkael nodded as if he expected my reaction. "Apparently, the Rift Stalker used some strange spells that Frederick had never heard of before. He stole Frederick's breath and somehow managed to pin Skell down."

I ground my teeth together when I heard his answer. "The spell that held Skell down. Was it like there was a massive weight pressing down on him even though there was nothing there?"

Malkael's eyebrow arched slightly at my question. "Yes. That is exactly how Frederick described it to us, but how did you know? No. I guess I don't even need to ask, do I? This Rift Stalker, Zeke, he's like you, isn't he?"

I simply nodded without meeting Malkael's gaze. "I don't think we're exactly the same, though."

"How so?"

"It's probably best if I don't say just yet. This is all speculation on my part at this point, after all. I'll need to question him the next time I see him. I just hope I'm wrong."

I glanced up at Malkael to find him looking down at me nervously. I was surprised. Typically, he maintained his composure no matter what happened, but my words seemed to have gotten to him. "Is it really that serious?"

"It's bad enough that he could throw the entire power balance of this world completely out of whack if I'm right. We'll have to wait and see, though." I took several deep breaths to try and clear my mind and walked past Malkael down the hall. "For now, let's get upstairs. We don't want to miss the first match."

I walked on for a bit before I realized Malkael wasn't following me. Turning around, I found him staring at me with a rather stern expression. It seemed like he had more to say, so I stopped and waited for him to find his words.

After a long moment, he started walking. As he passed me, he finally said what was on his mind. "I understand that you have some things you want to keep secret. We all do. That being said, if you keep holding back when we're facing such dangerous foes, then you and I are likely to find ourselves at odds."

Malkael kept walking without looking back at me. I watched him for a long moment, my feelings a jumbled mess. I understood what he was getting at. I probably could tip the scales against our foes.

I hadn't even considered it when I first arrived in this world because of how unfamiliar and strange everything was. Now that some time had passed, though, I realized just how much potential the knowledge from my old world had. In fact, that was precisely why I was keeping quiet about it. I was scared of what would happen to this world if I wasn't careful.

"I'll keep that in mind." My response was weak and non-committal, and I knew it, but Malkael didn't say anything. We simply walked in silence up to where we would watch Rose's match.

Rose's Semifinal

We arrived upstairs just in time for Rose's match to start. Both competitors had already entered the arena, and the crowd was bubbling with energy. Shouts and cheers echoed through the air even as the judge raised his hand overhead, preparing to start the match.

Rose stood on the opposite side of the arena, facing toward us. She still looked a bit nervous, but the determination in her gaze before hadn't diminished at all. In fact, she looked ever more pumped up than before.

Across from her stood a young girl who stood about a head shorter than her. Her blonde hair was tied up in twin tails that swayed side to side with her movements. Rose was staring her down, but the girl didn't waver at all. She jumped up and down, waving her arms in big circles.

Then, almost without warning, the judge brought his hand down and called for the match to begin. The crowd roared, and the sound seemed to propel Rose's opponent forward. In an instant, the girl had finished casting body enhancement magic and charged.

Rose's eyes widened in surprise, both at the girl's casting speed and the effectiveness of her spell. She was incredibly fast. In a split second, she had crossed half the arena. Her skills were clearly far above those of Rose's previous opponents.

Thankfully, Rose was used to facing off against powerful opponents by now. After all, Aurelia and Lesti were her usual sparring partners. She quickly threw up a stone wall to slow down her opponent and disappeared from view.

I expected the girl to slow down or cast some spell to try and break through

164

the wall, but she didn't let up in the least. Quickly closing in on the wall, she leapt straight over it. At the same time, she also cast an oddly familiar spell.

A portion of the arena crumbled into dust and quickly flowed like sand across the ground to join her. It formed into a wave of dirt that rose up to meet the girl in the air. Rose peppered her with spells from below, but the wave of earth intercepted them all.

"This is just like Lesti's duel with Alex," I muttered as the memory of that day on the training ground flashed through my mind.

Next to me, Malkael nodded. "I expected there to be some similarities considering the match-up, but there is far more in common than I was anticipating."

I wanted to ask Malkael who this girl was, but I didn't have time. The match below continued on at a breakneck pace. The blonde girl's wave of earth began to crash down toward Rose. Rather than throwing up another stone wall, she dodged.

Propelled by some force that I couldn't see, she launched herself high into the air. Flying over her opponent, she landed safely on the other side of the arena. The wave of dirt and sand the blonde girl had summoned crashed down where Rose had been standing moments before and dissipated.

I expected them to stop and take a moment to assess each other and adjust their plans, but the blonde girl apparently didn't have a slow setting. When the girl landed behind the wall Rose had summoned, it shattered into dozens of tiny stone shards that she launched across the arena. I quickly recognized the spell as Stone Bullet.

The attack was so fast that Rose barely had any time to react. She quickly threw up a series of layered barriers to deflect the stones that were heading at her. Dust clouds erupted nearby as the rocks were deflected and slammed into the walls and floor behind her. Despite how well she had placed them, several of the barriers shattered. The blonde girl was definitely wielding some serious power.

"As expected of a relative of the Bestroff family. She certainly does have some power behind her spells." Next to me, Malkael threw a curveball into his commentary.

"This girl is related to Alex?! Why is this the first I'm hearing about it?" I looked over at him in shock. If I had known about this, I would have done more to help Rose prepare.

Malkael simply shrugged. "You never asked. Besides, there wasn't much you could have done to prepare Rose for this. You were up all night just preparing Lesti, weren't you?"

I flicked my tail in agitation. He was right. Even if I had known, there wasn't anything that I could have done with the knowledge. That didn't mean I wouldn't complain about it later, but that could wait until the match was over.

The action continued at a lightning-fast pace as I turned my attention back to the arena. Rose's opponent charged her at full speed using body enhancement magic. I expected Rose to try and use spells to slow her opponent down and keep her distance. Close-range combat wasn't really her strong suit, and she hadn't gone through the same crash course that Lesti had. To my surprise, though, she cast her own body enhancement magic and fled across the arena.

That in and of itself wasn't all that odd. Using body enhancement magic would make it easier for her to keep her distance. What was strange was that she didn't use any other spells. The blonde-haired girl wasn't as good at Alex with this type of magic, so she couldn't catch up to Rose with that alone. This should have given Rose a brief opportunity to counterattack, but she didn't.

Her opponent quickly realized that she wouldn't be able to catch up and started firing off her own spells, trying to slow Rose down. Meanwhile, Rose continued to run away while desperately dodging and diverting her opponent's attacks. Fireballs, waterspouts, earthen spears, and various other spells whizzed by her ear and slammed into the surrounding arena. The arena was starting to look like a war zone with all the damage it was taking.

As the spells continued to fly at a rapid pace, the crowd grew louder and louder. Most voiced their appreciation for the spectacle of magic being put on by Rose's opponent, but my ears picked up on a few taunts and jeers thrown Rose's way as well. It made sense. Despite having several opportunities to counterattack, she had spent the entire match running away and defending. From an outsider's perspective, she looked like a cornered mouse.

There was one crucial detail that the people taunting her were missing, though. Despite how aggressively her opponent had been attacking her since the match started, she hadn't managed to land a single hit on Rose. Things had been a bit shaky at first, but once she had gotten past the opening stages of the match, her defenses had been perfect and relaxed.

"She's stalling," Malkael muttered under his breath with a confused look on his face. "Why, though? It would be more efficient for her to conserve her magical energy by ending the match quickly. She still has the finals to deal with after all."

I watched as Rose diverted another stone spear attack with a simple barrier. There was an intense focus in her eyes. She had a goal, and I had a pretty good idea of what it was. "She's buying time for Lesti to rest. She can't control the length of the other matches, but she can draw her own out for as long as possible to buy her time."

Even as I said that I could see the frustration growing for Rose's opponent. She hurled spells faster and faster, all the while desperately pouring more energy into her body enhancement spell. Her casting was now wild, reckless, and burning through her magical energy at an accelerated rate. Perhaps if she had as much magic as Alex, she could have gotten away with that.

She wasn't him, though. Even if she was related, she didn't have anywhere near the absurd amount of power he had. Her movements were already beginning to dull, and her spells quickly began to lose their edge. Rather than looking happy, Rose grimaced. It was clear that she wanted to buy more time.

There wasn't much more she could do to extend the match, though. At least, that's what I thought. In the next moment, she turned that idea on its head. Rose, who had been running away the entire match up until then, charged at her opponent.

It was so unexpected that even the blonde-haired girl couldn't react fast enough. Rose drew her fist back and threw an awkward punch at her. The blow landed and caused the girl to stagger and then tumble to the ground, carried forward by the momentum of her charge.

Even with her body enhancement magic running, Rose's attack hadn't done much damage at all to her opponent. The magical barrier that she needed to break to win the match was still completely intact. The main reason for that was that Rose wasn't great at hand-to-hand combat. She wasn't particularly strong or fast, and her technique left a lot to be desired.

Her opponent clearly recognized this. The blonde girl stood up where she had fallen and glared at her angrily. Rose squared up against her awkwardly, her stance full of holes. However, rather than rushing in to punish her, her opponent took more distance and launched a fireball at her.

The move caught Rose off-guard, and she barely managed to throw up a shield in time. Using the opportunity to take even more distance, the blonde-haired girl continued her ranged assault. Seeing this, Rose rushed after her in a desperate attempt to close the gap and stop her from casting more spells.

The crowd roared with delight. From their perspective, it must have looked like the girl that had been on the run and cornered the entire match had taken a desperate gamble and turned the tables on her opponent. But for the two girls, this had turned into a battle of pride; they knew the match's outcome was already decided.

There was no way for the blonde girl to make a comeback with Rose's skill and the gap in their remaining magical energy stores. Yet, rather than giving up, she desperately tried to continue the fight on her own terms. She burned through her own magical energy as fast as she could in the hopes she could somehow land a decisive comeback blow. Meanwhile, Rose chased after her, trying to pull her into hand-to-hand combat where she could draw out the fight.

As the chase continued, Rose began to pull more tricks out of her sleeve as she tried to slow her opponent down. Using earth magic, she tried to break the girl's footing by smashing or softening the ground under her feet. When that failed, she used ice magic to try and make her slip. Unfortunately, her foe had impressive footwork and balance.

No matter what tricks Rose tried, she couldn't close the gap. In fact, her own traps were slowing her down more than her opponent. As the arena became littered with them, it became harder and harder for Rose to keep up the chase. Growing impatient, she rushed at her foe, ignoring her own traps and trying to push through them with brute force.

She managed to get past the first few with no issue, but then she hit a patch of ice she had created shortly before and lost her footing. Her opponent immediately took a wide stance and began to gather what remained of her magical energy. Based on what I could see, this would be her last shot at winning the match.

A massive fireball formed in front of the girl, so large that Rose probably couldn't see her on the other side. Then, it shrank, or rather compressed, down to the size of a soccer ball. The fur on my back stood on end, and it felt like a surge of electricity shot through my body. Right before my eyes, this first year was copying Lesti's condensed fireball spell that she had developed based on my advice.

Rose stared at the girl in shock, completely forgetting about her vulnerable position for a moment. Then, her expression shifted to one of fear as the realization that this attack could actually turn the match around set in. A fierce prideful grin spread across the blonde girl's face as she launched the fireball.

It raced toward Rose at extraordinary speed. With her footing already unstable, there was no way she could dodge it in time. Realizing this, Rose quickly cast two spells, Earth Wall and Magic Barrier. A wall of earth sprang up before her to absorb the blast, a magical barrier behind it acting as a backup.

However, throwing up the hasty wall of earth turned out to be a mistake. The fireball slammed into it and exploded with enough force to instantly shatter the wall, turning it into deadly shrapnel. The barrier Rose had thrown up behind it was pummeled with stones and fire. It only held for a brief moment before it shattered, leaving her defenseless.

Smoke and fire washed over Rose, hiding her from view. A hushed silence fell over the crowd as they collectively held their breath. Rose's opponent fell to one knee, gasping for air as the exhaustion from overusing her magic caught up with her. Her gaze, like everyone else's, was fixed squarely on the cloud of smoke and dust on the other side of the arena.

After what felt like an eternity, the air began to clear. Emerging from the smoke was an exhausted but uninjured Rose. The judge took a single glance at her but made no other moves. With my eyes, I could see that the barrier protecting her was severely weakened but still intact. The match would continue.

An annoyed grimace crept across her opponent's face for a moment, quickly replaced by an exhausted smile. She tried to rise to her feet, but her legs gave out on her once more. Even that simple action left her looking pale and gasping for air. There was no way she could muster up the will to use any more magic. Even if she did, it would be incredibly dangerous.

Rose, realizing this, raised her hand toward the girl and began to cast a new spell. A strong breeze began to pick up within the arena, slowly building in intensity. It buffeted the blonde-haired girl as it grew in strength and began to push her back. In her weakened state, there wasn't much she could do to resist. A moment later, she was gently pushed off the edge of the arena and out of bounds.

The judge raised his hand high overhead. "Ring out! The winner of the first semifinal match is Rose!"

The crowd erupted in a chorus of cheers and applause. The entire match had been Rose stalling and trying to buy time for Lesti. It would have been over much faster if the two had fought head-on. In a way, the whole thing was one big farce. They didn't care, though. To them, it had been an exciting match between two first-year students that delivered more entertainment than expected.

Rose looked around at the cheering crowd and waved shyly as she headed over to her opponent. Reaching down, she tried to help the girl up but was met with an angry glare. Despite the crowd's appreciation for the match, it seemed her opponent was a little less than thrilled by how things had played out. There was a brief exchange of words between the two that only they could hear before several instructors arrived to escort them out of the arena.

The crew responsible for repairing the arena between matches looked over the area and began hurriedly trying to patch things up. However, with the damage as extensive as it was, it would take some time to fully fix it. I thought about getting up and roaming around the arena a bit, but before I could, there was a ruckus outside the doors to the suite.

"Halt! No one is allowed to enter this area without permission. Unless you have a summons, leave!"

It didn't seem like anyone else had noticed over all the talk about the last match, but my keen feline hearing could hear the shouting out in the hall. Whoever they were talking to wasn't quite as loud, so I couldn't hear them. Curious and with nothing better to do, I decided to go investigate. Malkael quickly followed me like he was my shadow. It seemed like he wasn't about to let me out of his sight.

As we approached the door, I became able to make out the voice of whoever the guards were shouting at. "Please, I need to see Instructor Malkael. If I can't enter, then can you please call for him?"

"And I told you, neither of us can leave our post. Go find a messenger elsewhere!"

The guard's angry retort, along with the fact that I recognized the other voice, made my fur bristle. That was no way to be talking to a young girl who was asking for help. It appeared that we were close enough that Malkael could hear what was going on as well. With a rather stern expression, he walked over and quickly opened the door.

"What is going on here?"

The guards snapped to attention. "My lord. We were just chasing off this intruder."

Malkael and I looked past the pair, both our eyes landing on the familiar figure of Rose. She was panting, and her cheeks were flushed. The fact that she had gotten here so quickly meant she must have run here, including up several flights of stairs.

Malkael narrowed his eyes at the guard. "I see no intruder, only a student of the academy."

"Sh-She doesn't have a summons, sir. Even if she is a student of the academy, she's still a commoner. We can't allow her through without a summons."

I hissed at the guard slightly, but Malkael held up a hand to stop me. "Even if what he says is unjust, he is simply following protocol. He hasn't done anything wrong, Astria." Once he was sure that I wasn't going to do anything foolish, he turned his attention back to the guard. "I know this girl; she's most likely here to see me. She has my permission to enter, so let her pass."

The guards both looked at each other hesitantly but stepped aside nonetheless. Rose ran up to the both of us, a relieved smile on her face. "Thank you, Instructor Malkael. I was asked to deliver this to you by Cl—someone. They said you would know what to do with it."

Rose held out a small slip of high-quality parchment that had been hastily folded in half. Malkael quickly unfolded it and read the contents. His expression grew puzzled and a little concerned. Once he was done reading, he recited a quick incantation and burned the parchment. "Both of you, come with me."

We turned and headed down the hall toward the suites used for private meetings with nobles. It felt like we walked for a good five minutes before Malkael came to a stop before one of the doors. Glancing in both directions to make sure no one was around, he knocked.

"Come in," a young girl's voice called out to us from the other side.

Malkael held the door open and ushered us all through, glancing around the whole while. Once we were all inside, he shut the door behind us and locked it. I wasn't sure what was causing him to be so cautious, but I imagined it had something to do with the young noble girl standing in front of me.

It was the girl Rose had just beaten in her semifinal match. She was still wearing her school uniform, and her entire body was covered in dirt. Looking at her up close, she was pretty short, maybe just a bit shorter than Lesti. She quickly curtsied, causing her blonde twin tails to bob ever so slightly.

"Thank you all for coming on such notice and under such strange circumstances. My name is Clara Belcrest. If you don't mind, I'd like to skip the formalities and get straight to the point. There is little time, after all. I have a favor I would like to ask of you."

"Um. What's going on?" Rose hesitantly interrupted, clearly confused. I could hardly blame her there. Everything was just happening way too fast. Even I was stuck with nothing but questions.

"Ah, yes." Malkael suddenly seemed to remember that we were both there and explained the situation. "You didn't read the letter, so you wouldn't know. Ms. Belcrest requested a meeting with me to discuss something relating to her cousin. The contents suggested that privacy was of the utmost importance, so that's why I was so cautious on our way here. I am sure she can explain the exact reason for calling us here herself."

"Thank you for your prudence, Instructor Malkael." Clara took control of the conversation back before I could even get a word in edgewise. My head was still spinning, but I didn't have any choice but to sit and listen. "My request has to do with certain private family matters that could cause issues if they get out, so our meeting must be kept secret."

"I understand. You said that there was little time, so I take it this has something to do with the tournament?" Malkael asked.

Clara nodded and took a deep breath as if preparing herself. "I want you to disqualify my cousin, Alexander Bestroff, from the tournament. Whatever happens. He mustn't compete."

We all stared at Clara in shock. I could barely believe what she was saying. She summoned us out of nowhere, and now she wanted us to disqualify her own cousin from the tournament. Something wasn't right here.

I wasn't the only one who seemed to think so either. Shaking her head as if trying to dispel the shock, Rose carefully questioned Clara. "I didn't mishear you, right? You want us to disqualify Alex?!"

"That's correct."

"I see. This certainly wasn't what I was expecting." Malkael furrowed his brow as he carefully watched Clara. "For what reason do you feel that he needs to be disqualified? I presume that he is cheating in some way?"

A troubled expression formed on Clara's face. "I'm afraid there isn't one.

He hasn't broken any of the rules."

"Ms. Belcrest. I'm sorry, but you'll have to give a better explanation than that." Malkael rubbed his temples and let out a heavy sigh. It looked like he was just as confused as I was now. "If Mr. Bestroff hasn't broken any of the rules, then why do you want him to be disqualified? This isn't some personal grudge, right?"

"O-Of course not! I have nothing but respect for Al. I would never try to sabotage him. It's just"— Clara lowered her eyes for a moment and tightly gripped her skirt. When she finally looked at us again, there was a clear sense of anguish in her gaze—"If he keeps fighting, I think that something terrible might happen to him."

"That's still not very much to go on." I finally wormed my way into the conversation, carefully watching Clara and trying my best to judge her intentions as I did so. "If you aren't willing to tell us exactly why he's in danger, then we won't be able to trust you."

As I pressured her, she shifted her gaze to look down at me for the first time. For a moment, she froze. Then a brilliant smile spread across her face. "You're...no. Now's not the time." Clara shook her head and forced a serious expression back onto her face. "You're absolutely right, Astria. Allow me to explain what I know."

Clara spent the next several minutes explaining what had happened over the last few weeks. From how Alex had been acting strange, up until his confession to her just the night before. Honestly, it all seemed rather flimsy. According to her, even Alex didn't seem to understand what would happen if he overused his magic. On top of that, there was something I just couldn't understand.

While Malkael and Rose quietly processed everything. I asked Clara about what was bothering me. "So why tell us all of this? Shouldn't you be talking to Lord Bestroff directly?"

She nodded as if she had expected the question. "I did consider talking to Al's father, but then I remembered the way Al acted when I suggested that we go talk to him together. He said that I mustn't talk to anyone about this."

Something about that hat struck me as odd. "Why would Alex confide in you and then tell you to stay quiet? It seems so contradictory."

"He didn't confide in me so much as I forced him to tell me what was going on. We've known each other for a long time, so I could tell something was wrong, and I couldn't just leave him alone." Clara shook her head as she corrected my mistake. "As for why, he didn't want me to talk to his father, well, there has to be something that caused Al's condition to become so unstable, right?"

"Is that so?" I asked as I looked over to Malkael for confirmation.

He nodded, his brow still furrowed in concentration. "Yes. I've never heard of any condition like this occurring naturally. If what Ms. Belcrest says is true, there would have to be some catalyst for the change. If that is some family secret, then Mr. Bestroff may have worried that her talking to Lord Bestroff would put her in danger."

"Yes. I suspect as much as well. Still, I couldn't just do nothing. I hoped that Al's father would stop him from competing, but since he didn't, I had to take matters into my own hands."

"So, you set up a secret meeting with me. With my connections to the headmistress, you assumed that we might be able to stop him from competing." Finally, the pieces of the puzzle fell into place as Malkael summarized Clara's intent.

"Yes. I can't go to the headmistress directly. That would be too obvious, but if I came through you, I thought perhaps I could at least delay being found out until after the tournament had ended. Then I could seek protection at the academy."

"I see. Very well. I'll see what I can do. It is the duty of the instructors of the academy to look after the well-being of our students, after all." Turning on his heel, Malkael headed for the door. "Let's go. There's no time to waste. We'll seek an audience with the headmistress immediately."

I quickly turned to follow him, along with Rose. Clara curtsied low and bowed her head. As she spoke, her voice was thick with emotion. "Thank you. Please save Al for me."

Hearing her plea, I couldn't help but want to reassure her. "Don't worry. We'll take care of this. You just worry about keeping a low profile. Alex would be furious with us if something happened to you."

Clara looked up at me, and her expression softened just a bit. "Thank you."

With that, I turned and followed Malkael down the hall. He was walking at a hurried pace, and both Rose and I had to trot to keep up with his long strides. We had covered half the distance back to the main party area in the blink of an eye. Then, I heard something that stopped me in my tracks.

"There you are."

Zeke's familiar voice rang through my head. I looked around nervously, my entire body on edge. Malkael, noticing that I wasn't moving, stopped and looked back at me. "Astria? Is something wrong?"

Just as he did, a small tear in reality ripped open behind him. Four tails snaked their way through and grabbed onto the edges of the rift, pulling it wider. Once it was open wide enough, Zeke stepped through and flashed me a cheerful grin.

"I've come to pick you up. Let's have a little chat."

Zeke's Ambitions

My fur bristled slightly as I watched Zeke close the portal behind him. Meanwhile, Malkael had finally realized what was going on and had already begun to silently build a spell. I was glad he was ready, but I would rather avoid a fight. Zeke had the power to take down Frederick and Skell. Taking him on was just dangerous.

"N-No." Next to me, I heard Rose's voice trembling as she muttered to herself. "W-What is he doing here?"

Glancing over at her, I could see that it wasn't just her voice that was shaky. The poor girl looked like she could collapse at any moment. Whatever had happened between her and Zeke when he was Arvis's familiar must have really traumatized her.

Stepping forward, I did my best to calm her down. "Don't worry, Rose, it'll be fine. I won't let him touch you, so long as I'm here."

"Oh, is that right?" Zeke seemed amused by my declaration. He turned to look over at Rose, a malicious grin spreading across his face as he did so. But as soon as his eyes fell on her, the look disappeared, replaced by surprise. "You. You're the girl that Arvis had me kidnap."

"You're the one who kidnapped Rose?!" My anger flared, and I shouted at Zeke before I could stop myself. "She was separated from her family because of you, forced to follow the orders of that goon, Arvis."

I expected him to shout back at me, but to my surprise, his reply was calm, somber even. "I know. I ripped you away from your one and only home. I may have been forced to by my pact, but that still doesn't excuse the harm I did to you. You have my deepest apologies."

Rose simply stared back at him, clearly unsure of what to say or even do. I couldn't really blame her for that. Even I hadn't expected Zeke to come out and apologize to her so wholeheartedly like that.

"While I appreciate the sentiment, Rift Stalker, we are in a bit of a hurry at the moment." Malkael, looking tenser than I had ever seen him, waved for Zeke to step aside. "State your business or be on your way."

Zeke snarled at him and bared his fangs. "Don't you dare talk to me like that. I'm not some animal for you to boss around. If you're in such a hurry, then move along. I'm just here to pick up Astria."

"Pick her up?" Malkael glanced back at me, his eyes asking me what was going on.

Honestly, I was just as confused as him. "Don't look at me like that. It's not like I asked for this." I looked past him at Zeke. "What do you want? Is it really just to talk?"

"That's right." Zeke sat down where he was standing, not making any moves to approach us. "Given what happened recently, I figured you might have heard some rumors about me. I wanted to come and clear the air while I had the chance."

"Clear the air? You're working with demons." I eyed him wearily, my tail swishing across the ground as if trying to defuse the tension in my body. "That's not exactly something you can just brush off with a few pretty words."

"I suppose that's true." A mischievous smile spread across Zeke's face. "I do have my reasons, though. And I'm almost positive that they would interest you as well."

"Interest me?" Despite myself, I found his words pulling me in. "Why me specifically?"

Zeke's tails began to flick through the air behind him, and another rift opened. "You already know the answer to that, I think. Follow me. We should continue this in private."

I felt a roiling sensation in my stomach at his words. If it only dealt with us, it had to be related to reincarnation and, most likely, Zeke's desire. I glanced at the rift that had opened. On the other side, I could see what looked like a hill overlooking an open field. It didn't seem dangerous, but I had no idea where in the world it was.

Following Zeke through that rift was risky, but I didn't feel like I had any choice. We couldn't fight against him, and we needed as much information about why he was helping Thel'al as we could get. I stood up and began to follow him when Malkael held a hand out to block my path. "I'm sorry, but I can't let you go. It's too dangerous to leave you alone with him."

"I'll be fine. Besides, doesn't this line up with our plans as well?" I looked up at Malkael, silently pleading for him to drop it, but he continued to block my path. Then, out of the corner of my eye, I saw Zeke's magic move. It was so fast that I couldn't react to counter it in time.

In an instant, the spell completed. The air around both Malkael and Rose shifted, somehow being distorted and changed by Zeke's magic, though I couldn't tell how. Malkael, sensing the change, released the spell he had been holding back. The walls and floors around Zeke splintered, turning into hundreds of small projectiles that launched themselves at him.

Without stopping his current spell, Zeke cast another. In the blink of an eye, a barrier formed around him. The stone projectiles bounced off of it harmlessly. Malkael's image-based casting had no chance of breaking through it.

I watched this entire sequence in awe. Zeke's casting speed was unbelievable. While the barrier had formed slower than his other spell, it had still been relatively quick.

I prepared to follow up and help Malkael, but as I did, he staggered forward, falling to a knee. A moment later, he collapsed entirely. Glancing over, I noticed that Rose had passed out as well.

A surge of panic welled up inside me. I quickly cast my own spells, preparing to charge and Zeke to try and stop whatever he was doing. Before I could even move, though, he ended the spell on his own.

"Relax. They're fine. I've just put them to sleep so that they don't interfere." Zeke pointed one of his tails toward the fallen Malkael.

Looking more closely, I could see his chest rising and falling slowly. The same was true of Rose. I let out a heavy sigh of relief and dismissed my spells. At least for now, he wasn't looking for a fight.

"Did you really have to do that?" I asked as I turned to face Zeke once more. "We could have just talked things out."

"That would have taken too long." Zeke brushed aside my complaints and headed into the rift behind him. "I've only got a limited amount of time, you know. Let's go."

With that, Zeke passed through the rift. On the other side, I saw him circle around to take a look back at me. I quickly used Power Cat to move Malkael and Rose into more comfortable positions. I would have felt bad just leaving them on the floor however they fell. Once that was done, I braced myself and followed Zeke through the portal.

As I stepped through, I felt my senses distort, and my stomach turn. I closed my eyes and took a deep breath, waiting for the sensation to pass. Once it had, I opened my eyes and looked around. I found myself standing on a hill overlooking extensive open grasslands. In the distance, I could see a towering mountain range. Nearby, on top of the hill, stood a lone tree.

Turning, I found him standing behind me with an eager smile. "Well, let's get down to business then, shall we?"

"So, you're from another world." I circled Zeke until the tree was at my back and sat in the shade. Trying to take control of the conversation, I probed him to see just how similar we really were. "Were you reincarnated by that weird voice, too?"

Zeke tilted his head at me. "Reincarnated? Weird voice? I'm not sure what you're talking about. I don't really remember much of my last moments in my old world. I believe there is a short gap in my memory. One minute I was sitting in my lab, and the next, I was suddenly standing in a summoning circle in this body."

I paused for a moment and considered Zeke's words. Although our circumstances seemed to be similar, they didn't appear to be exactly the same. Unlike me, Zeke didn't seem to know anything about how he had gotten here.

I considered prying into the matter more but decided against it. The voice had specifically mentioned that my memories would be erased the second time we met, but they hadn't been. It was probably better if I kept that info to myself. Besides, that wasn't what I had come here for. "So, just to confirm, do you have the rest of the memories of your past life?"

"That's right. I was a student in my old world." Zeke looked out over the field below as he started to talk. "I was just about to graduate and start my own research on interstellar travel techniques. I'd spent all four years working my ass off and held the top seat in my class the whole time. Research groups around the world were lining up for a chance to get me to join them."

"Then, one day, I woke up and found everything I worked for destroyed." A disgusted scowl flashed across his face as he continued. "I was pulled into this world by Baron Arvis and bound as his familiar against my will. Can you believe that? After everything I had done, all the hard work I had put in, I was transformed into some power-hungry noble's pet."

I could hear the anger in Zeke's voice, but something else he had said had frozen me on the spot, interstellar travel. From the start, I had been worried that he was like me and had knowledge that this world hadn't discovered yet. Even worse, it seemed like his own world was ahead of my own. I had to find out just how far that was.

"You said you were going to research interstellar travel techniques." I paused, trying to think of the best way to phrase my question. I didn't want Zeke to realize that my own knowledge was lacking compared to his if I could avoid it. "What was your specific focus, though?"

Zeke turned to look at me with a surprised expression for a moment before his eyes lit up. "You're curious, are you?! Well, if you must know, I was researching how to miniaturize wormhole generators and how to reduce their power consumption. You see, our existing wormhole generators were so large they were practically useless for anything outside of arc class ships. In order to truly make interstellar travel mainstream, we needed to be able to load the tech onto smaller ships."

I ground my teeth together as I listened to Zeke's explanation, trying my best to force down the panic I was feeling in my chest. "I see. That does make sense. Most technology only becomes mainstream once it becomes small and cheap enough for common people to afford."

"Exactly!" I suddenly found Zeke in my face as he excitedly pushed himself uncomfortably close. "If we could make the tech small enough to fit on even standard supply ships, we could much more easily transport goods across the universe. Trade would boom, and interstellar travel would become the norm."

"Right, right. I understand. You're too close, though." I leaned back just a bit, trying to create even a few inches of distance between us.

Thankfully, Zeke seemed to realize he was making me uncomfortable and sat back, turning to look out over the field once more. "My apologies. I got a little too excited there. Enough about me, though. What were you doing in your old world, Astria?"

I paused for a second, considering how I should answer, but decided that I could probably be honest about this particular subject. "Ah, I was a teacher for young children. Although, I had just started before I died."

"A teacher?" Zeke turned to look at me once more and tilted his head to the side. "You still had teachers in your world?"

"Of course we did. Why wouldn't we?"

"It's completely unnecessary with direct knowledge acquisition technology. Children can simply learn while they sleep by…" Zeke trailed off as he stared at me, a look of realization washing over his face. Then, he finally continued, standing up and walking over toward me as he did. "I see. So, you're not from my world after all, or perhaps you are but from a different time."

I smacked my tail on the ground in frustration. Without even realizing it, I had given away that my world wasn't as advanced as his. In fact, it didn't even appear to be close. Trying to brush it under the rug, I averted my gaze. "Well, who knows. Things might have just developed differently where I'm from, but that's not important."

Turning my gaze back, I found myself practically nose to nose with Zeke, his large form looming over me. He began to pace back and forth in front of me, keeping his gaze locked on me the whole time. The expression on his face told me he was deep in thought. Every fiber in my body was screaming for me to run as if I were some sort of cornered rabbit.

Then, his expression suddenly brightened, and he laid down casually in front of me. "Yes. I suppose you're right. What's important is that we've both been wronged by whoever it was that brought us here, no? I've already taken my revenge on Arvis, but you're still stuck under the thumb of that red-haired girl, right?"

"Under her thumb? I think you may be misunderstanding something." I glared at Zeke, my irritation flaring unexpectedly. "I'm not under anyone's thumb. Lesti and I are friends."

Zeke narrowed his eyes at me. "So, you're still saying that huh? I can't believe you're able to call someone who dragged you into this wretched backward world and forced you into a body like that your friend. From the start, she called you here to serve her own needs without any consideration for what you wanted. Am I wrong?"

My fur began to bristle as my anger flared. I was surprised at myself. It wasn't that I was angry at Zeke because what he said was wrong. In fact, it was the opposite. Even if Lesti hadn't been solely responsible for me arriving in this world, her summoning had been entirely driven by her own personal desires. She hadn't even considered how it would affect the person or creature being summoned.

I couldn't argue with Zeke's logic in that regard. At the same time, I hated the idea of him placing all the blame on Lesti. "Can you really blame her for that, though? Summoning is normal in this world, and despite being a child, she has a lot of problems of her own. In the end, she treats me like a friend and a partner. So what if I've become some sort of cat creature. It could be worse."

"It could be worse?!" Zeke jumped to his feet, looming over me with anger overflowing in his voice. "We should be human! Not pets whose only purpose is to fulfill the selfish desires of their owners. If anything, you and I should be leading this world into a new golden age! Think of all the things we could accomplish with our knowledge!"

"We died! We're lucky to be alive at all right now!" I shouted back at Zeke, a surprising amount of anger bubbling up within me. His words reeked of arrogance. "Besides, do you really think things would go that smoothly?! Even if you started to teach the people of this world about physics and science, a good portion of the nobles would just use it as an excuse to go to war."

Zeke glared back at me defiantly. "Then we just crush those fools that would abuse the knowledge we give them. Do you really think there's anyone in this world that could stand against us if we used our full power?"

"And what about all the innocent people that get caught in the crossfire? Do you really think you'd be able to chase after every single evil noble in the world and take them out individually?" With my own emotions boiling, I began to pace, circling Zeke as I went. "There would be war, and the majority of those fighting in them wouldn't be the corrupt nobles you hate so much. They'd be innocent people."

"Th-That's their own fault for choosing to fight against us. There's nothing I can do about that." Zeke turned and started circling as well, keeping me in his sights. It felt like a fight could break out any moment.

"Choosing to fight against you? So, it's either swear loyalty to you or die now? And you're assuming that they have the power or the means to flee from their lord." I felt my fangs bear unconsciously as I continued to rip into Zeke's logic. "The majority of the people in this world have neither. If they go against their lord, they'll be killed for sure."

"So, you're suggesting that we just leave this world in the dark ages?" A deep growl began to rumble from deep in his chest as our verbal sparring match continued. "You think we should just leave them to slave away under corrupt nobles for their benefit?"

"That's not what I'm saying! But—"

"But what?!" Zeke cut me off before I could explain, stepping closer as we continued to circle. "You have the power to change the entire course of this world, but you're not willing to take responsibility and do what needs to be done? Is that it?"

I froze on the spot as Zeke's words struck me deeper than I had expected. I'd struggled to decide if I should introduce the science and technology from my old world into this one since I had arrived. How many problems could I have solved if I had just tapped into that knowledge? Could we even have defeated Thel'al already?

Maybe I was just being a coward. While there were definitely consequences to introducing so much advanced knowledge into this world, there were also consequences to not doing it. How many people's lives could be improved or even saved?

As I struggled with that question, Zeke continued to circle me. Finally, he came to a stop in front of me, so close that we were nose to nose. To my surprise, his expression was neither cold nor angry. Instead, it was filled with disappointment.

He stared at me for a long moment before he spoke again. "Come on, Astria. Work with me. Together we can reclaim our humanity and lead this world to a bright new future."

Zeke finally got to the heart of the matter. I still didn't feel like I could answer him. In fact, I felt even more unsure about it after everything he had said. I needed to know more. "You keep saying that we can reclaim our humanity, but how?"

He leaned back, a thoughtful expression on his face. It was like he was trying to decide if he wanted to tell me something, I decided to give him a little push. "If you're not going to tell me, that's fine, but then I'm out. There's no way I can agree to something like this if I don't even know if you can actually do what you're saying you can do."

He let out a heavy sigh. "Fine. I suppose that's fair. In truth, I don't yet know how to do it. However, I believe it should be possible with magic. As far as I can tell, it can do anything as long as you have a well-constructed spell and enough magical energy."

"And just how do you intend to get either of those? I can't imagine you're a master at constructing spells, and even if you manage to craft the spell, the amount of energy it will take will be off the charts."

"Very true. Given enough time, I could probably solve the issue of the spell. The magical energy is another matter, though." Zeke turned and walked back a few feet before glancing back over his shoulder. "That's where the demons come in. With their knowledge, I should be able to build something like a battery. I can probably speed up creating the spell too."

"You'd work with demons just for that?" I asked in disbelief. I could understand Zeke's desire to become human again, but Thel'al and his minions were cruel and heartless. Working with them had to entail doing terrible things to others. There was no way that was worth it.

Zeke apparently saw things differently. "Yes. It doesn't matter if they're cruel monsters. They can help me accomplish my goals, so I'll use them. When I'm done with them. I'll make sure that they're taken care of afterward. In fact, arrangements are already being made."

I glared at him. My decision was settled at this point. The only reason I kept talking was that I was angry. "And all the people that will get hurt along the way? They don't matter to you at all?"

His expression shifted for just a moment, and then he looked away. "Sometimes, progress requires sacrifices. It'll be worth it in the end after we push this world forward."

"No one needs to be sacrificed for this world to move forward! The only thing they need to be sacrificed for is so that you can fulfill your own selfish desires!" I finally lost my cool and shouted at Zeke. "Even as a familiar, you could teach and guide the people of this world! I'd rather stay as a familiar the rest of my life than have people suffer!"

Zeke turned back toward me, snarling as he bared his fangs. "Fine! Have it your way. You can stay some little girl's pet for all I care."

I could hear the anger in his voice, and suddenly I realized I had screwed up. He was my only way back. I started to slowly stalk towards him as his tails rose into the air, ready to cut into the fabric of reality once more.

He turned and glanced back at me, an annoyed look on his face. "Perhaps if our interests had aligned better, I wouldn't have to do this. But I have to consider you a threat now. Goodbye, and good luck getting back, Astria."

Zeke's tails flicked through the air, a familiar scene of ruins appeared on the other side. It was the area where he had come from when he met me at the arena. Immediately upon seeing this, I raced toward him. I couldn't afford to have him leave me stranded out here. I leapt through the air, transforming into my tiger form as I tried to pounce on him.

As my claws extended toward Zeke, I felt a spell begin to form at a rapid speed. Tendrils of magical energy erupted from Zeke, manipulating the space around me. It was so fast, I couldn't even tell what the spell was doing. Thankfully, I didn't need to.

Reaching out with my own magical energy, I began blocking and hampering his spell. It wasn't enough to stop it entirely, but it was enough to slow it down. Zeke's eyes went wide as I closed in on him, but just before they could reach him, his tails flicked through the air, and a rift opened right in front of my face. Unable to adjust my momentum, I flew through the rift and came to a skidding halt on the other side.

In a panic, I turned and made to leap back through the rift. However, just as I did, the roar of the crowd exploded around me. Stopping to take in my surroundings for a moment, I realized that I was once again on the roof of the arena.

"Well, it looks like you win this round." Zeke's voice brought my attention back to the rift, which was already slowly closing before me. "I have to admit, I wasn't expecting you to be able to slow down my spell like that. I underestimated how advanced your old world was. It really is a shame. I was looking forward to working with you."

Zeke stared through the slowly closing portal at me. The look in his eyes was one of disappointment and loneliness. In a way, I understand exactly how he felt. We were probably the only two people in this entire world who could understand each other's situations. At the same time, there was no way that we could be allies.

The rift narrowed down to a tiny crack as I stared back at Zeke silently. He disappeared from sight, but before the rift completely closed, his voice drifted through one last time. "I'll see you again soon."

With that, the rift fully closed, and I was left standing on the roof of the arena by myself. I took a deep breath and started trying to process everything I had just learned. Most importantly, Zeke was a reincarnation from another world with advanced technology, like me.

On top of that, his willingness to work with Thel'al and sacrifice others made him even more dangerous. If he wanted to, he could cause incredible amounts of destruction. I needed to warn the others about just how much of a threat he posed.

Suddenly the roar of the crowd exploded once more, even louder than before. Apparently, an exciting match was going on down below. Standing there listening to their cheers, I realized that I wasn't sure how long I had been gone. It hadn't felt very long, but Lesti's match might have already started.

There was also the situation with Alex. I wasn't sure how long Zeke had knocked out Malkael and Rose. Were they able to stop the match in time?

Pushing the situation with Zeke, I transformed back into my normal form. As I did, I realized that behind the crowd's cheers, I could hear the sound of an intense battle going on in the background. I could hear the distinct cracking of stone as the arena was battered with powerful impacts. It certainly sounded like one of Lesti's battles.

Taking a breath, I stepped up to the edge of the arena roof, looked at the fight below, and froze. "You can't be serious."

The thought slipped unbidden from my mind as I watched the intense exchange unfolding before me. I had been expecting to see a fierce battle, but this was far beyond my expectations. The combatants were locked in an intense battle that had the crowd on the edge of their seats. In an instant, I was pulled into that atmosphere and found myself staring down at the fight in rapture.

Lesti vs. Sebastian

"-esti, Lesti," a familiar voice called to Lesti as someone shook her body gently. "It's time. Wake up."

Prying her weary eyes open, she found herself in an unfamiliar place. A simple stone room with plain wooden benches, no more than planks, really. It took a moment, but eventually, the fog of sleep cleared from her mind, and she remembered that this was the waiting room for combatants in the arena.

After spending all night with Astria practicing for their battle plan against Sebastian, she had been completely drained. All of that exhaustion caught up with her the moment she sat down, and before she realized it, she had fallen asleep. She expected her body to be sore, but she was oddly comfortable. Her head rested on a soft and surprisingly warm pillow.

"You awake?" The voice that had pulled her from her sleep came from directly above her. Rolling over on her back, Lesti found herself face to face with Aurelia. Her yellow eyes peered down at Lesti worriedly even as she allowed her friend to use her lap as a pillow.

"Auri, what are you doing here?" she asked, reaching up and playing with her friend's green braids. "I thought you were supposed to be meeting with Lord Valst?"

"Mm. I did. It went well." Aurelia nodded, her face remaining mostly passive. Still, something about her tone told Lesti that it didn't go as well as she was letting on. Most likely, Valst had used his negotiation skills to corner her into some odd agreements. Before she could ask about it, Aurelia changed the subject. "On my way back, Instructor Lania spotted me and sent me to check on you. She was worried that you wouldn't wake up in time for your match."

"Lani worries too much," Lesti replied, rolling over and snuggling against her friend's warm body.

A moment later, she was forced to roll back over and sit upright by the firm hands of Aurelia. "No. She was right. You would have slept right through your match. Hurry up. They're already calling for you."

At that moment, Lesti noticed a perturbed-looking instructor standing near the hallway that led out into the arena. Apparently, she was already running late, and they had sent someone to fetch her. The realization sent a spike of adrenaline through her body, washing away the last of her grogginess. Leaping to her feet, she dashed over to the instructor and started to head down the hall.

"Good luck."

Just as she passed into the hallway, she heard one final bit of encouragement from Aurelia. Looking back, she smiled brightly at her friend and gave a quick wave before disappearing down the tunnel. The moment she was out of sight, the nerves and doubts began to set in. Would she be able to pull off the plan Astria had come up with, or would she end up having to be saved again?

As the long walk down the tunnel continued, these thoughts assailed her faster and harder until finally, she reached the end. Light and noise from the crowd streamed in from outside, assaulting her senses. Lesti's heart pounded wildly, and her chest and legs felt heavy. A small smile formed on her lips.

It was always this way, ever since her parents had died. She always acted brave and tough, but deep down, she was worried and scared. She wouldn't let those feelings stop her, though. Taking a deep breath, she put her hands on her hips and forced herself to grin as hard as she could.

"Time to put all of the practice that we put in last night to work! I'm going to beat that brat, Sebastian, down and show him that I'm the best mage in the entire alliance!"

Her heart still pounded, but the racing thoughts that assailed her stopped just long enough. Using that brief moment of relief, she willed herself to step out from the tunnel into the open arena beyond. The sun shone down brightly, forcing her to shade her eyes for a moment until they adjusted. The crowd roared in approval as they caught sight of her.

As her eyes adjusted, she noticed that one person was far less happy to see her. Standing in the arena and glaring down at Lesti impatiently was Sebastian. Walking up the makeshift staircase, she stared back at him with a defiant gaze that masked her inner nerves.

"So, you decided to show up after all?" Sebastian taunted as he unfolded his arms from across his chest. "I thought for sure that you had chickened out after seeing my match yesterday and ran back to the countryside where you belong."

Lesti scoffed. "As if I would ever run away from a weakling like you. Don't go getting ahead of yourself just because you got lucky and won against Aurelia. If she had been allowed to use Fang, then you wouldn't have stood a chance."

"Oh, please. Having that filthy mutt around wouldn't have made any difference at all. Besides, being a mage who can't win on their own merits is nothing to brag about."

Lesti averted her eyes and kicked at the ground beneath her feet hard. Rather than giving at all, it simply jarred her leg, causing a tingling sensation. She clicked her tongue in annoyance as she continued to glare at Sebastian. "That's rich, coming from you."

He sneered at her angrily, but before he could say anything, the primary judge interrupted. "That's enough bickering, you two. We're already behind, so I'm starting the match."

The judge raised his hand in the air. Nearby, the drums began to bang in a slow rhythm that slowly built up, faster and faster. The crowd fell silent, and tension filled the air. Both Lesti and Sebastian crouched low as they continued to glare at each other. Soon, the pounding of the drums washed away everything else. At that moment, the judge swung his arm down.

"Begin!"

Sebastian was the first to strike. No sooner had the judge's arm fallen than he extended his arm forward and fired a powerful bolt of lightning at Lesti. She wanted to go on the offensive, but this wasn't an attack she could simply ignore. She quickly cast a spell of her own to ward it off. "Earth Wall!"

The ground between them exploded upward, blocking Sebastian's attack completely. Lesti knew how powerful his lightning attacks could be, so she had adjusted her spell on the fly, making it extra thick. And that wasn't the only adjustment she had made. Tweaking the variables, she had changed the length and shape of the wall, making it longer and curving it.

"Repeat ten!"

With a single command, she forced the spell to fire off in rapid succession, quickly forming a circle of earth around Sebastian. Not letting up, she followed up with two attacks in quick succession, pushing her casting speed to its limit. First, she cast another earth-based spell, causing spears of stone to explode from the ground inside the circle she created.

For some foes, this alone would have been enough to finish them off, but Lesti knew that wouldn't work on Sebastian. Immediately after that spell finished, a massive ball of fire began to form in the air above the arena. At that moment, Sebastian appeared in her view, having leapt up to avoid the spikes she had summoned. It was the same strategy she had used against Alex. Only this time, she was going all out.

"Take this! Condensed Fireball!" At her shout, the fireball floating in the air rapidly shrank down into a sphere the size of her head and launched itself toward Sebastian. In an instant, it was mere inches from his face, but just before it could connect, Sebastian used wind magic to push himself out of its path. That was also part of the plan, though.

The sphere crashed into the ground below and exploded with incredible force. The impact was so intense that it blasted away the thick wall that Sebastian had barely managed to dent as if it was nothing. Realizing that she might have overdone it a little, Lesti quickly threw up a barrier to protect herself from debris flying her way.

Sebastian threw up his own multi-layered barrier as well, imitating the technique he had used against Aurelia. Several layers shattered instantly, but in the end, they managed to absorb the blast. While they may have stopped the damage, they didn't prevent him from being blown even higher into the air, above even the arena roof.

"Fireball, repeat three hundred!" Seeing her opponent vulnerable, Lesti threw another series of attacks Sebastian's way. Countless balls of fire filled the air between the two, once again obscuring their vision of each other. Each one was only a fraction of the power that Lesti's previous spell had used, but the sheer amount would make it hard to avoid all of them. Or so she thought.

Rather than throwing up additional barriers or countering with a spell of his own, Sebastian simply began to fall. Lesti's attack fired off, and the numerous fireballs hovering in the sky flew toward him. The first wave closed in on him rapidly, but before they could connect, he cast Wind Blast behind him, accelerating his fall.

Lesti tried to adjust the course of the remaining fireballs to intercept him, but it was no use. He kept accelerating each time she would fire a new wave at him. Soon Sebastian's body was plummeting toward the ground like a meteorite. It looked like he would smash into the ground, but Lesti was sure he would use wind magic to break his fall.

Aiming for that moment, she redirected a number of her fireballs to that spot. He surprised her once again, though. Rather than coming to a complete stop at the bottom of his fall, he used bursts of air to level off his descent, converting his vertical momentum into horizontal momentum. Lesti's fireballs slammed into the empty space where she expected him to be with an explosive roar, leaving her completely exposed.

Sebastian raced toward her across the ground, using a continuous air blast to maintain his momentum. Using the speed he gained from falling, he rushed toward her like he had been shot out of a cannon. Lesti didn't even have time to throw up a single stone wall.

Panic sent a shot of adrenaline through her body, and thankfully she had the training to use that. At the last moment, her instincts took over, and she leapt to the side, rolling across the ground. At the same time, Sebastian's spell sputtered and then failed, and he was sent tumbling to the ground, completely unprepared.

Lesti jumped to her feet and ran across the arena, jumping up on the remains of the broken wall she had summoned at the beginning of the fight. A cloud of dirt and dust had formed where Sebastian had crashed landed. She looked on, hoping that when the dust cleared, he would have knocked himself out or broken his own shield on accident. Unfortunately, that wasn't meant to be.

A gust of wind swept through the arena, blowing away dust and revealing Sebastian brushing himself off, no worse for wear. He turned and glared at Lesti, hatred boiling in his eyes. "So, you got the mangy cat to teach you how to use spell jamming, huh? I'm surprised a failure like you could manage to pull it off in a situation like that."

"Spell jamming? I didn't do anything like that," she replied with a smug smile. "Didn't your spell just fail on its own?"

The scowl on Sebastian's face grew even more fierce. In a rage, he flung a rather haphazard fireball at Lesti. "Don't screw with me!"

The spell clearly wasn't intended to do any actual harm. It wasn't fast-moving or powerful. Lesti could easily have blocked it with one of her own. Instead, she simply took a single step backward so that she was on the inner portion of the remains of her wall.

The fireball closed in on her rapidly. Just as it looked like the spell would hit her directly in the face, it fell apart. Bright orange embers floated in the air in front of her, but they quickly cooled and disappeared. It was a nostalgic scene for Lesti. Astria had once done something similar in their fight with Thel'al, although on a much larger scale.

She continued to wear the smug smile she had from before, knowing that it was the best way to get under Sebastian's skin. It worked like a charm. Seeing his spell fail again, combined with her expression, caused his anger to bubble over. He turned and stalked toward Lesti angrily. "You little brat! Come down here and fight me like a proper noble instead of hiding behind your tricks!"

"I wouldn't do that—" Lesti halfheartedly tried to warn Sebastian, but it was too late.

"Gaaah!" Sebastian stepped forward just a bit too far. The ground below his foot glowed briefly before a small explosion erupted, throwing him backward a few feet. He immediately sat up and stared at the spot, eyes full of shock and confusion.

This was the plan that she had worked out with Astria. Starting from the moment Sebastian had been launched into the air, she had begun to use simple earth magic to carve magic circles into the arena floor. If he stepped on any of them, it would trigger a random spell, any of which would hurt quite badly. All the terrain surrounding her was now working in her favor.

"I tried to warn you. The entire arena is rigged with traps just like that one." The smug smile slid from Lesti's face, replaced by a confident grin. "Ready to give up? You can't get close to me without taking a ton of damage, and your spells can't reach me."

It'd be nice if he took the bait, but it's Sebastian we're talking about here. Despite her confident exterior, Lesti knew this plan was full of holes. She was really relying on Sebastian not having enough power to break through by brute force. Most of her magic had gone into her initial assault and setting up her traps. If he managed to get to her without wasting a ton of energy, then the battle would be over.

"As if I'd surrender to you of all people! You'd still be in the last class struggling to cast even the most basic of magic if it wasn't for that familiar of yours!" Sebastian raised his hand and fired off a lightning bolt at Lesti. It streaked through the air, faster than the eye could follow. Yet, just like the fireball before, it fizzled out just before reaching her, the magical energy absorbed by another nearby circle that sent the power to her traps.

"A backwater noble like you should learn their place!" Another lightning bolt, more potent than the previous one, shot toward Lesti only to fizzle again. Sebastian glared at her, seething hatred written across his face.

"And serve the real nobility like your parents did!" A final blast of lightning cut through the air along with Sebastian's shout and was once again absorbed, but Lesti barely noticed it.

"My parents didn't serve other nobles!" Something inside her snapped at Sebastian's words. Rage, unlike anything she had ever felt before in her life, bubbled up inside her. "They served our people! They listened to their worries, did their best to make sure they would have food on the table, and protected them with their lives like a real noble would!"

"Compressed Fireball, repeat ten!"

She poured all the rage boiling inside of her into her spell. Massive fireballs, larger than anything she had ever summoned before, formed into the air around her. The flames began to compress them down, further and further.

Typically, this barely took any effort, but since she had made the original fireballs so huge, it took a ton of energy to compress them and maintain the compression. None of that mattered to her right now, though. All she could think about was crushing the boy in front of her who had insulted her parents.

She launched the first wave of fireballs at Sebastian. Unable to dodge forward or to the side, he tried to flee in the only direction he could, up. Using a powerful burst of wind magic, he propelled himself into the air. Lesti knew that was his only option, though.

"Wind Blast!" As soon as Sebastian's feet left the ground, she cast her own wind spell, cranking up the power as high as she could. A torrent of wind slammed down on him from above, smashing him into the arena floor with enough force that it broke.

For most students, the impact alone would have broken the shield protecting them, ending the match. But Sebastian's reactions were good enough that he managed to throw up a barrier of his own just in time and absorb most of the impact. Usually, Lesti would have found that annoying, but she was glad that he was hanging in there right now. It meant the match would keep going.

A moment later, the first fireball slammed into the ground next to him. A massive explosion rocked the arena. The floor where the impact occurred was instantly obliterated, turning into shrapnel that peppered the barriers protecting the crowd and Sebastian. His body was flung across the arena even as the stone shrapnel pummeled the barrier he had hastily thrown up.

Then the second fireball hit on the other side, flinging his body back in the opposite direction. As soon as it hit, the barrier he had thrown up shattered. The stone shrapnel that it had been protecting him from slammed into the barrier cast by the judges, landing the first real blow of the match.

Lesti wasn't done, though. A third fireball slammed into the ground below Sebastian's rag-dolling body, hurling him further into the air. She could see him desperately trying to summon another shield. But with his body being flung around by the explosions and battered by the stones, he couldn't focus on the spell well enough.

For a brief moment, he floated in the air before plummeting toward the ground below, disappearing into a massive cloud of smoke and dust created by Lesti's spell. She glared into the cloud, her anger still raging, waiting impatiently for Sebastian to emerge from the dust and smoke so she could continue her onslaught. Yet, no matter how long she waited, he never appeared.

"Wind Blast!" Growing impatient, she cast another spell, lowering the power enough that it simply cleared the smoke and dust from the field. Her view now unobscured, she found Sebastian laying sprawled out on his back. The barrier that she needed to break to end the match was still in place.

Raising her hand, she prepared to send another fireball hurling toward him. Before she could, someone grabbed her wrist. The sudden contact shocked her, causing her body to start. Turning, she found the head judge standing over her with a grave expression on his face.

"Ms. Vilia, the match is over. Please release your spells."

"But the shield is still..." Lesti's voice trailed off as she turned to look back at Sebastian once more. He was unconscious, entirely out of magical energy. Defending from her attacks and then breaking his fall afterward had totally drained him. In her rage, Lesti hadn't noticed that he was utterly defenseless. If she had launched her next attack, there was a good chance she would have killed him.

As the realization that the match was over hit her, a wave of exhaustion swept over her body. She was dangerously close to collapsing herself. Yet, she couldn't simply cancel her spells like the judge had asked. If she did, all of the pressure would be released at once. Astria had warned her that she would need to slowly reverse the compression step to be safe, but she simply didn't have the energy left for that.

"Sorry about this," Lesti apologized to the judge beforehand, drawing a confused look from him. Then, she launched the remaining seven fireballs high into the air. After reaching a safe height, she released each one. They exploded with enough force that it shook the arena below slightly.

The judge glared down at her angrily, but she didn't even have the energy to look back at him. Her breathing was ragged, and her body felt like it was made of lead. For the first time in a long while, Lesti had overused her magic. It was a feeling she was all too familiar with, having experienced it countless times in the old classroom where she used to practice alone.

Seeing her condition, the judge simply grimaced and raised his hand, "The match is complete. Sebastian Cilias is unable to continue. The winner is Lesti Vilia!"

A wave of cheers went up from the crowd, but Lesti was so exhausted she could barely even hear them. Without waiting for instructions, she began to shuffle toward the tunnel leading back to the waiting room. Behind her, the staff immediately set out assisting Sebastian and repairing the arena for the next match. The damage from her last attack had left almost no trace of the battle area behind, so repairs would take a while.

As Lesti entered the tunnel, she heard the sound of footsteps approaching. Lifting her head, she saw Alex coming toward her. "What are you doing here? They haven't called for you yet, have they?"

He smiled at her, raising an eyebrow. "What kind of greeting is that? Well, I suppose it's understandable given your current state. I thought I would see if they could use any help repairing the arena. The explosions were so powerful that they shook the waiting room. I'm assuming that was you."

"Yeah. I might have overdone it a little," she replied, forcing a weak smile onto her face.

Alex smiled back at her. "That's probably a bit of an understatement. You look like you can barely walk." The smile faded from his face and was replaced by a troubled frown. "It's a shame. I was looking forward to our rematch. It's not going to be much of a fight with you like this, though"

Lesti ground her teeth but forced a smile onto her face. "Aren't you getting ahead of yourself? You still have to beat Elliot before you even get to face me. For all you know, he'll wear you out just as much as me."

"I suppose that is possible, if unlikely." Alex walked past her with a wave. "Thanks for the warning. I'll keep that in mind. Do your best to rest up."

"Yeah, yeah." Lesti dismissively waved him off, turning and heading further into the tunnel as he headed out into the arena. However, she didn't make it very far. As soon as she was sure that she couldn't be seen from the arena entrance, the exhaustion finally overtook her.

A wave of dizziness struck her, forcing her to lean on the wall to keep going. After only a few more steps, even that became impossible. The heaviness of her body became too much to bear, and she found she couldn't lift her feet anymore, no matter how hard she tried.

Her vision blurred, which confused Lesti. No matter how exhausted she had been in her training sessions in the classroom, this had never happened. Reaching up, she rubbed her eyes with her free hand only to find it came away wet with tears.

"So, that's it." Tears now freely rolled down her face as reality settled in for her. She wouldn't be able to beat Alex in her current state. She had used far too much magical energy in her last fight. It would be impossible to recover before the final match.

"I really screwed up." Letting the exhaustion and despair overtake her, she slumped against the wall. Staring up at the ceiling, she let the tears continue to flow freely. Slowly, her consciousness began to slip, and her vision began to fade into darkness.

The faint sound of footsteps reached her ears, coming to a stop before her. The person said a few simple words before moving on. Her heavy eyes couldn't open to see who was there. Nor could her foggy mind recognize the voice that floated to her ears. The words themselves did reach her, though.

"That look doesn't suit you at all."

Alex vs. Elliot

The arena below had been reduced to what amounted to a pile of rubble. Powerful spells flew through the air at an unbelievable rate, each one destroying more and more of the floor on impact. In the midst of all this chaos, the familiar form of Elliot dashed about at inhuman speeds, dodging the onslaught.

Opposite him stood Alex, an intense expression that I had never seen before plastered on his face. It was a look of combined concentration and frustration, like someone trying to crush an insect but couldn't quite catch it. He was hurling every type of spell you could think of at his opponent with reckless abandon, wielding his absurd magical energy stores to their maximum potential.

Yet, no matter how hard he tried, he could never hit his opponent. It wasn't as if his spells were slow or poorly aimed either. This was Alex, after all. No one could match him in power, and Lesti might be his only better when it came to technique. His opponent was just that fast. Elliot moved so quickly that my own eyes could barely track him, circling the edge of the arena and waiting for a chance to strike.

Then, he spotted an opening and made a mad dash toward Alex. Slipping between the barrage of spells, Elliot flew across the arena and leapt at Alex. Barely having any time to react to the attack, Alex threw up a barrier, pouring an absurd amount of magical energy into it.

Elliot's fist slammed into the barrier with enough force that it caused a shock wave. It was honestly surprising that it didn't break his arm. That was just how good he was at body enhancement magic, though. He wasn't making his body stronger but was also reinforcing it to withstand the effects of that increased strength.

Despite the impressive display of power, Alex's barrier didn't waver in the slightest, and Elliot's momentum was halted entirely. In that brief moment, their eyes locked, and they glared at each other with a fierce competitive spirit. It was the type of rivalry that was to be expected of the number one and former number two students.

Alex used the brief lull in Elliot's movement to try and launch a counterattack. Casting his spell at a speed that would make even some of the instructors look slow, he summoned several stone spears. Given the situation, it was a brilliant choice because it broke the ground near his opponent's feet and made it harder for him to move around.

At least that was the case in theory. The reality turned out to be far different. As fast as Alex could summon his stone spears, Elliot cast his own spell. Pushing off of seemingly nothing, he spun in mid-air and circled around behind Alex. Then, he threw one more punch before retreating to a safe distance. Unfortunately, Alex had been prepared for such a possibility, and his attack simply struck another barrier.

Still, I was stunned. The spell he had just used was one that I was incredibly familiar with, Air Walk. Elliot being able to use it wasn't really all that surprising. It was the fact that he even knew it at all that had me flabbergasted. I had never taught that spell to him, and I doubted that Frederick or Skell had been giving him private lessons while they were off hunting down Thel'al.

The action paused for a moment as the two took the opportunity to assess the situation. Alex stared Elliot down with a frown while Elliot stared back at him with a bright grin that reminded me a bit of Lesti, if a little wilder. I had missed the beginning of the match, so I wasn't sure how things had gotten to this point, but it seemed like Elliot had the advantage. Taking the lull in the action as my chance, I leapt down to the viewing area below, only to find Malkael staring out at the match while holding his head.

Seeing me, he let out a relieved sigh. Looking at him, it seemed like he had just woken up. That explained why Alex's match had been allowed to start. "Are you both okay?"

Malkael briefly checked himself over before nodding. Rose did the same before a panicked look spread over her face. "Wait, what about Alex's match?!"

As if in response to her question, the sounds of the battle picking back up drew our gazes below. Elliot was once again rapidly dashing around the arena, dodging the spells that Alex flung at him.

Without taking his eyes off the action below, Malkael let out a heavy sigh. "It seems we are too late. Even worse, it seems that Mr. Gambriel has the advantage. Things aren't looking good."

"Isn't there anything we can do to stop the match?" I looked at Malkael, desperately searching for some way to avoid a crisis.

He simply shook his head. "It's unlikely that we'll be able to stop the match at this point. All we can do is prepare for the worst. Ms. Rose, please head back to the preparation area and warn the instructors. Don't hesitate to use my name."

"Yes, sir." Rose immediately took off down the hall at a quick walk. It was obvious that she wanted to run, but her legs were simply too wobbly.

I turned to watch the fight once more. My eyes darted around the arena below, struggling to continue tracking Elliot. "What happened? Why is Alex just flinging spells like some sort of normal-ranged caster."

"I'm only guessing as I just woke up myself, but it appears that Mr. Bestroff can't keep up with Mr. Gambriel's speed. He's moving far quicker than I've ever seen before." Malkael closely analyzed the fight below as he held himself up by the railing. I could tell he wanted to run and get help, but apparently, Zeke's spell had affected him more than Rose. "His attacks seem to carry much more weight than usual as well."

"So, Alex was forced to switch to flinging spells, huh?" I watched the fight below with a strange mix of emotions. I was impressed by Elliot's growth, but his timing couldn't have been worse. It was evident that he was putting strain on Alex. If things kept going like this, then he might get pushed over the edge.

Even as the thought crossed my mind, the battle below began to shift.

Alex, who had been standing in one spot up until now, began to move again. He wasn't as fast as Elliot, but his speed was nothing to scoff at. He started to circle the battle-scarred arena, continuing to cast spells as he went.

Elliot, seeing this, moved to intercept him. Alex quickly threw a series of earth spells at him. None of them were particularly powerful, but each was carefully placed to impede Elliot's movement as efficiently as possible. Small spikes, half walls, and pits continuously popped up in his path, slowing him down significantly.

It was an incredible showing of skill from Alex's perspective. Firing off such a rapid series of efficient, tailored spells like that was no easy task. Yet, the entire thing struck me as weird. No matter how many of these spells he fired off, he would never stop Elliot or break his balance since he could use Air Walk. In fact, it would probably be more efficient to just throw up a big wall and hope he smacked into it.

"It seems like Alex is conserving his magical energy. It looks like Clara wasn't making things up." My thoughts slipped out as I watched the scene below unfold. Alex didn't seem like the type to hold back without reason, and I couldn't think of another one.

Next to me, Malkael glanced over at me with a surprised look. "Are you sure he isn't just worried about running out of energy? Mr. Gambriel was the number two student for quite some time before Ms. Vilia took his spot. He has a rather large store of magical energy himself, and he's been pressuring Mr. Bestroff the entire bout. It seems reasonable that he would conserve his magical energy."

I simply shook my head at Malkael's comments. They were reasonable, but this was Alex we were talking about. His stores of magical energy were anything but reasonable. "It might make sense if it was anyone but Alex. The amount of magical energy he produces is beyond anything I've seen another human pull off. Even if he used twice as much magical energy as Elliot, he would still outlast him."

"You surely exaggerate." Malkael turned to me wide-eyed. "If he had that much magical energy, the build-up would destroy his body."

"I wish I was kidding, but I'm not. The only other times that I've seen anything like it was with Thel'al and Skell. The stuff just flows out of him like water."

Malkael stared at the arena below, his surprise written clearly on his face. There was actually something bothering me about what he had said. He had assumed that having a large amount of magical energy would harm the body, and I saw something similar with Fang. Unfortunately, I didn't have a chance to ask about it as the action in the arena took another shift.

Elliot, who had been being kept at bay by Alex's spells, changed his tactics and began to fire off ranged attacks of his own. Fireballs quickly formed in the air around him and launched toward Alex. His casting speed surprised me, not to mention the control he had over the spell. The only thing lacking was that he used more magical energy than necessary. It was almost as if I was watching Lesti from a few months back.

As I wondered how he had managed to pull off such a feat without any of Lesti's knowledge, he used his spells to try and drive Alex into a corner. He slowly closed the distance between them while continuing to bombard his opponent. Meanwhile, Alex used his own barrage of spells to desperately maintain the distance between the two.

Yet, no matter how hard he tried, Elliot still slowly closed in on him as he circled the edge of the arena. Then, slipping past Alex's latest barrage of spells, he came within striking distance. At the same time, he cast his own magic, Earth Wall, twice in quick succession. Two walls of earth and stone sprang up on either side of Alex, pinning him in.

Elliot's foot slammed into the ground in front of Alex as he drew his fist back. It was an incredibly telegraphed but powerful attack. Alex was cornered and couldn't dodge to the sides because of the earth walls. Stepping back would likely force him out of the arena making only options ducking or taking to the air. The former would probably result in a powerful follow-up kick to his head, while the latter would make it hard for him to dodge any follow-up spells.

In the end, he chose not to do either. Elliot's attack plowed directly into his face, or more accurately, into the barrier he had thrown up a few inches in front of him. An audible boom could be heard even up where we were sitting.

The blow was incredibly powerful, but the barrier didn't even waver. Elliot threw another follow-up punch, but with the same result. Then another and another. He desperately pounded away at Alex's barrier, trying to break through it.

I knew it was hopeless, though. I could see the absurd amount of magical energy that Alex was pouring into his defenses with my eyes. It was like a golden cloud flowing out of his body, forming into a shield in front of him. It was so thick that I had to wonder if no one else could really see it. Yet, despite all of the energy he was using, I didn't see his power dwindling at all.

My teeth ground together in frustration at the absurd display of brute force before me. It was inefficient, reckless, and a complete waste of magical energy, but it was working. Alex was talented and skilled. That much was sure, but even if you overcame that, he had so much raw energy that he forcibly overpowered you.

Elliot shouted angrily as he pounded on the barrier, experiencing that same sense of frustration times ten. His own magical energy was dwindling, if slowly. At this point, Alex didn't have to do anything. Given enough time, he would win.

Something was odd, though. Even though it was unnecessary, Alex continued to pour even more magical energy into his barrier. I almost had to look away because the energy flowing around him was so bright to my eyes. That wasn't all he was up to either.

He muttered a spell, its name unheard under the sounds of Elliot's attacks. I felt the air in the arena shift as a strong wind picked up. Massive amounts of air were suddenly being drawn down toward Alex from above. At the same time, a powerful wind began to flow out from where he was standing in all directions at ground level.

The wind slowly increased in power, growing stronger and stronger until it slowly pushed Elliot back. It was like a small hurricane had formed in the middle of the arena. Dirt and stone from the shattered arena floor were tossed around like paper. Both the judges and Elliot were forced to throw up stone walls to protect themselves from the wind and debris. Thankfully, the crowd was safe behind their barrier.

The winds continued to pick up speed, roaring as they whipped around the arena below. Elliot huddled behind the hasty stone walls he had summoned, but even those were slowly being worn down by the insane strength of the winds. He slowly burned through his magic to keep repairing the parts that would get blown off.

In the midst of all of this, Alex raised his hand, pointing it toward Elliot. A fireball formed at the end and flew out into the storm. It only made it a few feet before the spell unraveled, and the flames were scattered by the powerful winds. Alex barely reacted. Instead, he silently formed another fireball, pouring even more magic into this one.

He fired it into the storm. This time it stayed together, but the wind sent it careening off into the barrier protecting the crowd. Alex adjusted his aim and fired again. But the winds were so erratic that they carried the spell off in a completely different direction this time, slamming it into the ground near one of the judges.

"This is bad. He's already lost control." Next to me, Malkael stared at the action below with a worried expression. "If that spell hits Elliot or one of the judges, there's a good chance that the winds will kill them."

Snapping out of the stupor caused by the unprecedented display of raw power Alex was putting on, I realized he was right. The wind was so strong it was hurling small boulders around the arena at this point and shearing off pieces of solid stone. If anyone got caught up in that, they'd get splattered like a bug.

"Someone needs to stop him." I glanced around the arena only to realize that all of the judges were pinned down by Alex's spell. None of them could stop the fight. "Malkael, go and gather the other instructors. We'll need as many people as we can to subdue him. I'll get in there and see what I can do."

"No. You stay here. There's no way that you can go into that madness on your own." Malkael turned and walked toward the exit, gritting his teeth as if he were forcing his legs to hold his weight.

"Wait!" I tried to call him back, but before I could, he was already out the door. I turned and looked back at the arena below. Alex's fireballs were getting closer to their target. With my eyes, I could tell he was pouring more and more magical energy into them to forcibly overcome the winds. At this rate, Malkael wouldn't make it in time.

Ignoring his instructions, I leapt off the balcony toward the crowd below. Even here, the air was turbulent from being pulled into Alex's spell. The worst of the chaos was being kept inside the barrier, though. Using Air Walk, I carefully descended down to ground level.

I was only a few feet from the battle area at this point. The power of Alex's spell was really apparent here. You could practically feel the force with which debris hit the barrier, and the sound of the wind was deafening. It was clearly making the crowd nervous, and most of the people near the front had abandoned their seats.

Nearby, I saw one of the teachers patrolling the crowd shouting and gesturing wildly, trying to get Alex's attention in vain. There was absolutely no way anyone was going to be able to stop him from outside the barrier. Even with my spell jamming, there was nothing I could do from out here. I had tried to extend my magic out to interrupt his spells, but I couldn't get past the barrier without disabling it, and that would put the crowd in danger.

That left me with only one option. I would have to go inside and try to stop his spell in the middle of that crazy storm. I took a deep breath to prepare myself and started casting my usual suite of body-enhancing magic. I decided not to transform myself as that would only make me a bigger target.

As I felt the power surge through my body, I began to piece together another spell using image-based magic. I knew it would be incredibly inefficient, but I didn't know the runes I could use to build it. Besides, I didn't have time to try and construct a perfect instruction-based spell using words due to the complexity. Closing my eyes, I began to imagine exactly what I wanted to happen.

I pictured myself standing in the storm, a magical barrier protecting me from Alex's attacks and the debris flying around the arena. The wind buffeted the barrier, but it didn't affect me on the inside. At the same time, I was still able to breathe and move around normally.

As I finished piecing together the image, I held back my magic from going to work. If I cast the spell now, I wouldn't be able to pass through the barrier. I would have to release it the moment that I was on the other side. Messing up the timing would either send me bouncing off the barrier or getting turned into a kitty pancake by the winds inside.

Taking a deep breath, I braced myself and began to watch the storm inside carefully. Debris continuously bounced off the barrier only to be carried back into the arena by the chaotic winds. If I jumped in at the wrong time, I would hop right into a boulder, so I watched and waited. Finally, I saw an opening. Not wanting to miss my chance, I leapt through the barrier and into the chaos beyond.

Astria vs. Alex

As soon as I passed through the barrier, I stopped holding my magical energy in check and released my spell. My timing was nearly perfect, but I still found myself flung several feet by the raging winds before the barrier could ultimately form. My momentum sent me hurtling toward the nearby wall. In a panic, I cast Air Walk to stop myself and leapt down to the ground.

Once my feet were on the arena floor, I took a moment to collect myself. The entire area was utterly trashed by this point. Chunks of stone and other debris dragged in by the intense winds flew in every direction. At the center of the chaos stood Alex, his hand outstretched toward the small stone outcropping where Elliot was hiding.

Even more magical energy poured out of him than before feeding the storm. Yet, there didn't seem to be any sign of him running out. My first order of business was to stop the storm. Unfortunately, Alex wasn't going to give me time to do that.

Even as I watched, more magical energy flowed out of his body and began to form a fireball in front of him. More and more power poured into the spell at an alarming rate, much of it gathering to try and force the fireball through the winds that threatened to whip it off course. If I allowed that spell to be fired off, it would definitely hit the spot where Elliot was hiding.

I began to run toward Alex, reaching out with my own magic at the same time to undo his spell. As I started to move, I felt my magical energy begin to drain rapidly. The barrier I had constructed was highly effective and allowed me to move around almost as if the storm raging inside the arena was nothing more than an illusion. Being an image-based spell, though, it was incredibly inefficient. I needed to end this quickly.

The fireball had nearly finished forming when my magic finally reached it. I began to tug and pull at the magical energy that held the spell together. It rapidly began to unravel before my eyes, and I breathed a sigh of relief, but then something unexpected started to happen. It began to repair itself.

As the spell began to crumble, Alex tilted his head to the side, seemingly perplexed. Then, he began to recklessly dump even more magical energy into it. Whether it was a conscious decision or not, I couldn't tell. Either way, the end effect was that the extra power poured into the spell started to overwhelm my spell jamming.

It became a battle to see whether or not I could unwind the spell faster than it could try and reform. Normally, winning a race like this would be easy for me, but I was distracted by trying to make my way through the storm while not getting hit by any of the larger debris. The barrier would protect me for the most part, but any significant impacts risked breaking it or draining my magical energy significantly.

As we battled back and forth, I began to pour more magical energy into my spell jamming, trying to overpower Alex. Every time I did, he would respond in kind. I could feel my power being drained rapidly. Meanwhile, Alex still seemed like a bottomless pit of magic. Realizing I would have to change my tactic, I stopped and created a stone shelter, similar to Elliot's.

No longer forced to focus on dodging, I threw all of my energy into dismantling Alex's spell. I searched for the weakest parts of it, pulling and tugging at them. As I did, Alex would pour more magical energy in, reinforcing those weaknesses. However, with my increased focus, I was able to shift the point of attack more rapidly, and Alex's spell soon began to fall apart faster than he could repair it.

A wave of relief washed over me as I realized that I was winning. Just then, Alex shouted, his scream wordless and devoid of any real emotion. A massive wave of magical energy surged forth from his body. Countless golden tendrils of power reached out and reinforced the fireball spell, causing it to rapidly begin to reform.

I struggled and pushed back as hard as I could, rapidly swapping between the spell's weak points at a feverish pace. Yet, no matter how fast I worked, I simply couldn't overcome the massive amounts of power that Alex was dumping into the spell. Anger and frustration began to well up inside me. My fur stood on end, and a hissing sound unlike anything I had made since gaining my new body escaped my throat.

The spell at the end of his hand grew larger, gaining shape as it prepared to fire. On top of that, it was no longer aimed at where Elliot was hiding. Instead, it was pointed directly at the small bunker I had made for myself. I had no doubt it would hit. I had been slowly closing the distance before I was forced to hunker down. At this range, the winds outside wouldn't carry the spell off course.

That was just fine with me, though. I gave up on trying to block Alex's spell. Without my resistance, it formed almost instantly. I quickly leapt from my hiding place out into the raging winds beyond. Just as I did, his spell fired. Using all my strength, I threw myself to the side, trying to gain as much distance as I could.

The fireball slammed into my little shelter and exploded on impact. An earth rattling boom resounded behind me, and a shock wave quickly passed over me. I felt a good chunk of my magical energy drain as it did. If it hadn't been for my barrier, I probably would have been sent flying by the blast.

I landed and turned my attention back to Alex. His gaze slowly followed me across the arena, tracking me like some sort of robot. I wasn't sure what was going on, but something wasn't right with him. The fact that he hadn't stopped fighting as soon as I jumped in the arena told me as much. It was almost like he was moving on pure instinct at this point.

At least I had his attention. Since he wasn't targeting the stationary Elliot anymore, I could focus on dodging and closing the distance between us. As long as I didn't move recklessly, I wouldn't have to worry about his spells hitting anyone else.

I began to move toward Alex once more, dodging and weaving through the debris that the storm tossed about. Hopefully, once I got close enough and could actually touch him, he would snap out of whatever crazy battle trance he was in. If not, I would have to try and knock him unconscious.

That idea was terrifying enough. Despite the powerful spells he was flinging about right now, Alex was actually a close combat specialist with body enhancement magic that put most adults to shame. I would be in trouble if he poured as much raw power into that as he was his other spells.

A powerful fireball shot past my ear as I dodged to the side and slammed into the barrier behind me. The sudden close call caused me to redouble my focus. I could worry about how to handle fighting Alex up close and personal once I actually managed to get near him. It didn't seem like that was going to happen without some serious effort.

Powerful fireballs continued to fly toward me. They moved incredibly fast, faster than any other fireball spell I had ever seen. I barely managed to get out of the way each time, causing bursts of intense heat to wash over me again and again. If I was hit by one of those things directly, I'd probably be reduced to ashes.

That wasn't my only problem. The amount of debris thrown about by the storm increased due to the fireballs colliding with the nearby terrain and destroying it. Dodging the shrapnel and the fireballs was quickly becoming an overwhelming task. I was still slowly managing to make progress, though.

At this point, I was only about thirty feet or so away from Alex. That distance still felt absurdly far, given the situation. If I kept going at the pace that I was, it would take me all day to get over to him. Not to mention, a single mistake could get me or someone else within the barrier killed. With that in mind, I decided to take a gamble.

I carefully watched Alex as he prepared his spell and braced myself. Not moving like I was doing now was basically asking to get smashed by debris, but that was okay. I still had my barrier. As long as it could last for just a little longer, everything would be fine. Even as I thought that, massive chunks of rock smashed into it, rapidly draining my magical energy.

Come on, hurry up and shoot off that fireball. I knew it had barely been a moment since I had stopped, but time seemed to drag on forever as I silently prayed for Alex to launch his spell. Then the moment came, and his fireball rocketed toward me. Using as much power as I could muster, I dipped under the attack and charged forward at full speed.

I blasted through several large chunks of debris, draining my magical energy even further, but the plan had worked. I was nearly on top of Alex in an instant. I looked up at him as I prepared for the final leap, only to find Alex staring down at me blankly, his hand extended directly at me.

I felt the ground begin to shift underneath me, but I ignored it. I couldn't back down here. Spikes exploded from the ground where I had just been standing, scraping my hind legs as I leapt up toward Alex's face. At such a close range, there was no way I could miss. But rather than feeling the satisfying contact of my paw smacking into his head, I simply felt nothing. Glancing back over my shoulder, I saw Alex standing just a few steps to the side of where he had been a moment ago. Somehow, he had dodged my attack.

It was exactly as I had feared this entire time. Alex hadn't just been pouring magical energy into the storm and his fireball spells but also directly into his body enhancement magic. The fact that he could follow my movements and react to them was proof enough of that.

I barely had time to worry about that, though. Alex sent another spell hurtling my way. At such a close range and stuck in mid-air, dodging it was no easy task. I barely managed to use Air Walk to throw myself to the side. The fireball went flying past, singing my hair as it went.

He didn't let up, immediately aiming another fireball my way. My reckless movement had left me in an awkward position, with my body turned sideways. In a panic, I twisted myself around so that I was entirely upside-down and threw myself toward the ground, doing a backflip at the same time.

I barely avoided the attack, only to find a massive stone block flying directly toward where I was going to land. Propelled by the storm raging inside the arena, it hurtled toward me at an incredible speed, giving me no time to react. I braced myself for the impact and focused on maintaining my shield.

The stone slammed into my shield and exploded. I felt a wave of exhaustion as a massive amount of magical energy was drained to keep the barrier from shattering. I could probably only keep going like this for a few more minutes, less if I took any more blows like that. I needed to stop this storm soon, or I was going to die.

Even as I had that realization, I was forced to continue fleeing for my life. The ground under my feet rumbled as Alex's spells forcibly molded it into stone projectiles, creating a sort of pit trap at the same time. I dashed to the side, avoiding the trap. The stones weren't far behind, though.

I ran in a zigzag pattern as I went avoiding the attacks, which smashed into the ground around me, only to be picked up and tossed about by the wind as more debris. In that sense, this spell was even more problematic than the fireball spells he had been firing before.

At the same time, it was far easier to dodge. The stones were far slower than the fireballs due to their weight. Plus, since he was controlling so many at once, it was probably using even more magical energy. Not that it really mattered. Glancing over at Alex, I saw the golden light still pouring out of his body like an endless fountain. He wasn't going to run out anytime soon, if at all.

Can I really win this? The thought rose unbidden in the back of my mind. Alex had a seemingly endless pool of magic at his disposal. This allowed him to put an absurd amount of power behind his spells. Even worse, he could still somehow focus on maintaining three spells at once. It was absurd.

Then, as if to mock me, Alex raised his hand toward me, and a fireball began to form in front of him. He was now maintaining four spells at the same time. I clenched my teeth in frustration and focused on moving as fast as I could, dodging stone spears, fireballs, and debris as I went. All the while, my own magical energy continued to dwindle.

My breathing started to grow ragged as exhaustion began to set in. My lungs burned, and my limbs felt heavy. Still, I continued to force my feet to move. Unlike before, there were no gaps for me to get an attack in. Alex was keeping me constantly on the defensive.

This was the most pressed I had felt since I fought against Thel'al. With attacks coming from so many directions, it felt like I would get battered to a pulp if my concentration slipped for a second. At least when I had fought the archdemon, his incessant taunting had given me room to breathe a little.

It's like he's turned into some sort of magic-wielding robot. I turned my gaze over to Alex for just a second, catching his glassy-eyed stare. I doubted he was actually a robot, but he clearly wasn't his usual self.

I leapt down to the ground as I thought once more about what was going on with him. That lapse in concentration ended up being a terrible mistake. The moment my feet hit the ground, I felt something hard wrap around my ankle.

Suddenly, my momentum came to a screeching halt wrenching my leg at an awkward angle that caused terrible pain to shoot through my body. It was so intense that a howl escaped my throat involuntarily. Glancing down, I saw my broken, mangled leg encased in stone.

For a moment, I was in complete shock. *How in the world did I not see his spell?* The answer quickly came to me, though. Dozens and dozens of golden tendrils of magic whipped through the air at Alex's command. The one for this spell simply slipped into the crowd and escaped my notice by coming from my blind spot.

I didn't have time to worry about that, though. I had to get moving again. Raising my other paw, I slammed it down on the stone encasing my leg, sending another intense jolt of pain through my body.

Ignoring the pain, I leapt to the side as a series of spells crashed down where I had been standing. Unable to land properly with only three legs, I stumbled and fell, skidding to a halt.

I quickly tried to rise to my feet, but I simply wasn't used to not having the use of all four legs. I was too slow. Another series of spells came crashing down on me. I shifted my focus, doing everything I could to maintain the magical barrier that was protecting me.

The first round of spells smashed into it, and I felt a wave of dizziness wash over me as a massive amount of my magical energy poured out of me to reinforce the barrier. It held, but I wasn't sure it would stand up to a second wave. Pinching my eyes shut, I focused as hard as I could and braced myself for the impact.

It never came. Opening my eyes once more, I found myself surrounded by a second barrier, cast by someone else. Spell after spell crashed into it, but it never wavered in the slightest. Confused, I began to look for the source.

Tracing back the tendrils of magic to their source, my eyes drifted over to the entrance of the arena the competitors had been using. Standing there, her arm flung over Aurelia's shoulder and leaning on her heavily was Lesti.

A similar barrier surrounded the pair. I wasn't sure how that was possible, though. Just maintaining my own barrier was running through my magical energy at an insane speed. Even with her incredible talent for making spells more efficient, it shouldn't be possible for her to protect us both.

Alex noticed the new combatants and turned to the side so he could see us both. Then, raising one hand, he fired off a series of his super-powered fireballs at Lesti and Aurelia. They rapidly closed in on the pair.

In a panic, I tried to drag myself to my feet, but the pain was too much. I crumpled back down to the ground as my vision blurred. I could only watch in a daze as their barrier was assaulted by the barrage.

The explosions that I expected never came, though. Instead, the fireballs all fizzled and dissipated just before they reached the pair. Almost as if the source of their power had dried up. At the same time, the barriers protecting us grew stronger.

I stared at her in shock as I realized what she had done. I had already seen this spell once before during our training sessions. It absorbed nearby magical energy that wasn't hers and used it to fuel a preset array of spells.

When she had used it before, it fired back tiny potshots at her opponent that were more annoying than anything. A lot of the energy went into maintaining the magic absorption and conversion of the spell, so there wasn't much leftover for attacking.

Yet, right now, she was using it to maintain two barriers at the same time. Not only had she completely changed what type of spell was being cast, but it seemed like she had managed to increase the efficiency drastically. Or maybe, it was just that there was so much magical energy being tossed around by Alex? Either way, it was amazing.

Still, despite the incredible feat she was pulling off, Lesti looked exhausted. She was clearly in no shape to fight. Even now, it looked like a simple push would knock her off her feet. Her breathing was ragged too.

I needed to move, to help her in some way, but I couldn't be reckless. Down one leg, my mobility was extremely limited. I wouldn't be able to dodge any of Alex's attacks if he turned his attention back to me.

Taking a deep breath, I thought about how I could best help her. Two options immediately sprang to mind. I was sure the first was the best one, but I wasn't sure if it would work at all. I hadn't seen anyone use a spell like the one I was thinking of since I came to this world.

With that in mind, I decided to focus on option two while testing out option one. It wouldn't be easy to concentrate on two tasks at once, but I had to give it a try. Closing my eyes, I carefully examined the flow of magic around me and within me. Tendrils of magic reached out toward the sky above while a spell began to take shape in my mind.

Giving Everything

I*t wasn't supposed to go this way.*

That thought raced through Alex's mind over and over as he watched the events around him unfold. He should be the one suffering the consequences of his actions. Yet, it was those around him who were suffering because of his mistake.

The moment he had lost control of his magic, he had lost control of his body as well. The dam had burst, and an unstoppable tide of magical energy had washed over him. He wasn't in pain or suffering in any way. Instead, it was like he was trapped inside himself, held back by the torrents of magical energy flowing through him.

He could see everything happening around him but was pulled back under whenever he tried to do anything to stop what was happening. It was as if the magical energy coursing through him had a mind of its own. Yet, all it chose to do was fight whoever was in front of them.

At first, that had been Elliot. However, another challenger had quickly arrived. Lesti's familiar, Astria, was currently doing her best to keep him in check. But it was only a matter of time until he wore her down. Even a high-level familiar couldn't fight against this much power.

He cursed himself as he watched her desperately dodge the onslaught of spells being thrown at her. If only he had listened to Clara, then all of this could have been avoided. No. That wasn't right. Even if it hadn't happened during the tournament, this was inevitable. This was simply the result of the experiments his family had been doing for generations.

Part of the responsibility fell upon him, but the entire problem was one caused by the Bestroff family as a whole. Yet, his father was nowhere to be found. Even though they had discussed matters last night, and he had promised that he would step in if anything went wrong. Whether something was preventing him from helping or he had simply chosen to abandon his son, Alex didn't know.

In the end, it didn't really matter. What did matter was that he was on his own. He had to regain control before he hurt someone, or even worse, killed them. Grabbing onto that desire, he began to push back against the swell of magic surging forth from within him.

Summoning all the strength he could, he struggled, clawed, and pushed his way toward the surface. Even as he did, the tide of magic buffeted against him, trying to keep him from regaining control. The progress was slow and grueling. Even worse, it offered him no control.

As he struggled desperately, the attacks on Astria became even more intense. Spell after spell kept her constantly on the run. He tried to reach out and hold back or interrupt the spells even just a little, but there was simply too much magic. The tiny bit that he could control hardly had any effect.

Then, he heard a loud snap and a cry of pain. His focus whipped back to Astria only to find her trapped, her leg trapped in stone and twisted at a horrible angle. She quickly broke free of the trap, but the damage was done. She dodged the next blow but fell to the ground where she landed, unable to move properly with her broken leg.

"Stop." The words fell from his mouth as his helplessness reached its peak. "Please, stop this. If anyone should get hurt here, it's me."

Even as he pleaded to no one in particular, his own resistance grew weaker. There was nothing he could do to stop the spell he felt forming. Astria wouldn't be able to dodge in time, and her barrier wouldn't hold. She would die, and it would be his fault.

"Anyone, please…" His voice trailed off as the first wave of spells smashed into her hastily prepared barrier. It held, but another round of attacks was forming. Astria didn't move. Unable to watch, he closed his eyes.

"Please, stop me!"

The spells fired and pummeled Astria's barrier. Even if he couldn't see it, he could still feel it through his magic. He waited for the sound of it shattering to reach his ears, but it never came. Confused, he opened his eyes, only to find a new barrier covering her. Someone had come.

His body slowly turned, and a pair of familiar figures entered his vision. Lesti stood there, her arm draped heavily over Aurelia's shoulder. She glared at him with eyes full of anger.

"How?"

He stared at her in shock. Having seen her after her match with Sebastian, he knew she was at her limit. There was no way she could have recovered in time. Just looking at her was enough to see how exhausted she was. Yet, she had somehow stopped his spells.

She took her arm off of her friend's shoulder and stood on her own power. Her legs seemed like they would buckle under her at any moment. Still, she stood, ready to face him with everything she had. Her words from the other night flashed through his mind.

"Put every ounce of your being into overcoming that obstacle."

A small flame lit within him at that moment as he came to a realization. "So, this is what she meant."

Up until now, Alex had never struggled in life. Everything had been easy for him. He didn't really know what it meant to give his everything. Maybe if he had, this all could have been avoided.

After seeing Lesti facing the overwhelming magic flowing through the air despite her exhaustion, he understood. That was just how far you had to go. Honestly, he wasn't sure he could do it.

One thing was certain, though. There was more that he could do. Reaching out the magic swirling around him, he got to work searching for even the tiniest foothold.

Lesti's Gamble

L esti stared at Alex with an abnormal amount of anger boiling within her. The sight of Astria's awkwardly bent leg was still burned into her mind. The boy standing before her, his eyes glazed over and power radiating from every pore in his body, was the one responsible.

It didn't seem like Alex was all there right now, but that didn't matter to her. He had hurt someone precious to her. She was going to stop him and make sure he was punished for what he had done.

Taking her arm off Aurelia's shoulder, she stood on her own two legs for the first time. They nearly gave out on her. That's simply how exhausted she was from her fight with Sebastian. If Aurelia hadn't found her passed out in the hallway, she'd probably still be sleeping there, completely unaware of what was going on in the arena.

That thought alone cooled her anger slightly. The whole reason she had ended up like that was that she had lost her cool in her fight with Sebastian. She couldn't afford to do the same thing again.

Glancing over at her friend, she couldn't help but smile a bit. Just like her, Aurelia was staring at Alex with anger in her eyes. That was good. She would need that kind of intense emotion to pull off what Lesti was about to ask her to do.

"Auri, I need you to keep Alex from getting close to me. I'm going to take him down, but I'm in no shape to be moving around. If he comes after me, I'll need you to hold him off. I know I'm asking a lot here, but do you think you can do it?"

Aurelia glanced her way without turning her head, constantly keeping one eye on Alex. A gentle smile spread across her face. "Mm. I was planning on it even if you didn't ask."

Bringing her fingers to her mouth, she blew, and a powerful shrieking whistle that seemed to cut through the storm around them pierced the air. In the next moment, Fang appeared out of seemingly nowhere to stand at her side. Without missing a beat, the pup growled aggressively at Alex.

Meanwhile, Lesti quickly adjusted the spell that was protecting them so it would cover Fang too. He was using his own barrier, which was similar to Astria's. She knew just how quickly a spell like that could drain one's magical energy.

In her mind, she saw the magic circle she had constructed and quickly made a copy of it. She then began tweaking the copy, adjusting the section of the spell that specified the targets for the outputs to include Fang. Once that was done, she swapped the position of the two spells, causing the copy to take the place of the original.

This was a new technique she had been working on as part of her research. The ability to change spells even while they were active. It was still in its early stages of development, and she hadn't even shown it to Astria yet. After all, it only seemed to work for long-running spells like this one at the moment, and most of her magic was relatively short in duration outside of body enhancement.

As soon as the images of the magic circles swapped in her mind, she felt the barriers around Aurelia, and herself, weaken slightly as a new barrier formed over Fang. Since another barrier was now being powered by the excess magic she was siphoning from the air, it meant each one had that much less energy to use. They were plenty strong to begin with, so she didn't expect any issues.

Alex had been carefully watching them since they entered the arena. But he hadn't taken his eye entirely off Astria either. Lesti expected him to switch his attention to them just like he had for Astria when she entered the arena. That was why his next move surprised her. Extending his left arm toward her familiar companion, a fireball began to form.

On the other side of him, Astria lay there unmoving with her eyes closed.

It almost looked like she was asleep, but Lesti knew better. She was up to something, and it had gotten Alex's attention too.

Seeing her companion continue to fight even while she was so seriously injured made Lesti feel both proud and angry. Proud of Astria for not giving up and trying to help her and mad at Alex for forcing her to push herself. With those emotions in the back of her mind, she once again copied the spell she was currently using and began to change it.

Lesti tossed away the parts of the magical circle that were creating the barriers around her and her companions. Then, she began to craft a new section that would instead cause the magic absorbed to be used in an attack spell, namely compressed fireball. Once the construction of the circle was done, she once again moved it in her mind.

Instead of replacing her other spell, though, she placed it next to it and connected it to a small and simple magical circle that the other one was connected to. This was her gate, one of them anyway. At this point, she had several layered gates that she could turn on and off with various commands. Each one had its own spell or spells set up behind it. Honestly, it was getting to be a bit much for her to keep track of.

As the spell she crafted began to function, the magic barriers around her and her friends weakened slightly once again. The magic that was powering them was partially diverted to this new spell. A massive fireball roared to life in front of Lesti, the heat so intense it caused her to wince.

The spell quickly shrank down to the size of a basketball and launched toward Alex. The roaring winds around them threatened to push the attack off course, but it didn't. Rather than using brute force like Alex had, Lesti built in a small section of the spell that would course-correct if anything pushed it off its intended path.

The spell collided with Alex before he could fire off his own fireball toward Astria. A massive explosion rocked the arena, propelling more debris into the air. Lesti grimaced at her mistake. That debris would only make it harder for her to maintain her barriers. She quickly set about adjusting the power of her spell as another fireball began to form in front of her.

At the same time, the dust cleared, quickly swept away by the chaotic winds. Alex stood there, completely unharmed, a barrier of his own surrounding him. Lesti clicked her tongue in frustration. She hadn't expected the spell to do much, but for it to do absolutely nothing was annoying. At the very least, her main goal had been accomplished, though. She had Alex's attention.

The arm he had been aiming at Astria swung around to point at Lesti. The fireball launched toward her at an astounding speed, an absolute torrent of magic forcing it forward through the winds. Lesti ignored it, continuing to work on her own spells. Aurelia and Fang, who stood at the ready, did the same.

In an instant, the fireball was on her. Then just as fast as it had arrived, it was gone. It would have appeared as if the spell simply dissipated to everyone watching, but that wasn't really the case. It had been absorbed.

The primary spell that Lesti was running right now was her trump card she had prepared just for Alex. It was a spell that took the latent magical energy from the air as well as any spells nearby and used them to power a set of preconfigured spells that were fired on repeat. The only spells that wouldn't get absorbed inside its range were those she cast herself and those generated by the absorption spell.

Seemingly confused, he fired several more spells at her. Each of them was absorbed, feeding the barriers protecting her companions and creating compressed fireballs to launch at him. A mischievous grin crept across Lesti's face. She had tested the spell out before, so she knew it would work, but she never expected to be using it in such ideal conditions.

The entire design was meant to give her the ability to compete with Alex's absurd stores of magical energy. After facing off against him once, she had quickly realized she would never be able to beat him, no matter how efficient she made her spells. He just had too much magical energy at his disposal. The gap between them was insurmountable.

So, if she couldn't close the gap, she thought that maybe she could use it to her advantage somehow. Alex was constantly using his magical energy in wasteful ways, and it practically poured out of him, according to Astria. So, Lesti had decided to try and harness that power for her own use. She would use his strength against him.

Apparently coming to the realization that his fireball spells wouldn't be effective, Alex lowered his hand. Lesti felt her body tense as she moved on to constructing a third spell. If ranged attacks weren't going to work, his next move would be to try close-range combat, his specialty. With how weak she currently was, there was no way she could hold him off and focus on her spells.

That was why she had asked Aurelia and Fang to cover for her. She glanced over at her friend, who wore a determined expression of her own as she raised her daggers to prepare. She most likely still had her loss to Sebastian in the back of her mind, but Lesti wasn't worried. With Fang at her side, Aurelia was way stronger than when she was alone.

There was a long pause as Alex stood there, staring at them blankly. Then, without a single word, he leapt forward from the heart of the storm. To Lesti's eyes, he almost seemed to blur with how quickly he moved. Her instincts screamed at her to flee, but she pushed those feelings down and continued focusing on her work.

In what must have been less than a second, Alex closed half the distance between them. Even Aurelia, who had already cast her own body enhancement magic, couldn't react in time. Fang was another story, though. With his sharp canine reflexes, he used his Shadow Step skill and cut Alex off.

The barriers protecting them collided and repelled each other. Both of them were sent staggering back a few steps. Aurelia didn't miss her chance and dove at Alex while he was still off-balance. Once again, the two barriers collided and bounced off each other, causing both combatants to get knocked back. Out of the corner of her eye, Lesti could see Aurelia's frustration.

As long as they were both using barriers, she couldn't attack Alex directly. Fang, on the other hand, didn't seem to mind the development. Just as Alex was recovering his footing, he dove at him again. This time, rather than letting their barriers collide, Alex jumped back.

Fang didn't let up, though. As soon his feet touched the ground, he leapt recklessly to the place where Alex had landed. Once again, he was forced to retreat. A smile formed on Aurelia's face as she realized what her companion was doing, and she rushed to join in.

The pair continuously rushed Alex forcing him to retreat over and over again. Even if they managed to make contact, they wouldn't hurt him, but that didn't matter. They just needed to buy Lesti time to finish her spell.

Seeing that the pair had everything under control, she turned all of her focus to the task at hand. The construction was something she had been working on ever since she asked Elliot about Alex's weaknesses. It was meant to wear Alex down and drain him of most of his energy.

Getting the chance to cast it would most likely have cost Lesti most of her stamina too, but that was fine. She was used to running on fumes from her training. If they were both fighting with the last dregs of their power, she was sure she could win.

That wouldn't work here, though. She needed to completely stop Alex, and his magical energy was on a scale she hadn't planned for when coming up with this spell. One mistake during construction could kill her, Alex, or even both of them. There wasn't any other choice, though. She would have to take that risk.

She quickly copied sections from other spells in her arsenal and began to weave them together. First, adding a component that would absorb nearby magical energy, then another portion that would use that energy to generate a barrier. Up until here, this was nearly identical to the spell she was using to protect them all from the storm.

The hard part was next, though. Lesti began to tweak the properties of the barrier, carefully removing specific runes. Normally, she would cast a spell like this on a test subject, namely herself. That wasn't possible in this case, though. She simply didn't have the energy to cast it twice, and even if she did, she probably wouldn't survive the first time.

Even as she thought that, another series of fireballs dissipated just before slamming into her barrier. Worse, though, was the attack that followed. Stone spears flew across the arena and collided with her shield. They lost a lot of their momentum before landing since the magic propelling them forward was absorbed, so they didn't do much damage. However, they did land, and she was sure Alex wouldn't miss that, even in his current state.

Continuing to work on her spell, she glanced up at him. Just like she had thought, he had noticed the weakness in her defenses and was preparing more stone spears. Thankfully, Aurelia and Fang were pressing him hard enough that he couldn't cast anything more significant.

Round after round of spells crashed into Lesti's barrier, more and more magical energy being put into increasing their speed. Thankfully, that extra energy was absorbed and used to strengthen the shield. Thus, even though the barrier was taking a beating, the net effect was neutral.

"Alright, I think that's it." A smile spread across Lesti's face as she finished tweaking the barrier portion of her spell but quickly fell off as she moved on to the next part. "Now, what to do about the absorption factor, and then there's the targeting element as well."

The targeting portion was easy enough to handle. Astria had told her quite a bit about how magical energy flowed through humans and where the source typically was located. Using all of their past conversations as a reference, she quickly created the targeting element. That left perhaps the most delicate portion of the spell, the absorption factor.

She suddenly wished that Astria was beside her. While she could tell that Alex was putting out an absurd amount of magical energy, she needed to know roughly how much it was, at least in relative terms. Astria could tell her that at a glance with her ability to see the flow of magic.

"If only I could contact her. Why did they have to make the barrier so that we couldn't talk anyway?" Lesti cursed the barrier surrounding the arena. Then, she paused and blinked for a moment. "Wait, aren't we both inside the barrier right now?"

Being so focused on what she was doing that she had forgotten that she was no longer separated from Astria by the barrier. All she had to do was reach out to her like she usually did, and they would be able to talk. Before she could do that, though, the battle with Alex took a sudden turn for the worse.

Out of the corner of her eye, Lesti saw him dodge another of Fang's lunges. Then, he slid past Fang, using his extreme speed to circle around the pup before he could recover. Aurelia quickly moved to fill the gap, trying to repel Alex with her own barrier. Just as she was about to make contact, The barrier protecting Alex suddenly shrank to fit his body like a glove.

The extra space created by shrinking his barrier gave him enough room to make it past Aurelia. With a powerful kick, he was behind both of them and began his rush toward Lesti. Fang tried to use his Shadow Step to cut him off, but Alex seemed to predict this move and quickly cast a stone wall, stopping the pup in his tracks.

A second later, Alex was on top of Lesti. Her instincts took over and quickly filled in the missing piece of her spell. Her hand shot forward toward Alex right as he entered the range of her magic absorption spell. The barrier protecting him dissipated as the magic was absorbed, causing her own shield to glow with extra power.

Not even a flicker of surprise registered on Alex's face. Seeing him up close like this, it was easy to see that he wasn't totally aware of his surroundings. It was almost as if the magic overflowing from his body was driving his actions. In a way, this made him vulnerable.

A fully aware Alex would have immediately retreated when his barrier disappeared. Instead of doing that, he pressed forward, slamming a magically enhanced fist into Lesti's barrier. The spell wavered slightly due to the incredible power of Alex's body enhancement spells. However, it held thanks to the magic Lesti had just absorbed from his own barrier spell.

Alex pulled his arm back, ready for another attack. That instant was Lesti's chance to cast her spell. All she had to do was activate the magic circle in her mind, and Alex wouldn't be able to react in time. The range was simply too short, and he was too focused on attacking her.

Something in the back of her mind stopped her from activating it, though. She knew that if she did, then Alex would probably die. The values she had thrust into her spell at the last moment had been added based on gut instinct, and casting on instinct never went exactly to plan.

There was no time to use another spell, and even if there was, she didn't have the energy to cast anything directly. Alex's fist descended toward her barrier like a hammer. This time, he would break through for sure.

However, just before his attack could land, a stone spear came flying from across the arena. The spell was aimed directly at Alex's head, forcing him to duck. It saved her life but clearly would have killed Alex if it had landed. Baffled, Lesti turned to look for the source of the spell.

Standing out in the open, unprotected, was Elliot. His face was contorted in anger as he glared at Alex. It was the first time Lesti had ever seen such a furious expression on his face.

Suddenly, she realized that it was strange that she could see him at all. The storm should be blocking her vision. Yet, she had a clear line of sight straight to Elliot. Actually, she could see the whole arena. The raging winds had stopped.

"Astria, now!"

Elliot's shout rang out clear as could be across the arena. Alex, who was still crouched down, leapt backward. In the next moment, a silver blur slammed into the ground right where he had been standing, sending even more debris and dust into the air.

"You okay, Lesti?" Astria glanced back over her shoulder at Lesti as the dust cleared.

She felt an uncontrollable grin creep over her face. "You sure took your time stopping that storm."

"Give me a break. I had to fix my leg at the same time." Astria waved her previously broken paw around. Lesti's eyes went wide in shock as she stared at it. Astria seemed to notice and quickly cut her off. "We can talk about that later. For now, we need to hurry up and finish this. The instructors need our help."

Lesti, confused, glanced out toward the crowd only to immediately spot Lani locked in battle with a small group of lesser demons. Then, she realized she could hear the sounds of battle all around her. The sounds of Alex's summoned storm had been covering them up before.

Suppressing her urge to scan the arena and survey the situation, Lesti turned her attention back to Alex. Astria was right. They needed to end this quickly. "My spell is almost ready. Just buy me a little more time, and I'll stop Alex."

Astria turned back to Alex. "You guys heard her! We need to buy a little more time. Let's go all out! Lesti, drop your barriers so we can fight normally."

Lesti quickly did as Astria instructed, turning off the barrier spell she had been running. As soon as she did, Astria leapt into action. Dashing toward Alex at full speed, she threw herself at him like a battering ram. It was a completely reckless attack that relied purely on speed, but that was precisely why Alex had a hard time dodging it. He was forced to throw himself to the side just to avoid getting hit.

As soon as he dodged Astria's attack, the other three combatants made their move. Aurelia and Fang dashed in close and began to slash and nip at Alex with a series of quick combination strikes. With the barriers no longer restricting them, their teamwork was able to shine.

Alex, who had already been put off balance by Astria's attack, was forced to quickly retreat. Every time he would try and counter one of them, the other would strike at the openings he left. Their combined attack put an extraordinary amount of pressure on him, despite his body enhancement magic.

That wasn't the only tool Alex had in his arsenal, though. He could also summon incredible spells. Yet, for some reason, he wasn't. Lesti doubted it was because of anything Aurelia and Fang were doing. That was when she spotted Astria.

Standing off to the side of the battle, she was staring Alex down with an intense look of concentration. Most likely, she was jamming his spells. It seemed to be taking quite a bit of effort on her part, she usually could fight and use spell jamming simultaneously, but that didn't seem to be the case here.

Meanwhile, Elliot constantly circled the fight, a spear made of stone in his hands. He could have joined in to try and overpower Alex, but he had never worked with Aurelia and Fang before. His getting involved would most likely disrupt their delicate teamwork and cause more harm than good.

Instead, he acted as their backup. By constantly circling as they moved around, he kept Alex's options limited. It also meant that he could quickly cut him off if he managed to break past the pair.

Seeing that her friends had things under control, Lesti got to work on her spell. "Astria. I need to know how much magical energy Alex is pumping out. Compare it to my own magical output if you could please."

Astria furrowed her brow without even glancing over at Lesti. "Compared to you? I'd say he's pumping out about one hundred times as much magical energy."

"One hundred times?!" Even as she absorbed the sheer gap in their raw potential, Lesti began to tweak her spell. "No wonder he lost control. How would you even manage that much power?"

Pushing the absurdity of Alex's magical energy generation out of her mind, she quickly manipulated the runes in her head. She knew her friends were holding off Alex for now, but there was no telling how long that would last. Opponents like him always seemed to have a knack for pulling something unexpected at the last second.

And, of course, this time was no exception. She heard Astria's voice echo in her mind. "Lesti, hurry it up. He's casting something big. I can't stop it!"

Lesti grit her teeth and pushed herself to work faster. "I'm almost done! Just stall him as long as you can!"

"I'll do what I can! Elliot, time to stop playing defense. Get in there!" She could hear the strain in Astria's voice as she started giving out instructions. Whatever Alex was doing was really pushing her to her limits.

Hearing the desperation in her voice, Elliot jumped in. Aurelia, seeing him coming, circled around to the far side of Alex. Now caught in a pincer attack with nowhere to retreat, Alex was forced to face Elliot's attack head-on.

Elliot rushed in and stabbed at Alex with his stone spear. Rather than stepping to the side or blocking, Alex shifted his weight slightly and stepped into the attack. The spear barely grazed his side. The barrier cast on him and Elliot at the beginning of the match shattered but protected him just enough so that the blow only caused a slight gash.

Once the spear was past him, Alex grabbed onto the shaft of the crudely made stone weapon and spun around rapidly before releasing it. The unexpected move caught Elliot off guard, and he was sent flying towards

Aurelia and Fang on the other side. Before crashing into them, he used Air Walk to stop his momentum and launched himself back at Alex.

Aurelia and Fang followed close behind him, but before any of them could reach him, Alex finished his spell. Raising both arms in the air, the earth seemed to swell around him, what remained of the stone floor of the arena crumbling to dust as it did. The wall of debris rose at a rapid rate, quickly filling Lesti's vision.

Then, it exploded outward at an extraordinary speed. Lesti could only stare in shock as a solid wall of earthen debris rushed out from where Alex had been standing. She was so shocked that she didn't even think to reactivate her absorption spell. Even if she had, it probably wouldn't have mattered. The sheer amount of magic packed into this spell would have been far beyond her ability to absorb.

The wall bore down on her rapidly, threatening to crush her. Then, almost as suddenly as it had filled her vision, it was gone. She felt her stomach drop as she was launched into the air. But there was no pain. Glancing down toward the arena floor, she spotted Astria in her tiger form.

For some reason, she was standing just beyond where Lesti herself had been standing a moment before, rushing toward the arena wall in a race with Alex's spell. Suddenly, Lesti's brain caught up with what was happening, and she realized that Astria must have rushed to save her by tossing her in the air.

There were just two problems. First, Astria was stuck in the spell's path now. Second, Lesti didn't have any way to slow her now inevitable descent back to the ground. Thankfully, it seemed Astria had planned things out better than she thought.

As her companion reached the arena wall, she jumped up and launched herself off of it. Using Air Walk, she then propelled herself even higher, barely clearing the wall of debris. A second later, it slammed into the arena walls and the barrier protecting the crowd, shattering it.

Dirt and debris poured into the lower seats where some instructors were fighting demons. The barrier had absorbed most of the momentum before breaking, so Lesti doubted that anyone was killed outright. But she saw several people and demons get swept away or buried in the debris.

Astria quickly joined up with her as she continued her descent back toward the ground. Grabbing onto the fur on her back, Lesti pulled herself close. Astria's warm coat was familiar and comfortable, but she pushed the sensation out of her mind, focusing instead on the task to come.

"I'm ready. Get me close to Alex, and then get out of the way."

"You expect me to leave you in there alone?!" Astria's voice was full of anger. "That's not going to happen."

"You have to. I think I have the targeting portion of the spell correct, but I'm not totally sure. If something goes wrong, you could get caught in it too." She patted Astria reassuringly on the back. "And I can't have that. Who's going to save me if you're out of commission too."

Astria paused for a moment but finally gave in. "Fine. Just don't hesitate to call me in if something goes wrong."

"You got it!"

With everything settled, Astria began her descent. Alex immediately launched a massive barrage of spells at them. Rather than dodging, Astria simply threw up a barrier and brute-forced her way through. She knew there wouldn't be a second chance, so she was leaving everything on the table.

Seeing their reckless assault, Alex threw even more power behind his spells. It wasn't enough to overcome Astria's barriers, though, and a moment later, they had closed the gap. Astria came to a skidding halt right in front of their target.

Lesti quickly rolled off her back and prepared to activate her spell. As soon as she was clear, Astria leapt back with one final shout. "Good luck!"

She didn't even have time to respond. Alex closed the remaining gap between them in an instant and pulled his fist back. With the spell she had been building up taking all of her focus, she couldn't even throw up the most minor defenses. Yet, before the blow could land, Alex froze in place.

For the first time since their battle began, she saw real emotion on his face. It was contorted in pain and desperation. Somehow, he had wrestled back control of his body, if only for a moment. Lesti was still nervous about her spell, but she couldn't let the opportunity Alex had created for her slip by. With a quick phrase, she activated the magic circle she had formed in her mind.

"Soul Siphon."

Lesti felt the last of her magic leave her body, draining her down to the dregs. At the same time, Alex stopped in his tracks, falling to his knees. Then, just as quickly as she had been drained, she felt a surge of power inside her own body.

She screamed. Searing pain ripped through Lesti's entire being. It was as though she was being ripped apart from the inside. Every fiber of her being cried out in agony as the pain overwhelmed her mind and the world went black.

Instability

My mind raced at a thousand miles an hour as I tried to stay conscious. Searing pain ripped through my body while memories and emotions that weren't my own flashed before me. I couldn't tell which was worse, the pain or the vague sense that my very being was being invaded.

I wanted nothing more than for the pain to stop and that uneasy feeling to go away, but I knew I couldn't give in. If I did, then Lesti would almost certainly die. The magic flowing through me right now would rip her to shreds.

What in the world was she thinking?

Despite the pain, I couldn't stop myself from asking that question. Through my blurred vision, I could see both her and Alex lying on the ground unconscious. The moment she had cast her spell, Lesti had cried out in pain, and they had both fallen to the ground. The cause was a combination of Lesti's absurd spell and Alex's own rampaging magical energy.

The crazy girl had made something absurd and incredibly dangerous. The moment her spell finished, a magical barrier, unlike anything I had seen before, formed inside Alex. It wrapped around his soul like a cocoon, and the magic surging from him had stopped for a brief moment. It didn't last, though.

The next thing I knew, a concentrated burst of magical energy had shot out of the barrier and headed straight for Lesti. On her side, she had another absorption spell backed up by automatic spell casting set up. It hadn't been enough.

As soon as the magical energy hit her absorption spell, it overwhelmed it. Unable to absorb and process all of that magic at once, the rest had flowed directly into Lesti. Almost immediately, her own magical energy had surged up to levels I had never seen from her before.

Thank goodness I was paying attention.

As soon as I saw what was happening, I used my spell jamming to redirect the extra magic to myself. Even now, it was flowing through me, threatening to rip my body and mind apart. It was simply too much.

Even for me, who had a much larger capacity for producing and holding magical energy than Lesti, the sheer amount was overwhelming. It threatened to build up in my body faster than it could be released. I had to start firing off random spells just to stabilize myself. Even now, I was firing fireballs straight up into the air as fast as I could, and it was still barely enough.

At the same time, I was struggling to hold on to my sense of self. Mixed in with his magical energy were Alex's memories and emotions. They flowed through my mind, mixing with my own. I experienced them as if I were Alex, which threatened to destroy my own sense of self. I had to distribute the magic faster somehow.

Yet, I found myself struggling to focus. My thoughts were slowly growing more muddled, blurred by the pain and Alex's memories flitting through my mind. I struggled to rise to the surface, but it felt like I was swimming through molasses.

"Lesti! Lesti! Wake up!" At that moment, Aurelia's desperate shouts pulled my own thoughts back to the surface. The usually cool and calm girl was clearly beside herself in panic. Seeing her like that, I redoubled my efforts.

Pushing through, I grabbed onto the thinnest of threads and began to cast a spell on the girl herself, body enhancement magic. I carefully adjusted the output to match her own magical energy levels, being careful not to overload her. It was slow and grueling work that wore on my mind. It felt like I would lose consciousness at any moment.

Then, my spell finished. Aurelia's head snapped up as she felt it take effect. She turned to stare at me wide-eyed. At the same time, I felt the pain lessen slightly, and the memories flashing through my mind faded just a bit.

I repeated the process once more. This time I targeted Elliot, who was kneeling next to Alex with a worried expression. Once again, I carefully adjusted the spell so as not to overwhelm him.

I finished and moved on to the next person I could think of, Lani. Then from her, I started casting on anyone I could see fighting demons in the stands. With each one, the fog lifted from my mind little by little.

I kept going, casting on twenty people before I was finally able to stop. After using my spell on so many people, the magical energy flowing out of Alex had reached equilibrium. I stood there breathing raggedly for a few seconds, trying to recover.

Vague, fuzzy images of his memories still flit through my mind as I redirected the magic. Unlike Lesti, I couldn't use absorption spells, so I was forced to take his magical energy directly. It wasn't so bad that I felt I was in any immediate danger, though. That taken care of, I turned my attention to the chaos erupting throughout the rest of the arena.

All around, people were fleeing or cowering in terror as a swarm of lesser demons chased them down. The instructors and some of the noble families were fighting back, doing their best to defend against the attack. They were heavily outnumbered, though. And the reason for that was the four rifts, through which more and more demons poured.

"Zeke..."

"You called?"

I felt my fur stand on end as the familiar voice called out to me. Aurelia, Fang, and Elliot all stood, turning toward the source of the sound as they readied themselves for a fight. A small rift opened just a few feet from us, and out stepped Zeke, a troubled look on his face.

He stood in front of all four of us confidently, his gaze drifting until he finally locked onto me. "Now, now. There's no need to be so alarmed. I'm not here to fight you. I'm just here to take care of an errand. If you just step out of my way, I can take care of my business and be on my way before you know it."

"As if I'd believe you." I stepped over Lesti, positioning myself to protect her. "You tried to leave me out in the middle of nowhere, and now you've summoned a whole swarm of demons. You're just as bad as Thel'al."

Zeke turned and glanced at the arena around us. "Well, I definitely see your point, but there's not much I could do in this situation. Even as strong as I am, I would have trouble securing our target with so many enemies around. I needed a distraction."

"Target?" I felt a rumbling rise up in my throat as I bared my fangs instinctively. Most likely, he was referring to Lesti. Thel'al wanted her dead ever since our fight with him. The only thing that had been stopping him was Frederick's persistent pursuit.

Zeke rolled his eyes at me, guessing my thoughts from my body language. "Oh, relax, would you? I'm not interested in your precious master. I'm here for the boy. Alexander was his name, I believe?"

"Alex? What in the world do you want with him?"

"I'll spare you the details. Based on the pathetic level of magic I've seen you perform up until now, you wouldn't understand it anyway." Zeke continued to stare at me, almost seeming disappointed. "Let's just say that he's the key to getting back to my old self."

"Hey, Astria," Elliot called out to me from his position by Alex, his gaze firmly fixed on Zeke. "I don't know what's going on, but it's safe to say this guy isn't your friend, right?"

I paused for a second, thinking of the best way to explain my relationship with Zeke. In the end, I settled for the simple truth. "Yeah. That's right. Right now, he's the one letting all those demons flow in, so that makes him our enemy."

"Great. So, it's fine if I cut him down." Elliot adjusted his grip on the stone spear in his hands.

"You're welcome to try." Zeke finally broke his gaze away from me and shot a toothy grin at Elliot. "I wouldn't advise it, though. There's no way you can defeat me."

"We'll see about that!" Elliot shouted as he lunged forward.

"Elliot, don't!" I tried to stop him, but it was too late. He had already closed the gap between them in the time it took me to shout. The body enhancement magic I had cast using Alex's excess magic boosted his speed to an insane level.

Zeke was faster, though. In the instant that it took Elliot to close that gap, he had managed to cast a spell of his own. An instantaneous explosion went off in the air right in front of Elliot. I barely managed to summon a barrier in time to protect him. He was sent flying backward, tumbling across the ground before leaping to his feet once more.

Zeke simply grinned, seemingly amused by his struggle. Another spell was already forming at lightning speed, but this time I was ready. Even with his absurd casting speed, I could still use my spell jamming to stop it if I knew it was coming.

Before the spell could finish, I blocked Zeke's magical energy. His eyes went wide as Elliot flew past the point where he had expected to intercept the attack. With a cry, Elliot brought his stone spear down on Zeke's head.

Rather than dodging or blocking, one of Zeke's tails flicked through the air. A rift opened directly between him and Elliot, and the spear passed harmlessly through it. A loud clang echoed from behind Zeke, and Aurelia was sent flying backward.

She had used Elliot's first attack to circle around behind Zeke to try and attack him from his blind spot. He had seen it coming, though, and redirected Elliot's attack with his rifts to repel her. Aurelia wasn't the only one timing her attack with Elliot's, though.

As Aurelia tumbled backward, Fang rushed past her and leapt at Zeke, paws outstretched. Before he could reach his prey, one of Zeke's tails flicked through the air at lightning speed colliding with Fang and sending him flying across the arena.

"So, it looks like you can't interfere with spells that only affect me at least." Zeke's gaze drifted back over to me. "I was suspicious after our last encounter, but now I'm sure of it. You can block magic somehow, right?"

"Don't go getting cocky now!" Elliot roared as he spun around the rift between him and Zeke and swung his spear horizontally, slashing along the length of Zeke's flank.

Before the spear could cut into Zeke's flesh, there was a blur of movement, and the stone spear exploded into fragments. The sudden change in weight of his weapon threw Elliot off balance. Zeke pounced on the opportunity, smashing another one of his tails into Elliot's side and sending him flying.

With no one standing between him and Alex anymore, Zeke began to casually walk toward the unconscious boy. I finally moved and dashed into his path. I didn't like the idea of leaving Lesti alone while she was defenseless. Still, I knew she would be furious with me if I didn't help Alex because of something like that.

Almost as soon as I moved, I saw Zeke try and cast another spell. I had expected it, so I quickly blocked it. His eyes narrowed as he looked over at me. "So, you can block my spells even while you're moving. That's rather troubling."

I felt my tail flick about in annoyance behind me. He was clearly testing me as the fight went on, trying to figure out the extent of my abilities. At some point, he would be able to come up with a counter-strategy. I needed to take him out or get him to leave before that could happen.

I started to prepare a spell as I tried to talk Zeke down. "Give it up, Zeke. You can't beat me without any spells. I'm way more experienced in combat than you at this point."

Attacking him directly was risky due to his ability to use rifts to redirect attacks. I could try and avoid them, but it would take split-second reactions. It wouldn't be easy. I'd rather avoid taking the risk if I could.

"Oh, you think so? Would you like to put that to the test?" Zeke just smiled at me confidently, seemingly not bothered at all by my boast.

Something about his confidence unnerved me, but I was sure I could win if it came down to it. I had been fighting quite a lot since coming to this world. That experience would be to my advantage.

I charged toward Zeke, using the full extent of my body enhancement magic. I felt the ground give way as I pushed off. Even my heightened senses struggled to keep up with the incredible speed. I barely even had time to cast the spell I had been building.

"Stone Wall!"

I summoned a miniaturized version of Stone Wall directly under Zeke.

It was only a couple of feet wide and equally long, making it more like a pillar. I aimed for his stomach since it would be harder for him to create a rift there. His tails could reach there, but twisting around like that would be pretty unnatural. Plus, the attack would be difficult to see in the first place.

Despite that, Zeke somehow sensed it coming and leapt to his right. I had planned for that much, though. It was rare for my first attack to work out, and I hadn't expected it to happen here. Using my momentum, I jumped up and pushed off the pillar to change my trajectory instantly.

I felt the pillar disintegrate as I pushed off of it, reducing my speed. This gave Zeke just enough time to react. As I hurtled toward him, a single tail flicked through the air and opened a rift directly in front of me.

Normally, I would have tumbled through that rift without having any time to react. I had expected this particular tactic, though, and had prepared a countermeasure. I shifted my form mid-flight, transforming into a miniaturized version of myself. At the same time, I cast another spell.

"Wind Rake!" I amped up the energy relatively high so that there was enough power in the spell to change my trajectory. I was forcibly thrown to the side, causing me to barely miss the rift. As soon as I was past it, I transformed back into my tiger form and used Air Walk to throw myself at Zeke once again.

Another tail began to move, trying to create a second rift between myself and Zeke. It didn't work this time. Since the surface I had pushed off didn't crumble, I was able to dash at max speed. I was on top of him before his tail could move more than a few inches.

I smashed into him, sending us both tumbling across the arena floor. I started to wrap my paws around him, intent on pinning him down. Just as I did, I saw several of his tails move out of the corner of my eye. Most of them tried to wrap me up and pull me closer.

My instincts cried out, telling me I was in danger. I quickly abandoned my plan and pushed myself away from Zeke. His tails reached out like tentacles and wrapped themselves around my limbs, trying to pull me back in. My heart rate spiked as I saw the one not entangling me flick through the air and open another rift directly in our path.

At the last second, I transformed back into my normal form. The sudden change in size gave me just enough time to escape Zeke's grip and throw myself out of the path of the rift. I tumbled roughly across the ground while Zeke disappeared into the tear in reality.

I quickly stood up and shook myself, and closed my eyes. A chaotic network of magic spread out before me. I hurriedly filtered out the noise, looking for Zeke's signal. Thankfully it was easy to spot. One moment it wasn't there, and then the next, it simply was. Opening my eyes, I spun around.

Tendrils of magic reached out from the other side of a new rift. They were quickly building a spell. Without wasting any time, I reached out with my own magic and stopped the construction. As soon as I did, the rift widened, and Zeke stepped through.

"I have to say. I'm impressed. I can't believe that none of that worked." Zeke flashed me a toothy smile. Rather than being annoyed or upset, he seemed to be enjoying himself. "I guess everything you said before wasn't just bluster. Having experience in real combat truly is different from having years of combat knowledge dumped directly into your head. How interesting."

"What? They never let you apply the knowledge that you learned? Seems like a waste to me." I decided to use Zeke's good mood to my advantage and buy time to come up with my next strategy. I needed to figure out how to deal with his ability to open rifts if I wanted any chance of winning.

"Well, it's not that they didn't let us. Time is unfortunately limited, even as advanced as our technology was. I chose to focus on other, more applicable subjects." Zeke began to circle around as he continued to talk. "Besides, there's not much I could have done to prepare for a battle like this anyway. We didn't have magic or shapeshifters back in my old world."

"Well, that's too bad. I guess I have the advantage in this category after all, then." I decided to bluff a little. While it was true that I had some combat experience, I could tell I didn't have much of an advantage over Zeke. He didn't need to know that, though.

Zeke continued circling, his brow furrowing in thought. I could only hope that he was deciding whether or not to retreat. Unluckily for me, that didn't seem to be the case. It turned out that I wasn't the only one using our conversation to stall for time.

Coming to a stop in front of the rift he originally arrived through, a malicious smile spread across Zeke's face. "Let's put that theory of yours to the test, shall we?"

He then leapt back through that rift, his tails quickly stitching reality back together afterward. I closed my eyes once more, waiting for him to reappear. It wasn't long before he did, and I started to open my eyes and spin around to face him, but something odd happened.

Zeke's signature appeared a second time and then a third. It kept on appearing all around me until there were too many to count. Confused, I opened my eyes to find myself surrounded by countless tiny rifts. Just large enough for a small animal to fit through.

On the other side of them was Zeke, sitting on a building in the middle of town. Each rift only gave me partial views of him from different angles. It was almost like looking at a torn-up painting, disorienting and confusing.

"Let's see how you handle this." Zeke's voice echoed in my mind, and I saw his magic begin to form on the other side of the rift. In the next moment, spells rained down on me from every direction.

A hail of stone spears, fireballs, and other assorted spells flew through the rifts. Each one was oddly simple, but it was still incredibly dangerous with this many firing off at once. Unable to dodge, I buckled down and focused my senses.

With less time to react, I couldn't undo all of the magic propelling the attacks. I tore down as many as I could and threw up a barrier to deflect the rest. I diverted some energy going toward my body enhancement to the shield to keep my magic from draining too quickly. Once I was sure it wasn't going to break, I turned my attention to counter attacking.

I couldn't just fire off spells through the rifts. If I missed, I would end up destroying the town. Stopping Zeke's attacks was my first priority. Closing my eyes, I decided to give a new technique I had been working on a shot. For a brief moment, I felt the assault against my barrier intensify as I stopped countering any spells.

I could see the hundreds of different views of Zeke's soul before me as the flow of magic expanded in my mind's eye. That wasn't good enough, though. I pushed my senses even further, focusing on the flow of magic outside of his body as well. Soon, hundreds of thin tendrils of magic filled my vision.

With so many rifts open, it was hard to tell if a spell I was seeing was different from another. I didn't have time to try and figure it out, so I decided to take the brute force approach. Reaching out with my magic in all directions, I ripped and tore at every single spell I could see forming.

Usually, I took a more detailed approach toward unwinding spells, pulling and tugging at their weak points. It was generally faster and more efficient. That didn't mean it was strictly necessary, though.

I slowly pushed back the spells coming at me, ripping and tearing them apart like a wild animal. Following Alex's example, I threw more and more power at the problem. It was a horribly inefficient use of magic, but that wasn't an issue. Thanks to Alex, there was plenty of energy to go around.

Soon, I had pushed my attack to the other side of the rifts, tearing Zeke's spells apart before they could even begin to form. I still couldn't quite stop them all. I could only control so many tendrils of my own magical energy at the same time. It would be one thing he was just copying the same spell over and over like Thel'al had, but each and every one was unique. Plus, they were coming at me from so many directions that it tested the limits of my focus.

"Impressive, so you can even handle high-frequency attacks from multiple directions. Perhaps you have some way to see or feel magic. How interesting." Zeke's voice cheerily observed me from the other side of the rift even as his attacks continued to pummel my barrier. "What about if I do something like this then?"

Suddenly, several concentrated spots of magical energy formed on the other side of the barrier. Something big was coming. I quickly shifted my focus to stopping these spells in particular, allowing more of the weak attacks through. For a moment, it looked like I would be able to stop them.

However, one finished before I could completely unwind it. Immediately, my instincts told me to run. I hastily threw myself to the side. A second later, a strange buzzing noise filled my ears, and there was an intense heat. I opened my eyes for just a moment to see what had happened.

Glancing over at where I had been standing, I felt my blood run cold. A line of melted stone ran along the ground where I had been just a moment before. I couldn't be exactly sure what had caused it, but I knew that if that had hit me, my barrier wouldn't have done a thing. Blocking each and every one of those spells was now my top priority.

I closed my eyes and focused entirely on countering the more powerful spells Zeke was casting. The weaker attacks continued to slam into my barrier, but I compensated for that by directing more power to it. As long as Zeke didn't rush at me, I would be fine. We were at a stalemate.

"So, you have to close your eyes to be able to counter my spells? No. That's not right. You were countering them earlier with your eyes open." Zeke continued to analyze my abilities as we fought. I was starting to get annoyed with his jabbering.

However, just as that thought crossed my mind, he got oddly silent. Then, I noticed something strange. There weren't as many copies of his soul surrounding me. That had to mean that there were also fewer rifts. At the same time, I noticed that the number of spells he was casting started to drop.

"What's the matter, getting tired already? I can do this all day, you know." After listening to him jabber on and on, I decided to take a shot at Zeke and see if I could rile him up. He responded in a way I didn't expect, though.

"Well, I don't feel tired. There is a bit of a problem, though." Something about the way he said that felt incredibly nostalgic. It reminded me of children I had dealt with in my class that had broken something by accident. Like he had realized he did something wrong but wasn't sure how bad it was.

Trying to figure out what was going on. I opened my eyes for a moment and froze. The hundreds of rifts that had been open in front of me before were much fewer now. They were also much broader.

"What in the world is going on?!" I glared at Zeke through one of the rifts.

He had stopped attacking me entirely by this point, but his brow was still knitted in focus.

"It seems that I've lost control of the rifts that I opened. They're growing larger even though I don't want them to." Zeke explained with a strained voice as his tails flicked through the air behind him.

"So close them!" I shouted at him. Even as we were speaking, the rifts were expanding. At this point, nearly all of them had merged into a single gaping maw through which I could see the town. It was incredibly disorienting and felt like the two places had almost become one.

"I would if I could," Zeke replied with a troubled voice. "In fact, I've been trying, but they don't seem to want to stitch closed."

"So, you're saying you can't fix this?! Aren't you supposed to be from a super-advanced civilization or something?!"

"We didn't exactly go around ripping open tears in reality with magic in my world, you know." Zeke's voice remained oddly calm. "If you have time to yell at me, I suggest you get as far away from here as you can. I don't know what will happen if this tear keeps widening, but I can't imagine it will be good. Two places combining into one seems like it would create a rather chaotic mess."

As he said that, Zeke's tail flicked through the air, and another small rift opened. He jumped through it, and the rift sealed up before I could even protest. He had run off and abandoned us after creating this whole mess.

"What a jerk!" I shouted at no one in particular.

But I got an unexpected response. "Yes. That was quite rude. I was hoping to have a quick chat with our friend about the mess he created. I suppose that will have to wait, though."

The voice came from directly behind me, where there shouldn't be anyone. I spun around as fast as I could, prepared for a fight only to freeze on the spot as soon as I did. Standing behind me was a being made of pure light. Rather, it was a being putting off so much magical energy that I couldn't even see its physical form.

The light shifted slightly, almost as if the body under it was moving, and then spoke once more. "So, Astria, we finally meet."

Unexpected Interference

Did they just say my name? They did, right? How do they know me?
My mind raced as I tried to understand why this creature with so much power knew who I was. I had never met them before. If I had, I would definitely remember it. After all, looking at them was like staring at the sun.

"Ah, right. Your ability must be making it rather tough for you right now. Let me fix that." The golden figure seeming to notice my discomfort waved a hand, and all at once, the normal flow of magic that I saw disappeared. "Better?"

I blinked a few times, not sure if my eyes were playing tricks on me. Standing before me was a young man, around the same age as me, with silver hair and bright blue eyes. That didn't really surprise me. After meeting enough people in this world, I had gotten used to strange hair and eye colors. It was the other features that were making me begin to question my sanity.

Sticking out of the top of the man's head was a second pair of furry cat ears, not unlike my own. His irises were also shaped like that of a cat. Rather than hands and feet, paws covered in silver fur were at the end of each of his limbs. Essentially, he was some sort of beast person.

That in and of itself wouldn't be all that strange. After all, this world had dragons and demons, but there were a couple of problems with that. First, I had never seen a single beast person, nor had anyone I knew ever mentioned their existence. Second, the clothes the man was wearing didn't fit this world's aesthetic at all.

Pajamas. That was the best way to describe what he was wearing. A loose baggy shirt and long pants made out of what appeared to be polyester. It was like an ordinary man had been ripped out of my old world and then had random cat parts attached to him.

"That should have fixed things. Yet, your silence tells me that something is still wrong." The man tilted his head to the side, looking somewhat perplexed by my silence.

"Oh, no." I hesitated for a moment, wondering how I should answer him. I didn't know who this guy was or what his personality was like, but I knew he could wipe me off the map without breaking a sweat. In the end, I decided to say exactly what was on my mind.

"Whatever you did got rid of the light. It's just that your appearance wasn't what I was expecting."

"Oh, I'd love to hear exactly how it is you see me in more detail, but that will have to wait." The man's eyes lit up for a brief moment before a more composed neutral look fell across his face once again. "First, I need to clean up this mess created by your fellow test subject."

"Fellow test subject?" The memory of my last encounter with the voice that had sent me here flashed through my mind briefly. At that time, it had referred to me as "T006" and mentioned some sort of soul transfer program. It wasn't something that I really understood all that well, but if this guy knew about it, it could only mean one thing.

"So, you're related to that voice that sent me to this world in the first place?" Without thinking, I once again said precisely what was on my mind.

The man quirked an eyebrow at me. "So, you do remember your interactions with the test system. I was worried that might happen. I suppose it's not that big of a deal. Not like you can go and tell the others."

"The others?"

"Oh, nothing. Just talking to myself. We should get to work. I can't interfere like this for very long, you know." The man quickly brushed aside my question. I honestly wanted to know who he was talking about, but he was right. There were more pressing matters to attend to.

Turning my attention back to rifts that Zeke had opened, I received yet another shock. They had stopped expanding. In fact, everything had come to a halt. The people on the other side of the rift, those fighting in the arena, and even spells that were mid-flight were all frozen solid.

Now that I had noticed it, I also realized that it was dead silent. The only sound was that of my own breathing. Even the man standing next to me didn't make a single noise as he moved about observing the rifts.

"What the heck is going on here?!" I suddenly found myself shouting. I simply couldn't take it anymore. "First, Zeke rips a hole in reality and runs off. Then, you show up out of nowhere, showing off enough magical energy to probably destroy the planet. And now, time is stopped?! This is insane."

The man looked at me, his face still completely neutral. Then, a faint smile came to his lips. "It's a lot to take in, I'm sure. So, let me summarize it in a way you can understand."

He paused for a moment, seeming to think about how to explain everything to me. "The one you call Zeke overdid it with his ability and caused the fabric of space to weaken. The system that is monitoring both of you detected this issue and notified me. Since it would be inconvenient for me if this world ended so abruptly, I came to fix his mistake. In order to do that, I slowed time down to be imperceptibly slow."

"So, you're like a god or something?" That was the only conclusion I could possibly think of. The stuff he was talking about was simply too high level for it to be anything else.

"From your perspective, I suppose that is the case, yes. You could think of me as the god who is responsible for maintaining this world. Although, that's a more recent development in the grand scheme of things."

So, it turned out that I was dealing with a literal god, although it sounded like there may be a bit more to it than that. Either way, he obviously had a lot of power and influence over this world. So, I decided to push my luck and see if he could help with some other things. "In that case, can you fix whatever is wrong with Alex too?"

Unexpectedly, his expression grew stern as his eyes drifted over to gaze at the immobile Alex. "I'm afraid that I can't do that. There are rules around how much I can directly interfere with the actions of sentient beings. I'm already bending those rules to their limits just by being here. Besides, I tried to warn him."

That last line came across as rather bitter and a little disappointed. There seemed to be a lot that this god was intentionally leaving unsaid. Although, based on Alex's memories that flashed through my mind, I had some idea of what he was talking about.

Still, I had more important things to worry about than his stupid rules. I was in a tight spot, and if things stayed how they were now, I wasn't sure how they would turn out. So, I kept pushing the matter.

I planted my feet and looked up at him defiantly. "So, what am I supposed to do, just keep redistributing all this magic forever? I mean, I'm fine right now, but I feel like this will wear on me if it keeps going. Are you really okay with one of your test subjects getting damaged?"

The man looked down at me, troubled. "I'm telling you, there's nothing that I can do about that. I can interfere with the rifts even though they were caused by Zeke because it directly damages the fabric of reality. Alex's case is different. There's nothing I can do."

"Perhaps I could be of assistance then?"

An unexpected second voice caused my heart to plummet into my stomach. Turning around, I found an oddly cheerful Rha'kul standing there, looking around at the frozen world with extreme interest. For some odd reason, he was able to move normally.

"Rha'kul. What are you doing on this side?" The calm, somewhat kind god I had been speaking to before suddenly changed his tune completely. His voice was now full of hatred and murderous intent. Startled by the sudden shift in tone, I had to do a double take to make sure someone else hadn't suddenly shown up.

"I do have to beg your forgiveness for that little transgression on my part." Rha'kul simply brushed off the god's threatening tone. He replied in an almost mocking way, clearly trying to push the god's buttons. "It was outside of my control, though. Fate deemed that Sebastian and I be brought together. Who am I to defy such divine providence?"

The god sneered at him and sniped back. "Summoning, then. To think that you would allow yourself to be bound into servitude. Perhaps you're trying to repent a little after all?"

Rha'kul fell silent at that jab, his expression becoming unreadable while the god stared at him with open hostility. These two clearly seemed to have some sort of history, and it obviously wasn't good. That was none of my business, though. So, I decided to ignore it and pushed my way into the middle of their conversation.

"You said you could help?" I asked Rha'kul, earning me an annoyed glare from the god standing beside me. "Is that true?"

"Most certainly." All of a sudden, a familiar-looking collar appeared in his hand. I couldn't see where it had come from. One minute it wasn't there, and then the next, it was. "All we have to do is put this collar on him. It will act as a limiter on his connection with your little friend there."

I hesitated for a moment. The collar that Rha'kul was holding was almost exactly like the one that Thel'al had placed on Fang before. The runes carved into it were far denser, so it obviously didn't do the same thing, but I still wasn't sure I could trust it. After all, it was coming from a demon.

"Astria. You're right to not trust Rha'kul." The god spoke once more, his gaze firmly fixed on the collar in Rha'kul's hands. "However, that collar does exactly what he says. It will solve your issue for the time being."

To my surprise, he seemed to approve of whatever Rha'kul was trying to do, even if he didn't fully trust him. That honestly made me feel a lot better. Even with that being the case, I wasn't about to let him put that thing on Alex just yet.

"I have a few questions first if that's alright with you?" I locked eyes with Rha'kul.

He simply shrugged. "Well, as I said before, I don't really want to harm you and your friends, so go ahead. Just don't go thinking you have any choice in this matter. I'll be putting the collar on the boy whether you like it or not."

The last bit of his response irked me, but I knew there was nothing I could do to stop him. So, I swallowed my pride and asked my questions. "Why exactly do you have something like that? It seems strange to me that you'd just be carrying it around."

"Oh, an astute observation." Rha'kul grinned, revealing his rows of razor-sharp teeth. "To be honest, we had been planning on doing this from the start. The original plan was to have Sebastian beat Alex in the finals and then place the collar on him while he was incapacitated. Quite a few things didn't go as expected, though, and here we are."

"You knew he was going to go berserk like that then?"

Rha'kul nodded, his magical eye wiggling about creepily as he did. "Yes. I could tell he was approaching the limits of his ability to control all that power. Still, I never expected him to lose it so quickly. In a way, that's actually your fault. The growth of your master and her friends is what pushed him over the edge sooner than expected."

"As if I could have known this would happen!" I shouted back at his assertion before taking a second to collect myself. There was no reason for me to get so worked up. Once I had calmed down a bit, I continued my questions while Rha'kul stared at me with amusement. "If you had a way to stop this, then why didn't you do something earlier?"

"Thel'al still doesn't know that I'm on this side." Rha'kul's voice turned cold as he mentioned his fellow demon. "If he learns that I'm over here, he'll be on his guard. So, I couldn't make a move with so many people watching. Don't worry though, I was keeping an eye on things the whole time and would have stepped in if it had truly gotten out of hand."

Rha'kul smiled and pointed at the pendant tied around my neck. A chill ran down my spine. With everything happening, I had completely forgotten that he was watching me through it. Doing my best to push my uneasiness down, I forced out a reply. "If you don't consider that out of hand, then I don't want to know what is."

"Indeed. Now, if you're quite satisfied, we're running out of time." Rha'kul began to walk over toward Alex, but I wasn't done yet. I dashed into his path, causing him to stop. He looked down at me, seeming rather annoyed. "Is there more?"

"Yeah. Actually, there is." There was still one last thing that was bothering me. It wasn't even all that important when it came to resolving our situation, but I felt like it was something I needed to know. "How are you moving around right now? Why isn't your time slowed down as well?"

A wicked smile came across Rha'kul's face as he glanced over at the silver-haired god. "Well, I wonder if it's alright to tell her?"

I turned my gaze to watch him as well. He glared back at Rha'kul, clearly annoyed, but only let out a heavy sigh. "You're free to do as you wish. I have no right to interfere, no matter how much I wish to. The only thing I can do is hope that the die I have cast come up in my favor."

Rha'kul didn't say anything for a long moment, simply staring at the god. It almost seemed as if he was taken aback by the response. Then another amused grin spread across his face as he turned back to me. "Die, huh? I see. So, that's the angle you're taking. How interesting. Very well, I'll play along for now."

He closed his eyes, seeming to think about how to answer my question. Finally, he opened them again and shrugged. "Well, to put it simply, you could call it my own special ability. It works a lot like how those eyes of yours do, although mine comes from the old source."

"Old source. You keep mentioning these sources, but what are they?" I tried to press Rha'kul for more information. However, before I could even finish asking, he was gone from in front of my eyes.

Suddenly, I heard his voice from behind me. "That's enough questions for now. It's time that we wrap things up here."

I wheeled around to find him kneeling over Alex, collar in hand. My tail twitched in agitation, but there was nothing I could do. Rha'kul was simply out of my league. I could only watch as he clasped the collar around Alex's neck.

Just before he did, though, he paused. Then he turned back to me. "Ah, right. Actually, there is something you could do here, little kitty. When I put this on him, the amount of magical energy the boy produces will drastically reduce. I need you to cancel your master's spell, or else it will kill him."

"Wait! I'm not sure I can—" I tried to stop Rha'kul, but he simply ignored me. Before I could even finish my sentence, he had clasped the collar around Alex's neck.

In a panic, I closed my eyes and practically threw my magic at Lesti's spell. I was worried that it would just absorb any magic that I tried to use to undo it, but that didn't seem to be the case. Apparently, it was set up to only absorb magic from Alex himself. I had to hand it to Lesti; she never slacked when it came to the little details like that.

In a few seconds, I had managed to disassemble the spell. I turned to glare at Rha'kul, but he wasn't even looking at me. Instead, he was staring at the god. "Looks like you've finished up on your end too. Excellent."

I followed his gaze and found that he was right. The massive rift that had formed, plus the other rifts the demons had been pouring through, were gone. In the few seconds that I had been working on undoing Lesti's spell, they had simply disappeared.

"Wow. That was fast," I muttered in awe. What seemed like a major disaster to me had been undone in a matter of seconds.

"Yes. Thankfully, the tear was still quite small." The god's reply seemed disappointed.

Actually, now that I thought about it, if he could clean things up so quickly, why did he take so long to do it in the first place? I didn't have to ponder that question for very long before I got my answer.

Turning toward me, the god smiled. "Well, Astria, a lot has happened, and I'm sure you have a lot of questions, but with the rifts closed, I have to take my leave. Things will only get more chaotic from here on out, so be on your guard. I'll be watching and hoping. Farewell."

"Hey, wait a—" I tried to stop him, but before I could, Rha'kul cut me off.

"Yes. It's time for me to take my leave as well. Good luck with the aftermath."

"Oh no. You're not going anywhere!" I turned back toward Rha'kul, intent on stopping him, but by the time I had turned my head, he was gone. I whipped my gaze toward where the god had been standing, only to find he too was missing. Then in the next moment, my ears were assaulted by a barrage of sound as time resumed its normal flow.

Cleanup and Healing

For a brief moment, I almost felt sick. The sudden assault on my physical senses after having time stopped around me combined with my magic sense suddenly returning was too much. I had to stand there with my eyes closed, just holding down my bile.

Then, a groggy voice from nearby called out to me. "Astria? What's going on? Are you okay?"

My eyes snapped open. I still felt sick, but none of that mattered. Turning toward the voice, I found Lesti sitting up on her elbows. A massive wave of relief washed over me, seeing her awake. Unable to control myself after everything that happened, I rushed over, climbed on top of her, and rubbed my face against hers, a happy thrumming echoing deep in my chest.

Surprised by my reaction, she turned her head away. Her smile told me she didn't hate it, though. "Hey! Wait! What are you doing? Come on, stop. I can't breathe!"

Forcing myself to at least stop rubbing up against her, I looked her directly in the eyes. "Sorry. I was just so glad to see you up, and a lot happened after Alex's magic knocked you out. Speaking of which, are you alright? Does anything feel weird?"

Lesti quickly looked herself over then nodded, although she wore an expression that looked like she had eaten some bad food. "Yeah. I feel fine. Although, I think I had some bizarre dreams or something about Alex. Wait! Alex!" She looked around in a panic. "Did my spell work?!"

I let out a relieved sigh. If she felt like Alex's memories were nothing more than dreams, then she would probably be alright. "It kind of worked.

258

Your absorption spell couldn't handle all the energy, so I had to manage the extra power. After that, a lot happened, but that'll have to wait until later. If you're feeling up for it, we need to go help Lani and the others."

I turned my gaze toward the arena where Lani, the other instructors, and some nobles fought the demons that had poured through the portals before. Thanks to the silver-haired god closing the rifts, their numbers were no longer going up, but they still drastically outnumbered the defenders. I was exhausted, and I'm sure Lesti was too, but we still had to help out any way that we could.

"Count us in too." I turned to find Elliot rubbing the back of his head as he winced. "I got pretty banged up back there, but I can still manage the front line."

"Mmm. Fang and I will be the vanguard." Aurelia and Fang walked up behind Elliot next, both looking a bit beat up, but fine for the most part. "We still have a lot of magic left, so you can be our backup."

Elliot let out a defeated sigh and shrugged his shoulders. "I'd honestly like to argue with you, but I'm not in any shape to do so." He turned his gaze back to Lesti and me. "What about you two? Are you really okay to keep fighting?"

Lesti pounded her chest once with a proud smile. "Who do you think you're talking to? If there's even a single drop of magical energy left in my body, then I can keep fighting."

I couldn't help but chuckle at seeing her usual enthusiasm. It helped to wash away just a tiny bit of my own exhaustion. "Yeah. I'm good to go as well. I spent a lot of magic fixing my leg, but almost everything else came from Alex's extra magic that we siphoned. I can still fight."

"Let's get going then." Elliot turned and ran toward the nearest battle, followed closely by Aurelia and Fang. I stood up and turned into my tiger form again, signaling for Lesti to jump on my back. Once she was on, we quickly picked up the still unconscious Alex and took off after the others.

"Hey, Astria?" I heard Lesti call from my back timidly as we ran.

"Yeah. What's up?"

"Thanks for bailing me out again."

I glanced back at her over my shoulder. Something seemed to be bothering her, and based on her choice of words, I had a hunch about what it was. "What are you talking about? We're partners, right? That means we help each other out when we need it. I would have been in serious trouble if you hadn't shown up back there, you know."

Lesti paused, staring at me for a long moment before a soft smile spread across her face. "Yeah. I guess you're right. Thank you, Astria."

"What are you even thanking me for now?" I teased her playfully before turning my attention back to the battle ahead of me. We'd be joining in soon.

She giggled and started forming a spell on my back. "I'm not even sure myself. I'm just really thankful to you, that's all."

With that final exchange, our little bit of time alone ran out, and we leapt into the battle. Aurelia, Fang, and Elliot were already on the front lines. With the three of them in the thick of things, the fight was already beginning to turn.

A glowing purple Aura covered Aurelia and Fang as they enhanced their link and cut a swath through the horde of demons. Elliot, meanwhile, helped to clean up any that managed to somehow slip through their assault, running them through with a spear he had taken from a fallen guard.

Lani wasn't slacking either. Despite looking absolutely exhausted, she continued to rain ice spears down on the horde of demons from above, thinning their numbers out little by little. Honestly, I was starting to wonder if we were even needed. Still, a little insurance never hurt.

I leapt onto the wall at the edge of the arena and threw myself as high as possible. Once we reached the highest point of my jump Lesti released her spell. "Compressed Fireball!"

Her specialty spell formed in an instant and flew into the center of the horde. The heat instantly incinerated the demons that were hit directly. The others that were nearby were sent flying by the subsequent explosion.

After our successful surprise attack, I landed by Lani. Lesti hopped off my back, pulling Alex down after her. She was already panting heavily. Honestly, I was worried about letting her fight like this. I knew there was no way she would agree to sit this out, though.

I wasn't the only one concerned, either. Lani, seeing her sorry state, immediately barked another order. "Lesti, you're forbidden from casting any more spells. I can't have you passing out on the battlefield. Astria, go help out Elliot, please."

Lesti simply stared back at Lani defiantly. "That's not going to happen, Lani. I'm helping. Don't worry. I've pushed myself to my limit so many times that I know it like the back of my own thumb. I won't be passing out."

Lani grimaced but quickly gave up trying to argue with her. "Fine, but if you do pass out, you're going to get an earful from me later. Astria, go!"

With the matter settled, I turned and leapt into the fray with Elliot. With the two of us holding the line, it freed Aurelia and Fang to go all out with their attack. The pair, who had been flitting about picking off demons that tried to break past them, suddenly dove directly into the swarm, dodging, weaving, slashing, and biting as they went.

Meanwhile, Lani and Lesti continued to bombard the swarm with spells from the rear. We quickly thinned out the demons that had spawned in this part of the arena, but there were still three more swarms to deal with after this. I wasn't sure that we would make it in time, but it turned out that my worries were for nothing.

As we continued to fight, there was a massive rumbling sound. Then, on the far side of the arena, a series of giant vines exploded up from the ground, entangling the demons that had been attacking that area. The teachers and guards that were over there seemed dumbfounded by the sudden development.

Behind them, an odd pair led a small group of reinforcements. Rose, her vibrant pink hair standing out against the dreary landscape of the battlefield, furrowed her brow in concentration as she maintained the spell. Next to her, Sebastian fired off a series of attacks into the entangled demons while yelling orders. Behind them, a group of students, many of whom I recognized from the tournament, fired off their own spells, obliterating their trapped foes.

Thanks to the pair's efforts, it appeared that we wouldn't have to worry about that part of the arena. I turned my attention back to cutting down the demons before me. The horde was thinning out, and we would be finished soon. Before that could happen, though, a cheer rose from another part of the arena.

I glanced over at the source of the noise to find the group counterclockwise from us had nearly finished defeating the swarm in their area too. Only a single group remained, and to my surprise, they were cowering in fear.

Standing before them was a tall, muscular man with blond hair and blue eyes, wielding only a sword. He was dressed in a simple outfit, with an ordinary blue shirt, brown trousers, and brown leather boots. His appearance was so plain that I wondered what he had done to terrify this group of demons so much.

Then, he moved. It was so fast that even my eyes could barely keep up. His sword blurred as it came down on the demons. They didn't even have a moment to react before their lives were over. I shivered slightly as I turned my attention back to our own fight.

That left just one group of demons to take care of. Lesti fired off another Compressed Fireball, which burned most of our remaining foes to a crisp. With their numbers severely reduced, Lani made a strategic decision. "Aurelia, Fang, and Astria, go help the final group. We can handle things here."

"Got it!" I turned and started to run toward the section of the arena clockwise from us. But before I could get more than a few feet, a massive shadow passed overhead. Looking up, I just caught the tip of a Skell's tail as it disappeared from view. However, in his place was Frederick, who stood as if floating in mid-air.

He looked down on the remaining group of demons and pointed a single finger at them. I suddenly saw an insane surge of magic as he uttered a single phrase, and in the next moment, a bolt of lightning rushed forth from his fingertip. It struck one of the demons below, burning it to a crisp.

However, the spell didn't end there; rather than stopping, the lightning arced from the struck demon to each of the nearby ones, setting off a chain reaction. In a split second, the lightning spread to all of the demons, killing them instantly. The battle was all too abruptly over.

* * *

In the aftermath, everyone seemed lost as to what to do. So much had happened so suddenly that it was hard to process. And despite our best efforts, quite a few people had died. The shock of it all caused some to break down on the spot.

Thankfully, there were a few people with strong enough composure to prevent a total collapse. Lani, Frederick, and the blond-haired swordsman immediately began to bark orders. They directed the guards to ensure that all the demons were indeed dead. Everyone else was tasked with checking on the wounded or looking for survivors.

Lesti and I were included in the group that was checking on the wounded. Neither of us had much medical experience, so we attended to those with less severe and urgent wounds. We only helped with the more injured patients when called to do so. There wasn't much that I could do since I didn't have hands, so I was stuck just watching what happened.

For the first time since coming to this world, I saw the usage of magical healing, and I immediately understood why it wasn't widely used. The people of this world simply didn't understand biology well enough. I watched as they crudely cast image-based magic that burned tons of energy just to close a single wound. The mages casting the spells were practically exhausted after one attempt. After watching them for a while, I grew frustrated and walked over to join them.

"Astria? Where are you going?" Lesti called out from behind me, but I ignored her. I was too focused on trying to recall as much information from my past studies as I could. I didn't think I would be able to cast a proper instruction-based spell, but the more I could envision what I wanted, the more effective my magic would be.

I arrived at a man who was pretty severely wounded. A demon's claws had torn a nasty-looking gash in his side, and the medics were struggling just to keep him from bleeding out. His wound was rather deep, but it didn't seem like his internal organs were damaged at all.

Focusing on the wound, I broke the healing process down into several stages in my mind. First, I imagined the bacteria and germs that could infect the wound being cleared away. My magic immediately got to work, it wasn't a very efficient process, and I couldn't tell how well it worked. Still, there was nothing I could do about that.

As soon as that ended, I once again assessed the wounds. They were large enough that they would need to be stitched shut. I obviously didn't have the tools or the hands for that, so I decided to just forcibly pull the wounds closed with magic. As I did, I imagined the wound clotting and the skin, muscle, and blood vessels underneath regrowing.

Once again, my magical energy interpreted my intentions well enough. The amount of magical energy that I lost, while not negligible, wasn't nearly as much as the other medics. Soon the wound had knitted itself closed before my very eyes and had started to scab over.

I stopped my spell at that point. The man's life was no longer in danger, and that was good enough. Others needed help. The medic and the man stared at the wound and then at me, looks of awe written on their faces. I ignored them and moved on to the next person.

After that, I don't know how long I spent going around and healing people. It must have been hours, but it seemed to end in an instant. There were some whose injuries were beyond my knowledge to repair, and I sadly was forced to leave them to their fate. I helped anyone and everyone that I could, though, until I was entirely out of magical energy.

The moment I hit my limit, I simply walked over to Lesti, who was watching me with as much shock on her face as everyone else. She must have realized that I was utterly burned out because she reached down and picked me up, cradling my exhausted body in her arms. As my consciousness slowly faded, I heard her whisper to me. "Good work, Astria. Get some sleep and leave the rest to me."

The last of her words confused me. I wasn't sure what was left to worry about, but I didn't have the energy to think about it. Unable to fight it any longer, I let my mind give in to the exhaustion and drifted off into a deep, restless sleep.

Epilogue

Lesti stared down at Astria as she fell asleep in her arms. A sense of immense pride flowed through her. She wasn't sure how she had done it, but Astria had used healing magic.

Not just any healing magic, either. It had been unlike anything she had ever seen before. Most likely, it had something to do with her memories from her previous life.

There was a lot that they needed to talk about, but that could wait until later. Right now, it was best to let her rest. Her poor familiar had gone through several battles and then healed the injured until she had nearly collapsed from exhaustion.

Still, some matters weren't going to wait. Turning around, Lesti came face to face with an imposing figure that almost everyone in the alliance was familiar with. A tall, muscular man with short blond hair and blue eyes stood over her with his hand on the sword at his hip. His plain clothing was more suited to combat than noble parties. On top of that, his hair was cut short, a style not popular amongst nobles. Even so, this man was one of the highest-ranking nobles in the alliance. This was Alex's father, Lord Bestroff.

Despite his intimidating aura, she made sure to meet him eye to eye. It wasn't out of respect, but rather because she was rather mad at him. She still didn't understand the dreams that she had after casting her spell on Alex, but she knew they most likely came from his memories. If that were the case and those memories were true, then this man was her enemy.

"Lord Bestroff. To what do I owe the honor?" Despite the anger swelling inside her, Lesti did her best to be cordial. She couldn't take action right now. "I would have expected you to have fallen back with the rest of the noble heads of house."

"Lady Vilia. A pleasure to see you as well." Lord Bestroff arched an eyebrow at her as he picked up on her hostility. "I could never retreat to safety while my men were still in danger. Such behavior would be ill-befitting of the Bestroff name."

Even as he spoke to her, his eyes quickly scanned the area. There was a chance he was just keeping a keen eye out for enemies, but to Lesti, it seemed more like he was looking for something. Then, it hit her. "If you're looking for Alex, he's been taken to the academy for a thorough inspection."

"Alex? I see you're quite close with my son." Lord Bestroff's stern gaze stopped looking around and fell directly on her. His intimidating aura threatened to overwhelm her, but Lesti was used to this sort of treatment. Adults had been trying to intimidate her ever since her parents had died. She made sure to hold his gaze without flinching.

After a moment, Lord Bestroff smiled slightly. "I see. You certainly do have an iron will, just like your parents."

The comment took Lesti by surprise. She knew that the current Lord Bestroff had met her with parents several times at social gatherings and council meetings, but she didn't think they were all that close. "You were friendly with my parents?"

"No. I wouldn't say that." Lord Bestroff shook his head. "But as a fellow noble, I truly respected them. No matter what others thought, they always did their best to serve their people. They were a breath of fresh air compared to the swine that surrounded them."

Usually, the praise that Lord Bestroff was heaping on her late parents would have made her feel proud, but not right now. The remnants of her dreams, or rather, Alex's memories, still floated around in the back of her mind. She simply couldn't ignore what she had seen.

"My parents always put the people before themselves, but even they had limits." Lesti paused for a moment, her heart pounding in her chest. She carefully chose her words to be just vague enough that they couldn't be taken as an accusation. "No matter how much it would have benefited the people to do otherwise, they would have put my health and happiness first."

Lord Bestroff stared down at her, his expression unreadable, before turning on his heel and walking away. "I see, then perhaps I overestimated them."

Lesti glared at his back as she walked off but didn't say more. There wasn't any need to. His response made it clear that he was her enemy. Like her parents, he seemed to take his position as a noble seriously. He viewed his position as one of service to the people. But what he was willing to sacrifice in the name of that service was simply unacceptable to Lesti.

As he walked away, a young girl about Rose's age with blonde twin tails called out to her. "Um, M-Ms. Vilia?"

Lesti, snapped out of her own thoughts by the girl's nervousness, turned to face her. "Yes, Can I help you?"

The girl's face turned bright red. "I-I just wanted to say thank you for today. I'm not entirely sure what happened, but you saved Al after he went berserk, right?"

"Al? Oh, you mean Alex? I tried, but my spell ended up backfiring." She glanced down at the silver ball of fur sleeping in her arms. "Astria here did most of the work. You should thank her."

"I see." The girl eyed Astria curiously and smiled softly. "Well, will you please let her know that she has my thanks when she wakes up?"

"Um, sure." Lesti smiled awkwardly at the girl. "I don't mind, but what name should I give her?"

"M-m-my name?! Right, I haven't given you my name! How rude of me." The girl gave a flustered curtsy. "My name is C-Clara. Clara Belcrest."

Lesti paused for a moment as she recognized the name Belcrest. If she remembered correctly, they were relatives of the Bestroff family. Suddenly feeling much more on guard, she forced out a reply. "Alright, Clara. I'll pass your message on to her then once she wakes up."

"Yes. A-Alright. I'll take my leave then. Thank you once again, Lady Vilia. If there is ever anything I can do to repay this debt, please don't hesitate to let me know."

With that, Clara turned on her heel and walked off in the same direction as Lord Bestroff. Every few feet, she would glance back at Lesti nervously until she was completely out of sight. Once she was finally gone, Lesti let out a sigh of relief.

Dealing with two of Alex's relatives had drained her more than should have been possible. She wanted nothing more than to find a quiet place and join Astria in her nap. At this point, she was running on fumes.

"Lesti. There you are." Just as she started to look around for a quiet place to get away, Lani's familiar voice called out to her. "I've been looking all over for you."

"Lani. Can it wait? I'm about to fall asleep on my feet here." Lesti had a bad feeling that she was about to get dragged into something rather annoying, and she tried her best to avoid it.

Lani looked at her sympathetically, but her response wasn't nearly as comforting. "I'm afraid not. An emergency meeting of the council has been called, and your attendance and Astria's has been requested."

"Are you serious? They called a meeting already, and they called us?" She looked at Lani, dumbfounded. "Don't they realize we just finished fighting for our lives? What do they want from us anyway?"

"I don't know. Both Frederick and the headmistress tried to convince them to wait until tomorrow, but they insisted that you were summoned immediately."

Lesti let out an exhausted sigh. "I see. I guess I don't have any choice then. Let's get going."

Straightening her back and sharpening her gaze, she followed after Lani. She didn't know what awaited her at the council meeting, but she would face it head-on, just like she always did.

Newsletter & Social Media

Thank you for reading my book! If you enjoyed it, please consider leaving a review. Want to know more about the latest releases, giveaways, and other news? Sign up for my newsletter now!

https://ranobepress.com/newsletter-signup/

If newsletters aren't your thing, consider following me on any of the following social media sites.

https://twitter.com/d_s_craig
https://www.facebook.com/dscraigauthor

Artist Information

Yura's arts is a talented freelance artist with a focus on anime-style illustrations. She is available to hire for both personal and commercial commissions and can be contacted via her Twitter.

Twitter

https://twitter.com/yura_s_arts

Made in United States
Troutdale, OR
12/11/2024

26307082R10170